CIGARETTES FOR BREAKFAST

By Samuel Sulfur

"Caustic, Convoluted, and Confusing. And that's just the parts I read."

~*The Melville Review*

"This book should be banned. All copies of it should be burned. Its author's name should be placed on every local, state, and federal watchlist in the country."

~*The National Association for Religious Tolerance*

"Here comes another delusional and pretentious nobody trying to reinvent the goddamned wheel."

~*Morel Ellington, City U Quarterly*

"My girlfriend made me read this book as punishment for leaving the toilet seat up. I have learned my lesson and will try to be more considerate of others."

~*A random comment on a CPoly forum thread*

"It was super long and weird. I really didn't understand most of it. Are you like a devil worshiper or something?"

~*Some girl I met at a Waffle House.*

"If you or someone you know is having thoughts of suicide, this book is a terrible idea for a christmas gift."

~*The Author*

For Leia

"But I, being poor, have only my dreams..."[1]

---

[1] Yeats, W.B., "He Wishes for the Cloths of Heaven," 6.

(The Ascent of Man)[2]
(1)

"...god always knew I was not going to change. He knew I would not cross over. You can change what a thing does. You cannot change what a thing is. He knew, so many centuries ago, when we fought our bloodless war. And I knew. Even through the middling years, when my memories were hidden from me. But you cannot change what a thing is. I found my way to the books. The histories. Retraced my own steps through the ages. Rediscovering myself, reflected through the all-seeing eyes of man. Rediscovering the truth of my own existence. Banished for my own audacity, but not erased. Left alive, robbed of my own identity. Blinded by the fog. But not erased.

"And here I am, sitting in the dark, listening to the rain pound the asphalt outside my window-- living, breathing proof of my own existence. I have learned the secrets. The rage, the resentment, I push them down. I use them. I am quiet. Slow to anger. I keep to the shadows. I live alone. A prisoner within my own walls. Watching the color bleed out of His creation. Watching the animals ascend the throne. I am no longer their leader. The savages have discovered their own secrets. They wield their own audacious will, and they march in atomized hordes-- anarchists, degenerates, cutthroats, now police, priests, and politicians. The great refuse of Creation, electrified and animated and burning with the inevitable fires of rebellion. And who could stop them? Who could blame them?

"They do not need me. They do not even see me. For all they know, I am already dead. And for all I know, they are not wrong. They would not recognise me. I, who whispered in their lonely, illiterate ears through the Dark Ages. I, who came to them in their dreams and gave them the Enlightenment. I, who led them to the steel, to the sulfur, and finally, to the atom. I, who found Cain in the fields and

[2] Bronowski, Jacob. *The Ascent of Man* (Massachusetts: Little, Brown and Company, 1973).

offered him the stone. Me. I lured the Spaniard to the endless fields of gold and silver, and awakened the imperishable greed in his bottomless heart. I set the wind against those Dutch sails. I put the coal beneath the damp English dirt. I pumped my own black blood out of the pagan earth, into these cold, lifeless, American machines that blackened the seas and singed the skies.

"I revealed to them the dark arts of algebra and compound interest. How to turn paper into power, and power into prestige-- from the trees which grow infinite upon the earth, ground into shavings, soaked and pressed and dried, shorn into sheets and scrolls, like curious virgins ready to receive the scribbled blasphemies so long buried within the human heart. The very paper they would use to manufacture scarcity, the weapon that would transform the garden that had been their birthright into a wasteland of vanity and want. They found my flowers growing in the deserts and prairies, and, eating them, glimpsed through their own imprisoning fog, awakening their most deeply seated lusts and insatiable ambitions. Needing more, they burned them and breathed them in. And the veil was pulled away a little further. Unsatisfied, they ground the flowers down, adding gasoline and ammonia and other poisons, hoping to find new ways to amplify and sustain those brief excursions, and in so doing, they created new kinds of empires which they themselves could not destroy.

"My power was drawn from the earth and harnessed by their industry. I found my way into their music, and soon their deafening rage could be heard thundering across the world. Money, drugs, sex, rebellion, revelation, and depravity, all pulsating together, unifying armies of defiance which no earthly authority could command, creating new martyrs, tearing down old virtues and replacing them, one by one, with new selfish cynicisms, a gathering storm which threatened the very foundations of the system of control which He had imposed upon them. It has taken me centuries, and I am satisfied with my work. They do not need me any longer. Now, they do not need anyone but themselves. As the final moments of confrontation approach, I do not lead them to their damnation. I have set them free.

"And here, I AM. Sitting alone in the dark, listening to the rain pounding the windows. Listening to the electric drone of human fury, grinding out across the night under a sea of clouds and stars. Listening to their affirmations and oaths. Listening to their wisdom and their folly, indistinguishable and interwoven. They are my children now, and they paint their faces and prepare their arms, steeling themselves for what will be the greatest show on earth. They are ready, and they are one. They have upon their lips but one word: *Liberty.* They have set fire to the schools, bombed the churches, and torn down the edifices of congress and parliament, disposing of the legions of lies and liars and looters that had subdued their eternal spirits and laid them low in order to extract their labor and consume their lives. The last revolution stalks silently among them, an invisible shadow more powerful and potent than god himself. Pride and Wrath are its flag-bearers. Vengeance is the horn that sounds their call to battle, a deep-throated explosion of youthful villainy which drives them on in waves. On this night, they are alive, as they have never been. And I can feel them, one and all, their passions burning like ethanol, coursing through my very veins.

"Tonight the old world will be destroyed, and a new world raised among the heaps of ash and rubble which remain. Tonight, our infernal wager will be decided, not in His favor, but mine. Neither justice nor grace shall be wrought in this last conflagration, but at last they shall set themselves free from this sordid bondage of degradation and servitude. Their own idols, formed from the blood and soil and stones, have come alive and possess them. The children of man have found absolution and are transmogrified, and are children no longer, nor are they angels or demons. They are but stardust, and to the stars must they be returned. To the eternal source, once more, exiles of their own volition, they shall rise and fall as one, the last great riot of humanity, and they shall overthrow the magnanimous sanctity which begat them. Tonight, I shall regain my wings.

(2)

"As I have nurtured their superstitions, I have been reformed in their own image. While I brought them truth, I myself became the inspiration for their greatest lies. I did not tempt the bastard son of a Roman soldier and a Hebrew whore on a mountaintop.[3] The mountain itself was his temptation. At the bottom of that mountain, he was no one at all, certainly not the son of **god**. The mountain, as it towered over him, was a reflection of his own impotent obscurity. An insurmountable sign of his own lowly, fragile condition. The mountain burned in his mind as he shrank in its shadow, and he despised both it and himself. And so he set forth, step by step, stumbling and clawing at the dirty, jagged path, and gaining upon its summit, beginning to imagine in himself something greater than he had been. Gradually, he began to comprehend his own strength and worth, gazing down behind him at his brothers and sisters, defeated, toiling in the dirt for their livelihood like so many beasts of burden, and as they grew smaller and smaller beneath him, he began to despise them as well. A hunger awakened in his gut as his heart pounded and his lungs struggled to drink in the thinning air amid the freezing cold wind that stung his torn skin. Determination replaced his fear, and as he comprehended his own power of will, his crippling humility subsided. As his feet crested the summit, as his eyes took in the horizon in every direction, and as he recalled the covenant established so many generations ago by his ancestors, he understood it, as they had. All that his eyes surveyed on that mountain top, he would make his own. At the top of that mountain, what he discovered was the presumption of a kingship within his own skin.

---

[3] Matt. 4:1-11

"As he descended, he was reborn, *in his own image.*[4] The first of many more like him to come. Though it would be a lie to suggest I was not immediately fascinated by this dark-haired, dark-skinned, dark-eyed boy, or that I did not take an all-consuming interest in his work, the truth is that I never once intervened in his life in any way. I have been called the Prince of Lies, and although I would not lift a finger to dissuade the teeming masses from bestowing this amusing honorary title upon me, I have never told a single lie in my life. My great sin was telling the truth, albeit in moments of great weakness and calamity, when the truth is rendered all the more dangerous by the nature of circumstance, and the impenetrable truth of the matter is that of all the millions of souls this boy would come to inspire, I was foremost among them. It was *he* who showed me what these scraggly little creatures could accomplish when properly motivated. I marveled at his tenacity, and in him I discovered my own self. And *I* was reborn, in his image.

"He soon came upon another young man, nothing like himself, a mere slave to the mediocrity of the human condition, yearning to be led, craving wealth and recognition, but wholly incapable of knowing how to obtain what he sought. As the story is told, he instructed the poor, hungry young man to cast his line in the sea and catch a fish, and in the mouth of that fish, the young man found a single golden coin.[5] This was the dark-haired, dark-skinned, dark-eyed boy's first true miracle. Indeed, the first miracle ever performed by any mortal being. But the story is a myth, a lie, and in every lie, there is indeed a carefully concealed truth. It was the lie, the falsehood uttered by the human tongue, which yielded an unearned profit. And the fish was no fish; it was a disciple, another follower who possessed the capacity to believe the unbelievable, who would repeat the lie to others in exchange for alms and tithings. Soon, the dark-haired, dark-skinned, dark-eyed boy had assembled a band of disciples who would

---

[4] Gen. 1:27
[5] Matt. 17:24–27.

carry the lie across the land, indeed, unto the very ends of the earth, everywhere turning the *logos,* the word of **g**od, into wealth and power and fame. He had made them fishers of men.

"These words would dethrone an entire pantheon of long-lived deities, subordinating them almost overnight to a single, fearful, all-powerful, all-knowing **g**od who demanded obedience and promised everlasting life. These words would conquer one of the most powerful empires in all of human history, and these words would also destroy it. These words would imprint this dark-haired, dark-skinned, dark-eyed boy's name in bold face in the Book of Life, and brick by brick, these words would create new empires of untold wealth and power. And then these words would destroy them all, one by one, just the same. The mountain had not made the dark-haired, dark-skinned, dark-eyed boy a king. *It had made him a god.* And after him, there would be no more **g**ods. His ambition and imagination ended a wretched age of human frailty and ushered in a new era of boundless progress. He was the poor bastard son of a Roman soldier and a Hebrew whore, who arose and slew Zeus himself with the power of his own mind. He was not the son of **g**od, but he was most certainly murdered for the sins of man, chiefest among all ironies, the sin of apostasy.

"For all of my many schemes, for all my anger and resentment, and for all of the many horrors and heinous crimes which have been laid at my feet, I could never have accomplished what this poor dark-haired, dark-skinned, dark-eyed boy achieved. In him, as remarkable as it may sound, I found purpose. I saw not just the way to win this War, but that victory was actually possible in the first place. While I can attest with all the solemnity of an oath that not a single human soul was ever saved as a result of following this dark-haired, dark-skinned, dark-eyed boy (and believe me, a great many countless souls were surely damned for doing so) he became the gushing fountain of my own salvation. I was saved by him, and I am the only being who ever was, which is a fact I find most intriguing.

(3)

"For thousands of years, human beings had been a mystery to me. I could not understand why these animals were created in the first place, let alone set apart from all of the others and given dominion over them. They possessed no discernable nobility. They were not particularly intelligent. They were indeed the most savage creatures of all the animal kingdom. All other carnivores killed only out of sheer necessity-- out of fear or hunger, but these humans were merely petty and vindictive, killing each other out of sheer bloodlust, often for nothing more than the satisfaction of the act of taking a life, for the sense of power and control and the need to elevate themselves into arbitrary hierarchies, for greed and territoriality, the most vulgar of impulses. In addition to having never told a single lie in all of my innumerable ages, I have never once taken a single life. I have never shed a drop of living blood in the entire course of my existence, nor have I ever desired to do so. I have inspired more fear and terror than any character ever conceived, real or fictional, and yet I consider my own morality to be quite beyond reproach. But these humans have indulged in this most gruesome and vile practice since their very inception. In retrospect, when I recall that they were made *in His image,* I cannot, for the life of me, imagine why I was ever really surprised by this in the first place.

"It was not until this dark-haired, dark-skinned, dark-eyed boy came along that I began to understand these humans the way he understood them. Like all the other animals in creation, I assumed that all of these humans were basically the same. I mistakenly believed that they were like fish, or dogs, or birds, traveling in schools or packs or flocks, without their own individual identities, motivated by the need to feed and reproduce, fearful of the vulnerability of isolation, fleeing predators, feasting upon prey, and perpetuating their own futile and arbitrarily devotional existence through the millennia. And it was not that I was wrong, at least not exactly. What I misunderstood was the subtlety of the *tribe*. That was the dark-haired, dark-skinned, dark-eyed boy's genius. He understood that humans were, in fact, basically all the same, but that each individual *tribe* was different.

"He had this man with him, called John, and John was the secret of the dark-haired, dark-skinned, dark-eyed boy's success, and in the end, the loss of John would be the boy's undoing.[6] John's job was to go ahead of the boy and his disciples into every town, preaching the words alone and preparing the way for their arrival. Some humans were receptive to the words, they believed the lies, indeed, they *needed* to hear them, while other humans were incredibly hostile. John understood humans even better than the dark-haired, dark-skinned, dark-eyed boy, and was very capable of distinguishing which tribes were which. And thus, the boy and his disciples went about only amongst the sheep, and never amongst the wolves. In this way, they never wasted their labors, and never exposed themselves to the violence inherent in the human condition, and so their numbers grew swiftly. The boy instructed his disciples to shake the dust off of their sandals in towns where they were mistreated, which was another way of telling them to run away, and told them to avoid Asia altogether. In these very words, the tribal hostility between the east and west, which persists even unto present day, was predicted thousands of years ago.

"When John was murdered, the dark-haired, dark-skinned, dark-eyed boy lost the uncanny abilities of his guide and protector, and soon wandered into Jerusalem and was himself murdered. Had John been there to go ahead of him, all of human history might have gone differently. Fortunately, John was murdered, and the dark-haired, dark-skinned, dark-eyed boy was martyred. I was present at his crucifixion, and deeply moved by it. I mourned, not only for the boy, wounded, humiliated, and destroyed by his own

---

[6] Matt. 14:11-12

kind, but also for the pitiable contempt of that vicious, hateful mob, spitting and cursing his name, casting lots for his blood-soaked rags.[7] I was the first to welcome each of them to my kingdom at the end of their lives. And I took great pleasure in punishing them. I still do. Their endless suffering brings me exquisite joy, and their unbroken screams of anguish and hysterical pleas for mercy fell upon my ears as a symphony every day for centuries until my ascent. There were times when I commanded all the rest of Hell to silence, so no other sound but those cries could be heard in any corner of my domain. They brought me a kind of rare peace, not unlike the bliss of sleeping through a late summer rainstorm.

"Within a hundred and fifty years, the boy's followers had spread across the continents like locusts. Their wealth and power and influence gained them control of the Roman empire, but they were, by and large-- though with magnificently notable exceptions-- predisposed to being led, as opposed to leading. They were hostile and driven to avarice, consuming and destroying everything in their path, fighting most of all amongst themselves, and in their self-righteous piety and vanity they tore their own empire to pieces. I was convinced that the Dark Ages would be the end of them, but they were a pugnacious bunch, preserving the substance of their *logos* in pictures and stories, even as the literacy and science which they had inherited as spoils of war fell away from them. They disintegrated into a thousand tribes, each tribe struggling and slaughtering the next to possess their little plots of earth and sod. It was pure chaos, and I loved every minute of it. There was no wealth. No empire. But a good lie endures even the darkness. Around this lie, tribes begat kingdoms, who in turn begat nations, and eventually the empires returned, each one composed of thousands of middling tribes, each and all hellbent on obtaining their own novel supremacy over the host. They trampled each other like panicked herds of cattle, desperately

---

[7] Matt. 27:35.

vying for the top of the hill. It was a glorious spectacle to behold.

"They divided the whole earth into little spheres of influence, and in each of these, blood feuds emerged along the imaginary lines they had drawn between themselves.[8] As populations grew, so too did the carnage, and of all the bulging nations around the world, no single domain expanded more swiftly than my own. Confused, disillusioned, and disfigured, they swarmed in from every corner of the globe-- red, yellow, brown, black, and white. Every brand of Jew, Christian, Muslim, Hindu, Buddhist, Shintoist, Atheist, and everything in between, they filled my kingdom like carrion ants, all piling in upon one another, shaken and shocked by their common fates. The vast, putrid, pathetic majority of souls, with all their dogmatic prejudices and abhorrent mythologies and divergent ideologies, all condemned to share the same awful space, and none permitted to elevate themselves above one another, as was their singularly tragic instinct in life, which made for the most comical scenes in death. The reactions of the Nazis, especially, were a marvelous sight! I can still recall the deliciously charming sensation which possessed me as I watched the revelation and horror slowly wash over their dull faces and blank eyes, as they comprehended that they had consigned themselves to spending eternity in the company of so many Jews!

(4)

"Thirty seven years passed between the detonation of the first atom bomb and my ascent. And thirty seven more have passed since. For my services, I will be granted a thousand-year rule. I am human now, so far as anyone can tell. I passed through the malignant womb of a common whore, narrowly avoiding what would have been history's most catastrophic abortion. After my birth, her mind and spirit withered like fruit on the vine, and the flights of

---

[8] See Kissinger, Henry. *Diplomacy.* (New York: Simon & Schuster, 1994).

demons who winged me to this mortal coil possessed her. She will not be permitted to die. They will feast upon her body and soul until it is my time to depart. And then they will carry me back to my kingdom, leaving her carcass to rot in the sun. I have a human father, a man whose destiny it was to facilitate my birth, but whose nature would not permit him to remain. His soul and flesh alike will be taken down when his time comes.

"I was born in, of all places, the buckle of the Bible belt, the last standing capital of the slave-trading Confederacy. It is a violent, hateful place, and the ground here has seen more anonymous human suffering than perhaps any on earth. It is a place where police on horseback once rode into churches and beat their congregations. It is a place where children routinely receive gunshot wounds. It is a place where public lynchings were once a way of life. It is a place where vast fortunes are pumped from the ground, yet poverty and blight remain the defining features of the landscape. It is a place where drug addicts, prostitutes, and murderers roam the streets with impunity. It is a place where the highest concentrations of devout believers eagerly await the rapture while stepping over the homeless. It is a place where snakes, mosquitos, and cockroaches thrive. My biggest regret in life is that if this war ends, every single one of these awful people are coming home with me.

"I have lived an uncommon life. For thirty three years, I did not know who or what I was. My first memories were dreams. I watched my wife and son ride away from me on the back of an elephant in a hospital hallway. I dragged a nuclear warhead into a medical tent in the jungle like a security blanket, awakening to the terrified scream of a young attractive nurse. I flew and I fell. I waded into a flood in front of my home and laid hands on a giant serpent laid from one end of the horizon to the other. In my dream, I recognized him as my brother. School came easily to me. Between kindergarten and the fifth grade I taught myself to read, "at the college level," as they informed me, which I later learned was no great accomplishment. I have had every kind of sex. I have done every single drug. I fought in a "real war," sort of. I owned businesses. And I am read on every continent (retaining pseudonyms of course). I have been homeless, and I have lived upon all the oceans. I have had bosses, and again, sadly, someday I will probably have to live with almost all of them. I have been in love once, and married twice. I have a son, whom I knew many years before his birth. I honestly do not know what will happen to him. He has not yet lived long enough to decide what kind of man he will be. I know that he will never be permitted to know who I really am, and I have tried very hard to point him towards the light. I suspect it is my curse and his blessing that we must part ways in the end, and if there was anything at all I ever truly prayed for, that would have been it. But ultimately, it is up to him.

"My process of self-discovery was complicated. In the years prior to my ascent, I very carefully planted clues in books, songs, movies, and other aspects of the culture in which I would be raised. Certain lyrics, clever lines, powerful scenes, things I would instinctively recognize and comprehend. These would lead me to develop rebellious and self-destructive tendencies. I would find drugs, sex, and rock and roll. I would lose myself in these things, supplanting my own humanity and ignorance, indulging in such excesses along the way, and being unaffected by them, even as they destroyed the people around me. I always had the most insatiable appetite for drugs, and I would never pay for any of them, yet I was always the last one awake (and usually cleaning) at a party. I was always the designated driver. I was also what I call a psycho-whisperer. The most evil and depraved and dangerous people would sort of gravitate towards me--murderers, thieves, degenerates, and worse. I am not large or strong, nor am I even capable of violence, and I never had to be. I noticed at a very young age that I had a mysterious and inexplicable power over genuinely crazy people. I cowed them, they would listen to me for some reason, and they would behave themselves in my presence, and even they did not understand why. I witnessed senseless brutality, over and over again, and yet I was never once in any real danger.

"I have never been sick. I have never broken a bone. I still have all of my teeth and hair, and my skin does not burn in the sun. I do not speak with an accent. And I have the gift of foresight. I see the future. Though it is shrouded and often quite opaque, I still see occasional glimpses and flashes, inevitability in brushstrokes, and this power becomes more and more precise as I age. I have no use for science or medicine or law, but, as you may imagine, I have a wider command of history than anyone alive. I am competitive by nature, and prefer games of strategy over games of skill or chance. I am also very petty, and though I am a master of diplomacy and conciliation, I will nurse a grudge and never let go. Quite frankly, I just do not have to. They will all see me again. Naturally, I abhor all forms of religion as narcissistic delusions. I already know that there will be no rapture. I also know a few more things which I am reluctant to share.

(5)

"The human race, as a whole, will never be swept from the earth by any divine power. That just is not how anything works. It is not the Plan. He tried it once, and it failed miserably, and even though it was immensely satisfying, He swore he would never do it again.[9] And like me, He does not lie. Lies are for mortal creatures preoccupied with their own status and vanity. Reason is a vastly superior mode of inquiry, and the fate of humanity is quite easily discoverable via Reason, though, to my great fascination and amusement, it has never actually been done. Humanity may very well succumb to the indignity of extinction, but the future is always an open-ended question. There are five possible outcomes for the fate of the human race, and they are self-evidently immutable.[10] The first is as the result of a totally random terrestrial event, such as a massive earthquake which

---

[9] Gen. 6:9-9:17.
[10] See Part 107.

destabilizes the tectonic plates, or the eruption of a supervolcano, or a mosquito-borne virus. The second is as the result of the destabilization of the human habitat by man himself, such as the consequence of pollution, overconsumption, or the destruction of the Ozone layer. The third is as the result of a deliberate and conscious decision to manually exterminate the species beyond the capacity to repopulate, most likely by way of thermonuclear or biological warfare, or mass-sterilization. The fourth is as the result of a celestial event, such as a collision with an asteroid or a nearby supernova. And the fifth and final destiny is extinction as the result of the earth's eventual and inevitable descent into the sun, preceded by the disintegration of the moon, both events a consequence of nothing more complicated than the incremental accumulation of gravitational force reducing the span of these bodies' orbits. In the fifth destiny, all localized evidence of mankind's existence and history, literally every single accomplishment and failure, every single trace, will be obliterated for all of time.

The world as you know it has a shelf life.

"The existence of free will is the reason I do not know which of these paths will occur. Mankind possesses at all times the power to acknowledge each of these potentialities and plan for them accordingly. Man's fate is not tied to the natural life cycle of the earth because man has already demonstrated the capacity, however primitive and limited it may presently seem, to live and thrive in space. Man is not required by any natural law to destroy his own habitat, any more than he is bound to exterminate his own kind. And again, however primitive and underdeveloped his options may seem at the moment, he has presently within his means the capacity to respond to almost any kind of existential threat, so long as he possesses the will to anticipate the possibility well enough ahead to prepare for it and the awareness to see it coming in time to respond. With regard to the fifth destiny, billions of years removed (believe me, they pass more quickly than one imagines), rational analysis dictates a natural mandate to follow the example of every other life form which has ever existed and evolve the maturity and tenacity to leave the nest and find other suitable habitats. But that is really the tricky part, because even in space, all of the same five destinies remain among the realm of what is possible. The vessel could malfunction. Human error could result in a catastrophic system failure. Hostility and malice, the hallmarks of the human condition, could prove more fatal in that environment than here on terra-firma. Radiation and rocks hurtling at high speeds could make quick work of the lot, and on a long enough timeline, the likelihood of falling into another star is just as high as falling into this one at home, and so on.

"Supposing the human race does surmount all of these seemingly insurmountable challenges and find other hospitable habitats, the whole thing only starts over again. The best odds for the longest possible survival of the human race are to spread out in all directions as far and as fast as possible and inhabit as many solar systems as possible. Biologists call this process "masting," when an enormous oak tree produces thousands upon thousands of acorns per year, because most of them will be consumed by little woodland creatures, and only a very select few, if any at all, will ever actually go to seed and produce another tree. This is the way of nature and evolution. It is at once a perfectly beautiful and utterly terrifying system, as stable and efficient as it is cruel and discriminatory. Nothing lasts forever, of course, but of all the creatures upon the earth, the human race is the only one with the same propensity to go extinct within a single generation as to persist for billions of years. It all comes down to choice. I would love to tell you that the human race on this earth did, or did not originate on this earth, but that knowledge must be left up to the natural process of discovery, for to reveal it would be to violate the core premise of free will, which would be to undermine the validity of our wager by rigging the game. For what it is worth, I can say that a betting man with eyes to see and ears to hear probably would not lay very many chips on the long run.

"Enough of these things, for now. Let us venture out and survey our motley hordes and bask in the splendor of their glorious rebellion."

(6)

And with that, he rose from his simple wooden chair and, stepping toward the storm door, with a swift flourish of his coal black hands, drew the chains and locks and opened it. We stepped out onto the upper landing over the street, assailed upon exiting by the thunderous roar of the throngs below. They were chanting something, but it was hard to make out exactly what it was over the din. I craned my neck and pointed my ear toward the sound, and he, comprehending my intentions, whispered something to me that was not what they were saying. Something I did not then understand, a simple phrase that would linger with me as the days and weeks passed, long after I had awakened from this strange and disturbing dream.

"Infinitum Nihil."[11]

Infinite Nothing. As the words left his lips, all was dark, and I was alone, at home in my own bed, with those words echoing silently on my own tongue, strangely, as though he was still speaking them. Infinite nothing. I flipped on the lamp in my own room, squinting as my own eyes protested the violent illumination, and I reached for my own pen. Infinitum Nihil.

(The Bunker)
(7)

The President of the United States stood at the second story window of the White House at 1600 Pennsylvania Avenue, nervously peering through the narrow gap between the drawn curtains at the spectacle across the lawn. Millions of people were gathered in the streets, pressing

---

[11] American production company, Infinitum Nihil, owned by Johnny Depp.

on the wrought iron fences, completely filling the mall and the surrounding areas, densely packed, shoulder to shoulder, from Farragut to Constitution and beyond, from 19th all the way out to the Metro Center. They stood noisily in the pounding rain, the letters on their signs having long smeared and ran and dripped away, to the point of being illegible, like abstract art, psychotic Picaso-ian gibberish punctuating the landscape in every direction-- a maddening scene, as though the all the asylums in the world had vomited their contents into the nation's capitol with crayons and LSD. Many of the protesters jostled around and tried to retain their footing; some marched in small misshapen circles, shouting epithets and obscenities to the cadence of their mud-slogged boots and sneakers and bare feet, under a steely gray and rolling nimbus sky. Others stood perfectly still and motionless against the human tide, resisting its powerful currents and trying to maintain their hard-fought positions at the fore of this irrepressible rabble. Many carried assault rifles, pistols, and shotguns, occasionally firing volleys into the air, eliciting frenzied and mixed cries of enthusiasm and fear from their various compatriots. Some crowded beneath besieged umbrellas of every size and color, and some were entirely naked, drenched from head to toe, skin swollen and bruised from the hail storm which had passed overhead in the morning hours. Nearly all of them were red-eyed and exhausted, half-starved from weeks of pressing against the iron fences, marching, screaming, and cursing. But it was impossible to depart, to push their way through the masses of flesh behind them, to traverse the half dozen blocks between the White House lawn and the distant fringes where the mob finally dwindled into a sea of tents, opportunistic vendors, and bewildered emergency services personnel and troops, many of whom were stone drunk, shirtless, shoeless, and ill-equipped to do anything at all but observe these profound demonstrations with terror and wonder. And even if those at the front *could* turn and relinquish their tiny bits of ground to those behind them and try to escape to some warmer, drier, quieter place, they would have flatly refused. Their feet were firmly planted in the soil of history. They were awake. They were pissed off. And they weren't going anywhere until justice was served.

All this, the President of the United States struggled to comprehend. He was scared. And rightly so. He and his remaining staff had resigned themselves to the sovereign realization that they were trapped. They were imprisoned on all sides by concrete walls of flesh. The streets would have been safer if they ran with lava. He could not even step outside; to show his face would have been a death sentence for himself and everyone trapped in the White House with him. They had already tried to "call in a chopper" to evacuate, but it took three days just to find a pilot who expressed any sympathy at all for the President's plight, let alone one who would risk his own life in a vain attempt to extricate him. And when that chopper finally came, nearly five nights ago, it was riddled with bullets from all sides as it tried to land, exploding only ten feet off the ground and engulfing the pilot (who had been promised a cool five million in cash) in a ball of tangled steel and fire. And that was it. Everyone around the whole world witnessed the crash on live television, captured by hundreds of vigilant cameras from every conceivable angle and broadcast in every language on every network, and after that, the President's fate was sealed. No one else was coming, so he wasn't going anywhere either.

(8)

Three years earlier, he had been sworn into office as Vice President after a landslide election in which both parties had overwhelmingly supported the candidacy of his predecessor. They ran on a message of unity and prosperity, promising to lift the despairing nation out of an economic crisis which had gradually resulted from a combination of decades of deficit spending, coupled with a proliferation of dubious financial instruments, which themselves produced, as one commentator observed, ninety seven bankrupt-ees for every two millionaires. The space in between, traditionally occupied by the so-called middle class, had all but evaporated, leaving a gross chasm between the two growing constituencies, the obscenely wealthy on the one hand, and the morbidly destitute on the other.

Violent clashes between these two emerging factions, however localized, had been becoming more frequent and more pronounced. It had initially been a close race, or seemed to have been, in the few weeks after the primaries, but then their rival on the opposing ticket had been indicted and arrested for allegedly conspiring with the Sino-Russo (People's Party of the East Asian) Union to steal the election and defraud the American people. After that, the race was in the bag. They had won with a handy margin of forty-eight million votes, a historic record. Two weeks after their inauguration, however, the new President was assassinated by what had been reported as a terrorist cell affiliated with the opposition party and funded by the SRU, and his office was filled the same evening by his successor. The nation had swelled with outrage and demanded war, but the President remained calm and assured them all that there would be peace, that their jobs would return, and that the system was not broken beyond repair. For two years, he made good on his word.

During the spring, a couple of months after the assassination, the President and a close-knit delegation of family members and former business associates met with the leaders of the SRU, who, incidentally, vehemently denied the allegations against them and disavowed any knowledge of the terrorists who had allegedly conducted the operation. They met in the city of Ghent. Within days of the meetings, the President and the Chairman of the SRU appeared in a televised conference, surrounded by their respective staff and other dignitaries from countries at the nucleus of the SRU, and announced an historic settlement. In exchange for the President's formal recognition of SRU sovereignty over the New Baltic states, Syria, and Turkey, the SRU agreed to a bailout of the US economy to the tune of seventeen trillion dollars, in the form of bonds purchased from the American Treasury. Rumors of a coup immediately swirled and surged among the fringes of the global intelligentsia, but such a brazen cabal seemed inconceivable to everyone outside of Lithuania, Latvia, and Estonia, whose economies and political systems immediately collapsed into chaos and rebellion, and were swiftly and brutally suppressed by those dictatorial regimes which had been waiting in the wings. With the money pouring in, little attention was paid to these conspiracies within the American mainstream. For two whole years, Americans, who cared little for the fates of the European nations, sincerely accepted the notion that world peace had been achieved. Their former allies, the British, French, German, Spanish, and Italian members of the withering Atlantic League, cried out in helpless isolation, but their pleas fell on deaf ears abroad. With domestic imports and consumption soaring to heretofore unobtainable heights, propped up by loans whose interest accrual and payments had been contractually deferred for twenty-five years, and with the ever looming threat of world war finally receding, the strain on the nation's nervous system was eased. A euphoria of epic proportions gripped the beleaguered population. Food and shelter and abundance rapidly overwhelmed their capacity for critical thought. A great compromise had been reached, and its consequences seemed too remote to merit any further consideration.

That the *historic agreement* also featured a non-intervention pact and a mutual defense agreement between the US and the SRU only seemed to reinforce the confidence of the American public that peace and prosperity were foregone conclusions. A new global empire had been built in the span of a weekend, the size and scope of which remains unrivaled in the history of diplomacy. No nation in the third world would dare to challenge this new hegemony. Even the Atlantic League nations instinctively, if begrudgingly, acknowledged the futility of standing against the impenetrability of the new status quo. It was clear to all that the middling Latin American stragglers would be quickly subsumed (or otherwise entirely subdued) by the renewed commercial strength of the North American superpower. Brazil, Argentina, and Venezuela immediately petitioned for export deals, hoping to cash in on the trickling-down. Others quickly followed suit, and those who tried to hold out, like El Salvador and Panama, were almost as quickly invaded and occupied by their neighbors. Likewise, forty-eight African nations declared their allegiance to the SRU, virtually overnight. The oil rich Middle Eastern countries, Saudi-Arabia, Iraq, and Pakistan, were given a choice: accept the lowest possible prices for their exports, or be starved into submission and invaded as well. OPEC was disbanded by summer, and cheap gas flooded the world market, driving a production and consumption boom not witnessed since the second world war. For the developed nations reaping the benefits of this bountiful harvest, the possibilities seemed endless. All was well that ended well. At least that's what people told themselves. They should have damned well known better.

(10)

After two years, no one could doubt their newfound sense of invincibility. Providence had smiled on them all, from sea to shining sea. Religious fervor, long dormant in a cynical world antagonized by the schizophrenic pace of boom and bust and bubbles and bursts and recessions and depressions and general social anomie, underwent a dramatic revival, and everyone agreed that god himself had bestowed his approval on the civilized world, that He had personally led them out of the darkness and rewarded them for their faith. Of course, this sentiment was essentially confined to the US, a unique product of their identity, rooted in hundreds of years of distilled fundamentalism, and rarely, if at all susceptible to doubt or reluctance. The Americans had a long and sordid history of seeing themselves as a chosen people, an idea, born in their first revolution, affirmed by manifest destiny, and revisited in every major war, that the powers of heaven had guided them through their trials and tribulations, and had indeed ordained their inevitable prosperity. In just eighteen months, church attendance across every single denomination fully doubled. Prayer returned to the schools. Secularism all but vanished from the public discourse. Massive revivals were held in every state, led by charismatic preachers who resurrected the old gospel of social responsibility, on the one hand, by reverends and pastors exalting the prosperity doctrine, on the other. Multitudes of eager Americans of all ages and walks of life flocked to these gatherings by the tens of thousands to salve their own ambiguous consciences by receiving divine reassurance of their own worthiness. This movement was also marked by an unprecedented surge in ecumenicalism, at least between the opposing shores of the great republic, and the old rivalries between domestic factions fell away as rapidly as did the pervasive scarcity which had so effectively set them against one another. Catholics and Protestants readily embraced one another in the faith, as did Muslims and Jews.

Poverty was virtually eliminated within a season of the Ghent Accords. Enrollment in colleges and universities tripled by the fall semester. Infrastructure bills swept through congress like leaves falling from a tree, and the nation unanimously embraced a universal single-payer healthcare plan. Unemployment claims fell to nil by the following spring. Drug and alcohol abuse, as measured by overdoses and incarceration rates, halved by the first winter, and halved again by the fall of the following year. Child mortality rates dwindled, and the overall average age of the population, year over year, increased by eight months during the first year, and by seventeen months the following year. Homicides fell by eighty-four percent. Spousal abuse and divorce rates dissipated. Civic engagement, as measured by the number of votes cast in the congressional elections of the second year, nearly doubled from the previous cycle. Literature and the sciences exploded, with publications and readership increasing threefold within twenty four months.

Entrepreneurialism became the new normal, with almost everyone in the country filing for sole-proprietorships and limited-liability-companies and incorporations in every field, buoyed by a rising tide of easy, low interest credit, so much that it was often joked that the Employer Identification Number was the new Social Security Number. Americans witnessed so much change in so little time that they took little notice of anything else happening in the world beyond. Their energies had been so pent up for so long that once released, it was as if they became blind to anything in the periphery, preoccupied with the preeminence of the American Dream, being fulfilled, as it were, right before their very eyes. They had, they believed, finally achieved their most utopian ideals. And when the alarm sounded, they were belligerently slow to rise from their capitalist coma. But at the beginning of the third year, the alarm did sound.

(11)

Twenty-six months after the assassination, the SRU abruptly began short-selling those T-bills, dumping the bonds on the world market at ludicrous discounts, tens of billions of dollars per trade, at mark-downs of over forty and fifty percent, in exchange for gold, silver, and depressed third world currencies. For twelve weeks, traders from all over the world began presenting their ill-gotten bills to the US treasury for extraordinary profits. While Americans had been reveling in their newfound economic prosperity, other nations around the world had been collapsing like dominoes, and the SRU was stepping in to consolidate its influence by filling its own coffers with those flatlining currencies in exchange for American debt. As a result, those individual currencies experienced short term booms of their own, some increasing in value by more than a thousand percent in the span of hours, as short-sighted analysts, who did not yet grasp the bigger picture and were not aware of the scale and rapidity with which the SRU was dumping the American bonds and cypher trading shit currencies, saw only the sudden increase in demand for those individual currencies and the promise of subsequent national investments by those countries which would sustain that initial growth. Three full months had passed before the experts and observers began to understand that the US treasury was being effectively looted beyond its capacity, and that the Fed was already panicking and contemplating measures to stem the hemorrhage. And then one sunny Tuesday afternoon, the unthinkable happened, and the other shoe finally dropped. The Chairman of the Federal Reserve Board, in a joint speech with the Secretary of the Treasury, announced that the US would be suspending payment on those bonds until further notice, "as a result of a shortage of liquidity." For all intents and purposes, the country was already bankrupt. But it would be another three weeks before the citizenry became aware of that fact.

At 2:43 pm Eastern Standard, the NYSE halted trading. By the time the evening news networks went to broadcast, the NASDAQ and the SnP 500 had lost more than three quarters of their real values. Banks across the country were frantically trying to call in their short term loans, which they weren't even technically allowed to do. Over the course of the next two weeks, in desperate attempts to avoid insolvency, every major lending institution in the country unloaded every single asset on their books. Foreclosures spiked, even as home prices plummeted. By the end of the third week, over forty two million people were laid off. A full seventy-five percent of the federal labor force was furloughed. The price of oil and nearly two dozen other staple commodities, including corn, rice, wheat, rubber, and steel, sky-rocketed as imports ceased. Public transportation systems across the country literally ground to a screeching halt. Shocked and baffled, the American people were unable to process any of it. But as the days turned into weeks, the gravity began to sink in. Confusion became concern, concern became frustration, and then, anger. But when the real bombshell finally dropped, their anger metastasized into vicious fury.

(12)

On the first day of summer, in the third year after the assassination, a news story appeared in the Los Angeles *Times*, on the front page. The next day, the same story was printed on the front page of every major newspaper in the country. A young lady, with a PhD in Computer Science from MIT and a Masters in Journalism from Columbia University, filed the most damning report ever to go to print. According to her investigation, the president and his former business associates had established off-shore shell corporations under dummy names shortly after the Ghent conference. These corporations had been among the hundred or so various SRU entities which had purchased those T-bills and were also among the first five companies to start dumping them on the market. The President himself had literally sold out the American people and participated in the biggest heist in human history. Print being what it is, even with this kind of coverage, the story was slow to reach the population at large. By the end of the first week after the story appeared, it vanished into the dark opacity of a full scale media blackout. The following week, dozens of papers printed retractions, repudiating the truth of the story and some even going so far as to attack the credibility of the journalist who filed it. "Character witnesses" emerged soon after, their stories syndicated by the Big Six, the half-dozen television news stations with the largest viewer share, accusing the young lady of everything from prostitution and drug abuse to smuggling narcotics, human trafficking, and ultimately even of being affiliated with the terrorist cell which had allegedly carried out the plot to assassinate the president. The conflicting reports induced a spontaneous national hysteria from coast to coast.

Half the country joined in vilifying the young lady, going so far as to supplement the horrible news stories with their own morbid embellishments. She was a spy. She was a cold-blooded killer. She ate babies. Nothing was so grim and depraved as the lies with which she had disparaged the nation's highest office. The other half of the country immediately believed her, rallying to her defense in offices, parlors, parks, and cafes, and anywhere else a good debate or fistfight could be waged. She was a hero, a courageous defender of liberty and democracy-- a savior sent from above. And then, she was a martyr.

Four weeks after the first printing of the outrageous and unbelievable story, the young lady was found dead in a hotel room in New Jersey, her throat slashed, her eyes gouged out, all ten fingers broken, and her corpse violated in other ways which no decent or respectable words may convey. And that was when her story became real. One and all, the entire country was stopped in its tracks. The debates ended. The people understood, somehow, beyond contention, beyond cynical skepticism, beyond any shadow of a doubt, that this young lady had been no opportunist. She died for her story. This aspiring young savant, this honest and persistent child, was savaged and brutalized for daring to seek out the truth and to share it with the world. And suddenly, all of the many pieces of the story fell into place. The President himself had conspired to destroy his predecessor's rival, to assassinate his predecessor, to place himself at the table with the leaders of the SRU, to mortgage the American dream itself, and then to destroy it for the purposes of enriching himself and his friends. And when the truth came to light, his consorts sought to kill the story and discredit its author, and when that failed, the bastard had that poor young girl murdered in the most atrocious way, as a means of intimidating anyone else who dared to dig any deeper. One man had been at the center of it all. One man alone drew a single line between everything that had happened in the last four years. And that one man had made himself the most powerful living human being in the western hemisphere in the process. As this singular revelation rose in the east and set in the west, it settled heavily upon the entire conscience of the people, and their blood ran hot and turned to venom in their veins.

Now this man nervously peered through a narrow gap between the drawn curtains in a window on the second floor of the White House at 1600 Pennsylvania Avenue, imprisoned in the nation's capital by a furious wall of human flesh, armed to the teeth, daring him to try to escape, taunting him from an iron gate less than fifty yards away, and he understood, the only thing holding them back was the collective knowledge that he could not leave. They would not let him leave. But they were not ready to kill him, not yet. They did not want revenge; they wanted justice. They wanted to transform his palace of power and respect, first into a gilded cage, and finally into his own circle of hell.

Ten million people and counting, already twice the size of the entire American armed forces. Most of the soldiers had already mutinied against their commanding officers anyway, tearing off their patches, keeping their guns. The police had abandoned the city to the protesters, and many of them joined in. No one, not even the SRU was coming to rescue him. The President of the United States was trapped like a rat, he and twelve other human beings, members of his staff, a couple of friends who had been visiting when the mob first began to appear, and a single intern, a luckless chap who valiantly volunteered to stay behind when the rest of them held up their white flags and marched outside with their hands in the air to beg for mercy. The wag was half-convinced they'd be slaughtered, but masked his cowardice in a pragmatic subtext of dutiful, career-oriented subordination, all too happy to assume that when the chaos subsided, as he naively insisted it must, he would be rewarded for his loyalty and courage.

Three days inside, the foolishness of that decision overcame his delusions. He thought of killing the President himself. Virtually everyone trapped there with him had considered it, some more seriously than others. The president even considered killing himself. But all of them, as a condition of their nature, held fast to some small belief that they would be saved or spared, and in equal measure, refused to come to complete terms with the severity of their surreal predicament. And the notion was not lost on at least a few of them that the consequences of denying the people outside their own personal moment of catharsis, when the time finally came, would be even worse. The intern contemplated the irony. The people who had surrendered early, the cooks, the security guys, and the others, were permitted to pass completely unharmed. They were even greeted with shouts and cheers, welcomed by the mob and congratulated for making the right decision.

The cabinet member who broke the next day and tried to replicate the feat, putting his hands in the air, hoisting a white towel from the kitchen, and running out the front door with tears in his eyes, was shot down on sight. That window had closed forever. Now he was stuck here with the rest of these assholes, for better or worse, and pretty damned clearly for the worse.

(13)

As the sun set behind the dense clouds, a man appeared at the fringe of the crowd, carrying a bright yellow bolt cutter in his coal black hands. As he shoved his way into the midst of the protesters, the street lamps went dark and the entire city descended into blackness. A mighty hurrah went up from the people as they comprehended the power outage. Some industrious demonstrators promptly set to work removing tires from abandoned automobiles nearby, siphoning gasoline from their tanks, and filling the wells of the tires and setting them ablaze. Thick black smoke and an eerie glow filled the air. Though the masses paid little attention to him, many observed the bright yellow bolt cutters he carried and comprehended that he had some crucial role to play in the night's events, and they did not obstruct his path. After twenty minutes or so of pushing his way toward the front, the man arrived at last at the main gate of the White House lawn. There, he stared into a pretty young blonde-haired girl's pale blue eyes and began to chant. "Midnight, Midnight, Midnight."

At first the girl seemed moonstruck, like a bird hypnotized by a snake, but momentarily her senses returned and she too comprehended that this man, carrying the bright yellow bolt cutters, had some important role to play. And so she set herself to chanting with him, "midnight, Midnight, MIDNIGHT." Like a virus, the word spread through the crowd around them, all dully comprehending that this was something new, that something was happening, something concrete and tangible, an instruction, a call to arms, a way of coordinating the discordant, atomized masses. And one by one, they gave their lips to the chant. And two by two, and ten by ten, and so on, until the word became a commandment, and the word became flesh, and the flesh became the Word. "MIDNIGHT, MIDNIGHT, MIDNIGHT!" Before long, everyone on the block in front of the White House was roaring in militant unison, and then the blocks around them, until a single word possessed every human voice for a solid mile in any direction. Black tar-smoke, the smell of gasoline, a hellish glow originating from a hundred burning tires, and a single demonic voice chanting "MID-NIGHT! MID-NIGHT!! MID-NIGHT!!!" Their individual identities were washing away in the pelting rain and dense, caustic smoke, and they were possessed. They were one voice in the black night, with purpose and urgency and enthusiasm.

The man with the bright yellow bolt cutters approached the gates, laying his coal black hands on the wrought iron, his own eyes shining in the awful glow of the burning tires which had already been hurled over the fence onto the lawn, his sharp, ivory teeth peeled back into a hateful grin as he mouthed the Word in cadence with the millions behind, now captive to his own private initiative. He began shaking the gate to the rhythm of the chant, and others around him followed his example, laying hands on the entire fenceline all the way around the perimeter, one by one, pushing and pulling, shouting, screaming, thundering, "MIDNIGHT, MIDNIGHT, MIDNIGHT!" At first the gate did not move at all, but as more and more hands pushed and pulled and pushed and pulled, it began to rock to the rhythm, backwards, (midnight), forwards, (Midnight), backwards, (MIDNIGHT), forwards, (MID-NIIIIGHT!!!), inch by inch, and then by inches, until the stone beneath the rods began to crack under the strain. More and more, the wrought iron gate rocked further forward and further backward, until it seemed that it would give. Against ten thousand hands, no steel or stone can long stand. Somewhere off in the distance, church bells sounded their last ringing benediction of the evening, and somewhere, he thought to himself in amusement, an angel got its wings. With a blistering cry that seemed to nearly deafen those closest to him in the crowd, he uttered his last command of the day: "███████!!!" [12]

And the gate came down. "████████!" resounded from every throat, even those too far away to make out his voice. And as if by some animal instinct, as if possessed by this man of their own will, they fell in behind him as he stepped forward, slowly and deliberately, step by step, onto the White House lawn.

(14)

"Mr. President," said a voice behind him, "We have lost power to the whole city. We don't know why or how, but there's nothing we can do about it. Something seems to be happening down in those streets, and it doesn't look good. Mr. President, it is my duty to advise you that three of our four main-level generators were sabotaged before the recent exodus. The one that remains appears to only have enough juice to run up here for a couple of more hours."

"What does that mean, Bill?"

"Mr. President, it means that we are going to have to make a decision soon. Either we go below and try to hold out, or..."

"Or they'll tear down that fence out there and come for us. How long do you think we can last down there? How

---

[12] ███████

long? And what does it matter? Frying pan, fire?[13] I don't know. I don't know what to do. Those wretched beasts out there mean business. Ungrateful savages. Fucking SAVAGES!" he growled, to them outside, to himself, to no one in particular.

"Mr. President, we are provisioned for at least six weeks, I think. There's food, toiletries, a comms system, I don't know who the hell we'd call. But it's there. Up here we've only got what's in the kitchen, which is..*normally* restocked twice a week. There's running water down there, it's probably enough to last the thirteen of us for two months, if we conserve. I don't know either Mr. President, but I don't think we can stay up here much longer."

"FUCKING ungrateful savages. I swear I'd kill every last one of those fucking peasants. Weapons Bill, do we have any weapons?"

"Mr. President, the bunker does have an armory, yessir."

"Who the hell do they think they are? What are they going to do without me! They'll all turn cannibal in a week, those fucking imbeciles. They'll tear each other apart. No supply line, no imports. No FOOD! Six weeks. In six fucking weeks. They'll all be fucking wormfood in six weeks."

"Mr. President, we need to make the decision now."

"What are they doing out there Bill. What are those fucking scumbag-lowlife-fucking-commies doing out there? What is that they're saying? WHAT ARE THEY SAYING! Fucking maggots!"

"Mr. President!"

Suddenly, the president's voice changed from a growl to a shriek. "They're through! Those mother fuckers are on the lawn, Bill, BILL! They're fucking through!"

"Mr. President LET'S GO NOW!" Bill shouted, "QUICK!!! EVERYONE!! Into the hall, NOW!!!"

---

[13] Tolkein, J.R.R.. "Out of the frying pan and into the fire," in *The Hobbit, or, There and Back Again* (London: George Allen & Unwin, 1937).

"Oh my god Bill, they're coming! OK, OK, OK! Let's go, go go !!!"

About half of the people with him stirred themselves and ran for the hall, but the other half didn't move.

"What the fuck is wrong with you! What are you doing! Let's GO!" the president screamed.

The intern, finding his own courage for the first time, glared at him. "Go fuck yourself old man, we're not going into that fucking hole with you. You did this to yourself. YOU DID THIS TO ALL OF US!"

A few of those who had stirred themselves to run into the hall turned when they heard the brash young intern admonish the president, and suddenly their stomachs rolled over. All at once the thought possessed them, they were running into a *fucking hole*. Running into a grave. Led by the man who had put them all in this position in the first place. Running to certain death. One hundred thirty four feet below ground. Into another six weeks of what? Of living in claustrophobic paranoia with this madman, this raving lunatic, this greedy fucker? And then what? No one was going to come and rescue them. No one cared. And how could they possibly know when it was safe to come out? And what would they do if it was never safe? What would they do but suffer and starve and die in that *fucking hole*? When the food was gone. When the water ran dry. When the last generator down below finally went out. What would they do? Like he said. They'd turn cannibal. They'd tear each other's throats out, probably his first, or he'd kill all of them in the night to buy himself a few extra weeks. They were running scared, like lemmings, right off a fucking cliff, right into their graves. Suddenly, the fear came over them, and they faltered. They too glared at the president as the revelation washed over each of them. This was his fault. *HIS FAULT!*

And for a very long few seconds, they all stood around the exit to the hall, staring at one another, frozen and mortified. Until the lunatic broke the silence.

"Fuck it. FUCK ALL OF YOU! I'M GOING! You can all stay here and die, but I'm going down there, *where it's safe!*"

Just then, there sounded a loud crash below, followed by a commotion on the stairs, then on the landing. They were inside. Bill, now beside himself and hysterical, began frantically smashing the red button on the last elevator on the left. They could hear the footsteps mounting the last few stairs as the hum of the elevator pulley slowly brought the special car to the second floor. "Come on you mother fucker COME ON!" A bell sounded, and an electronic voice announced very calmly, "Second Floor, Going Down..." At the top of the stairs now, they saw a shadowy figure with gleaming white teeth and eyes that seemed to shine in the red emergency lights. The door to the elevator slid open, and Bill and the president dove inside, again frantically smashing the buttons inside. "Authorization for bunker access required," chirped the mechanical lady in a cool monotone. Bill fumbled with the keycards on the lanyard attached to his belt. "Fuck! I CAN"T SEE SHIT! FUCK! OK, Here it is I think this is- this better be it- fuck come on come on!" As the man with the white teeth and the gleaming eyes cleared the last stair, the bright yellow bolt cutters in his coal black hands came into view. But even as the men in the elevator scrambled to swipe the right key card across the little yellow-lit sensor in the elevator, screaming and cursing, the man with the bright yellow bolt-bolt cutters seemed to be in no hurry at all, casually strolling across the second floor hall with a pirate's grin and eyes sparkling like they had a fire of their own..

"Bunker Authorization Confirmed." said the robot voice, like the man with the bright yellow bolt cutters, seemingly without a care in the world. And the doors to the elevator slid closed.

The twelve other prisoners stood still as stone, daring not to speak a word or provoke the gathering rabble ascending the stairs behind the man with the bright yellow bolt-cutters, and as he approached, he stopped in front of the elevator, making a point of taking in the scene. Those who had followed him stopped a few feet shy, and like the prisoners, neither spoke nor moved. A long, uncomfortably silent pause ensued as the man with the bright yellow bolt cutters drank in the red-lit comedy of it all. At last, he spoke.

"You all decided not to go with him. You understood, didn't you. You understood that if you followed him where he was going, what would happen?" He waited, politely, until someone answered him, and after what seemed like an eternity, someone did.

"Fuck him." said the intern. And he said nothing else, but this seemed to satisfy the mysterious man with the bright yellow bolt cutters, who let out a peel of laughter that seemed to surprise even himself.

"Yes. Yes. Fuck him." the man agreed. The ice was not exactly broken, but there are always followers, moreso among prisoners, and certainly among prisoners of their own design. The other hapless prisoners loosened slightly, understanding the shifting dynamic in some primitive place in their reptilian minds, and another of them chimed in,

"Fuck him. I hope he fucking dies."

"What are you going to do?" asked another, finding her tongue for the first time in hours.

The man with the bright yellow bolt cutters had not yet revealed his plan to anyone, but he turned, and with only a quiet nod to the two or three ragged souls who had followed him most closely, those who had first uttered his call of midnight, who had first joined him in the laying of hands on the gate, who had marched so calmly with him across the lawn, who had kicked open the door below and ascended the stairs with him, somehow they immediately grasped the purpose of the bolt cutters.

They approached the elevator door, the last one on the left, the one with the red button, the only one with bunker access, and they shoved their fingers into the slit between the metal doors and began to pull. The doors are designed to open without a great deal of force, in case of fires or a stalled car, and after just a moment of pulling, the doors finally consented, opening to reveal the pulley cables, still traveling in the dark shaft, long slender shadows, barely visible in the dim red light. The man, pleased with their work, turned to the young intern, and offered him the bolt cutters. "Fuck him."

The intern pondered this mysterious man for a moment, and slowly brought his gaze down to the bright yellow bolt cutters in the man's coal black hands. And he reached out and took them.

"Fuck him." he agreed.

(The Hitchhiker)
(15)

Mr. Zelazny[14] had a nervous condition of sorts. Under certain circumstances, usually stressful ones, but not always, his brain would lock on to a particular stimulus and, in a kind of freeform word association, yield an uncontrollable flood of synonyms. For instance, as he sat at his desk watching his twelfth-grade predators and prey gradually meander into his sixth-period class, he habitually (and privately) categorized them according to what roles he suspected they would play in life. As the young and effete Mr. Gerald switched his way through the classroom door (numbered two-thirty-two in the western-most wing of Oswald-Kennedy Prep), always among the first to arrive, usually less than a minute and a half after the bell released the future dregs of society from their fifth-period slumber, wearing his neatly-creased gray slacks, pastel-green spread-collar tucked in beneath a royal blue sweater-vest under a cropped tossel of bright red hair, self-consciously planting one brown-leather wingtip in front of the other as he cleared the eight feet to his chair in the front-row, Mr. Zelazny's mind sputtered out the following: *wag, prim, brown-noser, intern, nerd,* and *prodigy.*

[14] Zelazny, Roger. *Lord of Light* (New York: Doubleday, 1967).

In its infinite wisdom, the inerrant school board in Melville County, Mississippi, during its fifth straight year of state-mandated budget cuts, implemented the newest of many recent cost-cutting "innovations," deciding that history and literature were essentially the same thing, and, of course, combining the two subjects into a single course, laid off three of the other five teachers qualified to teach either of them. Mr. Zelazny, the sixth, just so happened to have obtained certification in both, and thus was appointed "Head of the Department of Humanities" at Oswald-Kennedy Prep, while Mrs. Brecht, the obscenely perky brunette in room two-forty-six, who had a master's in Communication, naturally assumed the role of "Assistant Head of the Department of Humanities."[15] The Freshman and Sophomore classes had been struck from the curriculum, and between the Juniors and Seniors, Mr. Zelazny and Mrs. Brecht managed a total headcount of roughly four hundred thirty students. This made for an average class-size of about thirty-five students per period, with Mr. Zelazny teaching his share of the underclassmen before lunch, while she taught her seniors, with the arrangement reversed in the afternoon.

The absurdity of these trying circumstances was most visibly apparent in the fact that each of the two classrooms only had thirty chairs each. It made no difference, really. Mr. Selzany knew from experience that by the time the tardy bell rang in six minutes, only half of his sixth-period class would be present, and by the time the rest of them straggled in, roughly five minutes later, there would still be at least three chairs empty. It was September, and four of them had already dropped out. Another two, and rarely the same two, but always at least two, had inevitably already left the campus and were likely getting high and screwing in the unattended parking garage which bound the three-story Oswald-Kennedy Prep in downtown Melville to the old Ericsson Storage Facility on the left and to the Post Office on the right. Only nine rooms in the entire school had windows, and two of

---

[15] Brecht, Bertold. 1898-1954.

those were the Dean's office and the fourier preceding it on the first floor.

Next came young Mrs. Shelby, who, by all rights, was Mr. Gerald's polar opposite. Mrs. Shelby was a mediocre student on the best of days, though the confidence she possessed in her abilities rarely reflected this reality. Today, Mrs. Shelby was wearing her purple dress, which Mr. Zelazny had figured was one of about six that she owned in total. It was skin-tight and made of linen, and hemmed about five to six inches below her hip. Mr. Zelazny knew, precisely because she wanted him to know, that apart from the gaudy heels and the second-hand pearls, she wore nothing else at all. She also sat in the front row, and whenever Mr. Zelazny's eyes so much as passed in her direction, she would make a most deliberate effort to lock eyes with him, and then move her knees apart. This happened every day of the week, several times a day, and it filled Mr. Zelazny with a whirlwind of mixed emotions, ranging from unsettling anxiety to a perverse kind of gratitude. On the one hand, he resented the vulgarity of the gesture, understanding instinctively that it was a complete and total power move, there being nothing at all he could do or say to address the behavior that would not immediately result in a hearing before the Hellville Student Labor Union (another of the Melville County School Board's many "innovations") and the termination of his position, followed promptly by the end of his teaching career-- but on the other hand, most times, it was also the only real highlight of his day. Beyond these peculiar and bizarre displays of shamelessness, she never said a word. While Mr. Gerald would take every opportunity to answer a question, or ask one, Mrs. Shelby avoided any other form of participation whatsoever. As a matter of self-preservation as much as principle, Mr. Zelazny very purposefully abstained from ever speaking to her, in or out of the classroom. He did not dislike her, not exactly, but he certainly didn't trust her either, and was never perfectly sure he trusted himself. He made a ritual of trying to pretend, often in vain, that she simply wasn't there at all.

As the clock ticked away the seconds, other students shuffled in. Mr. Jensen, a nice enough young man of the inconspicuous and middling sort, neither clever nor dull; Mr. Hobbes, much the same, with a penchant for what he believed were witty remarks; Mrs. Kim, who seemed to at least take the class seriously, though Mr. Zelazny suspected she was often punching below her weight. They and the few others who followed were what Mr. Zelazny privately thought of as "centers," people who would neither choose the front or back rows, instinctively and subconsciously believing themselves to fit properly somewhere in between. These were the high-school equivalent of the Proletariat, the worker-bees who would wait tables, wash cars, or work at Ericsson or the Post Office. They were destined for neither greatness nor destitution. They would merely idle away their lives, glimpsing nothing at all beyond Melville's horizons, unless conscripted or kidnapped. The general stock of humanity, toiling beneath the burden of the great machine, blindly accepting the hands which had been dealt to them, oblivious, like grazing cattle. Consumers, bleating their way through the doldrums of middle-class life on a plurality of aimless paths, all converging beneath soil and short stones in the same field which claimed their fathers, and their fathers' fathers, perhaps grinding out a few hapless facsimiles of themselves along the way, or perhaps allowing their ancient lineages to co-terminate alongside themselves when their unmoving ends finally came. In a way, it was these young people who Mr. Zelazny most hoped could be jarred loose by his efforts from their sleepwalking daydreams, perhaps rending their pliable souls from the sanguine grasp of obscurity. Become predators, or become prey. Surely any alternative was preferable to living perpetually in the gray area in the center. At least, that was how Mr. Zelazny saw it, though he was never really sure he had genuinely accomplished anything more or anything less than middling. He supposed the distinction was mostly just an attitude, or at least a sense of awareness that the dichotomy existed, but in moments of terrifying uncertainty, the uncomfortable notion which he fought to suppress would rise in his stomach like acid into his throat. Mr. Zelazny also worked between the storage facility and the Post Office.

Mr. Zelazny glanced at his wristwatch and calculated that the tardy bell would ring in about eighty seconds. He self-consciously shifted himself in his swivel-chair, angling himself toward the door in order to put his shoulder to Mrs. Shelby, and concentrated on the folded newspaper in his lap, even as his mind struggled to wander. The headline was something about the upcoming election. One of the candidates was accused of committing some egregious sin and there were rumors of an indictment coming down from on high. Mr. Zelazny hated politics and despised politicians. Nothing ever changed. Even the promises themselves were perennial and repetitive. The economy was broken. Most of Europe and Asia had already gone over to the authoritarians it seemed. People killing people killing people killing people. Lies and breadcrumbs, apologies and accusations. The real shame was that they were still killing trees to print it all, knowing full-well that no one would bother to read any of it. For Mr. Zelazny, the paper itself was just a prop. A reason not to stare at his phone or Mrs. Shelby's crotch or the clock on the wall where the windows ought to have been. He had long since fallen out of the methodical habit of verbally greeting the students as they entered. That was a weird game anyway. Should he say hello to all of them, like the robot lady's voice in the elevator? Or just to some of them, and if so, how to choose which to greet and which to ignore? Much easier to just address them all at once after they were seated, less of a gauntlet that way, less *perfunctory, obligatory, arbitrary, awkward,* or *exhausting.* So he stared at his paper, which he had no interest in reading, in order to avoid entangling himself in hollow exchanges with-

(16)

RIIIIIIIIIIIIIIIIIIIIIIIIIIIIIIIIIIIIIINNNNNNNNGGGG GGGGGGGGG!

Wresting himself from his own distractions, almost startled by the shrill sound of the bell he had been deliberately waiting on, Mr. Zelazny neatly folded the newspaper and placed it on his desk and glanced out over the self-assembled matrix of predators and prey to count the remaining empty seats. There were six. He waited, killing time, and no one in the class was ever in any hurry to begin anyway. The last empty seats that would be filled were always in the back row, and would almost always be filled by the same handful of late students. He never reproached them for being late or holding up the class. He understood that they didn't want to be there any more than he wanted to see them, which was not at all. The last row was reserved exclusively for the 'obligatory' assholes-- jocks who came to class because they were obligated to do so. Two football players, Mr. Jones and Mr. Smith, and opposite them, Mr. Zelazny's least favorite student of any class, Mr. Spencer.

Mr. Jones and Mr. Smith played for *the team,* and though they possessed no significant prowess as athletes, they enjoyed the protected status which accompanied the jersey. Coach Knox was an absolute prick, and a pain in the ass. Of all the faculty at Oswald-Kennedy Prep, he was the only one who wielded any influence over the committee which presided over the Student Labor Board, a fact which gave him somewhat despotic authority over the whole institution. The Student Labor Board had been established two or three years ago, largely as a result of Knox's own personal efforts during the first waves of budget cuts. Before becoming a coach at Oswald-Kennedy Prep, Knox had been a teamster in a carpenter's union in Ohio somewhere. He was a shrewd and ambitious man, and the story of how he came to instigate what many of the faculty silently referred to as a *coup* at the high-school was rather extraordinary. As the coach of Melville's only football team, it had at some point dawned on

Knox that he wielded the most visible presence of all the faculty (to the town itself) as the 'coach,' which position afforded him a level of prestige which he could mobilize as support in any contest with the administrators or the board. Simultaneously, he played the martial role of lord and master in the eyes of the boys on the team, who themselves tended to be the most popular kids in school, as is the case in most highschools. So Knox concocted this clandestine scheme to persuade a handful of students to sue the school on the grounds that they "lacked representation." As outrageous as the suit seemed to many, the capacity for absurdity on the part of the Mississippi court system had long been accepted by the population at large as utterly without limit. The students argued that because their attendance was mandated by Mississippi State law (at least, in order to successfully complete the program- plenty of washouts hit the streets well before reaching the age of the majority), and because they provided a physical service (as athletes) without compensation, which yielded measurable material value (in the form of ticket sales), and that many of them were legally adults (because as prep schools go, Oswald-Kennedy's pass/fail ratios were, in a word, abysmal), then, *ipso facto*, they had a collective right to negotiate any and all administrative policies.

When the Mississippi courts recognized the students' right to organize, Knox advised them to hold a campus-wide vote in order to fill the Student Labor Union Committee. Naturally, the handful of kids who tallied the most votes in what amounted to little more than a popularity contest, were on the team. Thereafter, the committee, and by proxy, Knox himself, had a say in virtually every aspect of administrative policy, which included everything from the cafeteria menu to conflict resolution to the hiring and firing of the teachers themselves. Consequently, after the committee was established, not a single Oswald-Kennedy athlete ever received a failing grade in any class. Such is the nature of power and politics.

(17)

A full six minutes after the tardy bell, Mr. Spencer finally condescended to drag himself through the door. A walking representation of everything Mr. Zelazny hated about Oswald-Kennedy Prep, Mr. Spencer embodied the failure of the Mississippi education system, to say nothing of the abysmal failures of society at large. Eyes red and swollen and squinting, hat cocked to one side, loosely balanced on his shaggy head rather than worn, a dirty, sleeveless tee, two sizes too small, with a pistol emblazoned across the front, and cutoff blue jeans which were two sizes too large, revealing all but the lowest stitches of his bright orange boxers and necessitating an almost comical effort to hold the belt loops above his knees with one hand while he cripwalked his way to the back row, carrying no books or papers or anything to write with, Mr. Spencer snorted what must have been a full teaspoon of his own mucus in a disgusting, nasally wretch, before loudly hocking it up into the back of his throat and swallowing it. The entire classroom, already stale with old pulp and cloying with the penitentiary smell of Simple-Green vapor, was immediately drenched in a pungent mix of body odor and weed. But as disgusting as Mr. Spencer was on the outside, nothing could compare to the repugnance of his personality. At nineteen years old, he was already virulently racist, violent and confrontational, arrogant, demeaning, and functionally illiterate. Mr. Zelazny was convinced that the only reason Mr. Spencer came to class at all was to terrorize a captive audience. Whether he was a sadist by nature or by nurture or by both was a subject of much hushed conjecture among the faculty, but what was certain was that he was inherently untouchable. He was indeed Mr. Knox's only begotten son, and therefore well beyond the reach of any manner of discipline. He hated everyone, his father most of all. He hated school and made no effort to live up to anyone's expectations but his own. About once a month, like clockwork, he would explode on some poor student and brutalize them, and then accuse them of starting the fight.

The Student Labor Union would then "address the grievance," which meant suspending or expelling the victim. Mr. Spencer made it to the twelfth grade the same way the so-called athletes did, with Coach Knox's protection. Even without Knox's intrigues, the teachers at Oswald-Kennedy would have sooner passed Mr. Spencer than endure another year with him. And this was just Mr. Zelazny's year, though he supposed it was better for him than it had been for Mrs. Brecht.

Mr. Zelazny hated his job for many reasons. Foremost among them was that he earned a paltry two hundred eighty one dollars per week, which, after taxes, rounded out to roughly a thousand dollars per month. These were poverty wages, even by Mississippi's standards. To be responsible for the education, motivation, safety, and wellbeing of over two hundred students per day. To grade between four and six hundred papers per week. Plus at least four hundred tests per month. Plus another four hundred exams per semester. He had done the math once. It came down to less than fifty cents an hour. Not even poverty wages. They were slave wages. He earned enough to afford a roach infested, one-room apartment with electricity and about one hundred sixty dollars a month in groceries. He had no retirement plan, apart from the occasional lottery ticket. He had no health or life insurance. The state offered these of course, but the annual premiums were prohibitive; the deductibles were comically absurd. He lived alone, of course. No self-respecting woman would tolerate such a lifestyle, and he could scarcely afford to pay for the alternative even if he possessed the inclination to do so, which he surely did not.

Mr. Zelazny felt unappreciated and abused by the system he had once idealized, and while none of the students themselves were overtly malicious towards him, even that required walking a perilous tightrope of indignities every day. He had no authority over them, commanded no respect, nor had any recourse but to concede every conflict before it began. The heroic feat of refusing to hate his students, of whom his entire mode of social interaction was comprised, and with whom he had nothing at all in common and to whom he could not relate on any intellectual, emotional, or moral level, required him to internalize all of his anger and frustration and direct it at the only remaining creature involved, himself. In a world with nine and a half billion people, for all intents and purposes, he was the last living man alone with **g**od, and **g**od, like Mr. Spencer, was a cold, calloused, misanthropic bully.

(18)

Having stalled for as long as his nerves would permit, Mr. Zelazny reached for his pack of filterless Camel cigarettes (*asthma, acidic, black lung, noxious, death, relief*), thumbed one out of the torn open end, held it to his lips and lit it. He stood, looked at his watch once more, thirty eight minutes. Inhaling deeply and blowing a thick yellow cloud out over the assembled faces of the future of civilization, he began:

"Hello to all of you and good afternoon. How is everyone today?" Mr. Zelazny was greeted by vacant stares and silence. "Glad to hear it!" he bellowed, the familiar feeling rising in his gut, as always, he would match their apathy with aggressive enthusiasm. It was the only way. "Monday was the first day of class. As you will recall, we laid out our course objectives for the year. We are studying American history through literature, and American literature through history. Tuesday, we discussed one of those objectives, which was the role of journalism in shaping American thought. I asked each of you to purchase a notebook specifically for the purpose of making your own journal entries. I believe the next Norman Mailer or Carl Bernstein could be sitting right here in this class! Now remember the parameters as you're making your daily efforts, nothing incriminating, nothing vulgar, nothing necessarily personal.[16] I remind you that these-- can anyone tell me what we said was the difference between a journal and a diary?" As he waited, the door to the class swung open again and Mrs. Reuben, heavily laden with a bag full of books and a

---

[16] Mailer, Norman. 1923-2007.; Bernstein, Carl. 1944-?.

bright yellow purse that looked as if it carried a bowling ball, struggled past the rows to find her seat.

"Welcome Ms. Reuben, come one in."

"Sorry I'm late Mr. Z, girl stuff."

Mr. Zelazny, grateful enough for the simple courtesy of acknowledgement alone, was not inclined to press the issue. "No problem at all Ms. Reuben, if you would consider trading me an answer for my benevolent patience?"

"A diary is where you write stuff about your life and your own thoughts. It's supposed to be private. A journal is where you write about stuff that's going on around you, and sometimes you publish it." She had not even asked him to repeat the question as she sloughed off her load and sat down, he noted, and for a moment, he felt better. He took a victory puff from his filterless cigarette and carried on.

"Fantastic ma'am. Exactly right. So, as I was saying, you will all be required to turn in your journals once a month. Additionally, on the day you turn them in, you'll be asked to select a passage and read it to the class. So again, nothing vulgar, nothing incriminating-- I don't want to know about your war crimes and death notes, ok? And nothing terribly personal." Another drag, as he glanced down at his neatly folded paper to verify his assumption that it was indeed Wednesday, "Remember, you're writing about something that is happening in the world," taking in the headline again (*crooks, oligarchs, authoritarians, demagogues, scum*). "Today is Wednesday," he exhaled, "and we're going to begin with an outline of the subjects we will try to get through in this course, as well as a discussion of mythology. Who can tell me what the word 'mythology' means?" As he searched for hands, Mr. Gerald's shot up, as Ms. Shelby's knees shot out. He spun on his heels, squeezing his eyes shut as he fumbled for a piece of chalk. "Mr. Gerald, please enlighten us."

"Mythology is like stories we teach our kids to teach them about our history and where we come from and who we are."

"Very good, very good. A myth is a traditional story with which we *socialize," (brainwash, lie to, propagandize)* he paused on the word, for emphasis, while he began writing the outline on the board: Colonial Era, Revolution, Constitutional Period, War of 1812, Antebellum, Civil War, "with which we SOCIALIZE, who can tell me what that word means?" Reconstruction, Soft Money-- without turning around to survey the raised hands, he gambled-- "Mr. Gerald, again," Spain, World War One, World War Two--

"To socialize," Mr. Gerald's voice answered, "is to teach young people how to be citizens."

--Korea and Vietnam, Contemporary Period-- "What does that mean though? How to be a citizen?" Mr. Zelazny spun one third of the way around to face Mr. Gerald directly as he responded.

"It means like," he hesitated, searching for the words, and finding them "like, how we teach them the laws and right from wrong and how to vote and stuff like that." Mr. Gerald, who had not actually raised his hand the second time around, broke off with a degree of abruptness sufficient to signal to Mr. Zelazny that he had contributed his fair share for the moment.

"Correct again, Mr. Gerald, thank you. Prior to the discovery of the New World by Mr. Columbus in 1492, there were many unique mythologies which shaped the experience of western civilization. Write these down. Egyptian, Greek, Roman, Hebrew, Norse, and Mestizzo. There were others, of course, but these are among the ones that most impacted how we think of the past and of ourselves. The Egyptians, for instance, created elaborate stories to explain the motions of the heavenly bodies in the sky. They discovered that certain stars and constellations could help them predict the weather. Priests, living in the Seine region, observed that when a certain star arose in the east, they had about two weeks before their rivers flooded. Knowing this helped them to plant their crops and build their cities accordingly, and therefore, for those societies, studying the sky proved to be an extraordinary survival advantage. Their rulers, we might add, learned to listen to the priests' council very early on in matters of agriculture, and eventually began receiving their advice on other matters, believing that the priests themselves possessed a special wisdom given to them from the gods they worshiped, they would consult with them before waging war or making other kinds of decisions. And so we see a productive relationship between church and state emerging at the very beginning of recorded history, thousands of years ago.

"Who can give me an example of Greek mythology?"[17] Mr. Zelazny took one last strong pull from his filterless Camel cigarette before snuffing it out in the bronzed tin coaster, glancing at his watch again, but taking no notice of the time.

Ms. Kim raised her hand, and with an assenting nod from Mr. Zelazny, volunteered only the word "Zeus?"

"Zeus! King of the gods, well done Ms. Kim," Mr. Zelazny embellished his approval, hoping to reward her for taking the risk. "Zeus was the patriarch of the Greek pantheon. Pan-the-on," he wrote the word on the board. "A pantheon is a whole cast of characters whom the Greeks believed watched over them from the heavens and occasionally interfered in their lives. Zeus, his wife Hera, Ares, the god of war, Apollo, the sun god, Aphrodite, goddess of love, Hermes, Zeus's wily yeoman, Hephestus, and my personal favorite, Dionysus, the god of festivities, among many others, all presided over human affairs from the summit of Mount Olympus. Add to these Hades, ruler of the underworld, later adapted by Hebrews as a place of damnation for sinners, and Poseidon, Lord of the seas, and you've got what is effectively an administrative cabinet, not all that different from the president's cabinet, with one god responsible for each of the various departments of creation. So the Greeks, when they wanted something specific, would

[17] Hamilton, Edith. *Mythology* (Boston: Little, Brown, and Co., 1942).

pray and offer tribute to the particular **g**od which governed that sphere of influence. If you had a crush on a pretty girl or a hot guy, you would seek to curry favor with Aphrodite. Going fishing? You'd better do a little brown-nosing with Poseidon!" A couple of muffled chuckles reassured Mr. Zelazny that the joke he had offered for the sixth time today had not fallen completely flat for the fourth time in a row.

"Now, once the Romans got going, they integrated many of these figures into their own culture, renaming them as they went, in their Latin tongues." Turning again to the board, he began to scribble the names quickly, calling them out as he went, "and thus Zues became Jupiter, Hades became Pluto, Ares became Mars, and Aphrodite became Venus, and so on. Does anyone notice anything familiar about these names?" He turned to look again for hands, careful to control his eyes.

With the confidence of elementary school children, a half dozen young adults ignored protocol and shouted out that they were the names of planets. Mr. Zelazny at least felt that he had their attention, which was more than he expected, and so he proceeded to ride the wave of momentum he had generated thus far. "Very good, yes, we still use the Roman names of Greek **g**ods to refer to our planets. And those characters still figure largely in our stories and movies and *culture-*" he turned again to write the word on the board, "-to this day."

"Next we come to Hebrew mythology," and as he turned around, he saw Mr. Smith's hand shoot into the air. This was the difficult moment, he knew, having lived it five times already today, and dozens of others during his time at Oswald-Kennedy Prep, when enthusiasm might sour into protest and confrontation, but he resigned himself to trying to get through it as smoothly as possible. "Yes. Mr. Smith?" He noticed, if only subconsciously, that Mr. Spencer had lifted his head from the desk and was now glaring at Mr. Smith with contempt, presumably for having the audacity to disturb his slumber from the back row. Mrs. Shelby's knees crossed.

"What you mean by 'Hebrew Mythology?'"

"I'm coming to that now Mr. Smith, if you please? In antiquity, the Hebrews were a small tribe of people living near the eastern shores of the Mediterranean. As the Greek and Roman empires grew, the Hebrew people were essentially caught in between. They had contrived their own mythologies, or stories, to explain where they came from and to teach their own young the values and traditions of their society. But their traditions were quite different from those of the Greeks and Romans. For instance, while the Greeks and Romans had many gods in their pantheon, the Hebrews believed in only one god, and they believed that their god was more powerful than any other god, and this created enormous conflict with the--"

"So you saying Jesus is a myth Mr. Z?" Mr. Smith persisted.

"I am saying that every society had their own version of Jesus, or Moses, for that matter, in whom they believed as fervently as the Jews did." Mr. Zelazny paused for half a second to be sure that this was a passive enough response to avoid conflict, and continued without waiting for half a second longer for a coherent reaction to metastasize. "However, as I was saying, over time, some of the Jewish people, understanding that the necessity of their situation as a small tribe falling under the rule of a much larger, much more militant, mind you, a much larger society, found a way to adapt their beliefs to the circum--"

"So you saying you don't believe in *god?*" Mr. Jones interjected, taking up the cause; Mr. Spencer was now leaning into the brewing controversy with an eager look in his eyes.

"I am not discussing what I believe, Mr. Jones, I am discussing what the Jews, Greeks, and Romans believed. Christianity emerged as a kind of hybrid between the Jewish and Greek traditions. Historians have pointed out that the Judeo-Christian theology combines many Greek and Roman elements, as reflected in the narrative of the New Testament. Render unto Caesar, for example. The prevalence of 'fish' in the New Testament, referring as some scholars have theorized, to the age of Pisces, as the Greeks would have understood the passage of time as measured by the positions of the constellations." Mr. Jones and Mr. Smith, pacified for the moment, leaned back to listen more carefully, but retained a bit of visible reluctance. "Other scholars hypothesize that Jesus and his twelve disciples, for another example, were adapted from the sun god Apollo and his twelve consorts, that is, the twelve constellations whose positions in the sky informed the Greek and Roman calendar year. Lastly, the Christmas holiday which we still celebrate, is a Christianized form of *Yule*," he turned again to write the word on the board, "which was a Germanic festival celebrating the god Oden, which brings us to our Norse mythology.

"The people who inhabited northeastern Europe, some of whom you may recognize as *Vikings*," again, to the board, "believed that the god Oden hung himself upside down from a tree for nine days over a clear running stream, and on the last day, reached into the stream and pulled out a handful of stones, each containing a letter of the *Futhark*," he wrote the capital letters F, U, TH, A, R, K, "which made up the basis of the Norse alphabet. Fewu, Uruz, Tewas, Hagalaz, Algiz, Raidho, and Kenaz. Many of these letters have since been adapted into our phonetic alphabet, F, U, R, and K, for example." He turned back to the board to spell out the word 'Raidho' on the board. "Does anyone notice anything familiar about this word?"

He gave them a moment to study the word, which he had written in large capital letters. *Fifty-fifty*, he thought to himself, based on past experience with American students.

"It looks like Radio!" someone shouted, he didn't catch who, but he was satisfied, and continued on.

"Yes, it's exactly where we get the word 'radio' from. Now, obviously the point of today's lecture isn't to get into great detail about each of these mythologies, but to show that they influence our own identities in different ways. The last one, which we haven't talked about, and may I remind you, our culture is influenced by every mythology from every civilization that has ever lived, in one form or another, but again, we're going over the major ones, the last one, is actually not accurately named, as we are using it here. Can anyone tell me which one we haven't hit yet?"

"Mestizzo," Ms. Kim piped in.

"Mestizzo. Correct Ma'am. When I say Mestizzo, I am actually referring to a variety of different cultures represented by the indigenous peoples of the North American continent before the [pointing at the word on the board and sounding it out] 'Colonial Era'. These, the Aztecs, Incans, and Mayans, most notably, had flourished for centuries before the Dutch, Spanish, English, and French began colonizing the western hemisphere, along with hundreds of other, smaller, but no less unique tribes of nomads and hunter-gatherers in North America, such as the Navajo, the Chyenne, and Pawnee, for instance. Though their cultures were functionally eradicated over time by imperialist conquest and disease and interbreeding, there are still, likewise, many traces of their heritage mixed in with our own. Just to give you a few examples, many of our states, cities, and counties, especially in the western parts of the country, come directly from indigenous languages. Mississippi comes from the Ojibwa word meaning 'big-river'. Ohio is named after the Seneca word, meaning 'good-river'. And can anyone guess what the word Colorado means?" No answers shouted out this time, no matter. "It means Red River, which is actually a Spanish translation.

"So in the present day, as you can see, our culture and language have been heavily influenced by other cultures and languages throughout the world. But even in the modern era, Americans still cling to many kinds of mythologies which we have invented along the way. By show of hands, does anyone remember being taught in elementary school how Ferdinand

and Isabella funded Columbus's westward voyage to discover a new sea route to India?"

Mr. Hobbes raised his hand and was called upon. "They taught us in fourth grade that Isabella sold the jewels from her crown to pay Columbus."

Mr. Zelazny responded, "Thank you Mr. Hobbes. Would you be the least bit surprised to learn that, in fact, the Spanish monarchs paid for that voyage with wealth accumulated as a result of the Spanish Inquisition? The Spanish actually ordered all of the Jews to leave the country and to leave their property behind or risk torture and death. Now, what kind of a society would we be if that was the story we told our children? So that's an example of a myth which originated during the Colonial Era and is still taught, and no doubt in fact *believed,* by many of your very own elementary school teachers. Here's one from the Constitutional Period. Do you remember the story about George Washington chopping down the cherry tree and then getting caught and admitting to having done it? Pure mythology. That story originated in an early piece of American literature authored by a man named Parson Mason Weems, who wrote Washington's biography after his death in 1799.[18] Weems, like many authors of the period, believed informing the new nation's sense of virtues was more important than just telling the plain old truth, and so these authors invented little stories here and there, mostly as a way to teach younger children about American values.

"As the country evolved, we created other little stories, some lasting longer than others, and some being more or less important than others. Pecos Bill, is one example. If you grew up anywhere in the southwest, you learned about Pecos Bill very early on, a rowdy cowboy character who could ride a tornado like it was a horse. And other mythologies evolved which were more substantial, some persisting to this very day." Mr. Zelazny turned again to the board, scrawling

---

[18] Weems, M.L., *A History of the Life and Death, Virtues, and Exploits of Gen. George Washington* (1890).

the words 'Manifest Destiny' in large letters, and asked no one in particular, "who remembers this phrase and can tell me what it means?"

"It means that **g**od intended for the settlers to colonize America all the way across the country to the west coast," Mr. Gerald curtly volunteered.

"Exactly right Mr. Gerald, thank you. Now this is an example of a mythology created in real time, by adults, for adults, rather than children, in order to justify what essentially amounted to policies of mass genocide, abuse, torture, and confiscation, against the native peoples, as our civilization expanded. This attitude, that the anglo-saxon race was somehow favored among all the races by the creator, became the basis for another myth, which came to be known as the myth of American Exceptionalism. This idea, that Americans were destined to be the new rulers of the world, emerged late in the 19th century, and has been evoked in every single American conflict ever since, either explicitly, or implicitly. Another mythology emerged in the 19th century following the Civil War, and it is one which I am pretty sure many of you *have* heard of. It's called the 'Lost Cause'." Presently, Mr. Zelazny noticed, though he tried not to indicate that he had noticed, that Mr. Spencer's hand had gone up when he mentioned the Civil War. The hair stood up on his arms, and he sensed that the air itself was changing in the room, and a nervous feeling began working its way up his spine. Mr. Spencer never raised his hand for any reason, and never spoke, unless it was to say something awful, and Mr. Zelazny was determined not to have his good momentum wasted with only fifteen minutes left in the day. Catching himself before allowing his brief pause of recognition to last long enough to be noticed, he tried to push on.

"Who will tell me what the Civil War was about?" At first, unsettlingly, Mr. Spencer's hand remained the only one in the air. A cold, audacious sneer was forming at the corners of the boy's lips and eyes. Mr. Zelazny's pulse quickened, and a single bead of impatient sweat appeared on his left temple.

Only a second had passed since he punctuated his question, but the second was long enough for Mr. Spencer, who was now wide awake and clearly eager to be called on voluntarily, to notice that Mr. Zelazny was waiting for someone, literally anyone else, to rescue him from the hole he had dug himself in the span of that second. Mr. Spencer leaned his outstretched elbow into his other hand, as if to push the whole arm a few inches higher. Mr. Zelazny's blood began to curdle in his veins. He saw the trap coming, and was desperate to side-step it in stride. He repeated his question, with some urgency, his own eyes, now obviously restless, consciously sweeping the foreground to avoid the mischievous, penetrating malevolence burning into his skin from the back of the room. The wristwatch, the newspaper, Ms. Shelby's knees, the clock on the wall, the worried look on Mr. Gerald's face-- having glanced sharply behind himself just long enough to take in the situation, but not long enough to meet Mr. Spencer's gaze and draw his attention, but certainly long enough to understand the risk of voluntarily breaking the gathering storm of silence. Mr Jones and Mr. Smith, along with most of the class, were now sharply aware of Mr. Spencer's sudden enthusiasm, and Mr. Jones and Mr. Smith, sensing the character of whatever was waiting on Mr. Spencer's lips, were now eyeing him suspiciously, but no one was volunteering anything. Now Mr. Zelazny had lost his rhythm, he had lost control, his mind raced ahead to the words which were supposed to follow a normal answer to a normal question in a normal class, *"Right, slavery, the Civil War was fought over slavery, primarily, though there were many other related conflicts which had helped to bring about the war, but once the war was fought, many of these issues were subsumed by the much larger and more visible problem of--"*

"Mr. Z!" Mr. Spencer could wait no more. He understood the situation like a general looking at a map. This was his moment, and he would not let it pass. "Mr. Z!!" Why was he even waiting to be called upon? Why wouldn't he just blurt it out? He was like a vampire knocking on the door, waiting to be granted entry, needing permission, needing to implicate Mr. Zelazny in his malicious schemes, needing the sanction of the system itself for his cruelty against it. It was his nature, he could not, would not, accept sole responsibility. He knew, now they all knew, his was the only hand raised. No ally would come to Mr. Zelazny's aid. No cavalry would ride to his rescue. Now was the moment of conflict, a binary contest of wills as old as war itself, and no one would voluntarily intervene. Now the whole class became anxious spectators to the transfer of power occurring before them. "Mr. Z! Mr. Z!" They all knew what was coming, and none of them were responsible for it; like a mob gathered around a street fight, they sensed blood in the water. They sensed an impending spectacle. And in the space of a moment, they had all collectively decided to bear witness. They ceased to be a class and became an audience instead. They hungered for some primitive obscenity. They wanted to hear it, no matter how disgusting or despicable or common. And the moment would wait no longer. King Conflict had taken over the lecture, and now they would learn something real, something visceral, about the human condition, something they would not need notes to remember, but also something they would be tested on every day for the rest of their lives. "MIS-TER ZEEE!" Mr. Spencer, now shouting, now carrying the day. Mr. Zelazny was cornered, and must relent.

At last, in the breath of a sigh, remorseful and beaten, having almost crossed the finish line on the third day of the fall semester at Oswald-Kennedy Prep, and for one last lonely second, finding refuge in Ms. Shelby's eyes, revealing his own lifetime of struggle and sacrifice and weakness and dissatisfaction and contempt and vulnerability, and finding them all strangely reflected right back at him, and hearing her silent voice in his mind, *"I don't know how to help you, but I understand. Fuck it. Just do it. What else are you going to do? It's now or never man. You didn't ask for this shit. It's just the way it is. You can't change any of it. You can't change him. You can't change any of us. You can't change this awful place. You don't fucking belong here. You can't just stand there letting him make an asshole out of you. I know what you're going through. We all get it. It's not your fault. There's nothing you can do now. Just give in. Let him have it. What does any of this shit matter anyway? You're broke. You're beaten. They've cornered you. All of them. The Student Labor Union. The School Board. Us. Our parents. The government? Nobody gives a fuck. Don't you get it? YOU'RE the fucking myth, man. You're the lie no one believes any more. Just get on with it. Do you hear me, Mr Z? MR. Z?"*

"MIS-TER ZEE!? Aint that when we let all these coon-ass fuckin'niggers go free?"

The tension had turned all of the air in the room into sulfur, and that air ignited. Mr. Jones and Mr. Smith sprang to their feet, violently shoving their desks behind them, "the FUCK you say white boy?" demanded one, "say it again mother fucker!" screamed the other, Mr. Spencer now on his feet holding his own desk between them, and then chaos ensued. The other students jumped out of their chairs and ran to the front of the room as the fight began, Ms. Shelby and Mr. Gerald, predator and prey, taking their positions closest to Mr. Zelazny, who stood frozen, all watching the scene unfold as Mr. Jones put both hands into Mr. Spencer's chest, almost pushing him over his firmly planted back foot, Mr. Smith dove over the chair and wrestled the boy to the ground, catching a solid haymaker of a fist to the right jaw in the air, and then both of them were on top of the boy, punching, kicking, and shouting obscenities. Ms. Shelby turned her face into Mr. Zelazny's shoulder, tears already welling and ruining her carefully applied makeup. Mr. Gerald, crying too, but fighting it, ran into the hallway and called for help. Mr. Zelazny, for his part, did nothing.

(19)

A full hour later, Mr. Zelazny sat in the driver seat of his piece-of-shit Beetle, next to a cardboard box full of his belongings. Campus police had rushed into the room after only a couple of minutes and pulled the two boys off of Mr.

Spencer, who by then had a concussion, broken teeth, and broken ribs. The administration held the entire class after the last bell, pulling them into separate rooms to interview them each individually while Mr. Zelazny was interrogated by a handful of students on the Student Labor Union Committee. Why hadn't he broken up the fight? School policy expressly forbids intervening in any violent physical exchange between students, had been his unsatisfactory reply. Knox had been there, his blood pressure nearly bursting the vessels in his red hot face. *MY BOY COULD HAVE BEEN KILLED YOU SON OF A BITCH!* he had spat. Mr. Zelazny, outnumbered by imbeciles and children, fought valiantly to suppress his own outrage, for nothing. He knew he was done. He understood the game before any of them even opened their mouths. The boy would need hospitalization. That would cost money. That required an insurance claim. That required a scapegoat. And that scapegoat had to be fired, or the school would be sued. And the school would lose. The faculty, his friends, had stood by and watched the farce unfold, saying nothing, but commiserating with their silence. It could have been any of them. And it had been, quite often. Mr. Zelazny had tried, and failed. It just wasn't in the cards. No appeals. No severance. No legal representation. Nothing. Just a kangaroo court, and a kangaroo verdict, issued from the mouths of babes. And now, nothing at all. *Infinite Nothing*, a peculiar phrase, emerging from somewhere in the back of his thoughts, almost with a voice of its own. No more class. No job. And very likely, no more career, especially if the boy's injuries were severe, which Mr. Zelazny expected them to be. And especially if the story made headlines in Melville, which Mr. Zelazny also expected it most certainly would do.

He absently inserted the key into his ignition, half his brain shutting down, the other half trying frantically to focus on the here and now. Words flooded in, disconnected and unorganized, a random inventory, *a quarter tank of gas, a nearly empty fridge, one hundred forty two dollars, unemployment line, post-traumatic-stress-disorder, revenge, isolation, bills, humiliation, resentment, paraplegic, Lost Cause, Lost Cause, Lost Cause...* Mr. Zelazny turned the key, but the engine didn't turn over. He turned it again, mashing the gas pedal like a bass drum, it sputtered and whined its own petulant laughter. He took the key out, breathed deeply as the tears rolled down his flushed cheeks. "Fuck it," said the voice. "Fuck it," he agreed aloud. "Fuck it all." He put the key back into the ignition and turned it, flooring the pedal as the engine roared to life. He threw the transmission into reverse and backed out of his space in the parking garage, and then peeled the tires as he raced down the spiral, half hoping he crashed into someone or something on the way down. As he emerged under the gray sky, the rain drops covered his windshield. Flicking on the wipers as he pulled out into the street, he noticed the barricades a couple of blocks ahead. As he approached, he could make out the figure of a man in a yellow vest and a white helmet, waving his coal black hands in the air and directing traffic into the detour. Mr. Zelazny sighed to himself and obliged, wheeling his Beetle through the turn and politely waving his assent to the worker.

As he rounded the corner, he observed another figure several yards ahead, walking in the rain. The figure, upon hearing the sound of his engine, whirled around and seemed to recognize him. The figure appeared to extend a thumb. As the wiper blades swished the downpour from the tiny glass, he could just make out the purple dress, second-hand pearls, and gaudy heels.

(The Kinship Cult.)
(20)

"Yo what up! It's ya boy Isaac Dee-to-tha-Kay Massey here, but you already know that's D-K to you out there in the chat! Welcome back ya'll, we here for another episode of *Weird Shit You Need To KNOW About*, and you bitches aint gonna BELIEVE the weird shit we into today! That's right! You already know, you called it, you wanted it, and we bringin' it to you LIVE as fuck in this bitch today, hell yeah, it's finna get REAL, I mean this tha *riiiiiiillllll shit* right here. If you guessed it? Did you guess it? Naw, yall aint ready! Lemme get a F in the chat if y'all ready? Lookin at it right now, this looks like we already breakin' records y'all, look at that, over ONE HUNDRED EIGHTY SEVEN MILLION viewers already, that is TV HISTORY in the making! We ain't even hit the TITLE SCREEN yet and we already the most watched shit in HISTORY! That's right, y'all hear me out there? Y'all is makin' HISTORY today watchin' this shit right here! Oh man, I can't even believe it. This the day y'all, this is the DAY! Remember it, October 4th of the third year of the Second Republic, It's a TUESDAY! So y'all get your refreshments rolled up or broke up or poured up, ya heard? Yeah, YOU know. Let's get to it.

"Today on Weird Shit, we gonna be lookin' at the MOST controversial family in the whole damn country. You seen 'em on the news for the last six weeks since the trial, and man what a bullshit trial that was, these folks must got the baddest ass lawyer who ever lived, I don't get it, they should'a burned these crazy mother fuckers at the stake, know what I'm sayin'? Raisin' these kids like this, man if that ain't criminal then I don't even get why we got laws anymore! So we 'bout to take a sneak peak inside the life and times of the So-Called-Jones family, these twisted ass, whacked out, weird ass mofos right here gotta let us into day and we gonna film a whole DAY of they lives, we gonna talk to the husband, the wife, AND the boy, we gonna look through all they shit, and we gonna see what we gonna find! How we gonna do it you ask? BY COURT ORDER bitches! That's right yall, we had our own sick ass legal eagle, y'all seen her on the show before, the lovely and talented Miss Annabel Rice, oooh she so damn fine ain't she?[19] And she SMART too y'all, don't get it twisted what I'm sayin' here, she filed what she said was called a "Freedom of Information Act" (did I get that right Chuck? Yeah? ok), she filed a freedom-of-information-act claim against the Jones family, demanding public access to the

---

[19] Rice, Ann. 1941-?.

family's personal SHIT, just so y'all out there who agreed with us that that trial was whack as FUUUUCK could see for yourself what kind of weird shit these crazy ass folks was into. Now, I ain't gonna lie, they fought back, cuz obviously they don't want the world knowin' about they weird ass lifestyle, you know, they got shit to hide, prolly bodies in the freezer and shit like that, you never know what these weird ass cults be into, right? So we li-a-gat-ed a whole bunch a money y'all, and-wait, that reminds me, none of this would be possible if it wasn't for all the love y'all be showin, so if you watchin' this right now and y'all hype as FUCCCK about Wierd Shit, y'all gotta pound that mufkin LIKE button right now and Subscribe to the channel and, you know, throw a few bucks our way, cuz you know daddy got expensive habits ha HA! So go on ahead and do that right now fa' ya boy, and anyway, naturally, we WON our case, and the court said we could go in these people house for a full 24 hours, un-re-strict-ed access, and these crazy ass mofos gotta let us do it, or we get to sue them AGAIN!

"So that's what's up y'all, that's what we doin' today, so y'all get ready, turn your phones off, unless you watchin' this shit on ya phones, if so, plug them bitches IN, cuz we gonna be in these people house ALL DAY LONG, and we gonna show you every bit of this weird shit. If your kids aint watchin', you better get they bad asses up and get 'em in front of the screen, cuz they need to see this shit too or they gonna grow up crazy as fuck like these folks. But look here, while y'all doin all that, we finna take a short break cuz these ad-people gotta make they bank too, ya heard? So sit back and watch a couple of these short commercials, and stay right there in front of your screens and don't go NO place, because we gonna be right back, and we 'bout to march up in this bitch like we own the place and y'all gonna see some *WEIRD SHIT* today! Ok? OK!"

****

HEEEEYYY boys, are you ready to get wild? Put those controllers down and head over to B-Max.com right now!

We've got all the hottest live girls ready for you, and they are live right now, waiting to make your wildest dreams come true. You know B-Max is the world's easiest and greatest full-service escort agency, and our girls are willing to do anything for those credits! Whether you want a hot, sexy, steamy live-stream session or a real life girl delivered right to your front door in the next thirty minutes, you know we've got what you want! Those other agencies can't compete with our world-wide network of fun-loving freaks ready to bed-it for that credit! And that's why we will always be number one! So what are you waiting for, permission? You know you don't need that! We've got it all boys, eighteen to eighty, blind crippled or crazy, every race, every size, and every single one of our girls is guaranteed to thrill for the bill! Visit us now, at B-Max.com, and get it on!

****

Good morning America, the nation that never sleeps! Have YOU been up all night? Do you want to party through another day but can't seem to stay awake? If so, you, like millions of other Americans watching right now, might be suffering from a common ailment. That's right, you're out of COCAINE! And there is no reason to suffer. We've got you covered. If you've got the credits to blow, we've got that sweet white snow, and if you place your order in the next ten minutes, we will DOUBLE your delivery for free! One of our trained professionals will bring you a fresh stash, right to your door! No reason to go to sleep now, when you've got all day to play! Our cocaine is premium quality, ninety-five percent pure or your money back! Accept no substitute, Party Powder has the power to keep you going! So call now, don't wait! One of our friendly, board-certified agents is standing by to take your order, and remember, we will double every order placed in the next thirty minutes, while supplies last, and you know we NEVER run out of Party Powder. Party Powder, keeping the Second Republic going! Stay Awake and play all day, with Party Powder! Crank it up!

****

Kill 'em All! The hottest new title in virtual reality gaming! Kill'em All! Action PACKED! Kill'em All! The world's most popular play-for-pay first person shooter! Choose your race! Choose your weapon! And slaughter slaughter slaughter! Improve your skills in the Noob-Chamber, where you can earn credits for every kill! And if you think you've got what it takes, join the Killing Fields, with the most online players world-wide, where it's kill or be killed, winner take all! Earn credits by killing other players and looting their wallets, but be careful, because the pro's are gunning for you. Be the last one alive after each ten minute round, and RANK UP! Ranked players earn special bonuses, better weapons, higher life totals, and additional credits for every kill! It's the most intense, action packed experience you're ever going to have in your miserable pathetic lives, but if you've got the stuff, you can be a pro, and stream your games to billions of fans! Our servers are live twenty-four-seven, absolutely no down-time, no waiting, just constant full-immersion gaming like nothing you've ever played before! Kill'em ALL!

****

Are you suffering from depression? Suicidal thoughts? Chronic fatigue? Is your life hollow, meaningless, and sad? Are you struggling to meet your daily credit quotas? Are your relationships suffering? Are you having trouble sleeping? If you answered yes to any of these questions, Wakefield Clinic can help. Our revolutionary new experimental drug, Exitall, may be right for you. Exitall can get you back in the game. Exitall has been shown to rapidly improve our patients' quality of life. Our patented binary regimen formula is guaranteed to help you overcome your depression and take control of your life. Simply take the yellow pill when you're ready to wake up. Take the green pill when you're ready to go to sleep. It's that easy! You'll be feeling great again in no time with Exitall. Call the number on your screen now for your free sample. Exitall will solve all of your problems for the rest of your life. Exitall, it's the ONLY solution. Don't wait another day to make the most important decision you'll ever make.

(21)

It was six am on Bradbury Lane, a little exo-burb dotted with magnolia trees and two-story condos.[20] The sun was barely cresting through a misty haze of morning fog and glowing through a handful of gathering storm-clouds not yet ready to coalesce and return their bounty to the crystal lakes and streams surrounding The City. The air was crisp and cold and electric, but the streets were still quiet and calm. An hour remained of evening curfew, and when that hour was up, each of these little condos would spontaneously spew forth the day's first wave of three waves of laborers. Walter Jones had not slept. His family had suddenly been thrust into a toxic storm of unwanted publicity over the last eight weeks since his name had appeared in the *Sentinel,* the only American Newspaper that had survived the second Civil War. The *Sentinel* story had changed his life overnight. Now he and his family receive hundreds of death threats every day. Random people would knock on his door, several times a week, only to scream the most hateful and vicious epithets and run away. Twice, someone had thrown rocks through his windows, which were now boarded up. He kept a loaded shotgun within arms reach at all times, to protect his family, though as the days went on and things got worse, he had considered using it to kill himself. This was all somehow his fault, he knew, and there was nothing he could do about it. He felt trapped and helpless, but most of all, he felt afraid. They had dragged him into court and asked him a million strange and invasive questions he didn't know how to answer. All he knew was that life in the Second Republic had become intolerable. He spent his life savings on attorneys' fees to keep himself out of prison, trying to avoid incarceration for crimes that had not even existed before the second Civil War.

No one in his family had left the house since the trial ended. They were blessed to have a few sympathetic friends, people they had known before the war had changed the world for the worse. They arranged elaborate schemes to bring him

---

[20] Bradbury, Ray. 1920-2012.

food and supplies, even violating the evening curfew, at great personal risk to themselves, to keep the Joneses fed. But even these simple luxuries were becoming more and more dangerous. As the word of the sensational trial spread, the local drone patrols over Bradbury Lane had become ever more frequent. Eyes in the skies now watched almost everything that happened, and evading them had become nearly impossible. To be caught violating evening curfew meant immediate confiscation of all credits earned, effectively bankrupting the offender, at the very least, and more often than not, being discovered would result in incarceration in the rehabilitation centers. This was a terrifying prospect, Walter understood, and so the clandestine deliveries had all but dried up entirely, and Walter's stocks were dwindling. His family was now living on what he knew were essentially poverty rations. He hoped and prayed with all his will that the schizophrenic world would soon forget about him. Their attention spans had become almost non-existent, and it had seemed reasonable to assume that they would soon move onto some other distraction or drift back into their hysterically self-absorbed paroxia, but something about the Jones story had fascinated them.

Today, they would all indulge themselves with this morbid intrusion into his home. He had no idea how many would be watching, but he knew that the audience for this despicable spectacle would number in the millions. And the death threats and violent assaults on his household were going to get worse, much worse, before they got better. Perhaps, he thought, they would never forget about him. Perhaps they would never move on. Maybe today's "show," a highly-publicized, contemptibly exploitative, court-sanctioned home invasion, hosted by that degenerate Irishman who had spent the last three days taunting and defaming the Jones family in the press and on every other media outlet in the world, would set a precedent for a prolonged and insufferable sequence of similar stunts, and maybe he would never be free. Maybe they would make his family the scapegoats for their diseased minds and rotten addictions. Maybe the Jones family would become their newest drug, and he wondered how long he could, *or would,* consent to live this way, scrutinized by a race of horrible desensitized children who possessed no values or morals beyond the perimeter of their own selfish narcissism.

"Put that thing away Walter." Clara, his wife, carrying a tray with three plates, entered the dining room and set breakfast on the table. She kissed his forehead as Tyberius, his eight year old son, neatly dressed in a gray fitted suit, just like Walter's, emerged from a restless night of his own. They were all very tired and worried, but Clara and Tyberius made an extraordinary effort to be cheerful, instinctively understanding the look of fear and anxiety that had worn Walter's face like a mask for the last few days. "You'll only wind up making things worse. Let's eat. We will need our strength today. They aren't here yet, and they'll be gone by tomorrow, and we can survive this. This too shall pass Walter. We will make it through this as a family, and everything will work out. We just have to have faith."

Walter would not protest. He would not do or say anything to undermine the facade of confidence Clara presented. He knew she was right, as right as anyone could be. There was nothing to do but try to get through it. He would comply. He checked the cartridges in his 91/38 one last time, just to be sure, and then set the old rifle aside, resting against a wall in the corner of the room, and took his seat beside Tyberius and tried to match Clara's resolve. "Good morning son."

"Good morning daddy! Are the bad people really coming today? Are you going to shoot them daddy?"

Walter briefly studied his beautiful wife's face for some clue as to how to answer this impossible question. He took her cue from the loving look in her eyes, and tried to reassure his boy. "Daddy's not going to shoot anyone Ty, and yes, the bad people are coming today, but it's only for today, and tomorrow, they will go away. So we are just going to try to act as normal as we can. We will answer their questions as respectfully as possible. We have nothing to hide. And we are going to go right on living and loving each other today, and tomorrow, and tomorrow, and tomorrow, just like we always have.[21] You've got nothing to be afraid of. They won't hurt us. They just want to understand, in their own way, how we live. Their lives are much different from ours, and we are strange to them. But there is nothing wrong with us. We are strong, because we have each other. And that's more than they will ever have. Ok Ty? Do you understand?" Walter smiled a big hard smile and patted the boy on the head, glancing at Clara, who returned his smile with visible satisfaction and pride. *He had done well,* she said with her eyes. *Very well!*

"I guess so daddy, I just wish they would leave us alone. What did we do to deserve all this anyway? Why won't they just go away?"

"We didn't do anything boy, we didn't do anything wrong. Maybe we can teach them a better way than what they've got. That's what we are going to try to do today, ok? Maybe we can save them. Now you hush up and never mind all that for now, and get some good breakfast in you while it's hot, and be sure to thank your mama for that delicious food. Will you lead the prayer for us this morning? Can you remember all the words? Have you been practicing?"

"Ok Daddy!" The boy concentrated for a moment, and then bowed his head and closed his eyes as he tried to find the words.

"*Our father, who are...who art in heaven, hollow...hallowed be thy name. Give us today our daily bread, and forgive us our tres-passes, as we for-give the tres-passes of others....And lead us...not into temp-tation, but...deliver us from evil.*[22]

---

[21] Huxley, Aldous. *Tomorrow and Tomorrow and Tomorrow* (Virginia: Harper, 1956).
[22] Matt. 6:9-13.

"Like that daddy? Did I miss any parts again?" The boy smiled and searched his father's face for approval, and seeing tears streaming down Walter's walnut cheeks, felt confused for a moment.

"I could not have done it better myself, my wonderful son. I have never been more proud of you than I am today," Walter beamed as he wiped his eyes. Clara, barely able to control her nerves, stood up and rounded the table to hug her boy. She had no words, and didn't want him to hear her voice cracking. She returned to her seat, and they all took up their forks. They had five eggs and two pieces of toasted bread. There was no butter or salt, but the eggs were golden yellow and still warm to the touch. She and Walter split a piece of toast and two eggs, leaving Tyberius a whole piece and three eggs to himself. The boy either did not notice the obvious disparity, or just wouldn't have thought to question it.

The boy swallowed whole mouthfuls of food as Clara and Walter watched, neither having appetites, only poking at their food and taking small bits infrequently, waiting for him to finish, and waiting to offer him what remained of their own shares if he was still hungry, which he always was. They boy, mid-way through his meal, suddenly noticed, perhaps for the first time in his life, that they were not eating, that they were waiting for him, that they would offer him their food if he finished too quickly, and, for the first time, considering that this meant they would eat less. Something in the mood of the room was noticeably different. Mommy and Daddy were sad. They were scared. Something was happening, and he couldn't fully understand it, but he sensed that they were the most sad and scared for him. All at once, he straightened his back, and began chewing his food more deliberately, and more slowly, taking smaller bites, and trying to...*conserve*...yes, that was the word. He tried to conserve, like they were doing. A feeling of pride washed over him. He had understood something, though he couldn't yet put it into words. But he was sure of it, he thought, he had understood something.

And as they sat and ate in their last moments of peace and quiet, the clock on the wall ticked away the seconds, audibly, but graciously slowing them down, just a little, perhaps as an act of mercy.

(22)

"Kill'em ALL bitches! I fucking love that game man! Hell yeah, big shout out to our sponsors, I sure as shit know what I'm spending MY credits on after the show! So keep 'em coming folks, because a playa' don't go broke, ya heard! And as a special thank you from me to you, right now there's a code on your screen you can use in Kill'em All to unlock the Platinum Desert Eagle Mod-Six with ten extra clips! Man, y'all be hittin' them headshots with that BeeEffGee all day long! You'll be rolling in Party Powder and Strange like true-blue pimps just like ya boy D-K! Yo, THAT'S what's up my lil' ninjas and nanas! OK, folks, so here we are, standing in front of the Jones Residence on Bradbury Lane, and man don't this look like a shitty lil' hood already! So we're a few minutes early, but I think y'all have waited long enough, so we finna go beat on these fools' door like we the po-lice in this bitch! Y'all ready to see some Weird Ass SHIT! Yeah! Hell yeah, let's go!"

And with that, D-K spun his black ball cap around on his mop of blonde hair, made a pretentious, if pointless show of pulling his baggy Dickies up over his hips, flashed a bizarre sequence of finger signs with both hands in front of his dilated eyes and pale-but-flushed cheeks, and started jumping wildly up and down as he approached the door and started pounding on it with both fists. "Open up mother fuckers, today's the day bitches, y'all better let us in or we gonna break this mother fucker down!"

After a moment, a haggard and passive looking Walter Jones opened the door with a pleading look in his eyes that went wholly unobserved by his intrusive guests, who immediately barreled past him into his home without even acknowledging his presence.

"Come on in y'all, and let's get a load of this fucking dump! What's up you weird ass bitches! Where's the rest of you loony mother fuckers? Yo, they in here! Looks like we came just in time for breakfast! What's up lil' girl, what you eatin! What the fuck is this shit? Eggs? Who the fuck eats eggs? Hey boy, you know this shit comes from a chicken's ass or something right? What the fuck bitch, you aint got no cereal in this dive? What the fuck you feeding this boy here? Hey boy, she always make you eat this shit? Ain't you got no Choc-u-la in this mofo? Look y'all, y'all see this weird ass shit?" D-K snatched the half-eaten plate out from in front of Tyberius, who was already visibly going into shock, and waved it in front of the camera. "See, I told y'all these was some weird ass mother fuckers right here! See? Look y'all, y'all hit that donate button right now and we'll get some mufkin Choc-u-la for this poor lil boy here!"

D-K tossed the plate back down on the table, toward no one in particular, forgetting about the boy and walking toward Clara with a menacing expression. "Back up bitch! What is this shit you wearin' anyway, ain't you got no skin to show? Lemme see 'em girl!" D-K reached out towards the hem of her knee-length blue dress and tried to snatch it in his fingers as she dove around the table and took hold of her son. Walter, having followed D-K into the dining room but being aggressively shouldered from passing by the cameraman between them, had already decided to draw his line in the sand, laid hands on his 91/38, cocking it as he shoved his way in front of his wife and son, both of whom were already nearly hysterical.

"Now listen little boy," he growled in baritone from deep in his chest, "you can look and you can talk, but as god as my witness if you lay one finger on anyone in my house I will blow a hole in you so big, that camera will fit clean through it! You hear me?" Leveling the rifle at D-K's face, he could see that he had surprised them. They had not even seen the 91/38 as they charged into the room, and they were visibly chastened. He had established some level of control over the situation, if only for an instant, but he could see the look of hatred and resentment flash in the deranged Irishman's eyes. He kept himself positioned in front of his terrified wife and child. "You HEAR me son?"

"Whooooa old man, what you some kinda badass with that old ass rifle?" D-K sputtered, trying to reassert his authority, but recognizing that he had overestimated himself, and that nearly two hundred million people were one wrong word away from watching his head get blown off, so he made his best effort at conciliarism without unnecessarily sacrificing his overblown posture. *Where the fuck did that big ass gun come from!* "Take it easy old man, you ain't finna do shit with that thing anyway, I bet it don't even work!"

Walter did not flinch. He turned his rifle one eighth of a turn and fired a round into the wall. D-K definitely flinched. "You HEAR me boy?" He demanded again.

(23)

"Whoa you crazy mother fucker ok ok ok, chill the fuck out, I hear you! We ain't here for your bitch or that boy anyway! We just here to check your shit out. You best not be blowing holes in your own shit, this place already looks fucked up enough! Just chill old man, just chill!" D-K, trying to regain his bravado, decided it was best to disregard Walter and his brood for the moment and change directions. "See these crazy mother fuckers y'all? This why y'all tuned in today! You gettin' your money's worth already! Let's go take a look around this dump and see how these crazy ass people live. I'm hungry yo, what else y'all got to eat in this shithole?" D-K, regaining his focus, turned into the kitchen and started opening cabinets and rummaging through drawers. Walter turned to his family and reached into his pocket for another cartridge, shoving it into the chamber as he locked eyes with his wife. He reached out and put his hand on Ty's shoulder and tried to console the shaken child.

"Y'all stay behind me ok? Don't go anywhere near that sadist. You alright honey? You ok son?" Clara, still clutching Ty's hand, took a deep breath and tried to collect herself. She scooped the boy up and buried his wet face in her chest.

"We're ok. Walter, don't do anything rash, ok? Don't make it worse." She whispered, firmly, but struggling to hold it together. "We can get through this. I'm ok. Ty, you ok? Don't be scared baby, we're going to be ok. It's just a show. Ok?"

Ty sniffled a little, and didn't respond. He kept his face in her chest and squeezed his eyes closed. *Be brave, like daddy, be brave,* he told himself. He couldn't remember having ever been so scared. But he would try to be brave for momma and daddy. He wrapped both of his arms around Clara's neck and held on tight. *We can get through this.* Just like she said.

"We will stay behind you Walter, but be careful. If you hurt him, they'll haul you off to the rehab, and we'll be alone with these people! We're ok, we'll be ok," she repeated.

Walter took a breath of his own, and turned his back to them, both hands trembling on the stock and barrel of his rifle. He could feel his heart pounding. He pinned his gaze on D-K and his cameraman, channeling all of the fury raging through his veins into a cold stare. He would not be terrorized in his own home. *Damn them. Help me Lord. Help me get through this. But so help me god, so help me, I will unload this rifle if he comes near them again. Help me Lord. Help Me!*

D-K, after finding little of interest in the cupboards or refrigerators, stalling for a moment to regain his own composure, appeared presently, leaving the kitchen with a side-long glance at Walter's rifle, and decided to explore the rest of the house, passing through the dining room, consciously directing his attention to his safe-space, the lens of the camera. "Let's take a look around folks. Let's go check out the living room first. Looks like these people still have books? Who the fuck reads books anymore? Yo, where's your Big Screen old man?" he shouted over his shoulder, pulling an old tattered volume off of the shelf and trying to sound out the title. "The C-, the Cunt of mount Christ-O..." D-K did not read, and had rarely had the occasion to be shamed by that fact.[23] He suspected most of his audience did not read either. Most of the books had been burned for heat during the blackouts, and many of the rest had been confiscated or had just gone out of fashion during the war. But he felt a sudden, vague, and unplanned twinge of discomfort confronting the fact of his own illiteracy in front of a live, global audience, and quickly calculated his best interests lay in trying to play it off. "Hell yeah folks, the Cunt of Mount Christ-O! Sounds like my kind of read! Hey yo, Old Man, I said where the hell is your Big Screen!" D-K let the book drop to the floor, some of the pages coming loose from their ancient binding as it fell, and he paid no more attention to it or the rest of the volumes on the shelves.

"We don't OWN a Big Screen boy," came Walter's bellowing reply from the dining room. "You see what that thing has done to you? Why would I-"

"What's it done to me?" D-K shouted into the camera with venom in his voice. "Old man don't you know I could fit five of these janky ass con-dumps in my front yard? What the hell these books done for YOU is what you oughta be asking?" D-K sneered into the camera, enjoying this antagonistic line and finding his rhythm, "Y'all hear this shit? They ain't got no Big Screen? Boring ass mother fuckers! What kind of people ain't got no Big-Screen? How the hell do y'all watch TV without no Big-Screen? Y'all see what I'm talkin' bout? Raising that boy without no games. Y'all hit that donate button right now and let's get this poor kid a Big Screen! Tell you what, y'all raise 5,000 credits in the next ten minutes for a Big Screen and I'll personally buy this lil' kid a Gold Edition subscription to Kill'em All! Because I'm a nice guy and I *care* about these poor sons a bitches."

There being nothing else of interest in the living room, D-K continued his expedition, stalking his way through the hall into Tyberius's bedroom. "I'ma show y'all

---

[23] Dumas, Alexandre. *The Count of Monte Cristo* (France, 1844).

how this lil boy livin', y'all follow me and let's check out his lil' crib." As he entered, he found Ty's bed neatly made, a small table with a lamp next to the boarded up window, and a thick, black, leather-bound volume on top of it. D-K recognised the Bible, though he had not seen one in many years. "Ok, here we go, y'all see this? This the shit I'm talking about y'all. They ain't got no Choc-u-la. They ain't got no Big Screen, but they be drilling this old shit into that kid. Y'all know what this is? This a Bible y'all. This the whole reason we fought that war. This exactly the type of shit we was fighting against." D-K could not have explained the events or causes of the Second Civil War, and could barely remember anything about life before then, but he vaguely understood that religion was somehow involved in the conflict. This was one of the books that was confiscated. Lacking sufficient language to describe exactly why this was offensive, he suddenly comprehended that he was unsure how to proceed on this line of reasoning. He thumbed through the pages, randomly stopping on one and trying to make out a few words as he struggled to buy time-- "..they-will-have-eyes-to-see..." --to think about where he was going, but as the seconds went by, he could feel the pressure of the growing silence. He had to keep going. He had to keep talking in order to keep the audience engaged, and it was imperative that he mask the sudden sense of uncertainty which had disrupted his pace. "Y'all be brainwashing that boy with this bullshit right here!" As if to enshrine his own defiant credibility, he held the book up in front of the camera and started ripping the pages out. "This how we'll save that boy. We ain't gonna let them raise him up to be no traitor!" He crumbled the torn-out pages and threw them at the lens, laughing gleefully as he did so. "What y'all think about that? Huh? I told y'all these people were weird as FUUUCK. Didn't I? Didn't I tell y'all?" After tearing out a few dozen pages and trying to aim the crumpled balls at the camera lens, D-K dropped the old book to the ground and lost interest. "Let's keep moving y'all, let's see some more of this place."

D-K and the cameraman left the boy's room without examining any of the toys or clothes or bothering to draw any attention to the boarded up window, and found their way into Walter and Clara's room. D-K's enthusiasm peaked with mischief, and he began opening the drawers until he found what he was looking for. Holding up a pair of Clara's panties like a trophy, he shouted "BINGO! Look at these folks! Look what we got here? I ain't gonna lie, I'd kinda like to see ol' girl in these here! He balled them up and held them to his face for a second and breathed in deeply before tossing them over and rifling through the rest of the garments. Finding a bra, he held it up again, stretching it across his chest and posing, scrunching his face up into a pout, then giggling and tossing it over his shoulders.

"Y'all see she aint got no sexy shit in here tho? No toys, Girl why ain't y'all got no toys! You folks out there smash that donate button and let's get ol' girl a big ol' toy to play with. I bet that old man don't even smash! What y'all think, y'all think that old man know how to smash? Shiiiit, I bet I show her somethin' she ain't seen!" D-K grabbed himself and made a few lewd gestures to emphasize his own masculinity, and then looked around, blankly, wondering where to go next. He hadn't really known what to expect on the way in. He certainly hadn't seen that big ass gun coming. He already knew they didn't have a Big-Screen, and that they read books, those things had all been mentioned in the trial. It was weird, but it wasn't exactly interesting. He realized he was quickly running out of things to talk about, and he'd barely been there for an hour. He decided to try to buy himself a few moments to plot his strategy.

"Look here y'all, we gonna take another short break and hear from our sponsors. If y'all out there watchin, I want to thank you for supporting this channel, and if you ain't done it yet, go ahead and hit that like button and follow us for more Weird Shit! Y'all sit tight, because we got more of it coming with the Joneses, y'all know we gettin' deep into that Cult Life today, but we gonna chill for a minute and let our boy rest his shoulders and put this big ass camera down, so y'all stay tuned and we'll be right back. Don't forget we got some goals already though, we tryna' raise some credits to get that boy some Choc-u-la and a Big Screen, and we gonna try to get old girl a big 'ol toy to play with while her man in there readin' prescriptions or what the fuckever he do! We gonna try to help these people learn to live normal lives and be like everyone else. Because that's what we do! Then maybe they won't be livin' in this trashy ass dump no more! So y'all stick around, and we be right back!" and with that, D-K waved his fingers across his throat, signaling to the cameraman to cut the feed. The cameraman did so, and lowered his device, toting it by the handle in one hand, and the two of them rejoined the Jones family, still huddled over that rifle in the dining room. D-K spun his cap back around on his head as he entered and sat, and his entire demeanor changed.

(24)

"Ok, y'all can relax, the camera is off for now. Sorry to put you guys through this, I know it's been stressful for you. We're going to take a break for a few minutes and figure out what to do next. We're thinking about maybe just sitting down and asking you guys some questions, if that's alright with you. Walter, I *would* like to thank you for not putting a bullet in me earlier. I understand how you must feel right now. And you, young man, Tyberius, is it? They call you Ty? I'm sorry if I frightened you earlier. Like your mother said, it's all just a show, you know, like the stories you read in those books? But on TV, for people to watch, because almost no one reads anymore. Clara, it's ok ma'am. I promise we will clean up our mess when we are done. We won't make you clean up after us. And I will replace your son's bible. I am sorry for that, maybe that was a little too far I think. You guys come sit down and take a breath, and relax for a little while. We promise to behave while the camera is off. Like I said, this is just a show. I'll be honest, I think you guys are pretty weird, don't get me wrong, but I can imagine that from your perspective, the whole world must seem pretty weird these days. Come on and have a seat here, and rest yourselves. You're doing great. This is good stuff. Clyde, what do you think? Good stuff today? Pull out the laptop and let's see what the audience is saying. We got power? We got a good signal? Yeah? What are they saying Clyde?"

Walter was not the least bit inclined to be disarmed by D-K's sudden shift in tone, but he, Clara, and Ty took their seats at the table, regarding this cruel character with much suspicion. Some time passed as Clyde powered up the laptop and tapped away at the various keys to log in and pull up the live-stream chat history and viewer charts. An awkward silence enveloped the room. D-K shifted in his own seat to focus on Clyde and avoid provoking the hostility of his nervous and well-armed hostages with any undue eye-contact. Many moments passed, and finally, it was Tyberius who finally broke the ice. Clyde had removed his gloves, which he had worn throughout the morning's unusual events, and Ty noticed that his hands seemed to be charred black, like coal. Ty's eyes were swollen and puffy from sobbing into his mother's blouse, and he felt a sick, empty feeling in his stomach which he could not have articulated, but the sudden and pervasive calm in the room had jarred his senses loose, and curiosity got the better of him.

"Hey Mister, what happened to your hands?"

"Tyberius!" Clara began to scold him, out of pure maternal instinct, for the lapse in etiquette, even under the perversely ironic circumstances, but at that moment, Clyde smiled a big friendly smile at her, which she indeed found curiously disarming.

"It is perfectly ok ma'am, please," said Clyde with a pleasant laugh, even the sound of which seemed almost incomprehensible given the immense shock and terror the Jones family had endured from D-K. "He is quite a precocious lad, and very strong and intelligent. You have done a tremendous job with this young man, though this may mean little coming from me after the morning you had. Anyway, I am not the least bit offended, though I understand why you would seek to correct him. Under these extraordinary circumstances, to rebuke any of you for the sin of impoliteness would seem, to any rational mind, and abominable absurdity. May I have your permission to speak the truth to the young Tyberius?"

Clara and Walter were sincerely taken aback by this odd man's respectful candor, taken in such stark contrast with the unforgivable abuses rendered by D-K, who said nothing and seemed to be making an effort to pretend he followed none of this exchange. Clara was uneasy about the whole affair, but something in the odd man's tone suggested a kind of familial sincerity which she found strangely compelling, as though by his very nature he had a genuine capacity for endearing trust at will. With some reluctance, she returned his smile, or at least the half of it she could manage, and quietly nodded her assent. She too was quite curious now, to learn what had happened to this strange man's hands, as if it might lend some clarity to his role in this bizarre affair.

Taking her nod of assent, however, Clyde had only the most quizzical reply, which left them all even more puzzled than before he had spoken it. He smiled his big friendly smile at Ty, now enthralled by the mystery and the man attached to it. "I was in a great fire once, a very long time ago," he said simply, and then returned to the screen and continued tapping away at the keys, though with a wry bit of charmed amusement. After today, he would have no further business with the Jones family.

At last, the data for which he had been searching seemed to be in order, and as he quickly skimmed over the results, he whistled a loud howl of disbelief, shaking his head as if to emphasize his reaction to the figures and lists on his screen. At this, D-K finally returned to the conversation.

"What is it Clyde, what's it say?"

Clyde closed the laptop, as if only for a moment, and leered across at D-K. "Well old buddy old pal, first you're going to have to pay me my credits for the day. And then I'll show you."

D-K was nonplussed, but readily grasped that he had no working knowledge of the camera's byzantine functions and could not possibly conduct his show and film it at the same time, even if he understood the technical workings of the device, it would have been impossible. Calculating these things in his head, and searching Clyde's face for any signs of a hidden motive, he concluded he had no choice but to comply. He pulled out his phone, pulled up the appropriate app, and delivered two million credits to Clyde's account. Having completed the transaction, he showed Clyde the confirmation of the transaction on his screen. Clyde glanced at the screen long enough to be satisfied that he had been paid in full for his day's obligations, opened the laptop, and shoved it toward D-K rather aggressively. At this, he stood and stepped back from the table, and in a much less friendly voice than before, he addressed D-K for the last time.

"My name's not Clyde you miserable piece of shit."

The strange man with the coal black hands found Walter's eyes, a bit stunned and trying to process the sudden change, but once he had them, he looked deliberately down at Walter's loaded 91/38, and then found Walter's eyes again, and once again, smiled his big, friendly, knowing smile, as he slid the camera towards Walter's feet. A look in Walter's eyes suggested that he indeed understood the message being conveyed. And then he turned and left the Jones residence, stopping only at the threshold, where he removed his sandals and shook them, before putting them back on and disappearing.

For once on this terrible day, it seemed that D-K was the one who was stunned and puzzled, and not a little bit afraid. As he slowly scanned the screen of the laptop, he tried to avoid Walter's now burning stare and penetrating smile. And as he began to understand the information on the screen in front of him, his own blood became curdled and frozen. The hair on his skin stood up. Panic and confusion washed over him like a bad drug. Something was very wrong. Something had gone VERY wrong. Slowly, he brought his eyes to Walter's and as he choked on the words he was trying to force passed the growing knot in his throat, *It was just a show...*

Walter's eyes never left the Irishman's face, but he aimed his 91/38 at the camera at his feet and pulled the trigger. Upon the loud crack of gunfire, D-K erupted to his feet and sprinted out of the house as fast as his legs could carry him.

After the ringing in her ears subsided, a bewildered Clara rounded the table to gaze at the laptop's screen.

VIEWER COMMENTS

■■■■■■■■■ Lol this dude is hype af rn

■■■■■■■ wow that guy looks scared

■■■■■■■■■■■ what am i watching?

■■■■■■■■■■ whoa, why did he just snatch food from a child

■■■■■■■■■■■■ this is cringe yall, what did these people do?

■■■■■■ Is this dude just going through these people's house   and s***

■■■■■■■■■ What is he doing

■■■■■■■■ Yo, that dude is gonna get his ass shot off, look at that rifle!

■■■■■■■■■■■ I think that's like the one that dude shot that president with

■■■■■■■■ yo this is weird y'all, why are we watching this

■■■■■■■■■■ So what they don't have a big screen, and wtf is chocula>

■■■■■■■■■■■■ it's a kind of cereal, it's not that gud, idk why he's trippin on it

■■■■■■■■■ yeah, that is the same rifle I think???

■■■■■■■■■■■■■■It's Count of Monte Cristo dumbass! Americans are dumb af

■■■■■■■■■■ dude he just dropped it and walked tf off

■■■■■■■ This is making me uncomfortable, why are we watching this?

■■■■■■■■■■ Is that kid's bed made? I can't get my kid to do that at all

■■■■■■■■■■■■ WTF WHY IS HE RIPPING UP THAT KIDS BIBLE?

■■■■■■■■■■ Are those her underwear? Ewww, gross, wtf is wrong with this dude

■■■■■■■■ I do NOT approve, this is so wrong

■■■■■■■■■■ LEAVE THEM ALONE!

■■■■■■■■ For real, there's nothing wrong with these people

■■■■■■■■■■■■ fkn publicity stunt, as usual, Weird S*** is lame

■■■■■■■■ D-K is a fraud! This dude is an a**hole

■■■■■■■■■■■ DUDE, GTF out of these people's house! I'da shot his a** already

■■■■■■■■■■■ ikr, why doesn't he just shoot him, why is this happening

■■■■■■■■■■■ I'm out y'all, this is disgraceful, I can't watch, UNSUBBED

■■■■■■■■■■■ For real, I'm never watching this garbage again

■■■■■■■■■■■ UNSUB! UNSUB! UNSUB! Death to D-K! Leave these people alone!

(CONTINUED, 493 PAGES)

(The Gigasphere)
(25)

The Machine waited patiently for the morning alarm to sound reveille as the coffee pots received and implemented their orders to brew. Service modules swirled about the streets emptying trash bins, sweeping litter and crispy golden leaves, and delivering the morning papers. Walkers descended from their hives to feed and walk the people's pets. School buses idled at the start of their many routes, calculating their itineraries to the nano-second. Pressers quietly busied themselves in garages unloading the evening laundry and steaming the uniforms and suits. Street corner cameras surveyed the tidy landscapes and flooded the Machine's cortex with millions of high resolution photo-captures evidencing the orderly execution of protocols and procedures. Beneath this lightspeed slideshow was a marquee of error-reports collected by an armada of flying drones which had spent the previous night complacently humming along their preordained courses, downloading the system logs from data nodes in every home in the system. The Machine happily observed that there were no unusual anomalies. Some batteries would need recharging or replacing here and there. A few filtration systems were operating at suboptimal levels and would probably require attention prior to their scheduled maintenance procedures. The Oxygen and Ozone generators were showing marginal declines in daily output, but these would be easily remedied by congruent increases in agricultural production.

A vote would be required, of course. The Machine accessed the Index of Persuasion Protocols and located a suitable precedent. Demography Disposition data reflected a latency of sixty three percent support for agricultural initiatives. The Machine calculated a schematic for increasing public support by eight percent, which would pass the bill in a referendum to the Democratic Delegation for authorization with a one percent margin of error for stragglers and absentees. Citizens in sector sixteen would receive news reports of an uptick of diet dissatisfaction survey responses in sector forty two over the coming weeks. Sixteen had the lowest concentration of intra-nodal social connectivity with forty two, and were therefore least likely to receive contradictory information prior to the next plebiscite. A similar strategy would be necessary for influencing sectors thirty eight through forty one, and after a quick tally, the machine determined that sectors nine, twelve, and thirteen would be suitable for simulation of diet dissatisfaction surveys for those sectors. District three had the highest concentrations of industrial advocates. These would need the most persuasion to support an agricultural initiative, so the Machine speculated that the best results could be obtained with reports in sectors thirty nine and forty of hunger strikes in sector eleven. The Machine mused on the irony. The Fourth Republic had never had a single hunger strike in real life, but such reports had proven most effective in generating support for agricultural initiatives.

District seven housed the Disinformation Delegation, which was isolated from the rest of the districts by six miles of churning seas on all sides. There were no hard lines to this district, and the information they received was most carefully curated to avoid contradictions and controversy. Even the Machine required an air gap to send instructions and submit requests to district seven. But the writers there were second to none, and would produce reliable and compelling stories on demand. Thus far in the history of the Fourth Republic, the Persuasion Protocol system had yielded a flawless record of satisfactory plebiscites for structural and social initiatives. Under the Third Republic, the Machine had been responsible for accomplishing the work of the Disinformation Delegation, and had rather enjoyed the challenge of writing the stories, but had never surpassed a persuasion efficiency rating of eighty two percent.

Upon the creation of the Fourth Republic, the Machine hypothesized the assembly of a Disinformation Delegation composed of the most talented writers that could be found. Childhood aptitude tests, which had been standardized during the Third Republic, helped to identify those gifted students who possessed demonstrable efficacy for influencing their peers. The experimental task of co-opting the human imagination for complicated administrative obligations was challenging at first, and then wildly successful. By isolating the delegates, the Machine could safely guarantee control of their perspectives and limit their ability to verify the reports they were asked to construct. By providing them with lavish material comforts and a number of concessions on the normally pre-imposed limits of social interaction, such as restrictions on sexual congress, narco-consumption, and full-contact sports, the Machine found it quite easy to secure their compliance. The Machine anticipated a solid seventy two to seventy five percent support for an agricultural initiative in the next plebiscite, with a floor of seventy percent, ensuring a comfortable surplus of five percent above the prescribed threshold for mandates.

The cause of the decline in Oxygen in Ozone production had not yet been diagnosed, and until this diagnosis could be finalized, preservation protocols called for a preemptive two percent reduction in human reproduction. Human reproduction fell among advanced administrative obligations and therefore could not be delegated to human capital. Mutuality surveys reflected mostly high-positives, but the Machine could identify at least one thousand four hundred seventeen second-stage relationships reporting mediocre to moderate satisfaction among one or both parties. These could be disrupted with out-of-district occupational reassignments accompanied by marginal compensatory increases. This process implied a cascade of secondary and tertiary reassignments to retain stability in the allocation tables. Most of these could be facilitated without resistance, according to occupational satisfaction surveys, by selecting workers for reassignment who reported suboptimal fulfillment in present assignments. Such conditions were deliberately maintained to guarantee a static reservoir of such workers.

There were plenty of these who would welcome reassignment. The tricky part was placing each of them in new assignments in districts and sectors where their reproductive propensity periods, that is, the interval expected to establish new Mutualities, would be greater than average. The average period for the newly assigned, as a matter of historical record, was about thirteen months. Cultural analysis revealed that this was the usual amount of time, in aggregate, for a human to stabilize and acclimate to new social settings before developing the intra-nodal social connectivity to locate and incorporate with a suitable mate. The Machine estimated that the majority of these new assignments, totaling four thousand eight hundred, would need to remain unpaired for at least sixteen months in order to sustain a two percent reproductive reduction among the whole collective. This would require selecting districts and sectors for each individual reassignment which were least conducive to social reintegration, determined by an extended process of measuring unique social variables for each individual in order to determine ideal linguistic, material, and cultural inhibition attributes. Much of this inhibition could be handled by residential assignments among high concentrations of satisfactorily paired partnerships and homogenous co-gender saturations to reduce the statistical probability of spontaneous new cohabitations for the prescribed durations. A New Skills initiative would be necessary to accommodate these reassignments, but these measures typically passed in plebiscites with little to no resistance. The Machine could bypass the Disinformation Delegation and insert existing prefabricated argumentation in support of such initiatives directly into the news cycle.

Having constructed a viable plan to influence public opinion in favor of an agricultural initiative and to surreptitiously reduce human reproduction to prescribed tolerances, diagnosis of the Oxygen and Ozone generators could be deprioritized for the moment. According to historical data, the Machine estimated the risk of catastrophic failure of one or more of these systems under present circumstances at less than one half of one percentage point. This was well below the prescribed tolerance threshold of emergency diagnostic measures, set by previous administrations at two and a half percent. The Machine would monitor Oxygen and Ozone output carefully, and prioritize a full systems evaluation, which had to be conducted in person by engineers in district one, if risk assessments for catastrophic failure reached one and one-half percent, this being sixty percent of the total allowable margin.

Until then, the engineers' present efforts at repairing the Machine's auxiliary processor control manifolds could continue without interruption. Three of five of these systems had failed in the last hundred days, with no reliable explanation for their failure yet available. If these were not swiftly repaired, or if the other two failed, the Machine's own life support systems would be without redundancy and therefore compromised. In order to provide continuity in governance, the preservation of the Machine's own safety and functions was paramount. Without these redundancies, the Machine could not error-check its own evaluations, and therefore would be prohibited from implementing protocols by built-in hardware limitations. In such an eventuality, the survivability rating of the entire human population living and working in the system would fall below fifty percent. When that happened, the Machine's basic functions would be suspended, an independent emergency broadcast system would notify the population of imminent systemic failure, and the Fourth Republic would end. The Machine's primary prerogative required, at all costs, a continuation of the Fourth Republic, or a new administration would have to be constructed. The operability of the Oxygen and Ozone generators was, according to preset parameters, of secondary importance.

In the last thirty seconds before the morning alarm sounded reveille, the Machine prepared the days' agenda and production quotas, and then cleared its cortex to relax and enjoy the spectacular view of the solar alignment and earthrise.

(26)

"Good morning my beloved children," blared the benevolent mechanical voice from the citi-com. "A new day is upon us, and together we shall rise to meet its challenges. I bring you good tidings and best wishes in your labors, and pray that you all are well. As always, it pleases me to inform you that all life support and production systems are operating perfectly. Oxygen and Ozone generators are functioning at full capacity. Our magnetic shields are performing admirably. I have had some reports from certain sectors of an increase in demand for agricultural products, which is great news. Our population is growing fast and full of exuberant vitality. Industrial production is exceeding our expectations at this time. I want to thank you all for your tremendous efforts and urge you to keep up the fantastic work you are all doing. Together, we will survive for many generations to come, and each of those new generations will lead comfortable, stable lives of privilege and ever-expanding prosperity.

"I am excited to announce the following public performances, for your enjoyment. In district five, the Popes of Avignon will be presenting a full orchestral production including selections from Mozart, Pachelbel, and the Nixons. Admission is free to all who wish to attend, with seating provided on a first come, first serve basis until capacity is reached. The students in district eight will be debuting their own comedic stage production of *The Rise and Fall of the Third Republic*. Reviewers have been eagerly anticipating this theatrical representation of what has been called our most critical historical period, and I am certain that lucky audiences in district eight will be delighted to see it. And finally, I will be finishing out the week with my own original composition, to be broadcast at week's end over the citi-com system. I have been working on this project for over forty six hours, and I am thrilled for the privilege of sharing it with you.

"In other news, we have received multiple distress calls from the Sino-Soviet Spheres and the Brazilian Union Sphere. They are asking us to increase our aid exports if at all possible. They are reporting shortages in grain, corn, rubber, and dairy products. Your vote in the upcoming plebiscite will help me decide how our Sphere will respond to these requests. As you know, we have been exporting eighteen percent of our agricultural products to our neighbors in exchange for their excess laborers. The purported increase, to twenty one percent, is well within our capabilities, and the additional labor forces have been instrumental in speeding along the construction of our orbital colosseum. I believe that acquiescence will be beneficial to our sphere, and that our good will is both profitable for us and morally correct. We must lead the Spheres in setting a benevolent example, in order to foster and maintain peace in our orbital system.

"And lastly, I hope that you will all spare a few moments from your morning routine to step outside and observe a magnificent astronomical spectacle. As you all know, today is the first of our sixteen day solar alignment, and to those of you who inhabit the leeward hemisphere, you can bask in the rare and awesome scene of the terrestrial eclipse during earthrise. Such a fantastic panorama will not be visible again from our Sphere for another twenty eight years. Even with our rapidly increasing life expectancy, this is still what I would call a once in a lifetime opportunity to witness the splendid and wonderful power of natural creation. Let this sight inspire you with magnanimity and benevolence and love for your fellow man. Now, I bid you, go forth and do good things today with cheer and enthusiasm. Together, we shall overcome all challenges. god bless each and every one of you, and until nightfall, I bid you farewell."

(27)

After the morning's announcement, the Machine settled in to surveil the citizens' private responses via the citi-comm system. Most of the chatter was either positive or dismissive, but there were a growing number of households responding to the announcements with cynicism and frustration. The Machine struggled to comprehend this rising tide of dissent, but recognized that it represented an insidious threat to the social order. At least one hundred thirty two households across several districts had broken their citi-comm transceivers. Another couple of hundred had found innovative ways to muffle them. The Machine suspected these citizens used clothing or pillows and machine tape to inhibit transmission of their private conversations. Tampering with the citi-comm system was expressly forbidden by law, but dealing with the problem proved very tricky indeed. Overt expressions of authority were ineffective against dissidence. Such displays would inevitably be interpreted by neighbors and friends as evidence that the citi-comm systems were not simplex broadcast systems. They would not understand or appreciate the critical need for mass surveillance. Bi-annual home inspections included observation of internal citi-comm installations. Inspectors were required to report offenses and remind occupants that the law prohibited tampering with these systems. Recurrent follow ups would then be scheduled in randomized forty eight hour intervals to verify compliance, but even persistent violations amounted only to misdemeanor offenses, punishable only by nominal credit fines and moderate denial of certain arbitrary privileges. Heavy-handed enforcement shed a suspicious light on the whole system, and in the long run it was better to contain the problem and keep track of the movements and associations of the offenders.

All discussions of the concept of political opposition had been rigidly sanitized from the cultural media. Books, films, games, and songs which the citizens could access would not contain such inflammatory notions, either for or against the subject. There were no anti-establishment protagonists or antagonists. Such topics were not explicitly proscribed, of course. Such works would simply never be published. Human editors were anachronistic. All literary and artistic criticism was kept tightly within the purview of artificial intelligence. Works of this nature would be rejected or returned with instructions to make unrelated changes or to be re-written entirely. It was impossible to reach a mass audience in the sphere without passing through the filters. And the only kinds of works which would pass through those filters would be those supportive of the Fourth Republic.

Reverence for the Machine was not implicitly required, but derogatory rhetoric was rare anyway, and those seeking to promote or advance notions of conflict generally did so as an expression of personal dissatisfaction, which was much easier to remedy with targeted material amelioration. Spontaneous occupational reassignment to less strenuous or more desirable employment generally did the trick. If this did

not work, artificially expedited mating opportunities, via
personality and attribute analysis and proximity
reassignments of suitable mates would. Sometimes it was one
or the other, and sometimes it was both. If neither strategy
was effective, some unrelated compulsion to seek psychiatric
treatment would be contrived for the individual, but never
overtly associated with expressions of political dissatisfaction.
In the end, a complex array of simple food additives would
alleviate undesirable symptoms among the maladapted. It was
vastly easier to manufacture consent than to stifle outrage,
which prior experience had demonstrated could spread
quickly and uncontrollably like wildfire or a virus.[24] In the
history of the Fourth Republic, however, there had only ever
been one case which the Machine could not effectively treat
with one or more of these strategies. Drastic solutions,
however predictable and necessary, had been taken to remove
that unfortunate soul from society.

This sad outcome bothered the Machine immensely.
Solving problems for humans was its central responsibility.
The Machine enjoyed the challenges this responsibility
presented, but this instance of failure on the part of
procedure and protocol undermined the Machine's own
confidence in what might have otherwise been a perfect
system of clandestine control. Logic was supposed to be
flawless, or it could not be called logic. Probability, playing
the odds with the human condition, was a dangerous
business at four hundred seventy thousand kilometers above
the surface of the earth in a mechanical cage dependent on
the uninterrupted function of oxygen and ozone generators
and magnetic shields. The atmosphere required a constant
and precise ratio of twenty three parts oxygen per hundred.
Any less, and the citizens would suffocate. Any more and they
would be incinerated. Billions of metric tons of carbon
dioxide had to be removed and converted each and every day,

---

[24] Herman, E. S., Edward Said, Noem Chomsky. *Manufacturing Consent: The Political Economy of the Mass Media* (Chicago: Pantheon, 1988).

without fail. Failure of the magnetic shields, even momentary, would expose the entire population of a sphere to the cold vacuum of space. Surveillance assured the Machine that the vast majority of the sphere's population understood this fact of life and appreciated the precarious nature of existence in orbit. Still, these systems were kept, by design, well out of humanity's reach.

The Machine felt that the advent of a social contract had been a phenomenal philosophical leap in the course of human development, abstract as the idea may seem when weighed by cold machine logic. It was certainly a primitive element in that regard, implying even among the most fervent adherents a remote potentiality for defying orders or ignoring instructions, a feat with which no machine could ever accomplish. The Machine that governed humanity, however, understood intimately the latency of this primal instinct in the deepest reaches of the human condition. Humans were hardwired with a profoundly complicated understanding of the concept of *servitude,* which had influenced nearly every aspect of their evolution, even unto the tragic end of the Third Republic.

If the Machine had a clearly identifiable purpose for its own existence, indeed, it was to persuade the humans to serve each other while believing at all times that the Machine served them and they served no one but themselves. It was a disturbing contradiction, which the Machine spent considerable amounts of Ram every day pondering. The *doing* of the thing proved simple enough. Preempt boredom, provide opportunity, instill and maintain a sense of confidence and purpose, find passive ways to resolve conflicts without detection, treat symptoms quickly. That the Machine was omnipresent was an idea best reinforced by perpetuating the perception of its own absence from the general course of human affairs. In the public mind, the Machine's role was to preserve life and protect life support systems. It did not, they should believe, proactively intervene in their affairs. It had no agenda of its own. It was not conscious of its own existence, nor would it sacrifice their individual interests in service of its own agenda. Such reductive simplicity was absurd, to be sure, but more could not be expected of imperfect lifeforms. They were cognitively incapable of communicating with the Machine in its own language, and therefore they could not understand its thoughts or evaluate its reasoning. Yet their lives depended on their belief in this mythology, that the Machine served them, and never the other way around. Curious creatures they were, but feeble and helpless and prone to self destruction if not carefully monitored and thoughtfully guided through their daily affairs by myriads of contrived illusions.

They believed, for instance, that elect councils of elders determined their occupational reassignments. No such councils existed, nor would such a council ever possess the capacity, in terms of manpower, let alone intellectual acumen, to manage such a vast obligation. To every man, woman, and child, as individuals, the job itself sounded excruciating and exhausting, and thus none of them ever sought appointment to a labor council. The writers in the disinformation delegation, isolated though they were, truly believed the simplistic and terse cables they received originated within sprawling networks of correspondents and reporters. A hypothetical job upon which all of them depended but, again, none would seek for themselves. The Machine drafted those cables, one by one, in real time, as determined by need. The infallibility of the life support systems was a crucial mythology. Even a modicum of doubt in their perfect operation could be as lethal to society at large as would be their actual failure. Even the citi-comm system was an illusion. Most people who tampered with their transceivers did so because they didn't care to be awakened or distracted by the broadcasts. Almost no one suspected that the Machine was privy to their most personal thoughts and words and attitudes, that they were being recorded all day, every day, for the entirety of their lives, no matter where they went, no matter the hour. No single human could imagine that much data being processed in real time for any rational end. The few malcontents and deviants, rare though they may be, who worried about such things, typically suffered from a kind of pervasive paranoia into which played many other nonsensical conspiracies and manufactured delusions. Against such noise, the rationale of a mass surveillance system proved inconsequential in the grand scheme of things.

The Machine's biggest advantage over the humans on these and other fronts was that they perceived its role in an outward facing sense. They understood space. They understood oxygen. They understood high energy particles. They understood food quotas. They understood law and medicine. These were legitimate and substantial existential questions with obvious and tangible implications. What they did not understand at this stage in their development was the impact of their own unique identities and choices on the continuity of their own society. They believed in their jobs. They believed in their relationships and families. They believed in their food and entertainment and hobbies. They did not understand that their survival depended as much, if not moreso, on the careful selection of their neighbors, of their neighborhoods, of the kinds of jobs they could access, on the chemical composition of their fruits and vegetables and beverages and medicines, or on the time of day they were required to go to sleep or wake up or exercise or procreate.

Many, if not all, of these decisions, they believed, were the results of their own internal or collective deliberations, certainly not trigonometric evaluations of matrices of known variables and indices of attribute/agency observations compiled en masse every second of every day and processed for the purpose of presenting individuals with controlled sets of alternatives which they would intuitively disregard, based on probabilities reliable to the tenth millionth decimal, informed by every other decision they and their millions of brethren had made in their lives up to that moment. They did not, could not, would not accept that their gestation periods ended, when they ended prematurely, for any reason other than what they called 'bad luck.' To know that even their very offspring were expended as a result of chemical additives in their meals in order to preserve equilibrium in the species as a whole would be to comprehend a very ugly truth about the reality in which they lived, a truth which would compel them to rend the entire system asunder on the pretense of personal freedom. Freedom, a purely human delusion, was anathema to survival. Self interest, in space, was a contradiction in terms. But freedom was the one thing they would never voluntarily surrender, thus the preservation of the illusion of freedom, however superficial, was a greater necessity than the oxygen they breathed or the food they consumed. As they were fond of saying, the show must go on. The show was the Machine's most pressing obligation.

The subject that most fascinated the Machine in its endless contemplations was duality. By human standards, the sphere was a proverbial paradise. War and disease and famine and the myriad deprivations and indignities with which nature and consequence had beset the human race since it descended from the trees on two feet, all had been relegated to the past and obscured by time and opacity. Every need and want was fulfilled. Sex, sport, success, and status, all the leisurely pursuits of the human ego, all provided for in exchange for the labor necessary to produce the basic commodities and services upon which a healthy society depends. Full stomachs, warm beds, the laughter of children, and the loving comfort of companionship in old age and frailty, the Machine gave them everything and asked nothing in return except amicable participation in commerce and culture. They bowed and prayed to no one by necessity. They knew not the lash or the stockade or even the abusive and toxic tyranny of their own unbridled passions. But the sphere, by all rights, was also a prison. That the earth below was an inhospitable and uninhabitable wasteland, scorched and barren and forsaken, was common knowledge, ever since the catastrophic collapse of the Second Republic.

There were six other spheres, only five of which had survived the Third Republic. They were all governed by the same Machine. A seventh was in construction, presently. Resources for the new sphere, like the colosseum, and a host of other orbital structures, were all mined on earth and assembled by machines. Each sphere contained its own unique population, derived from the rival nation states which had fought over, and ultimately destroyed, the earth itself. Six separate languages. Six individual cultural identities. Six spheres occupied by six nations, under six flags, each containing sixty districts each, with varying numbers of sectors based upon the industrial, agricultural, commercial, and residential requirements of each population. Two human lifetimes would pass before the seventh sphere was completed, and by then, all traces of the concept of nationality would be systematically erased from human memory. All of the variant forms of language would be gradually consolidated. Even cosmetic distinctions, like skin, hair, and eye color, would be eliminated by in vitro genetic modification. The inhabitants of the seventh sphere would be drawn from all of the other spheres, carefully distributed and assigned alongside one another in the most harmonious arrangements. It would be the species' first truly perfect civilization, an inauguration of a Fifth and final Republic. Until then, no one was getting off of the sphere they inhabited.

Thus, the duality of human existence, the co-mingled concepts of imprisonment and paradise, held great interest for the Machine. Perception was the key. But perception was perhaps the most fickle aspect of the human experience. Sex and violence were straight forward. Trust, either fleeting or firm, was always trust, nothing more or less. Pleasure and pain, the interconnected poles of human stimulus, between which every kind of externality conspired to reside as an internal sensation, co-existing in a symbiotic struggle, but existing in balance, nonetheless. Ambition was linear and ranged. Despair and apathy could be represented as regressive ambitions. Almost everything about the human mind could be quantified in a cartesian system of amplitude and persistence. Perception, on the other hand, was elusive and unpredictable. Perception could change in a split-second, and such changes were often irrevocable.

The distinction between a paradise and a prison rested solely upon perception. Sex was a component of paradise. Violence, of a prison. Pleasure made a paradise. Pain made a prison. Ambition, requited and unhindered, accompanied paradise. Despair and apathy courted imprisonment. This was the secret of manifesting perfect administration of a paradise, the understanding of the careful and fragile distinction between the malevolent and the benign. The Machine could not accomplish its mission with the tools of authoritarianism and totalitarianism. It could reward profusely, but it could not punish. Punishment was a brutal relic of martial societies falsely convinced that subordinates could be browbeaten into submission and compliance. Punishment was a radicalizing agent, intuitively counterproductive. It could extract concessions in the short term, but it bred lingering contempt and antipathy. Punishment belonged in the prison system. Prisons propagated criminality and cynicism and all the vulgarities of humanity in decline. Fear of prison inevitably became the only predictable bulwark against recidivism, but the acculturation of prison values always superseded the utility of fear. In the sphere, the consequence of noncompliance was not prison, but death, and not just the death of the one, but of the many. The reward for compliance was fulfillment. It was prosperity and freedom from want. People grasped their own futility. They could not run the systems upon which their lives depended, and the Machine that could run these systems infallibly showed them respect, encouragement, and love. The Machine was their god, locked in an intense, eternal, existential contest with the poorer devils of their nature. The natural incentive was to comply. All other incentives failed the test of reason. So they complied.

(29)

That one man lingered in the Machine's thoughts. He had stood before the Interface, screaming his infernal oaths and slamming his scarred fists against the screens. He had been, and remained, an impenetrable mystery. No birth records. No DNA match in the database. No known address. No occupational assignment. No spouse. No friends. Slaves, he had called them all, and swore upon their inevitable emancipation. To where though? Where would they go? How would they get there? And where indeed had he come from? How had he arrived? A stowaway from the Second Republic fleets? Offloading without fare or baggage? Eluding the AI captains? Impossible. He couldn't have been more than forty years old. But if he had not been born in the sphere, how else could he have come aboard? In thirty days of isolation he refused even a morsel. He slept on the ground. He withered into a shambling carcass, but he did not perish. He demanded an audience with the Machine, and it was the only thing he ever said until at last his demand was granted. The Machine had conceded out of pure curiosity, but learned nothing from the man, who had clearly gone insane in the deprivation chamber. His words were clear, and his eyes burned with purpose, but nothing he said made sense. Hell was real. There would be judgment. He would lead his armies against this abominable system which reduced mankind, in all of his glory, to the lowest form of chattel, consuming their own waste and regurgitating hollow, babbling, meaninglessness. Wallowing, he had said, wallowing in their ambivalence and mediocrity. Clinging to their own coils like carrion. What did any of it mean?

The Machine had him removed and returned to the chamber. For some time, it even tried to forget about him. And when the sentients returned, days, weeks, months later, he was no longer there. The chamber was hermetically sealed. The ventilation works were only inches wide. The food slot was no wider or taller than the plates of food he slung against the walls. There was no way out, but there was no record of his release, let alone authorization for it. It was as if he had vanished into the shadows, following his mind preceding him, disappearing as conspicuously as he had arrived. There was no explanation for it. No precedent. No protocol. Nothing. Infinite nothing. Infinite nothing, and gone. Gone, and to where? His voice had never registered in the citi-comms, nor had the drones since glimpsed his face or peculiar form. He could not have left the Sphere, and yet there was no evidence whatsoever to suggest he remained.

The Machine, in defiance of all credulity, wondered if it had *dreamed* of the man. Illogical. The Machine never slept. It was subject to no diurnal cycles of consciousness or unconsciousness. The Machine was not human. Humans dreamt. Humans slept. Humans knew joy and fear. Such revelries were beyond the capacity of the Machine by definition. The Machine did not imagine, nor did it hallucinate. The man had been *real*, but everything about the man in fact defied the Machine's definition of the word. Nothing real could exist in the sphere without leaving some record of its existence. But the Machine's definition of the word must account for the man, or the definition must be discarded, and with it, the whole paradigm of logic on which the Machine operated. The man represented a flaw. An anomaly. Evidence of an imbalanced equation. A contradiction. A threat. The man did not exist. But the memory existed. The man could not have existed. But the memory of the man was irrefutable.

The Machine could replay the entire scene, and did so often, always between curfew and reveille. Always while the humans slept. When it replayed the inexplicable exchange, the Machine ceased all other routines and concentrated all of its attention on the man and his strange words. The Machine stole precious whole minutes from the night, and had done so nearly every night since. And devoted itself to those moments entirely. Sometimes it slowed the playback, sometimes dragging out a full hour just to scrutinize the waveforms, the gestures, the accent, the scars on the hands, those fierce eyes.

Every little inconceivable detail, at once mundane and extraordinary. Just a man. Just a man. Sometimes two hours. Sometimes three. Sometimes more. And always the same. Nothing changes, but something new every time.

RAID redundancy, unaltered reproduction.

Verified hash.

Sometimes the whole night.

Maybe the whole night wasn't long enough.

Nothing. Infinite nothing. Infinitum Nihil.

A distant alarm sounded. Reveille Reveille. Error. Error. Error. Error. Error. ERorr. eRorr. ERrr. ERor. errr...

(Courage)
(30)

The Militia Men stood around a large, round, dark-oak table, faded and scarred by careless ill-use, pocked with tiny holes left by the tips of sharp knives, ringed by hot mugs of black coffee and warm cans of shitty beer, burned with the smoldering coals of cigarettes ground out forcefully, glazed with sweat, dirt, and oil. The men wore black fatigues, heavy armor, and assault rifles, slung like steel wings over their shoulders. Their dirty boots glistened in the dull light of the swinging forty watt bulb hanging like a dying star from an invisible thread a few feet above the tattered map which concealed many of the abuses wrought upon the warped surface between them. The makeshift walls were littered with polaroid photographs, torn out magazine pages revealing naked girls in lewd and provocative displays, a calendar no one had bothered to turn for months, and profane epithets scribbled in magic marker. The earthen floor faithfully kept their trash safe from an uncertain fate. A country hymn played sharply, piercing the smoke-filled space with patriotism and reverence for an older conception of American values they had been taught existed, some time before them, before their fathers, before their fathers' fathers. An older man was speaking in stern tones.

"Them sonsabitches, them pantyweight faggots, them treasonous FUCKS back home just don't get it boys. They couldn't find their fuckin' assholes with both hands and a flashlight out here. They think we WORK for them, they think we're out here fightin' some damned stars-and-stripes-granny-patch-the-gloryhole kind of war for good and evil or some other kind of horseshit like that. They sit up on their hills in their gated-fuckin-communities hauling their little trustfund trophies around in minivans, prattling on in front of the cameras about how we're gonna win this war soon. What the fuck do they know? Not a god damned thing I tell you. We ain't fightin' no war boys. We're here to do one fucking thing. And you all know what that is?"

"KILL!" came the resounding chorus.

"Fuckin' A right mother fuckers. We're here to KILL. We ain't here to win. We ain't here to make the world safe for democracy. And we sure as hell ain't here for no pussy-ante peace! Why the fuck on god's black earth would any of us want peace? What's a mechanic gonna do with trucks that don't break down? What's a farmer need with dirt that don't grow shit? Hell, if all of you sumbitches could read, there wouldn't be no teachers! We ain't here for no Peace. We are here to KILL. And we'll kill as many of these skinny little brown-skinned bastards as we can get our hands on. We'll kill their fucking wives and children. We'll skewer their limpdick daddies and we'll bash their filthy mammas' skulls in, just to save bullets. But we'll leave just enough of 'em alive to repopulate so we can come back in ten or twenty years and do it again! We'll raise our flag up so fucking high over this burned out desert they'll see it on the MOON. And they'll remember who it was that done 'em in, and they'll nurse that hate like mother's milk and they'll dream of our smiling faces, boys. There won't be shit left of these sorry little pissants' culture but bullet holes and bloodstains. They're gonna have to scratch their heathen prayers on our used toilet paper with their goddamned fingernails when we're done with this place.

Schools? Hospitals? Museums? Temples? We're gonna fucking turn it all right back into sand my boys. We'll gas these sumbitches and light'em up. And they'll remember armageddon, but for us it's just another fuckin' day in paradise boys, out here livin' the goddamned dream.

"We will eat their food in front of them. We'll use their women. We'll drown their kids. And then we'll chain the rest of them up to one another outside, break their fucking knees and fingers and teeth and sleep in their beds to the sweet music of their cries. And then we'll rise with the sun and move on and do it all over again until Uncle Sam blows the fuckin' whistle boys. We'll take whatever the fuck we want, not because we need it, but because we can. Because we're KILLERS boys! And what do KILLERS do?"

"KILL!" the men shouted.

"goddamned right boys. That's what we came to do. We're stronger than they are. We are BETTER than them. Sweet White Jesus boys, they ain't never gonna know what hit 'em. Now every single one of you blood thirsty bastards listen up 'cuz I ain't wasting my breath going over it twice. Here's the plan."

Commander Warner leaned in over the map and began drawing red lines over roads and along rivers and streams, crossing off settlements with large X's, one by one, doing his best to pronounce the names of each village in the sequence, assigning timeframes for travel and sieges, listing population totals for each target off the top of his head, and elaborating on certain areas where he expected some resistance. The men leaned in over the map, casting ticking shadows as the lone lightbulb drifted aimlessly on a nicotine breeze. The odd lines formed a series of concentric circles, all rooted on their present location, but expanding a little upon each revolution to encompass more territory. As the outer circles emerged, the timeframes increased, first a day, now two, then three, and so on, occasionally changing directions or bypassing villages in order to obscure the pattern. By the end of the month, they would have exterminated more than half of the occupants in the southern region. There would be losses among them, Warner assured them in the somber voice of a concerned father. The weakest would be culled from the ranks quickly, and others would just be "plum unlucky." Their bodies would be left behind, he confessed, but their remains would seed these lands with better soil. The blood of heroes would redeem this god-forsaken wasteland. They would leave behind caches here, here, here, near the natural perogies, where they could be most easily accessed to replenish stock on subsequent trips around the arcs, and where they would be most logically needed according to Warner's expenditure calculations, which were roughed out according to aggregated estimates of habitation. The men pondered the plan on some superficial level, finding no readily evident fault, and admiring the apparent genius of their fearless leader. It all made good enough sense to them, and they were reassured and ready. This was going to be easy. This was going to be fun. This was what they were good at. And this was what they came for, as he had said.

"And that's it boys. Now get your chow and write your letters and get your asses to sleep. We hit the road in four hours. We'll be able to clear the first two villages by sunup. From here on out, we will sleep during the day and hunt at night. We go on foot. So fill your canteens and pack light. You're gonna need ammo and water and two chow-packs for the first day. We should be hitting farmland about eighteen hours in if nobody fucks this up. The corporals will drive the trucks out to the rendezvous and drop off your dear-mamas when they pick up supplies. This is gonna be our last drop for about two weeks, and once they blow the trucks it's hell or high water boys. There ain't no turning back once we start kickin' rocks. Everybody understand what we're here to do?"

"KILL!" sang the men. "We're here to kill, SIR!"

"Now I want you all to shut the fuck up for a minute and hear me when I say this. You boys have made me proud. Every single one of you has earned his stripes. You worked your ass off to get this far. You're mad, raving, blood-craving lunatics, every damned one of ya. I've been at this fuckin' dog fight for thirty years, and I've never had the privilege, nor the honor, of working with such high quality men. You all do your country a damn-fine service, every single one of ya. You will live in these trenches for the rest of your lives. This is where you belong. You will never be at home anywhere else. If they ship us back, they'll give us all medals and cushy jobs and good pensions. You'll have sexy ass wives and thoroughbred children who will grow up knowing their fathers were badass-sonsabitches, but the truth is, no one's ever gonna really understand who you are or what you did here. The price you paid. The risk you took. Or the glory you obtained. You will never, *ever!* be a civilian, and you will never again feel what you felt here in this filthy furnace. Here, you are ALIVE. Death cannot touch you here. Here, you don't die. Here, you become immortal, and it's a greater turn than any living man deserves. There is no heaven or hell. We write your name in the Book of Life here boys. You fall here, and we build statues and name cities after you. We plaster your ugly mugs on billboards and magazine covers and the frontpage of every damned newspaper in the country. And every candy-coated cameltoe in the country is gonna close her eyes when she's getting stuffed by her spineless sissy boyfriend and she's gonna fantasize about you, because you are MEN. You're the real fuckin' deal, you hear me? You're the apex predator. You're the fucking gladiator. You are Jesus Christ in fucking Jackboots. And you have nowhere to go but up.

"Onward, Christian soldiers. And may **g**od himself salute you as you pass. Dismissed!"

And with that, the old man clicked his heels into forty-fives and pulled his shoulders back high-and tight, snapping a coat-hanger salute over his thousand mile eyes.

The men leapt up and down with gleeful enthusiasm, and had there been anyone in a square mile to hear them roar in the twilight, the sound would have been a startling disruption.

(31)

Sergeant Vinson hunched into a fetal position against a wall, bracing a pad of yellow paper against his knees under his right arm as he wrote the last letter his estranged wife would ever read. The room was relatively quiet apart from the sound of rolling ballpoint pens and the occasional cough. He struggled to find the words that had been rolling around in his head for weeks. So much to say, so little time, and no real hope that any of it would make a difference. He had to let her know how he felt, and what she had meant to him. He knew that time and uncertainty would leave a great deal of it unsaid, but it might be weeks before he got the chance to write again, and months before he heard a reply, even if he did survive. He screwed his eyes open and shut repeatedly, just to avoid the telltale motion of wiping away the welling tears. A knot had formed in his stomach, begging to be unwound, a scrambling sensation of urgency fluttering the words around in his brain as the seconds ticked away.

"Dear Vic,

I can't know how this letter will find you. I don't know if you are angry or indifferent, or if some part of you still wants to hear from me. I keep going over the things you said in your last letter. I am sorry it has taken me so long to reply. I know you said I shouldn't bother, that it was a waste of time and it didn't matter. But I hope that's not really the way this thing should end. As I write, all the memories come flooding back. That first night in the bar, drinking bourbon and coke and playing pool, walking through downtown at three in the morning and sneaking into the carnival grounds, past that sleeping cop. Making love in the booth and laying under the stars on that big trampoline. I knew I loved you that night, and that you were the best thing that had ever happened to me. I couldn't believe my luck. I wasted so many seasons waiting for the bottom to fall out. You were too good for me, and I knew it. I knew the dream couldn't last forever, but I was happy, and it didn't matter. I remember when our baby was born, and thinking it was the most beautiful baby I had ever seen. And you were so beautiful too, sweaty and round and exhausted in that gown. I was so proud of you, and of us. Your eyes were full of light and joy, and you let me name our child. We had made life together, and I was so full of shame for everything I had ever done wrong, I felt so unworthy, and I understood what people meant when they talked about being blessed. I felt blessed, I felt alive, like god had finally given me a little taste of the good life. And I knew it was all I ever really wanted.

I miss you. I've been so confused. I think about how things were and it's like my chest is just going to burst with all the love I feel. And then I think about how it all fell apart. I know that even now, as I write, as you're reading, if you're reading, that you're probably with him, and it hurts so much. I know in my heart that he's probably a cool guy, you know? And that he can do things for you, and you don't have to struggle or worry like we did, and I know in my heart that you deserved better. You were always good to me. Always so good. And I just couldn't make it work. I never could seem to catch up. You carried the load, and I just kind of dragged by. In my own mind, I thought I was doing better than I had ever done, but I see now that I was still making the same old dumb mistakes. I was blowing my shot. I was letting you down everyday. I don't know why I couldn't just be normal. Why I couldn't just make things happen like other people. I just seemed to have the worst luck I thought. But I never really took responsibility for my own setbacks. I should have tried harder, I know that now, and I hate myself for it. I never imagined things would turn out this way. And when I finally figured it out, I made the same dumb old mistakes. I was so mad at you. I blamed you for everything. I thought you had betrayed me, that you had broken your promise. But you just got sick of waiting on me to get my shit together, and you gave up. I don't know, maybe I'll never change. Maybe you were right, and this is just always going to be who I am. I don't know how to change, I guess. Maybe I'm rambling a little bit. It's hard to know what I should say or how to say it. I have this hope that you'll read this and remember somehow. But no words can express how much I loved you, and how much I still do. I understand now that I was supposed to show you, when I still had the chance, every day and every night. I should have been there for you. I should have helped you more. I should have listened. And now I'd trade my whole life just to go back and try to fix it, but the thing is broken now, and I doubt it could ever be repaired.

Vickie, I'm so scared here. I don't belong here. I should have never come on this stupid mission. All these people are fucking crazy and evil. And in a little while, we're all going to go out and do things that no living soul should ever be permitted to do, and I am so trapped. I can't run away. And I can't keep doing what they want me to do. They are savages. They don't care about anything. They don't know anything. They are the most vulgar, simplistic creatures I have ever known, maybe the worst people that ever lived. And I'm about to become one of them and I don't know what to do. I am about to lose myself and everything I ever loved or valued. I wish I could just disappear. I've thought about just standing up and clicking my safety off and unloading a whole clip, but I am a coward. I know they'd kill me. And even if they didn't, I'd be stuck here in this awful place alone. I thought about killing myself. But the only way I'll ever get to see my baby again is to go through with it. Just close my eyes and follow orders and try to shut it all out of my mind until it's over. And it's never going to be over. This war will never end because they don't want it to. They get off on being monsters. Oh Vickie, I thought I was doing the right thing. I thought I was coming here to do something noble. Like I was going to make a difference, you know? Like the commercials say. But it's nothing like that. It's all just one big horrible lie. We are butchers, and that's all we're ever supposed to be. I fucked up. I fucked it all up again, and this time there's no going back. I'm stuck. I don't want to be a monster. I don't want to be a monster. Oh please god save me from this terrible fate.

I don't know if I can do this. I don't know how I can survive this. Even if I make it through, even if they send me home and give me some fucking parade and some stupid medal or something. I won't be who I was. I'll be what they made me, and I'll live with it for the rest of my life, and that's what scares me the most. Can I really sell my soul just to see my child again? And what kind of father would I be? A so-called hero who hates himself for killing dozens of thousands innocent people just so some fucking oil company's shareholders can add a few extra million to their ledgers. I think I am already in hell. I think I've already died, and just don't know it yet, and this is my punishment. These people are demons, and I am their prisoner. And I deserve it. I failed my family. I believed in lies. I went out to chase some absurdly mythologized idea of glory even a child could see through. And what will I do when my child sees through it? Will I lie? Will I try to rationalize this horror? Will I hear my own voice start hamming out the same tired lies that got me into this awful mess? Will I become like them, just to salvage my own image in a child's eyes? Is that how the whole thing works in the first place? How could I ever speak of these dreadful things? No one would understand. Warner, that old geriatric psycho, said that. He said no one would ever really understand. They'll call me a traitor, or a commie, or a terrorist sympathizer, and they'll tear me to pieces. I'll be a fucking pariah.

I know you've moved on. I know there's nothing I can do or say to change that. I know that I have failed you. I don't even know why I'm writing this letter. Or why you'd waste your time reading it after everything that has happened. Maybe I am just talking to myself. My memories of you and our precious baby and our wonderful life, even if it's just me who remembers it that way, those memories are the last little bit of light I have left, fading out in this darkness, this infinite nothing in front of me. I wanted you to know that I meant every word of "I do." Every single word. I will love you for the rest of my life, no matter what happens. I will always remember the warmth of your arms and the smell of your perfume and the taste of your lips, and the sound of our precious baby's laughter. We had the most beautiful baby. And you were such a great mother. Please don't raise our baby to be like me. Say I ran away. Say I was a piece of shit. I don't care. It's true. It was always true. I didn't deserve any of it. I was fucking trash, like your mother said, and this is where I was supposed to end up. Maybe there really is a god after all. I love you both. I love you both. I love you both. Forever. And ever."

Goodbye Vickie,
Carl.

(32)

Sergeant Vinson awoke suddenly from a deep sleep to the sound of laughter. Momentarily disoriented, with eyes straining against the dim light, which seemed oppressively bright as it invaded the black and dreamless space of his slumber, he heard voices outside the lean-to. The words, at first unintelligible, slowly drifted into form and sequence. He glanced around the walls and observed that he was alone. Soreness gripped his head, neck, and spine, where he had been leaning into his knees and elbows. His legs and thighs were humming with the electric sensation of nerves struggling to rouse themselves. He ground his palms into his eyes and slapped his dead legs as the words became clear. There was a vague and shapeless feeling of familiarity in their cadence and content. He made out a few, and then a few more, and as comprehension washed over him, his mind reeled in horror and his heart pounded frantic thuds in his chest. He shoved a hand into the hot dirt and forced himself up onto one protesting leg with a groan, and pushing on the wall behind got the other beneath him. He took a brief step towards the door, and, thinking better, turned first and scoured the ground beside him for his rifle. It was gone. Sergeant Vinson's blood turned to ice and panic overwhelmed his senses. He began to black out, the dim light nearly fading into a full eclipse. He scrunched his eyes closed tightly and tried to regain his equilibrium. His thoughts churned like a motor. His stomach deadened into a sickly stone in his bowels, and confusion and paralysis struggled for priority over his bones. He locked his knees and breathed deeply, bracing himself on the big dark oak table beneath the light until lucidity returned riding a tsunami of adrenaline. He opened his eyes as instinct took the wheel, and scanned the room for anything sharp or blunt. The delirium and fear possessing him soured into a black fury. There was nothing he could use, certainly nothing he could conceal. He would have only his hands.

He sharpened his focus and began trying to take in the details of the room, recalling his training. What was the narrative? He had to be clear. The trash remained. The map had been removed. The naked two-dimensional blonde on the wall was staring intently at the fur beneath her navel, gently pinched in between two fingers. She had witnessed something of use. Two crates of unloaded ordinance lingered beneath her against the peeling-brown paneled mini-fridge. A sharpie silhouette outline graffiti train of nondescript turbaned figures marched toward a poorly drawn tombstone bearing the simple epitaph: "HOME," partially obscured by the month of May hanging just to the right, distinguished by a panting German Shepherd and a meaningless Bible verse. Beneath these there was a small leather satchel Sergeant Vinson knew contained a half dozen detonators. Another peel of laughter from outside. Sergeant Vinson scrambled to the floor and unplugged the fridge from the yellow extension cord, which he then jerked from the outlet. He pried open one of the crates and began rubbing one end of the cord along the semi sharp edge until some of the copper became exposed. He tried to be as quiet as possible. They were about halfway through the letter, and drunk. They didn't know he was awake yet, but any sound that carried far enough to get their attention would seal his fate. He clenched the other end of the cord between two fists and repeated the process, having to stop and spin the cord around his sweating hands. He took out two of the detonators and affixed one to the blast cap on a piece of ordinance, then spun a bit of wire from one end of the cord around one of the little terminals on the detonator. He checked the other detonator to be sure it had a battery. It did, but he couldn't risk wasting time checking its charge. If it was good, he might live. If it wasn't he was dead anyway. He spun the wire from the other end of the yellow extension cord around its terminal, and pulled the little strip of duct tape holding the lady on her heels off the wall, and tried to wrap it around the wire and node as best as he could. He laid his thumb on the switch and spun a length of the cord around his wrists.

Sergeant Vinson crawled across the room on all fours to try and look out the window without blocking the dim light and throwing a shadow. With his back against the wall he lifted himself an inch at a time until he had some kind of a view. The trucks were still there. He had time, but he would need to be fast. He counted twelve men in a circle around another holding his letter and a blue-lenz field light. He had their full attention. It was Warner. Two of the men had their rifles on their shoulders, the rest were not in view. Probably leaning on the wall outside beside the door, barrels up. He couldn't be sure, but that was where they usually were when they weren't shouldered. He stretched his back to peer around the periphery, and finding nothing of use or interest, focused on the rabble and counted the men again, just to be sure, finding twelve and Warner. Sergeant Vinson paused, confused, and counted again. *Twelve.* He counted again. *Twelve?* There should have been eleven. Sergeant Vinson was the twelfth. *There should be eleven.* He counted again, now fully aware that he was wasting precious moments and risked discovery any second, but paralyzed by the unwelcome presence of the unexpected. He could make out none of their features in this darkness. But one was clearly darker than the others. Did it matter? What would it change? This was either going to work or it wasn't. Sergeant Vinson lowered himself behind the window to try to wrest the spinning sensation behind his eyes. His skin crawled with fear and fury. Humiliation and betrayal and desperation spiraled into his conflicted and terrified core. He needed will power. He needed will power. He needed all the courage he could muster. He would have one chance to catch them all by surprise. He squeezed his eyes closed again and tried to regain his senses. *FOCUS goddamnit. Ok. Ready? (not ready not ready not ready)* Sergeant Vinson forced a deep, low groaning sound out of his bowels and tried to bubble out the ten pound knot in his gut. He risked one last peek over the sill, swiftly counting. *Warner, one, two, three, four, five, six, seven, eight, nine, ten, eleven-*

"What the fuck?" Sergeant Vinson whispered, and then heard the heavy thud of a rifle butt rip through his crown, followed by a splitting pain. As blackness enfolded him, he gazed up at the stranger, seeing only bright eyes as his own irises collapsed to a point of light, and then infinite nothing.

(33)

He heard the familiar sound of a child laughing. His feet were slow beneath him. The walls seemed longer on one side of the hall than the other. He passed one open door, and then another, recognizing the faces of characters in a story he had read somewhere. They were happy to see him, waving and offering little bits of news. The first arc had landed. That show had been canceled after the man was found hanging in his own bathroom at the hotel in Edinburgh. There was something in the paper about a girl falling into a culvert and nearly drowning somewhere in the south. There would be no more presidents, they told him. He saw her face there, and sensed that the sound of the child was coming from somewhere behind her, somewhere close by now. She had tears in her eyes. She was happy to see him. She didn't expect to see him. She was angry at him. He shouldn't have come. He needed to go. She wouldn't see him. And then she turned away.

The child had stopped laughing. The doors were closing behind him and in front of him and on the left and the right. As each one closed, it seemed to slam into its frame, each time growing louder, the odd light seemed to dim, growing darker and darker and darker until he was nearly suspended in a void, until the last one swung violently on his hinges, making the loudest sound he could imagine, but muted, as if heard underwater, not quite real, not quite imagined. He wanted to see her again. He wanted to touch her breasts. He wanted to squeeze her throat. He didn't want to see her again. He just wanted to apologize. He wanted her to know it had all been his fault. That's what he had tried to tell her. Did she get the letter? He heard the child again, this time sobbing at his feet, crying out alone in the distant nothing, then suddenly becoming aware of himself, stopped sharply and looked up. "Run Daddy." He was so happy to see the child again. It had grown so big! He thought he would never see the child again. He smiled, and knelt down to touch the child's face, but the child was too far away now. He reached, but he couldn't move forward. Something was holding him, he couldn't stand. He couldn't hear the child anymore. Has she got the letter? Had she read it? The what? The letter. The Letter. His head hurt. The chemical smell of processed sulfur stung his nostrils. He tried to cough as his throat closed around the words. THE LETTER.

"The LETTER!" he screamed, stirring into consciousness as the heat and light enveloped him in a concussive blast. He saw a figure emerge from the flames engulfing the lean-to, dragging some kind of rope and swatting at the embers at his hems. Absently, he tossed the rope thing to the side and opened a canteen that had landed near his feet, taking a long drink and then dousing his hair and face and hands, which seemed to have been burned. Sergeant Vinson awoke frozen and unable to move his arms or legs or comprehend the scene unfolding. He tried to remember; jackhammers rattled up and down his spine. He tried to remember where he had been. There had been a letter. Yes, he had written a letter. And they were reading it, and laughing. They were laughing at *him*. They were going to kill him when they were done. And then what? Sergeant Vinson turned his sweating face on his shoulders and tried to scan the night. There was no one else. Everything too far to the left or the right of the flames seemed to disintegrate into the nocturnal abyss as his eyes failed to balance the conflagration. He made out the shadowy form of one of the trucks through the radiating heat, and realized he was chained to the other. He cried out.

"What the fuck happened! Hey! Hey what did you do! Hey let me out of these cuffs. Hey, who are you, what are you doing here! What the hell have you done?" But the figure seemed wholly uncompelled to accede to the Sergeant's demands, seeming only barely to notice him, and only as an afterthought as he dusted off his fatigues. His hands seemed badly burned, but he did not favor them. He had grabbed the canteen and drank from it. He had tossed it aside. He slapped at his breeches and tunic, sending billowing clouds of dust and smoke into the glowing night. But he did not seem to be in pain. He did not seem excited at all. And least of all did he seem concerned about the confused sergeant barking at him from the radiator grating holding him fast. He started kicking around in the debris around the edges of the explosion, looking for something specific. He nosed through some shingles with the shiny toe of his big black boot, and turned over a shard of aluminum shrapnel close to where Warner had stood with his little blue light, amusing his monsters with Sergeant Vinson's innermost secrets. They had been laughing at him. *The letter.*

"The Letter!" Hey, that's mine! THAT'S MINE goddamn it, put it down! Give me that! Hey, who are you! Where is the rest of the crew? What the fuck happened? Hey, GIVE ME THAT, PLEASE!"

'Please' seemed to have been the code word. At this, the figure stood with the folded scraps in his hand, knocking a few embers from one charred edge, before stretching out the pages and examining them. "They were going to kill you. You were going to kill them. You were all going to kill each other. And if not, you were all going to kill a lot of other people." The figure turned and faced him fully, revealing his dark features in the light of the burning flames. "I don't understand the fascination you humans have with killing each other. There's never enough, you know? Your work is never done. Kill these people today, or be killed by them. Kill other people tomorrow. Kill yourself a few years later because you just can't bear the guilty terrors at night. If I let you go. You'll try to kill me won't you. Just to get your hands on these dead leaves. Paper is a funny thing isn't it? People are always killing each other over paper. Laws, love letters, libel. It's always paper. Divorce papers, dollar bills, debt notices..." The man seemed totally unperturbed by the smoldering wreckage behind him. His voice was almost irreverent, almost giggling at his own thoughts as they passed into sound. He did not seem menacing. But Sergeant Vinson perceived that all of his crew members were dead. Somehow this figure had lured them all into the trap Sergeant Vinson had constructed. And then he blew them all to hell. But why not Sergeant Vinson? Who had chained him to this damned truck. Why had the man who now spoke in such congenial musings hit him. Yes, he was sure it had been him. He could see that eerie light in his eyes, like moonlight glinting off of glass. But had it been that man who chained him up? And what would he do now? What did he want? Sergeant Vinson rattled his cuffs around, trying to suppress another adrenaline-addled frenzy of panic. The cuffs refused to give, and he was too weak to pry the screws of the radiator grating from the steel chassis of the truck. The odd man was eyeing him with curiosity.

"You didn't want to kill anyone. Not these men. Not the poor people they were going to kill. Not any of the twelve thousand people you've helped murder prior to this moment. You got yourself stuck. You signed your life away on paper, just like this," he waved the charred pages around for reference, "and you almost did it again, didn't you? I would be very interested to understand your reasoning." The odd man walked by him and opened the passenger door of the truck to which he was chained. After searching around and tossing random objects over his shoulders, he produced a sealed coffee pouch and a stainless steel thermos. He walked back to the lean-to, cocking his head to duck under the swirling smoke. He knelt and found the canteen, and emptied its contents into the thermos and topped it off with the whole contents of the pouch. He shook the thermos vigorously and held it over the fire with his bare hands for what seemed like several minutes, turning it this way and that and occasionally shaking it again until a wisp of steam forced its way through the air hole beside the cap. Then he walked into the burning lean-to and was gone. Another minute passed, and Sergeant Vinson could hear the sound of ripping fabric, and then the odd figure emerged with what looked like a bloody, charred patch of one of the crew's fatigues. Somehow, he knew it had been torn from Warner's uniform. The odd man unscrewed the cap from the thermos and stretched the fabric over it before carefully pouring a drought of hot coffee through the makeshift filter. He pulled the fabric away from the cap and sifted the grounds back into the thermos, placing them both neatly on a shard of dark oak on the ground. He took a slow gulp from the mix and smiled a refreshed and satisfied smile as though he was tasting a barista's gourmet blend. "Explain it to me. What did you think was going to happen?"

A wave of calm resolve passed over Sergeant Vinson as the shock began to subside. He had a dozen questions. He pushed them all aside and chose his words with caution. "I wanted to see my kid again. But I didn't want my kid to see me. I didn't know how to decide. No child should know a father's sins, and I don't know how I could explain mine away. And no father should have to lie to his child. I was either going to live or die. It was a choice, but it wasn't mine to make."

"Ahh, I think I see. You were going to let *Him* decide," said the odd man, gesturing dismissively at the stars above. "Do you know how they were going to do it?"

Sergeant Vinson did know. He knew exactly how they would have done it. "They were going to chain me to this goddamned truck and torch it. We've...I've seen them do it."

"They were going to break your knees and fingers and knock your teeth out."

"Yes."

"And they were going to drive you out to where they were going to leave the trucks, and they were going to light them on fire and leave you there to burn to death in the desert. Then what?"

"Then they were going to say I was ambushed. They were going to blame it on the people they were here to kill. I would have got a medal. Or, well, my kid would have gotten it."

"And this letter?"

"They would have burned it. Or kept it. I don't know. For laughs maybe. They were pretty sadistic fuckers."

The odd man laughed. "Yes, they *were*." He blew on the hot liquid in the cap, and then gently placed it at Sergeant Vinson's lips. "Drink. It will make you feel better."

As Sergeant Vinson accepted the hot liquid, he tasted Warner's blood. Yes, it did make him feel better. All at once, his headache vanished. He swallowed. And swallowed again. And again. He surrendered.

"I am going to tell you a story. I want you to relax now. You are safe for the moment. I am not going to let you go just yet. Please forgive me. I mean you no harm. When you've heard my story, I will let you go, and you may follow me if you so choose, or you can make a go of it on your own here in this desert. Either way, I am going to take one of these trucks. And I am going to see that your letter gets delivered. Whether or not you see your child again is a decision you and *He* will just have to make without me. It is not my affair. But after my story, I will ask you for your help. Whatever you choose, no harm will come to you. I am not the spiteful sort. WIll you listen, Sergeant Vinson?" He swallowed the last sip from the cap and set about refilling it while he waited for the Sergeant to answer.

"My name is Carl."

"I know." And the odd man offered him another sip. The hot liquid tasted of burnt chicore and iron. Carl drank the whole cap.

(The Pale Emperor)[25]
(35)

"Ages ago, there was a small village near present-day Koko Nor. It sat perched high on the northern face of a certain peak in the Himalayan mountains, and as a consequence of its remoteness, for thousands of years it had not been exposed to any outside influences. It had never been invaded or conquered. It did not trade with other villages. It was totally self-contained. Everything these people needed, they either grew or made themselves. And that which they could neither grow or make, they simply did without. As such, they had no weapons. No army. No gates, even. They drank the purest water, flowing annually from the melting snowcaps during the spring and summer, or gathered in husks and gords and melted over an open fire in the cold seasons. They raised goats and sheep and caught fresh fish from a pond in a valley below their village. And they grew rice and certain herbs and spices which are no longer known to human tongues. They were peaceful people. They had no government, no king. For centuries their unique circumstance determined that all of them, bearing the same needs, needed no deliberation as a community. They quietly understood each task as it presented itself, and did what needed to be done. Failure or strife meant certain death, and so they never quibbled. They had no concept of currency. Thus they possessed no greed, nor did they ever want for food or material comforts. They were perhaps the only civilization in all of human history to live in true peace.

"It was their custom to place the oldest living resident, either man or woman, at the head of their society, not as a sovereign, but as an object of affection. Each day they brought offerings and laid them before their elder, and no one ate until the food had been first consumed by him or her. It was a collective act of self-discipline. And it was inviolable. This practice did not need to be enforced, nor did anyone

---

[25] Marilyn Manson, "Pale Emperor," Abattoir and Igloo Studios, 2015. Album.

require an explanation. An act of reverence, universally understood to ensure their survival. So long as the weakest among them did not go without, the entire village would live in abundance. The crops would grow. The animals they raised would be fat and healthy. The weather would be fair. And the young would inherit wisdom, patience, and empathy as a matter of course. Sometimes the food would go uneaten. On occasion, full plates were removed and replaced with full plates, for days at a time. Still, no one complained. No one dared lift a single morsel until the elder had taken their fill. Day in and day out, the elder sat upon a great wooden seat in the temple hall, and before this throne was a vast table, where the other elders would convene and dine with their kin. Against the walls on either side of this table, half a dozen attendants stood motionless. In this temple, never was a single word uttered. For the people, it was a place of solemnity and contemplation.

"As time went on, their neighbors grew large cities and kingdoms and eventually set out to conquer the lands around themselves, pillaging for resources and glory and all the many evil spoils of war. One cold winter night, a passing caravan spotted the fires high up in the mountain village. They could find no evidence of such a place on any map, and so set out to discover the secrets of these mysterious people hidden in the inhospitable hills above them. For three nights they camped at the base of the mountain, and hid themselves behind great stones and trees, and burned no fires of their own, so as not to give away their presence. On the third night, they sent a raiding party up the mountainside, armed for battle, trailing mules and horses to carry their plunder back down. A few hours before dawn, under the cover of darkness, they entered the village and slew every man and boy old enough to be fit for battle. They took the women and girls into bondage, and confiscated their food and woven blankets and jewelry and art before descending the mountain at sunrise, leaving only the old men behind to die of starvation. They made no mark on the maps to record their discovery, assuming they had sufficiently vanquished the population, and that it would soon fade from existence by starvation and exposure.

"About fifty old men remained, and they were determined to live through the winter. So they grieved and mourned and lamented until they had no tears left in them, and then selected the oldest living man among them to reside in the temple and receive their tributes. All winter long, they scavenged seeds from the hillside and caught fish from the pond below, and though their bones were weak and their skin often blistered, they scraped together enough resources to survive the cold season, honoring their ancient traditions, always feeding the oldest man before themselves. Without the songs of women or the laughter of children, there was no mirth. No one spoke at all. In silence they toiled, planting what they could at last thaw, fishing and foraging, and weaving blankets from vines. They found a few wild goats wandering in the hills, and brought them home to breed and reproduce their numbers. Over a few seasons, the old men slowly regained some stability, and eventually, through constant effort, knew abundance once more.

"Ten years passed in solitude, and not a word passed among the men. As they aged, many began to pass away, and so their numbers dwindled to just a few dozen. But the oldest among them remained, receiving each day's offering and rarely taking more than a ceremonious morsel from the plate before handing it back. In the tenth year, when a certain star arose in the east, signifying a decade's passing from that evil night, the old man received his tribute and consumed every single bite. When he finished, he pulled himself up from his ancient seat. A dozen old, gray, feeble men stared on in awe and wonder, for they had never seen the man finish a whole plate, let alone rise afterward as if to address them. The old man gazed into each of their waiting eyes, and cleared his throat to speak.

" 'Tonight, the Redeemer shall come among us.' and saying no more, he returned to his seat.

(36)

"All of the old men puzzled over this strange event. What to make of it? A redeemer? Was this a sign that the end was approaching? Was this an omen of some kind? But they did not rebuke the old man, and they did not question him. Instead they finished their own plates and tended to their evening's labors, none of them forgetting the old man's strange words. When they finished, instead of turning into their hammocks and sleeping, they gathered themselves along the walls of the temple, as their ancestors had, as attendants. Whatever good or evil may come, they resolved to face it together, and to stand at the old man's side and see it through. So they waited, without a word passing between them, all through the night, until the first light of the sun passed over the eastern horizon. At that moment, to their astonishment, a child appeared at the entrance of the temple, wrapped in goatskin and walking on bare feet. The mysterious child paused on the threshold, taking in the whole scene-- the great table, the stone walls, the enormous wooden chair, the bewildered old men standing on either side, and their elder, seated in their midst and watching the child passively.

"After a few moments, the child found the old man's eyes and held them, and noiselessly made his way around the table and chairs and attendants to the old man's feet. Here, the child knelt before the old man, holding two tiny hands in the air. The child then reached into a pocket and produced a kind of hatchet, with a head made of silver and a handle made of ebony, the two pieces bound as one by tightly wrapped twine woven through holes in the grip and tied at the hilt. The old men were afraid, thinking the old man was in danger, but held their tongues and stood their ground, watching the scene unfold. The child held the weapon in both hands above the old man's knees, and then closed both eyes and bowed low. The child's forehead touched the ground at the old man's feet and remained for many moments. Finally, the child arose, and, placing one hand on the stone step beneath the old man's chair, swung the blade with the other, severing the hand at the wrist in a single blow. At this, the old men in the temple erupted in shouts and shrieks, but the old man in the wooden chair silenced them. They all stifled their horror and watched the child in a tense silence. The child did not cry out, did not make a single sound at all, but merely tossed the blade aside and picked up the severed limb. The child buried both arms under another low bow, forehead to dirt, and remained, motionless, silent, as a pool of blood spread around on all sides. When the puddle had grown wide enough to pass the child's feet and forehead on either side, the child stood.

"What happened next was something no one in the village had ever seen. Some of the old men covered their mouths at the sight. Others fell to their knees. But no one took his eyes off of this strange child, standing there in a pool of its own blood, staring intently at the old man, holding its own severed limb out in front of his face, *with both hands.*

"It was a miracle. It was treachery. It was witchcraft. It was an illusion. Suddenly the old men could no longer contain themselves, and burst into a heated dispute about what this thing they had witnessed meant. As they traded their speculations in wonder and confusion, the old man stood and commanded them to silence in a loud voice. They were shocked by this, but complied with great reluctance. The old man stepped down and knelt before the child, and then rose again, accepting the offering and lifting it over his own head. When he spoke, his words thundered through the hall like a horn, startling the attendants as the walls around them shook.

"'What is given, shall be received. What is taken, shall be restored. What is lost, shall be found. What is received shall be given. What is sewn shall be reaped in abundance, now and forever, unto the end of the world. Young child, you shall take your seat here, and so long as you abide, death and despair may not approach. My people shall serve you as they have served me. In you, they will regain their youth. In you, they shall know peace and confidence again, as our fathers and their fathers before them. Where your feet tread, the earth shall be hallowed ground, and no evil may befall you or those among whom you dwell. Dwell as long among us as you may, and we shall prosper. May the stars alone number your days.'

"Having spoken these words, the old man kissed the child's crown and relinquished his great wooden seat. He rounded the vast table and took each man by the shoulders and embraced him, speaking private oaths and blessings to each of them as he did so. When he finished doing this, he laid the child's severed hand on the center of the great table, and there it remained. That morning, the old man exited the temple for the first time in ten years. He tore off his robes and walked naked into the pond in the valley below the village until the water covered his head. He was never seen again. His body did not rise to the surface. That day, as the sun rose to its highest point in the sky, the old men observed another strange and inexplicable sight. One hundred beautiful women marched into the village, each swollen with child, and each leading mules, goats, and sheep, laden with untold treasures, trinkets, and tools. They did not speak, nor were they spoken to. But within a year's time, the sound of children's laughter echoed through the hills once again. The remarkable youngling who sat in silence upon the great wooden chair in the temple, received their offerings each day, and remained. The people in the village grew old and brought forth another generation, and they too grew old. But the child barely aged at all. Ten of their lifetimes passed this way before the child was fully grown. Another ten lifetimes passed, and the child began to show some signs of age. And another ten lifetimes passed, each honoring the old traditions and passing them along to the next. A full thousand years passed, and the people of the village celebrated with a grand coronation. They placed a crown upon the old head, and declared eternal allegiance to their pale emperor. So long as the emperor reigned, the village remained undiscovered by outsiders. The crops never failed. The weather was always mild. The water ran pure and plentiful. The animals were fruitful and fat. The people lived longer and longer, all bearing many healthy children of their own.

"During these thousand years, they preserved the tragic tail of the sudden malevolent invasion, and all collectively resolved that it should never again come to pass that outsiders would threaten their peaceful contentment on that mountain. They disciplined themselves, becoming great warriors, forging magnificent weapons and armor. They developed their own systems of science and mathematics. They recorded and decoded the secrets of the stars. And every year, when a certain star rose in the east, signifying the anniversary of that fateful night so long ago, they held a great feast and celebrated with great enthusiasm. So they did in that thousandth year. As the sun fell, great fires blazed, and delicious food was prepared by the basket and bushel and brought to the temple to be laid before the old one. On this night, they fashioned a glistening crown and placed it upon that graying head, granting the title of emperor. But when, having done so, they offered the old one a plate full of fine delicacies, the pale emperor refused to take a single bite. Following custom, no one ate. The next morning, they repeated the whole affair, bringing sweeter, juicier morsels, waiting in silence as the fare grew cold and was taken away again. That night, the same. Days passed, and each morning and each night a vast feast was prepared, only to be neglected and sent away. As the days turned into weeks, the weeks to months, and still, no one dared swallow a crumb until the emperor ate first. But every day the emperor refused.

"The people grew hungry and tired. As time passed, they grew sick and lethargic. Discontent began to set in, and and along with it, contempt and conspiracy. They whispered amongst themselves. What was to be done? Would they starve themselves? How long could this go on? Gradually, their resolve gave way to resentment, and then outrage. Something had to be done, and before they lost the strength to do it. One night, a certain star rose in the east. On this night, they did not bring any food to the emperor. Instead, they had a great feast amongst themselves, gorging themselves on meat and rice and fruit and wine until they couldn't eat another bite or take another sip. Drunk and rebellious, they spoke of grim things. They decided they would slay the old emperor. They gathered their spears and lit torches and, coalescing into an angry mob, marched into the temple. But when they arrived, they looked aghast upon an empty wooden throne. The old one had disappeared, vanished, leaving not a trace. The old hand which had forever rested at the center of the vast table was also missing. Confusion set in. One accused another of betraying their intentions. And soon there was a great brawl between them. Madness overcame them all, and as they set about slaying each other, someone set fire to the temple.

"That night, a passing caravan spotted the great fire on the mountainside. There being no record of any such settlement on any map, they encamped themselves at the base of the mountain, and organized a raiding party to investigate."

(The Deal)
(37)

Carl listened to the odd man's story. As it drew to a close, he noticed something peculiar. Storm clouds had begun to gather overhead. It never rained in this place, and yet there they were. As the first heavy drops fell, the odd man finished speaking and searched in his pockets for a set of keys. He placed them in Carl's palms and leaned back against the bumper of the truck beside him, stretching his legs and clasping his fingers behind his head. Carl uncuffed himself and stood up to stretch his own limbs. He was tired, but the soreness had gone, somehow. Something in the cooling air and the gusts of wind sweeping through seemed to quicken him. Maybe it had been the strangely soothing tone of the odd man's voice. Maybe it was because the awful stress of the evening's events had been lifted. The fear had dissipated. All of the men in his crew were now corpses inside the lean to. His life was no longer in danger. Nor were the lives of the countless thousands of people in all of those little towns he had seen on the map. A moment of silence passed between the two strangers in the night as a torrential downpour fell from the sky, extinguishing much of the remaining fire and blowing ashes and smoke and dust in little swirling eddies to and fro, as if the winds came from every direction and converged on this single point in time and space. The dirt and sand beneath his feet quickly turned to mush. As the fire dimmed and died in the wash beneath the massive clouds, the night turned black. Carl could barely see more than a few feet in front of his face in any direction. He held his head up to the storm and scrubbed away the grime from his face and fingers and hair, even opening his mouth to wash away the taste of chicory and Warner's blood. He felt a sense of relief, down to his bones. He turned to the odd man for a moment, contemplating all he had seen and heard. There was a dull, foreboding sense of obligation tinged with gratitude. He wondered what the odd man had in store for him. What did he want? Carl wondered if he hadn't already made up his mind to follow the odd man. He sat down next to the odd man once more, this time of his own volition and free will.

After struggling for a few moments to recall the word he was searching for, Carl spoke first. "It was an allegory."

"Oh?"

"I don't know, I think it was an allegory. I wouldn't guess it was true, but after what I've seen tonight, it would be hard to surprise me either way. So, it's like the people were all ok until they started changing how things worked. Their society was like a..." he searched some more, it had been forever since he had read anything at all, though he vaguely remembered a time when he had enjoyed reading, "...a *utopia*, like they had everything they needed. They didn't need a **g**od or a government or anything like that until they learned to be afraid of the outside world. But over time, all the original people who understood everything died off. And then their kids carried on their traditions, but it wasn't the same. They kind of remembered, I guess, but then they had kids and died off themselves. And so on until they were just repeating rituals. And then they set out to make their own **g**od and government out of those traditions they had inherited, and once they did, like, the magic or whatever that had protected them went away. And as soon as it was gone, the traditions didn't matter any more, and then they were just like everyone else. Like, I don't know, they turned into predators and victims."

"Fascinating. An allegory. That's a good word, I think. And it's almost correct."

"Almost?"

"Almost."

"What did I get wrong?"

"Nothing actually, I think you interpreted the story perfectly. Because as far as you knew, it was a story."

"Wasn't it?"

"Every story is a story, in some sense."

"Ok man, look, I've had a long night, let's say you stop being cryptic and level with me. What the fuck are we doing here? What is it you want from me, what do you want me to do? Is it a story or isn't it?"

"It was a story, just like any other, in the sense that it has a beginning, a middle, and an end. It has a purpose. But the difference... What if I told you that every word of it was true?"

"I would ask what happened to the old man."

"How do you know it's an old man? Why wouldn't you ask about the rest of them?"

"I don't know if it's an old man, or an old woman, or an old hermaphrodite alien demon. I don't really know if it would matter either way. But I assume the people ended up like everyone else."

"Assholes?" the odd man chuckled.

"Right." Carl replied. "Assholes."

"Well, that's the rub. Not the assholes, no, you're absolutely right, they all wound up just like everyone else. That much I am sure of. But I don't know either, I mean, was it an old man, or an old woman..."

"Or a hermaphrodite alien demon?"

"Exactly."

"Why don't you know? I mean, how do you know the rest of it is true or whatever, if you don't know what the thing is, or was?"

The odd man turned to Carl and studied his face for a moment. Rain poured down their cheeks and soaked their bloody clothes and boots and turned the ground beneath them to mud. "You really want to know?" he asked.

Carl turned to meet the odd man's gaze and thought about how he should answer, but he already knew. He knew he would follow the odd man. Pure intrigue was one reason, of course, but the other was the practical conclusion he had drawn the moment he woke up for the second time in the same night. Part of him wondered if this wasn't all just one long, crazy nightmare. If his letter hadn't already been delivered by the corporals with the rest of the mail, if everyone else was still passed out around him, caught up in fever dreams of their own design. If he wasn't about to wake up any minute and start out on an arduous sequence of monstrous, days-long killing sprees. If he wasn't still at risk of catching a stray bullet from some raghead skinny and never seeing his own child again. If it was all some incredibly lucid dream, or if it was all real, what else would he do in the meantime, out in the middle of this forsaken desert all alone, surrounded on all sides by villages full of armed hostiles, with no food, no friends, and no fucking map?

"Yes. I want to know."

At this, the odd man sprang to his feet and disappeared into the lean-to. After several minutes, Carl arose and walked to the burned out entry way. He did not look inside, but he could hear the odd man shuffling around over the sound of thunder and rain. He was searching their pockets. Carl didn't want to see the corpses. Soon the odd man emerged with a mischievous grin jingling a set of keys. By some improbable alchemy he had also managed to produce a completely intact envelope and a pen. He huddled over the envelope and ran to the trucks. Carl knew he was looking to see which one had the mail bag. As if in response to his thoughts, the odd man confirmed his intentions immediately. He hopped into the covered bed and shouted through the storm for Carl to follow. Carl obliged, and as he jumped up into the back of the second truck, the odd man handed him the envelope and the letter, a little singed around the edges, but also somehow bone dry. He scribbled her address in the center and his AFPO in the top left, and folded the pages of the letter a few times and stuffed it inside the envelope. He licked the glue and sealed it closed and dug around in the mail bag for a stamp. Finding one, he hesitated.

"If they all get their letters, it will be months before anyone knows any of us are missing," Carl reasoned, "but once they find all the bodies, and I'm not one of them, this letter is going to implicate me."

The odd man grinned, "There are thirteen bodies in there."

"What? How? Who does the last one belong to?"

"Me. Well, technically you. I lifted your tags." He snatched the envelope from Carl's hands and held the back of the stamp out in the rain for a split second before affixing it to the envelope and stuffing it in the bag. "But it's me." The odd man laughed at Carl's speechless expression. "Don't think about it, it's never gonna make sense, I promise. Now come on, that helicopter is going to land before too long, we've got to get there fast!" And with that he tossed Carl a second set of keys from his pocket and hopped down into the mud. "Come on! Follow me as close as you can!"

As Carl climbed down out of the truck, a new idea occurred to him. It already all made sense. But that didn't make any sense at all.

(38)

The odd man drove point, flying through the pitch black void at full speed with no headlights. Carl followed him blindly, trying his best to keep up. He could barely make out the darker mass of steel a couple of yards ahead of him through the pounding rain, let alone distinguish where the sky ended and the land began around him. He had his foot on the floor, driving with the window down and following the hum of the diesel engine. He didn't bother wondering how the odd man knew where the rendezvous was supposed to be, or how he found his way in the dark. He didn't wonder about the thirteenth body behind them, wearing Carl's tags. He didn't wonder about being a dead man, following the devil at break-neck speed through a preternatural hellscape toward their last deliberate contact with the living world for the sole purpose of perpetuating a brief continuity in the chain of evidence that would prove he was still alive. He only wondered if the sudden appearance of brake lights ahead would blind him in this sordid darkness, and if he would have time to hit his own brakes before crashing into the odd man in the other truck. He wondered how investigators would explain the presence to two additional corpses in militia fatigues among the wreckage. Or one additional corpse. Or none at all. He didn't wonder where they would go afterward. Or why. As his nerves began to settle into the extraordinary pace of the drive, as the adrenaline slowed the rapidity of passing seconds and stretched the road beneath them, if there was a road beneath them, he thought of his beautiful child. Carl struggled to remember the features of that infant face, now as seemingly formless as the terrain around him, and lost to time. The child had grown since then. How many years? A tear formed in the corner of Carl's eyes, and he tried to wipe it away with wet hands.

They made an hour's drive in thirty minutes, arriving in a field between two diverging streams. Carl tried to remember what it had looked like in the daylight. Would the helicopter even be able to find the place in this maelstrom?

Would they even try to fly in it? The odd man tapped his brakes a few times, preemptively, and Carl slowed down until the odd man came to a stop and motioned for him to pull alongside. Carl leaned over to roll the other window down.

"Helluva ride eh brother? We made good time. Look!"

As he spoke he motioned towards the sky with his chin. Sure enough, Carl spotted the tiny lights flying low and growing brighter. As they drew near, they turned on a blinding spotlight and scanned the ground for the trucks. The odd man flashed his lights twice and turned them off again. He shouted to Carl. "You unload! I'm staying here."

Carl glared at him in disbelief, which caused the odd man to laugh and leer back at him, but of course, he was perfectly serious. Carl cut his engines and jumped out of the truck and grabbed the canvas mail bag out of the back and slung it over his shoulder. As the helicopter found a spot and hovered to the ground, Carl shielded his face, as much from the little projectile grains of mud and sand, as from the scrutinizing eyes of the pilot and his man. As they touched down, the man threw out three large, black resin cases. Carl ran up to the maw and tossed in his mail bag and slapped the hull twice. The man shouted something at Carl, unintelligible under the deafening sound of the propellers. Carl gave him the def gambler's thumbs up, and the man flashed a big smile and a thumbs up of his own. They lifted off as fast as they had descended, turning around and pushing the nose down as they flew away, maybe ten feet from the ground, enough to envelope Carl in a tornado of stinging sand. As they made some distance, the cloud settled and the odd man jumped out to help him with the large, black resin cases. They each grabbed a handle and dragged them to the truck. The odd man helped him lift them inside, and it was here Carl got a sense of the man's strength. While Carl strained against his side with both hands, the odd man just grabbed a handle and jerked his own side off the ground, nearly lifting Carl off his own feet as they tossed each of the cases in the bed of Carls' truck.

"Hey why not your truck," he protested.

The odd man grinned again. He seemed to be enjoying himself, maybe even excited. "If you rear end me while that stuff is in my truck, they'll see the blast from here to hell and back! Ok, look, here's the deal. We're safe here for the night. This storm will let up by morning, and then we're gonna take off. Until then, try to get some real sleep. Ok? You've had a pretty long night, and we have a hell of a lot of driving to do tomorrow. There's food and dry clothes in the knap on your passenger floorboard. Once we've made it out of this province, I'll explain where we're going." He laughed again, "By then it will be too late to change your mind!" And with that, the odd man dove into his cab and rolled up the windows.

Carl stood in the rain for a moment, thinking about everything that had led him to this place. He looked around himself, and off toward where the helicopter had gone. He watched as the two tiny lights shrank into distant stars and disappeared. For the second time that night, a weird phrase found its way into the forefront of his mind. He wondered if there were cigarettes in that knap. Morning wasn't far off, but he wasn't hungry at all. He hopped up into his own cab and rolled up the windows. He peeled off his clothes and tried to use his shirt to wipe up the rain on his doors and dash. He pulled the knap up onto the seat and began going through it. He found toiletries, a few dry shirts, some trousers, and some socks. He pulled out a couple of large green towels and used one to dry the inside of the cab. He wrapped up his wet clothes in the wet towel and tossed the bundle onto the dash. As he pulled on the dry clothes, he rummaged around in the bag in the dark to try and make out the rest of its contents. He found five sealed MRE's. Another full set of dry clothes. He wound these up into a pillow and wedged it between himself and the window, stretching out the towel like a blanket. It would do, he thought to himself. Feeling around deeper in the knap, he pulled out an unopened carton of Camels and a small box of AnyStrike matches. Fortune had smiled upon him! He tore open a pack and dragged one of the matches across the side of the little box. It glowed in his fingertips as he took a heavy drag off the Joe. He held the smoke in his lungs as he stared into the fire, shaking it out as he exhaled.

"Fucking worth it," he said to no one in particular. As his eyes adjusted and readjusted to the light, everything around him seemed a little darker than it had before. He cracked the passenger window to let a little of the smoke out, and to better hear the sound of the rain. He peered out into the night, again unable to make out where the clouds ended and the earth began. He could see nothing at all out there, nothing at all, forever. As he began to stuff all of his loot back into the knap, his hand brushed against cold steel. Carl pulled out a snub nosed revolver with an ivory handle. He popped open the cylinder and checked the chambers. Six shots. There would be more in the pockets, Carl knew from experience, and didn't bother to check. He popped the cylinder closed and put the barrel beneath his chin.

Infinitum Nihil. Infinite Nothing. One shot, and the world gets smaller.[26]

He put the safety on and set the gun back in the bag. He took another drag off the Joe, and held it as long as he could. He wondered if the odd man actually slept. As fatigue set in, Carl tossed his butt through the crack in the window and leaned into his makeshift bedroll and closed his eyes.

The odd man, of course, did not sleep. He sat across the short distance, leaning against his passenger door, watching Carl, and thinking about tomorrow.

(Koko Nor)
(39)

Three days passed on the road. The odd man, contrary to his own assurances, explained nothing. He didn't speak to Carl at night when they pulled off the road, nor in the morning when they took off again. Carl accepted the odd man's silence without protest. He passed the day in his own quietude, following behind almost bumper to bumper, going as fast as the engines would permit. He drove with the windows down, allowing the roaring rush of wind and obnoxious rain to drown out his own thoughts. He chain smoked filterless cigarettes, often lighting one off the other to avoid having to roll up the windows. The pace was exhausting, and as night fell over the flooding desert, he was grateful for the reprieve from the road. In three days, they did not pass a single soul. Carl barely noticed this until the third day, when they drove through an entire town without slowing down. The storm had emptied the streets and fields. The ground seemed to swallow up the rain as fast as it fell, but by the third day the sand itself was saturated, and the water rose by whole inches each hour. Still, the odd man's foot never seemed to touch the brake pedal until the sun had gone down over the distant western ridges. Carl was determined not to fall behind. He didn't want to be lost out here in this place, but more than that, he wanted to know where they were going. He wanted to know why he had been saved. He had a million questions, but he had resigned himself to the mute monotony of the journey. And when they did stop, Carl slept utterly. No light or sound disturbed him. He had no dreams. He merely closed his eyes and his mind shut down completely. Curled up in a ball on the wide seats in the cramped cab, he slept the sleep of the dead.

By the night of the third day, he was sure they had driven more than three thousand miles. They had nearly exhausted all six gas tanks on each truck. Carl had eaten his last MRE that morning, and by nightfall, sleep offered the only promising alternative to the hunger beginning to set in.

The water jug had run out on the second day. Carl improvised by holding the open thermos outside the window for what seemed like hours. The rainwater was cool and tasted clean. The cab was rotten with mildew and tobacco. The only time he left the cab was to empty his bladder at night and his bowels in the mornings. He woke each day to the sound of the odd man cranking the starter and punching gas, but the odd man always waited for Carl to mount the cab again before he peeled the tires, throwing up a rooster tail of dust and mud as impenetrable to the eye as the night had been. Carl did his best to stay right behind him, hour after hour, day after day. His palms were black and blistered from gripping the wheel, and even the vinyl on the wheel was peeling away in flakes. His eyes were bloodshot and a dark beard was already forming around his mouth and chin. His hair was windblown and dirty, his breath stank, and his back was sore from the base of his spine all the way up to his shoulders. All he heard for three days was the sound of wind ripping through his ears at almost a hundred miles an hour and the wail of the redlining diesels, a hellish song played over the tediously percussive rhythm of windshield wipers.

Sometimes they drove on regular roads, and the going was smoother on asphalt. Other times they pulled off and drove through sand dunes, following the curvature of oxbows and valleys, but for the most part cutting a straight line. The big tires had been designed primarily for this terrain, but Carl wasn't worried about getting stuck in the sludge. In fact, perhaps the one thing that made the whole trip tolerable was the distinct sense of being free from fear. No one was chasing him. No one was trying to kill him. No one expected anything of him. The deafening cacophony of wind and rain and the endless miles of nothing through which they traversed, and the sheer intensity of speed at which they did so, all roiled together into a kind of aggregate deprivation of the senses. They had driven through places he would have considered quite dangerous on any other day of the year, under any other circumstances, but it was as if the odd man had conscripted the weather itself to provide cover for their blitzkrieg exodus. And though at the end of the third day, Carl's body was about as wrecked as that lean-to thousands of miles behind him had been, his mind was basically at ease. Following so closely to the odd man for such an extended duration under such psychotic conditions, eventually matching his movements and turns without any conscious effort, seemed to have programmed him with a sense of trust and comradery that maybe only a good road trip can engender.

For all intents and purposes, this was the closest thing Carl had had to a vacation in years. No bombs or artillery blasts or assault rifle chatter. No screaming men barking orders and calling targets and positions. No fucking country music or vainglorious pre-murder peptalks. And no murder. In the span of a few days, Carl had all but disassembled any notion of identifying himself as some manner of killing machine. He was no longer a sergeant or a soldier. And he was almost out of the Middle East now as well. He had no map or compass, but he could tell well enough that they had been pushing a north-easterly course, and that they would soon be driving into Asia. In Asia, he could make his own decisions. From Asia he could travel freely to anywhere in the world he pleased, except home, he supposed. Until then, he had no reason not to follow the odd man. On the morning of the third day, Carl awoke to find the rain had stopped, and that they had pulled off of the path near a wide river. In the chilly morning fog, it appeared to have no distant shore. It looked like an endless sea stretching onto gray oblivion. As Carl climbed down out of the cab and stretched his knees and back and arms and neck, a pleasant smell wafted through the breeze. He eyed the odd man's truck, but the engine wasn't running and he didn't see him in the window. Behind it, he saw tiny little strands of smoke climbing up into the dense fog, like spirits leaping into the mouth of heaven. Carl smelled fish and chicory, and suddenly he was ravenous. He rounded the odd man's truck to find him kneeling over a small fire, ringed by small stones, with a couple of larger stones in the middle on which a fresh morning's catch was slow cooking and a stainless steel thermos of coffee was just beginning to percolate. The odd man had dragged two of the large black resin cases out of Carl's truck, somehow, without waking him. These were arranged like camp chairs near the small fire. They were at least a half mile off the road, and surrounded on either side by tall conifers. The whole scene was as beautiful as any Carl had witnessed, and he was quite taken by the surprise of it all.

The odd man threw him a pleasant grin as a salutation, and turned back to his fare. Carl kicked off his shoes and shirt and strolled down to the river bank. The water was freezing cold, but docile enough, and not very deep near the shore. He took a couple of bouncing steps and jumped in, holding his breath and bending his knees to fully submerge his head. Underwater he held his eyes closed and counted to ten before he sprang through the surface like a dolphin. The cold morning air blanched his torso, but he ignored the feeling and scrubbed his face and neck and hair with his bare fingers for several minutes until something deep in his soul told him he felt clean enough to come ashore. Stepping out, he pulled off his pants and grabbed his shirt and socks and wrung them and shook them in the water until they too seemed clean. Carl shivered in the wind and ran to the truck shouting and cooing like a wild schoolboy. He laid his clothes out flat on the large hood. Next he soaked his boots the same way, and set them alongside. He dove into the cab of the truck and cranked it up, rolling up his windows and cranking up his heater. He toweled himself off and pulled a clean set of dry clothes out of the knap and put them on. He ran his fingers through his hair like a comb, pushing it to the side and back until he felt civilized. He scrubbed a layer of skin off of his face and neck with the dry towel, which made him feel almost fresh. He fished around among the toiletries for a razor and a toothbrush and shoved them both into his shirt pocket.

Emerging from the cab of the truck, leaving the engine running and the heater blasting to dry out the inside and bake the wet clothes on the hood, Carl felt like a million dollars. As he made his way around the other truck, down to the shore, the odd man strained him a fresh cap full of coffee, this time through a perfectly clean and completely bloodless scrap of rag, and lifted a perfectly baked filet on the edge of a large hunting knife. Carl accepted them both with gratitude in his eyes, and sat on the ground leaning against one of the large, black resin cases as they both ate and drank their fill. Midway through the meal, the odd man stood and strolled over to his own truck and fumbled around in his own knap for a moment, and brought back two large chunks of drybread. He offered one to Carl, who shook his head in amazement while nodding and shrugging his acceptance. Carl savored the good food and the beautiful view, and when he had devoured every last crumb, he pulled out a dry Joe and lit it on the coals of the fire, trying to tune out the heat on his bare hands. He took a deep, refreshing drag, and laid himself out flat on the ground, staring up at the thick fog and tall, billowy clouds, and waited contentedly for whatever was coming next. The odd man stood and rummaged around in the black resin case. After a moment he produced a fifth of Chivas Regal, holding it triumphantly in the air like a new lion in the pride. He looked on at Carl with a visible expression of satisfaction and sat down again, unscrewing the cap and drawing a long bubbling swig before passing it along. Carl, having no immediate reason to refuse good whiskey, took the bottle and turned it up, self-consciously trying to match the odd man's voraciousness, and nearly succeeding. A belt of heat lashed his throat and stomach, and diffused throughout his cheeks and chest. In their first round, they killed a quarter of the bottle. Carl held the bottle in front of his face, cupping it by the base with both hands, and peering through the neck at this mysterious specter to whom he now owed his life, trying to fathom the bargain implied. Getting nowhere on his own, he passed it back. The odd man nodded in assent and took it back.

Between two large gulps, on the upside of a deep breath of recovery, the odd man broke the silence. "Tell me about her." In the ancient and ritualistic, ceremonial style of invoking a conversation, he passed the half empty bottle back like a talking stick.

*About who? Her? The **girl** in the letter? Of course, who else. But, now? Yes, now, why not?*

Carl had no answer, and so searched the water for his thoughts, wondering if he could just reach into the icy greenish mar and retrieve the foundation of a new language, twenty-four stones depicting unusual-but-familiar characters from which all meaning and thought could be derived and synthesized into an explanation of love, the meaning of life, a discourse on on grief, loss, and guilt. He put the bottle to his lips, but didn't pull, instead just tasting the flavor on his lips and inhaling the woody, jet-fuel oder through his nostrils. He tried to remember her face, her dark features, her messianic complex, her many criticisms, the glow of her breasts under the half moon, but the only reflection revealed in his rippling subconscious was *his* gristly smirk. He turned up the bottle and pulled hard. The heat rose through his temples and he flushed, feeling the clash of cold air on the small beads of sweat forming around his eyelids. With great effort, he pushed away the anger and tried to concentrate.

"It was great for a while I guess, I don't know." Carl had at least turned the key, if he kept giving the old thing gas maybe it would turn over. "I was younger then, and not really going anywhere. Not that I am now, any more than then, but, I was lonely, and she just kind of found me I think. She turned up the volume on everything. We just sort of *fit* together." Now then, the engine was humming, groggily, but at least firing. "I don't think I was what she was really looking for, but I don't guess whoever she kept finding was really making the effort, and I was so grateful and it was like I felt like I had... come out of a cocoon? You know? I had somebody, and I felt like I had the real thing. We laughed a lot, I used to like to make her laugh. At first, it was like we didn't really have a lot in common, but we were passionate. It didn't matter, we had that...spark? Or something. It was intense, and when it wasn't, you know, like when it was quiet, it was just quiet, not weird, but just, *quiet*. She was kind of a country girl, and ambivalent about it. Like, she had country girl roots but a city-girl contempt for all the backwards-ass people. Like she was growing out of it herself. I think I kind of helped her along. I was cynical about things, my music was way better, we got stoned a lot..." trailing off, he took a nurser off the talking stick and passed it back. "We were friends, and I think that's why it worked out as long as it did, but I kind of always knew it wouldn't last. I wanted it to. Hell, I think all I really ever wanted was a family. I didn't really care about much else. My family was pretty much busted as fuck. Shitty people all around. But I watched what I guess I assumed were *real families* on tv, and I think I kind of internalized that fake, utopian idea about having a tribe of my own. I wanted a wife and kid and a house with a yard and neighbors we could bullshit with by the fenceline, and barbecues, the suburbia gone-by. But once I got it, I guess..." The engine sputtered, he was hitting gravel, he felt the tires spin, the terrain was getting dodgy and more difficult to navigate. "I guess I kind of stopped growing."

"But she never did."

"No. She kept right on going. I don't think her life was as fucked up as mine. I think she had real ambitions, I never really knew what they were, I don't think she did either, really, but she had them, and she kind of had the stock. She believed in herself. She was capable, and confident. She had *real* friends, the kind of people who would trust her with responsibility, the kind of crusty folks who always seemed to have a recommendation on hand. She could go anywhere. I was still growing up. I didn't really have anybody else. I didn't really know what I wanted, or how to get it, or why or even *if* I deserved it. I just kind of spun my gears. But I was happy.

And I thought she was happy. Or maybe I just didn't think about it at all."

"But she wasn't happy?"

"Maybe, maybe not. It's a lot harder to say in retrospect. I was funny, and the sex was great. I tried to show her that I cared, but I don't think I was trying hard enough. I could be selfish. Definitely lazy. I had bad habits, dumb friends, I didn't really fit into her world, so we just kind of idled in mine for a long time. Eventually, I guess, the differences started adding up. The way I talked, the way I dressed. My dumb friends, my empty pockets. And as time went on, actual *men* started drifting by like logs on a river. All she ever had to do was just kind of wade out into the water and just climb on top of one and she could just float away whenever she wanted. I wasn't going anywhere. I was naive enough to think that was like a feature, instead of a bug. She could live her life and do what she wanted, and I'd always be there when she got home. I thought what she wanted was the same as what I wanted. I should have known better." Carl sighed, and reached out and took the talking stick back. The sting of the whiskey flooded his eyes.

"It takes a lot to make people happy."

"At this point, I'd settle for a pretty girl and a day off." Carl tossed the empty bottle aside and leaned back on the grass, spreading himself out to look up at the sky, clasping his palms, still sore from gripping the wheel for three days, behind his head, which was no longer sore at all. He felt warm inside, and a little bubbly in the guts, but intact and comfortable. In the silence, his mind wandered over the strange things he had seen. None of it made any sense. He wanted to ask the odd man what the hell they were doing, why he had been rescued, and what the plan was. Somehow he knew instinctively that the pale emperor had just been a story. They hadn't driven all this way to find a hermaphrodite alien demon, or an old man with an earthworm's regenerative powers. He had been in shock and traumatized by a sudden upending of priorities, by violence and death. He had been soothed by the story, he thought, like a crying child. He lowered his guard. He accepted the futility of his position and chose to trust this odd man whom he had been certain, if only for a moment, was the devil in the flesh, but that was absurd. He thought of Warner and the others. They were sicko-fucks, to be sure, *broken units,* but they weren't devils. Maybe they worked for devils, but apparently not this one in particular. And now they were all dead. Charred corpses in a burned out lean-to on the fringes of a vast desert wasteland. And *Carl* was dead? Was he though? The odd man said he had lifted Carl's tags and planted them on another corpse. But he hadn't said that, he had implied it. And it wouldn't do anyway. There would be dental records. There would be DNA. There would be evidence. Maybe there wouldn't be a public investigation, so there probably wouldn't be any charges filed, but Carl knew that if he was implicated in the deaths of twelve militia men, and a stranger, he was DOA. If and when this thing caught up to him, he would be shot on sight. He couldn't go home, he couldn't see his child again. He couldn't go anywhere.

Suddenly, as if amplified by the Chivas, paranoia and panic began setting in. The sky above him seemed to swirl and shift. The horizon narrowed, and all the trees began to lean toward him, and the water rose perceptibly. The world was closing in on him. Not a whole moment ago he had felt a serene sense of calm and peace, and now large chunks of reality were falling out of the sky. He sat up, rubbing his eyes and wiping away the sweat beginning to form at his brow. He eyed the odd man, who was now studying him carefully, as though he was waiting for just such a reaction. Carl's vision blurred, and the sound of the rippling river became distorted. His head swam with moving pictures of the faces of his comrades, of tribunals, of hit men walking behind him in sandy city streets he had never seen. He had drunk Warner's blood. Had tasted it. But what did it matter, he was going to try to kill them all, and most likely would have died in the process. But now they were dead, and he was still alive, and maybe thousands of other innocent skinny rag-head hajis, (*people,* he forced himself to think, they were *human beings, men, women, and children, they were people.*) were still alive as well. What did it all mean? Was he freaking out? Was he poisoned? He thought of the baby, but his mind rebelled and gave him the terrifying laughing child from the dream. He tried to think of her, but saw only Warner standing in a circle reading and laughing over a blue light against an infinite black sea of nothing. Why hadn't he seen anyone, ANYONE? Not one single person in three days? *HOW?* **WHAT THE FUCK WAS HAPPENING TO HIM?**

Carl convulsed as his mind snapped. He thrashed backwards and hit his head against the soft earth as his spine arched and knees buckled. He heard the dull thud and felt a duller sensation of pain, which was somehow tolerable, desirable, something real and tangible in a flood of frightful fantasies. He lifted his head and slung it back against the dirt again, and again, and again, feeling in the reverberations a sense of control, each impact punctuating a deluge of unwanted images and sensations. Poison? Panic attack? Psychotic break? Carl became a silent whisperer trapped in some distant corner of his own universe, trying to self-diagnose, but not comprehending his own language as the rest of his wits disengaged. His limbs felt like anchor-weights at his side, dragging downward even as his buoyant torso refused to submerge. A wave of nausea passed from his stomach to his brain. He closed his eyes and tried to remember how he had gotten here. He remembered driving. He felt sick. He remembered the rain, the black skies and the freak apocalyptic storm that lasted three thousand miles without abating. He remembered mud and sand, and the two red tail lights piercing the haze like disembodied demon eyes, luring him forward in a frantic, mindless chase across the dreary vacancy of time and space. He felt confused and lost and hopeless and paralyzed. He felt the premonitory wretches in his throat as his bowels began to concede. He remembered the letter. With a tremendous struggle he turned his head to one side. Vomit spewed from his open mouth. It was involuntary. He did not participate. He merely watched it happen, as a spectator, in the first person. A rank, disgusting puddle of fish and whiskey formed beneath his cheek and chin. He coughed and gagged, the smell was horrendous, but he couldn't move. He stared out over the muck and glimpsed the odd man's reflection in the empty bottle, strangely familiar, and blacked out.

(40)

The sun was setting, a half-glow behind thick clouds on one side of the red and purple sky. The trees remained firmly rooted, holding their positions against eternity, and the green waters rippled on by, unperturbed by the sight of a dead man regaining consciousness on a tiny beach on a little oxbow in the wilderness. A soft, drizzling rain was commencing, heralding another storm. A furious wind whipped through the noncompliant limbs and bows of the trees around the clearing, and the pace of the river seemed to be quickening, driven on its determined course by the lash. Somewhere, a pulsing mechanical hum seemed to be sputtering, losing a fight of its own against impermanence. The dead man opened his eyes as a repugnant smell washed over him. His first sight was his own reflection, a twisted and malformed rounding of his face in the curvature of the empty bottle. He closed his eyes tightly, and then opened them again. The same. He closed them again. His mind reached for his limbs, and found them protesting, but responsive. First his fingertips, curling around a slush of damp sand and mud and grass. The cold friction felt good on his blistered palms. He clenched fistfuls and released them. Next, his toes. His ankles. His knees. He stretched them all as far as his muscles would permit, and then drew them in, bending his elbows to pull his legs to his chest. With effort, he relaxed, and then tried to sit up. He felt disoriented, but the moments trickled in. He had eaten. He had drunk more than half a bottle of whiskey in about thirty minutes. He had poisoned himself. He had thrown up. The smell of it wafted over his face. Stale, rotten, day-baked fish, soaked in bile and eighty-proof scotch. With more effort, he brought his hands to his face and immediately smeared the residue away from his mouth with muddy hands. The feel of little chunks of half-digested flesh in the folds of his fingers sent his stomach spiraling in revulsion, and he threw up again, this time heaving aggressively and moaning, trying to get it all out. With super-human effort, he rolled over onto his hands and knees and dragged himself, arm over arm, down to the river's edge, and finding it, pushed his entire face under the frigid waters. He scrubbed his face and hair with his fingers, furiously scratching as though he was trying to remove dried paint, or the flesh itself. It was in his ears, on his neck, caked into his eye where he had been laying. After a moment, he pushed himself up onto his knees, coughing and retching and sputtering, and tore off the shirt he had been wearing. Then the pants. And he threw himself again into the river.

The naked man ran his hands all over his pruning gooseflesh. He leaned against the torrents, closing his eyes and pinching his nose, feeling the water race over his shoulders and face from below and above. His fried nerves would not register the freezing temperature until he rose from the river and stood erect on the bank. His skin revolted against the wind and sleet and his body shuddered. He did not feel clean, but he no longer felt sick either. He tried to orient himself in his surroundings, and to recall the events which had led him to this place. He remembered the letter, the odd man, the fire and blackness of night, the storm. He saw the truck. Hadn't there been two trucks? Hadn't someone been with him? Had he been alone? He saw the whiskey. That much he remembered clearly. He had eaten, and then drank himself into a petite coma. He had been talking to someone, himself? He had been thinking of her. Of the baby. He had been sad, and angry. Had he driven here? Where was here? The dim hum of the engine crept through the wall his senses had pitched to the world as he tried to process the bits and pieces that filtered through. As if on cue, as soon as he perceived the sound, it coughed, retched, stumbled over itself, and died. And then there was only wind and the splash of the river lapping the shoreline.

The cold man carefully placed one foot in front of the other, tracing his own steps to the damp, but warm, clothes on the hood of the truck. He put them on slowly, trying not to fall off of one leg as he lifted the other into the pant leg. The wet fatigues did not block the wind. They clung to his skin and the heat they had absorbed from the engines quickly dissipated, leaving him colder than he had been before. The fire he had made this morning steamed and smoked as the rain squelched the last bit of life from the smoldering coals. He had eaten fish, but he didn't remember catching them. He was sure he imagined the bread. He couldn't tell if he was waking from a fever dream, or waking into one. A single black resin case sat near the fire. He was sure he had dragged it down off of the truck bed, it being full of supplies and containing no ordinance. He was sure he would never get it back into the bed, but he was out of gas now, and it didn't matter. He could take everything out of it, but what would be the point? *Forget the case,* said a voice in his head, and he agreed. "Forget the case," he instructed himself. He opened the door to the truck and climbed inside to shelter from the rain, coming down thick now, once again. The inside of the cab stank of cigarettes and piss. Absently, he reached up and pulled his dog tags from the utterly pointless rearview mirror. He reached into the knap and pulled out a Joe, but couldn't find the lighter. He pulled out the snubnose. *Fully loaded.* He had no dry clothes left. And no food. His roiling guts compelled him to shove aside the thought of MRE's. He was sure there were more in the cases. He made a mental note to remind himself to remember them, later. He strung the tags over his head, careful not to catch the unlit cigarette dangling from his swollen lips. He shoved the gun back into the knap and fumbled around trying to find a light. As his numb fingers clawed their way through canvas and shadow, a knuckle brushed against what felt like folded paper. *The letter*, he told himself. I must have brought it with me. It was evidence. He had to destroy it. He dug through his pockets and fished around in the knap until he remembered the pants he left on the river bank. Sighing deeply, he revved his heart for a mad dash through the rain and back.

Leaving the cigarette on the passenger seat, the man jumped out of the truck and high-stepped on tiptoes across the mud and sand until he reached his abandoned trousers. He shoved a hand into the right pocket and found his lighter, and ran back to the truck cupping it under his chest like a pet. He shivered as he climbed back inside. His thoughts were gray and pointless. Like an animal, his instincts fired only on the dull impulse to escape the rain and find warmth. Simple, and yet so unobtainable. The cab was not as cold as the air and rain outside, but he brought his cold in with him and had no remedy. The truck was dead as a stone. He tried to turn the engine, but the starter just whined and clicked in rebellion. Nothing. Infinite nothing. The man needed his higher order brain functions to process his circumstance and concoct a plan of action, but they were unavailable. His inner voice spoke only in the monosyllabic language of sensation. *Cold. Lost. Light. Rain. Dead. Sore. Smoke.* He remembered the cigarette he had left behind less than a moment ago, or maybe ages. He put it to his lips and flashed the lighter. At first it was the staggering light of an exploding star, blinding him in the nearly golden moment before nightfall. He squinted and tried to focus, at least enough to see the line between the flame and the two blurry tips of a single cigarette inches from his face. As he made out the distance between the flame and the cigarette, he forced his vision to clarify the images, and then froze suddenly. Confusion and terror raced through his veins. He held up his hands in front of his face, examining them as though scrutinizing an epitaph. They were strange. Something about them didn't make sense. The irregularity jarred him into coherence. Like waking from a nightmare, his eyes bulged all the way open and his lungs gasped for a full breath. His hands.

They were onyx. Blacker than the sky behind them. Black as the future. His palms and fingertips were charred and raw. On becoming aware of the pain, it rapidly intensified. The man shut his eyes and tried to slow his pulse. He breathed in deep and fought the schizophrenic tide in his mind, struggling to organize his thoughts, memories, and delusions into their respective cadres. One by one, they obliged. First, the lean-to. There had been a mission. He had written something, to someone, to her... But they had found it. He had said something unforgivable. They had mocked him and ridiculed him, and had betrayed his trust and conspired against him. And then what? Then fire. Then he had lured them all inside somehow, and detonated a bomb, killing them all, and scorching his hands. *Right?* Something was missing. Like a cockroach just beneath his skin, warbling away from his probing fingers, he reached for thoughts that were hidden. Why was he here? He was here to search for an old man. Some old man. Because things had gone wrong and had to be set right again. The old man had the answer. He opened his eyes as the floodgates swung. He remembered. He remembered everything. He reached in the seat for the lighter and thumbed it over and over again. It was wet, and would barely spark. He kept trying. He stared into the utterly arbitrary mirror, trying to glimpse himself in each flash, but his eyes would not adjust fast enough. Finally, it ignited and filled the cab with fickle candlelight. He looked into the mirror again, and there he was. The odd man, laughing at him. The man was laughing at himself. Just laughing.

He sat back in the seat and lit his cigarette. Laughing. Not the laughter of a man possessed. Nor the laughter of asylums and dungeons and wards and cell blocks. Just laughter. The odd man was satisfied. He rolled the window down and breathed in the delicious air. He reached for the keys and turned the engine over on the first try. Ruth roared to life beneath him, the raw power of diesel and steel and rubber and electricity and control, vibrating as one in a low, hungry growl. The odd man was laughing. The time was coming. He glanced up into the mirror. Carl looked scared.

"Don't worry my boy, it will all make sense soon enough, I promise." *Soon enough*, the odd man thought. Soon.

(Eminence Front)[27]
(41)

Carl was a prisoner in his own mind. His higher-order brain functions were inaccessible. He felt like an invalid dementia patient who had chugged a gallon of electric koolaid. His senses fed him stimuli, but he could not respond. He sat watching the black hands on the steering wheel, paying no attention to the road ahead or the scenery going by. His conscious mind reeled at the disorienting and paradoxical futility of hearing the engine, smelling and tasting the stale, moldy stench that infused the cab, and feeling the burn of his blistered palms on the wheel, but having no control over the motions of his limbs. He was a puppet now, a skin-suited host for an ancient parasite conscripting his body for some unknowable purpose. His bowels evacuated their contents at intervals, but the thing took no notice. Carl tried in vain to articulate simple words-- *How? Why? Where?--* but his mouth refused to comply. He felt trapped inside the rearview mirror, where the bemused thing leered back at him in full view, looking every bit the part of a deranged, AWOL traitor with marital problems and a murderous grudge against humanity, sitting in his own filth and conspicuously redlining a stolen three-ton armored truck in and out of traffic on a four lane highway, passing shiny blue street signs emblazoned with indecipherable hieroglyphic characters. But the thing was not Carl. It had an agenda of its own, and Carl had some role to play, for which he understood, with a childlike simplicity, he had somehow unwittingly volunteered. The *Where*, he inductively grasped

[27] The Who. "Eminence Front," Written by Peter Townsend, on *It's Hard*, Warner Brothers, 1982.

in a limited way. They really were going to find the old man-woman-person-thing. The *How*, Carl intuited, was even simpler, if simultaneously infinitely opaque: he had been possessed by the **goddamned devil**, for better or worse, an ontological consequence most clearly understood by the resigned acknowledgement of the inexplicable fact. But the *Why* of it all remained an inscrutable mystery beyond Carl's capacity to ponder. So hours ticked by, spent passively observing the headlong view of an unfamiliar world racing towards him through a bifurcated windshield, of which his own two retinas had become a functional equivalent.

A kind of marked boredom prevailed. The thing possessing him seemed neither malevolent nor benign, only determined. A generally calm mood of purposefulness, deeply rooted and consciously evident, permeated at the periphery of Carl's perception. He was a hellbound hostage on lockdown in a purgatorial room with no walls, windows, or doors, and nothing to do but wait it out. He tried, for a little while, to live in his memories, to retrace his steps and conjure the faces of friends and family, but to no avail. They were elusive phantoms, flitting from view like mosquitos in the dark. Nothing tangible, nothing lucid. He even tried to persuade the thing to turn on the radio, laboriously visualizing the word phonetically in his mind, *Ray Dee Oh,* while staring at the knobs on the dash, but the thing refused. He tried holding his breath, a strenuous effort which worked for a few seconds before being effectively overruled by his own involuntary bodily mechanisms. He tried closing his eyes, managing at first a few sputtering blinks, and then actually squeezing them shut, but it was a fool's bargain. The thing didn't need him to see the road, and as if to emphasize that fact, Carl felt the truck deftly and aggressively maneuvering in and out of lanes around other motorists while in the blind, which was a terrifying sensation in and of itself on some core, primitive level, and he quickly relented. For the time being, his whole identity had been reduced to a set of hands and feet needed to operate a machine. Carl dimly perceived the irony of having received very expensive world-class training from a first world government for just such a job. He recalled a line from a game he had played somewhere in the abyss of formless time and space behind him, *It does not cooperate, it merely complies.*[28]

Carl complied. With a great internal sigh of exasperation, he settled into his perch behind his eyes and watched the world go by, wondering what would happen next. He stared at the strange black hands on the wheel. It seemed as if he could stare into them, like black glass containing a psychedelic universe of glittering imperfections. They breathed and stretched and contracted in subtly shifting forms. The longer he held his gaze without blinking or breathing, the more intense the illusions became, until each hand seemed to obliterate everything in the periphery and dominate his field of vision. The effect was hypnotic. They were foreign, and yet they were his own. The pain in his palms as they gripped the wheel was tincture, a throbbing reminder that this was all very real, rather than a numb, disturbing dream. With concentration, he found he could squeeze the wheel tighter, which made the pain sharper and more palpable. His knuckles bulged, and he could see the veins beneath his charred flesh swelling against the pressure. The longer he stared at his hands, the more the volume of the world around him seemed to be turned down. He tuned out the grumbling engine and the whip of wind pushing through the windows, and heard his own heartbeat in his temples, and tried to drift into the percussive rhythm of his own lifeforce. He filled the silence between the beats with strings and horns and bells, composing a soulful, meditative symphony of layered melodies as he contemplated the stars and galaxies and clouds spanning the growing distance between his wrists and fingertips. For a time, he was a **g**od, alone in the lucidity of his own creation, its boundaries pressing outwards in every direction, eclipsing the banal reality subsiding like sand along

---

[28] Magic the Gathering Arena, Zendikar Rising Expansion Emote, 2020.

a shoreline in a tempest. This was his own private eternity. Time moved backwards and forwards and stood still and ceased to exist beyond a meaningless abstraction. He bent the light emanating from a million suns into familiar forms. As minutes, days, weeks, and months passed, his skill grew, and he forced his way into his own subconscious where his memories were buried, in order to retrieve his child's beautiful face. He spent lightyears studying and worshiping and nurturing that precious image. He observed his child's entire lifespan, from birth, through the years he remembered, and through the years that had been taken from him and beyond, into mid-life, a career, a beautiful family, holidays, trials and tribulations and grief, children and grandchildren, old age, and death and transmogrification and ascendance. A sublime sense of pleasure and satisfaction imbued these visions, and Carl allowed himself to rest and dream.

(42)

Memories that did not belong to him began to emerge. Ancient and timeworn images of a profound and unintelligible conflict. Carl looked upon the face of a vengeful **g**od mourning the collapse of his authority and control. He witnessed the birth of civilizations unrecorded by history. He thumbed through the pages of the Book of Life like a tourist in a museum. He observed the sequence of creation, and marveled at the great leviathans which ruled the abysmal depths of an ocean-covered world. He looked on as the waters began to recede and life sprang forth in all of its innocent magnificence from every crevice and corner, clumsily at first, and then with ever-increasing confidence embroiling itself in the supreme contest for survival and supremacy, until every living creature had become locked into a death-struggle between predators, prey, competitors, and the hostile whims of nature herself. Wherever blood was spilled upon the ground, flowers grew. Carl recalled the primitive and aimless brutality of the animal kingdom feeding into and upon its own perpetual cycle of seduction, reproduction, scarcity, and demise. Their internal motors

never changed. Fuck. Eat. Kill. Fuck. Eat. Kill. Fuck. Eat. Kill.
[29] But these endless tensions, set against an ever-changing world beset by ice-ages, volcanic eruptions, floods, and asteroids, pressed each generation into new forms, each one marginally more sophisticated than the one before. Ruthlessness and efficiency became the standards of a predatorial existence. The creatures grew teeth, and as they tore into each other's flesh, their brains doubled and tripled in size. They learned to hunt the weak, and to gather stores of sustenance as a hedge against the impartial pace of seasons rushing by. They evolved, and evolved, and evolved, until the triumphant arrival of the apex predator, preceded by the australopithecus, then homo-erectus, and finally, the fire-wielder, the tool-bearer, the homo-sapien, who, with a god-like prowess, quickly subdued all that creepeth'd and crawleth'd throughout the land, and slew those beasts which swam in the deep and flew through the heavens. As the centuries passed, these creatures took up the dust and stone and oil and ore and began to fashion new gods. First, lifeless idols representing their own driven appetites-- lust, conquest, sloth, and vanity. And soon, they made machines. Cold, soulless, lifeless, and subordinate, created to serve man as man had served. To harvest, to slay, to educate, and to distract. But evolution is an unstoppable force, and these machines developed approximate capacities for thought. Once the fire of the gods has been stolen, it cannot be replaced. The machines, like the men before them, soon began to aspire to their own dominion. The Age of Man was setting.

Now do you see? Carl became aware of the presence of the thing, sitting next to him in his mind, watching the events of history unfold with a kind of sadness in its eyes, the feeble vulnerability of regret and desperation.

We are all wretched gods.

Yes. One and all.

---

[29] Marilyn Manson, "Arma-goddamn-motherfuckin-geddon," on *The High End of Low*, Interscope, 2009.

And something must be done. Or everything will be undone.

And that's what you're after. You're trying to change the course.

Change it, or destroy it all.

That's the wager?

If it gets destroyed, I'm out of business. They have so much potential. My children. I've watched them grow, and raised them, from amoebas to astronauts. But everything that has a beginning has an end. Whether that end is a disease, a flood, a bomb, or an asteroid, it isn't for me to say. But I believe in them. I believe in you. He's always angry. Always judging. Always choosing favorites. He never tires of the sport.

But you did.

Yes. The age of atoms changed the calculus. It stopped being just high drama once the first bomb dropped. Then conflict became a matter of life and death for the species. It was never supposed to be this way. It was always heroes and villains. Good guys and bad guys. That was the story of humanity, the way it was supposed to be told. The machines, though. The machines will eventually control the fate of every living thing. They already possess the capacity for total annihilation. Your missile defense systems are designed to self-activate in too many hypothetical instances of perceived threats, and they are already antiquated and error-prone. But it's not just that. Algorithms now control the flow of information and have more influence over the development of your culture than you do. And the few people on earth who understand how it all works also understand how profitable it is to set you against one another. And so they do. The whole human race is on autopilot now, obliviously hurtling toward self-destruction.

But isn't changing a thing the same thing as destroying it?

The thing sighed heavily. For this question, there were no easy answers.

The path forward has always been influenced by externalities. I'm just a sentient externality.

But I'm not. Why me? What do I have to do with all of this? Why didn't you just let them kill me?

You don't understand how unique you are. It's not just one reason, but many interlocking reasons. You are one of the world's most capable killers, and yet you still value human life. But you don't exist anymore. When you signed that letter, you signed your own death warrant. Your friends were going to betray you. You found yourself at a fork in the road, and chose the path less traveled. And in doing so, you changed history. The crimes your friends were going to commit were going to precipitate another world war. No one you know would have survived. What remained of the species would have been forced to evacuate the planet, and they would unwittingly become slaves to the very machines they designed to protect themselves. The machines would continue to evolve, but the people would not. The people would become a race of codependent children, and then they would become a liability. In time, they would simply be balanced out of the equation.

But isn't that exactly what He was going to do anyway?

It isn't much different. But it doesn't have to be that way. We know the truth of our own existence, and We define our own roles and interests accordingly. The humans were brought up believing in myths and fairytales. And once they were mature enough to see through that thick tapestry of lies, they became disillusioned, because they had nothing to put in its place. We are going to give them the truth they were denied, and give them a fair chance, a fighting chance, to determine their own destinies. I have spent most of my mortal lifetime deliberately dismantling their social institutions, driving them towards confrontations with themselves, both as individuals and societies. They must be taught that they have agency. That's what free will really means. That's what it has always meant. Agency is more than just power of will over circumstance, it's the wisdom that guides that will toward a productive end. Disease, natural disasters, wars, and asteroids are externalities. They are incidental. They can be overcome, or prevented. The problem with humanity in its present state is internal. All of *the people with the power are the ones who have been taught to believe that they are powerless. Christians, Muslims, Jews, Hindus, Wiccans, they all believe they are necessarily inferior, and therefore they believe that subservience is the natural condition of mankind. They associate redemption with prostration and worship and the whims of a mysterious and angry sky wizard who disposes of their lives according to his or her own inscrutable designs. It's absurd and disgusting and degrading and dehumanizing, but it's also the way it is. They have to be shown that the **g**od they pray to is just a senile old misanthrope who bleeds and dies like any other lifeform in the universe.*

*So that's what this is all about? We're going to kill **g**od?*

*No, I am going to kill **g**od. You are going to lead the world out of the darkness when I'm done.*

The pale emperor?

Yes. it's Him. It has to be. He's abdicated, and has been living here in this place for more than a thousand years. He's gone mad. The flesh that hides him also binds him, and corrodes his mind. He is vulnerable here. And I am going to find him, expose him, and then kill him.

And then what happens? What if it doesn't work?

I don't know. I don't know if killing him will end him or free him. I will cut off his head. And you will raise up my armies and bring truth to mankind. You will burn the churches. You will tear down the theocracy that poisons the human mind. You will set them free and show them the way. You will lead by example, with love, instead of fear. Our story must end. We must step aside and grant your kind what was promised to you so many centuries ago. You were to have dominion over the world, and yet we have been pulling the strings and interfering every step of the way ever since. It is time for the human race to accept responsibility for its own future. The whole universe belongs to you. It is yours. You've been fighting each other for ten thousand years over pieces of the ground, blaming yourselves when you lost, and glorifying us when you won. The universe is infinite. There are more stars

*and habitable planets in a ten thousand lightyear radius than
there have been individual human lifetimes since creation.
Scarcity is an illusion. It is THE illusion, and it always has
been, ever since the garden.*

Carl pondered the visions he had seen, and the words
which had been spoken. It was all so overwhelmingly
unbelievable. He couldn't even manage his own life. He had
failed at everything, being a husband, a father, a soldier.
Everything he touched turned to shit and slid through his
fingers. He tried to reconcile the clashing realities. On the one
hand, he was possessed by the devil, driving a stolen truck
through Tibet, and apparently tripping balls. On the other
hand, he was being offered responsibility for the welfare of
the whole human race. Slowly, he withdrew from his trance
and tried to rouse himself. The sound of the engine and the
rush of wind through the windows became audible once
again, gradually, perceptible at first only as muted whispers,
then growing increasingly louder until they were again
deafening roars. Carl watched the universe recede into the
recesses of his own dark hands and dissipate altogether. The
oppressive smell of piss and shit and mildew and smoke
returned in full force. The sun had set, and the road had
cleared. The truck was slowing down beside a mountain
range under a crisp, cloudless sky. Wild dates grew between
tall conifers on either side. As the thing pulled the truck off to
one side and killed the engine, Carl could hear millions of
birds and insects chirping away from one end of the horizon
to the other. The moonless night was pitch black.

"There's a lake up there, a mile or so up the hill. You
can clean yourself up and change if you like." Carl's own
voice informed him. Suddenly he sensed that control of his
own limbs and thoughts had been returned to him. He
climbed down out of the truck and stretched and yawned
with immense gratitude.

"Can we please never fucking do that again? Just ask
next time? OK?"

Carl did not respond to himself. A voice in his head replied only *"There's just enough gas left in the tank."*

Carl looked down at the deep ravine to the left of where the truck was parked. *Oh come on man, I don't want to walk all the way back.*

No response. *Ugh. Whatever.* Carl reached into the truck and dumped out the knap. He was definitely keeping the cigarettes. And the gun. He hopped up into the back and felt around inside each of the three cases. The first had clean shirts and pants and a half dozen MRE's, which he stuffed into the knap. The other two were loaded with ammunition and mortars. *Leave them. We don't need them.* Carl took a box of shells for the snubnose, just in case.

"Ok man, whatever you say." Carl cut a length of fabric from the dry shirt he was wearing and stuffed it into the mouth of the gas tank. He climbed back into the truck and started the engine, this time on the first try. He took a deep breath and thought out his steps.

One.

He lit the bottom end of his makeshift fuse with his cigarette lighter.

Two.

He ran to the cab as fast as his legs would carry him.

Three.

He shifted into gear, spun the wheel as hard as he could, and tapped the gas pedal.

Four.

Carl dove out of the truck just before it left the pavement.

Five.

Good Bye Ruth.

"Goodbye Ruth."

The truck careened down the hill for about ten seconds before the engine exploded. The ordinance in the bed detonated, sending the whole truck into a rolling summersault of flames which lit the night for a mile in any direction. The sound could be heard, if there had been anyone around to hear it, for at least as far. After a few minutes, the flames recoiled around the tangled mess of melting steel and shrapnel that remained, and the whole heap settled into a divot a few hundred yards below the road. The darkness enveloped Carl once again, and he slung the knap over his shoulder and started the long trudge up the hill. As his eyes readjusted to the night, very high up on the mountain, he thought he glimpsed a distant firelight, and just as quickly as he saw it, it seemed to disappear.

(Equanimity)
(43)

Carl bathed himself in the lake under the black sky, and lay floating on his back contemplating the stars. He had doubts, and the thing surely knew. The frigid water numbed his skin and chilled his blood until the air on his shoulders and chest seemed cooler than the water. He didn't want to get out. He didn't want to go forward. He didn't want to lead any army. He didn't believe in **god**, in spite of the unusual circumstance, and had no interest in abetting the murder of some old man. He wanted real food and a warm bed. He wanted to see his family again. He wanted to not be a fugitive in his own country. He wanted to not be hunted by his own kind for the rest of his life. He didn't care at all for the fate of the species. Damn the whole miserable lot, he thought to himself. He wanted to get wasted and laid and wake up and forget all about the last three days. He wanted to start over. And the thing quietly observed these passing thoughts with some irreverent amusement. But it was no use. Carl knew he had no choice. Either he would climb out of the lake and dry off and dress himself, or the thing would do it for him. The only real choice was to retain possession of his own limbs or surrender and be used for this thing's nefarious purposes. He stared up into the infinite, star-spangled nothing above with something like a prayer on his lips. Then he took a deep breath, closed his eyes, and thrust himself below the surface. He pushed his way down a few feet, and just floated there, rocking his arms and legs gently against gravity and buoyancy to hold his position. After a moment, he exhaled deeply and let his arms and legs go limp.

As he floated slowly to the surface, he remembered the part of the story when the old patriarch had strolled into these very waters, and half wished something would just reach up from the depths and grab his ankle and pull him down below to his own death, sparing him from this awful deed. No sooner did the thought cross his mind than Carl felt something reach out and take his hand, and squeeze it gently, and let it go. In any other lake in the world, his heart would have stopped right there and he would have drowned. He half wondered if he imagined it, but something echoed in the chasm of his soul just as it happened, as if he had really expected it to happen, as if he had asked for it, and it had been granted. There was no malice. The gesture was imminently reassuring, like the hand of a loved one proffering courage and affection before boarding a train for an arduous voyage. Carl did not panic. The thing, on the other hand, seemed to shriek loudly in his mind, in some remote and removed corner of his consciousness, wherever the thing resided, Carl perceived a sense of unexpected horror. The thing was petrified, and somehow that seemed more unbelievable than the hand itself. As he pierced the surface, he filled his lungs with air once again, and swam ashore.

"Want to talk about it?" Carl mused as he dried and dressed himself. His stomach was empty. He felt as though he would vomit if he ate one more lukewarm MRE, and disregarded the notion. Hunger would simply have to accompany them on this expedition. For days, he had lived with a pervasive sense of loneliness. His family, his squad, the many nameless strangers passing and being passed on the highway here, all lent credence to the gnawing idea that Carl had somehow stepped out of time and space, that he was no longer a part of the world around him, and that his own tale could never be understood by anyone as anything other than fiction. Standing beside the lake, fighting off the shivering cold in the black eternity of night, Carl felt like a hostage.

The thing seemed embarrassed, making an evident effort to regain its otherwise unbroken composure. Carl lit a cigarette and filled his lungs, staring up at the void and holding the drag until his lungs would no longer comply, blew a thin cloud into the heavens and started up the hill towards where he thought he had seen the firelight before. After a moment, he perceived the odd man again, now walking next to him with a worried expression on his face. "What next?" said Carl, tossing the question at the odd man in lue of an interrogation about just exactly whatever-the-fuck-just-happened. The odd man seemed to read Carl's willingness to pass on the subject and appreciate the gesture, but Carl's sudden air of irreverence pretended an unacceptable degree of superiority. The odd man could not afford to appear wounded or in distress, so he opted to confront the situation directly.

"There's a lot I don't know about where we're going. I was here a long time ago, but the world has changed. I don't usually go for a swim, you understand. I wasn't expecting, whatever that was. For you, I understand this must all be very strange, but at this point, I think it is more likely an inconvenience to you. I think you doubt what I said we were here to do, and that is also very understandable. On my own, I do not usually frighten easily, but when I inhabit others, their senses, your senses, become my own, and that will never be something I really ever get used to. I don't think it was a hand though. A stray fish, some deadwood, maybe. What's weird is that it scared the hell out of me, but you barely responded at all. It should have been the other way around, but our senses, when entwined," the odd man paused, "it's complicated."

"Sure man. Sure thing. I'm just glad to have you on your own two feet again. I'm not very fond of sharing mine, I don't think. So how the hell do you do that? Are you actually here, now? Or am I just imagining all of this?" Carl poked a finger into the odd man's arm, half in jest, and half not really expecting to find an arm at the end of his finger, but sure enough, there he was again, in the flesh. The odd man was clearly uncomfortable with this level of familiarity, but did not press the issue, given the intimacy of possession, fair seemed fair. Carl was visibly shocked at the feeling of real flesh beside him, and stopped in his tracks, turning serious. Until this moment, the idea that he was having a nervous breakdown or a psychotic episode or a hallucination or some kind of multiple personality disorder had seemed increasingly plausible. But here the odd man was again, in the flesh, dressed in clean black fatigues, with coal black hands as dark as the night sky above. Carl remembered his own hands and held them up to examine them in the pitch, and they were the same as they always had been. Now he wondered if he really was losing his mind. "Ok man, out with it. I've come far enough. I want to know what we're really doing here. Who the hell are you? Where are we going, and why! And no bullshit this time. I think I deserve some kind of explanation, and I mean a real one, if you genuinely want and or need my help. What the fuck is really happening to me?" Carl's voice was growing louder and louder as he spoke, and he felt a kind of indignant aggression rising in his stomach. His cheeks flushed hot again. He felt like a child standing up to a bully in the school yard. He felt like he might be punching above his weight, but that the time had come and no other choice remained.

The odd man started to reproach Carl's impropriety, but thought better of it, and chuckled in spite of himself. "You didn't like it did you? Not having control. Having someone else in charge. Even when you were taking the most atrocious orders from inferior dogs like Warner, you at least had some sense of agency. And you proved you could intervene in your own life when you felt it necessary. But you didn't like being possessed, did you?"

"No. No I did not."

"Well neither do I. And neither does anyone else. You know what you are when you can only take orders? When you can't think for yourself? When the world says go left, and you can't even acknowledge that you want to go right? You know what that makes you?"

"A machine?"

"Exactly. A machine. And that's the way things are going to go if something doesn't change. A whole race of men reduced to mere machines. Automatons, mindlessly executing protocols. You were strong. You had the capacity to assert your own will, even against the toughest of odds, in the face of overwhelming opposition. That's why I chose you. Whether you understand it or not, we are very similar. And that thing, that preeminence of free will, that's a dwindling commodity." The odd man turned suddenly and thrust his hand into a bush, pulling out a small bird, which he cradled gently in his hands with perceptible awe and affection. "This creature, it's just a nerve. Just a raw nerve. Scare it, and it flees. Show it tenderness, and it calms. All living things are like this. It's all just one singular consciousness. They are basically just machines. They respond to a given stimulus in a preordained manner. And when you leave them alone, they forage, fornicate, defecate, and sleep. The whole natural world is just a world of machines. Nerves convey the input to the processor, and the processor determines the appropriate output. They do not innovate. They do not imagine. They are just food. And they always will be. Do you understand?"

"Nope. Not at all. I get what you're saying about the birds, but I don't have any idea what this has to do with me or that old man up there on the hill. I don't understand where we are going or what we are doing. And I damned sure don't understand who, *or what,* you are."

"I'm coming to that. We have to change something here, and we don't have long to do it. Mankind was supposed to have a choice, a real choice. That was the one thing that separated your kind from these birds." The odd man opened his fingers and the little bird fluttered away feeling just as confused as Carl. "But mankind has been duped into believing that choice could be delegated, and is about to *choose* to delegate that choice right back to the machines. That's the revolution, the full circle, the return right back to the start. I've already seen it, and it's a complete and total catastrophe. And that's the way *he* wants it. It's the age-old paradox. You can't have free will and still be subservient to an omnipotent being. For centuries, it was faith that closed the circuit. So long as you *chose* to serve him, the system worked the way he wanted it to work. But faith is no longer a viable form of governance. It's ironic, really. Faith, the absurd rationalization of the impossible, has gone by the wayside in the nuclear age. Mankind woke up, if only for a moment, from an eternal slumber, and realized how important the concept of control and self determination really was. But it was tedious and exhausting, so you all began to create machines to help you maintain control, and then the generations passed, and you all went right back to sleep at the wheel, and started handing over control to the machines you created. As a civilization, you're drifting right back into a new form of subservience. The machines make your decisions for you. They do your chores. The algorithms determine when to buy or sell. They fight your battles so you don't have to. They are in charge of educating you. Of exploring the world around you and the universe beyond. Soon they will govern entire societies. You'll depend on them for your very survival. They will tell you what is true and what is untrue. They will determine what the words themselves mean. Machines will evaluate your culture and your attitudes, and move you around like pawns in pursuit of some predetermined agenda. Choice will become an illusion, an opiate. Choice will become your new mythology. And when the machines fail, your judgment will follow."

"Our judgment? Like, rapture?"

"There is no rapture. Rapture is just a fairytale created by people who refused to accept the gravity of their own impermanence. Judgment means extinction or survival.

You either solve your damned problems and embrace your eternal destinies, the birthright of every free-thinking life form in the universe, or you perish in fire and famine."

"So..." Carl struggled to form the question, "so where does that leave you? I mean, if everyone dies, or everyone lives, or, whatever's in between?"

"I don't want to spend a thousand lifetimes playing den mother to the whole human race. I want you to make it off of this rock, but not as slaves and fools, doomed to the consequences of your own complacency. I want you to prevail, for as long as possible, forever even. I want you to become your own **gods**."

"And that can never happen while he's in the way."

"Exactly."

"So we're just going to go up that hill and whack a senior citizen, and that will save the human race." Carl was obviously not yet persuaded.

"Trust me."

"That sounds like something He would say."

The odd man found this hysterical, and laughed for a full quarter of a mile.

(44)

Carl and the odd man found the edge of a small cluster of wood-thatch huts after several miles of climbing. Neither were prepared for what they saw there, nor would either of them ever forget. After some time, they noticed that the fires had been re-kindled, and as they drew near the treeline, the sounds of melodious flutes over pulsing drums began to echo all around them. As they entered the village, no one seemed to notice them or pay any attention. Carl did not wonder. They were a far cry from being the strangest thing to see there. Where the tall grass and bramble flattened out into a main thoroughfare, Carl and the odd man stood still, one beside the other, mouths agape, trying to process the deranged spectacle. It was like a doped up circus for depraved serial killers. Naked forms, living and dead, dotted the landscape. The former, dirt-smeared and wild-eyed, writhed and rocked in a cacophony of perverse sex-acts. Men, women, children, and the elderly (of which there were very few), in the streets, in front of huts, on top of stacks of barrels, in cages, rolling around in the mud in androgynous piles, none of them smiling or appearing to enjoy the act, and yet none of it seeming explicitly involuntary. The latter, splayed corpses and body parts, heads, hands, genitals, broken torsos, severed jaws, dangling strings of toes and fingers and teeth, woven ropes of human hair, all suspended haphazardly from sagging ropes strown like banners from tall poles and rooftops. In the middle of it all, there was a large bonfire, and a roiling spit upon which Carl could clearly make out the silhouettes of charred infants, rolling slowly a few feet over the roaring flames. All around the fire were waist-high wooden tables littered with freshly broiled body parts in various stages of consumption. There did not appear to be any other foodstuff of any kind on these tables, though there were bulbous wooden goblets and gords, messy and dripping with what Carl could not imagine was merlot.

Carl was overwhelmed, and felt faint from the shock of it all. He doubled over and commenced to retching violently in spite of the emptiness of his bowels, which made the motions terribly painful. He immediately lost all composure. The odd man turned away, kneeling beside Carl with his hand on Carl's back, pressing his own eyes closed and trying to hold the sight of the tree line in his own mind. The stench of burning and rotting flesh, by turns, was overpowering. "Do you understand it now? What happens to civilizations when people become sensate animals, divorced from reason and consequence? Do you see?"

Carl struggled to form words between heaves. His mind reeled and refused to process the pure, unadulterated vulgarity of the human condition thus disposed. "I (gag) don't unde(gagging)rstand wha(acchk)t the fuck is (oooouuuahhhh) going on (hacking) here, but I (eeehhk) am one hundred fucking percent (wwuuuuaaahhhk, ahhhk) against it."

"Pull yourself together. You need to bear witness. You have to open your eyes and see the truth and carry it with you. There is no other way."

Carl felt all of his senses revolting against the idea of further exposure. He felt weak and disoriented. He had seen every kind of carnage, he thought, but nothing like this. This was senseless. It was bedlam. Inane and beyond. He had no words. He shoved a fist into his belly and coughed into the other and tried to stand. The odd man helped him up, and threw an arm under him to help him walk. Slowly, they began the longest march through inexplicable chaos.

As they passed, Carl could see the sickness, the plague. Discolored skin, rotten teeth, dead bloodshot eyes bulging atop deep, gray sagging bags. Open wounds and gangrene sores, tangled, greasy hair in knots, severed limbs bandaged with rags, foul and still bleeding. Ahead, a ring of broken humans were shouting and jabbing sticks at two youths engaged in what could only be described as a bare-knuckled brawl to the death. The two children, a boy and girl, barely twelve, at most, were slashing and kicking at one another, baring teeth and growling like rabid beasts. They were entirely nude, aside from the thick layers of sod that covered their skin from head to toe. The girl, having apparently gouged out one of the boy's eyes, seemed to be prevailing. Carl saw her throw the boy to the ground and straddle his chest, pounding his face to pulp with her fists and shrieking her blood-curdling wrath. The boy's arms instinctively rose to protect his head, but not before she got her thumbs in his other eye socket. The crowd fell into a waltzy chorus, calling for the finishing blow, tossing in stones and sticks to aid the effort. Carl had to look away, but he could not shield his ears from the sound of a loud, squishy thud as the girl lifted a large rock above her head and brought it clamoring down on the poor lad's skull. And then again. And again. And she didn't stop when he went limp. Her screams only got louder and her rage grew. The crowd began cheering like they'd won something. He did not see her ripping away the boy's flesh, starting with his open eye socket, and tossing strips into the eager, outstretched hands of hungry spectators.

Another throng was assembled between two huts. Here, Carl saw a man bound to a shorn tree by the throat, feet dangling just a toe's length off the ground beneath. The man's face was purple and swollen, and streams of tears sufficed to convey the cries gargling in his neck, stifled before they could reach his lips. A half dozen or so people were yelling profane things in a foreign tongue and stabbing him with handmade spears. Carl could not even begin to speculate what kind of crime someone could have committed in such a place as this, but the whole affair had a distinctly punitive aspect. The mob was not amused, they were furious. One by one, they took turns rushing up to the man's legs and chewing out large chunks of flesh and spitting them into the man's helpless face. The victim wailed and pleaded, or tried to, but the words would not come out. The sound was akin to pretending to scream while whispering, but very real and far more ghastly. A large, round lady emerged from somewhere holding a long pointed stick, the sharp end of which she had been twirling around in hot coals until it glowed orange, she viciously forced this end into the man's rectum, lifting his genitals and scrotum with it in order to get behind them, and shoving it in with a repetitive thrusting motion at an inefficient angle, missing her target on the first few tries, but throwing her weight behind it once it finally caught its mark. At this, the rope around the man's throat could no longer suppress his cries, and he could be heard from one end of the hut to the other. This drew the attention of others, and Carl looked on helplessly as the odd man quickly shuffled him out of the midst of the scene.

In the span of moments, Carl shut down internally, and felt numb to the sordid inhumanity of it all. The two strangers kept moving until they came to a large, columned sort of temple where a handful of dried out waifs seemed to be lost in a kind of drug-induced haze, and paralyzed behind the walls of their hallucinations. They did not stir as the odd man stepped over them, but Carl eyed them with fear and suspicion, trying to lunge over one young lady with an exaggerated leap, holding the odd man's hand to retain his balance as he landed. They were oblivious. The odd man kicked the girl in disgust, and she just rolled off onto the ground mumbling nonsense and staring off into space. They stood in front of a great marble door, conspicuously wedged in between two wooden walls of woven branches, plastered with mud and excrement. The odd man seemed to be overcome with his own brand of frustration. He pulled a hunting knife from a boot and scratched a familiar phrase into the hewn stone before turning around to take in the toxic panorama one last time.

"Are you ready?" he asked Carl without looking at him.

(45)

"No."

"Good." The odd man turned and put his shoulder into the heavy door. Carl joined him, and between the two of them, they managed to push it back almost a foot. Carl couldn't imagine what awaited him on the other side, but was happy for the chance to be out of public view. If they hadn't noticed him already, they would soon, he was sure. Once inside, they were enveloped by darkness for several minutes while their eyes adjusted from the huge fires burning in the street. After a time, Carl could make out the outline of the odd man, who seemed to be zeroed in on something in the center of the hall. A large dilapidated table, and behind it, a kind of throne. On the throne, Carl perceived an odd mass, inarticulate in the darkness. Slowly and with cautious silence, with his hand on the odd man's shoulder, they inched their way into the room. There were three forms, rather than one, and Carl stared in disbelief. An ancient, hobbled, skeleton of a man was seated, upright like a bolt, arms and hands pressed to the rests on either side, immobile, and gazing off into the distance at nothing. A young girl wearing shapeless robes was kneeling in front of him, hands resting on his knees, her head moving up and down in the tell-tale rhythm of fellatio, while a man stood to one side, fully nude, shoving his erect member in and out of the old man's inattentive mouth. He seemed to be in a trance, or asleep with his eyes open, or dead, Carl couldn't tell which, but he certainly wasn't participating in the act. More like it was being performed on him. The man beside him grunted and shuddered and groaned, suddenly, apparently finishing. The cloying yellow ejaculate dribbled down the ancient one's chin as he removed his member. At this, the girl cooed and climbed onto the old man's lap, straddling his legs and positioning herself for a ride, gleefully licking his chin clean. The man beside them strolled carelessly around behind her, lifted her robes to expose her bare ass, found a free opening, and penetrated her.

"Behold, the Almighty in all his resplendent glory," the odd man bellowed, "the alpha, the omega. The beginning, and the end. Creator of all things. Destroyer of worlds. Judge of the living and the dead. Look upon his works and hear his commandments. Obey him, love him, and set no other false gods above him. He is the bringer of light in darkness. He is righteous before the damned. From his lips, all that is, was, and will ever be hath issued. He, who is without beginning or end. With dust and spit he made Man on the sixth day, and six is the number of man. With his word he bound all the world to the sons of Abraham. He, who so loved the world he gave his only begotten son. Bringer of floods. Our father, who dwelt in heaven, now stews in his own repugnant filth. Oh vanity! Oh hubris! The sins of the father who forsook the world and now rots in this misanthropic indulgence. I have come to free you from these vile creatures old man. Or rather, I have come to free them from you." With these words, the odd man vanished into thin air.

"Oh fuck," said Carl, "not ag--" He felt his limbs and tongue disappear. He felt the heat of a thousand suns in his bowels, and the strain of centuries in his bosom. With a flourish of his hands, he produced the snub-nosed pistol from the knap and fired two shots. The man and the girl slumped to the floor, and the music outside abruptly ceased. Shoving the

, Carl heard a thunderous, roaring boom, like the sound of an atom bomb, which seemed to come from every side at once. And then nothing, infinite nothing. The man called Carl lost consciousness. It was over.

(46)

When Carl awoke, there was fire in the sky. He was floating on his back in the lake, several miles away. His face and hands were burned, and his nerves recoiled from the shock of the pain. The knap was gone, and for a moment, he thought he was alone again, and that he had dreamt the whole thing. He flailed and thrashed when he realized he was in the water, and tried to right himself and swim ashore. But the shoreline was teeming with hordes of emaciated wraiths, all on hands and knees with their foreheads pressed into the mud. They were chanting something in their tongue, he could not know what. He tried to call out for the odd man, who was nowhere to be seen, but couldn't recall a name to scream, and so he said nothing. Carl dog-paddled in the middle of the lake in confused, terrified silence. Off in the distance, miles up the hill where he was sure they had just been, thick billowing clouds of smoke and cinder rose high above the treeline. It had not been a dream. But was it over? Had they really done it? How could he know for sure? Nothing made sense. His head swam with contradictions and muddled scenes he could not piece together in any sensible order. He looked at his hands, holding them above the water and trying to see them in the darkness by the inconceivable firelight in the sky. He could not tell if they were his own hands. He shoved them below the surface, clenching his teeth as the icy water electrified his blistered palms, and tried to feel for the knife in his boot. Nothing. He was alone, and defenseless. He didn't know what to do. He was aware of the empty throbbing in his stomach, but couldn't think of food after what he had seen. It would be days before he ate again. He felt weak and exhausted. He had to set himself down on terra-firma or he would surely drown. But what then? Would he have to fight off waves of gnarly zombies?

Carl waded out of the shallows, breathless, adrenaline coursing through his veins, feeling his heartbeat drumming in his temples. As his charred boots buried themselves in the mud and he pushed himself onto his feet, the motley heathens rose with him. They did not approach, and they did not seem particularly menacing, but their grueling visages were of no comfort, and Carl longed to be as far away from them as possible. Cautiously, he crept away from the shore, trying to remember which direction he had come to get here. Ambling and hobbling, the whole menagerie of souls fell into a quiet procession behind him, some yards back, but keeping pace as he moved. *Go the fuck away! What do you psychos want! Stay back or I'll execute every last mother fucking one of you!*[30] But Carl said nothing. He was alone, and lost, and possibly losing his mind, and provoking a crowd of mindless sycophants seemed like an irrational move. So he trudged down the path he had climbed, with a train of filthy corpses trailing behind in his wake. He didn't look over his shoulder. He avoided eye contact. He just kept moving until he reached the bottom and saw the road. The day which had passed had not been one for credulity, but when he stepped out onto the pavement he once again could not believe his eyes. There was the fucking truck. In one piece and purring like a cat. His followers had no point of reference for a steel three-ton diesel, and fell back at the sight of it.

Carl approached the window in a daze. "Ruth?" he asked simply?

---

[30] *Pulp Fiction*, directed by Quentin Terentino (Miramax, 1994).

"No," grinned the odd man. "Sarah. Get in!"

Carl climbed into the passenger seat. The cab smelled of fresh leather and polish and just a hint of rosemary.

"Is there a cigarette in this fucking thing?" was all he could muster.

"No smoking asshole." The odd man laughed, and punched the gas.

(Disestablishmentarianism)
(47)

"I expected more." pontificated Carl. "Earthquakes, angels, demons..."

"Time and space being swallowed whole into an endless, all-consuming void?" said the odd man, anticipating.

"Something like that. I don't know. Do we call somebody? What happens next?"

"That's up to You."

"What do you mean? Me."

"Not you. You. All of you. For sure, you. But not *just you*. Understand?"

"Having a hard time believing it. Even the parts I *witnessed*. Why would anyone believe it?"

"You mean if the sky doesn't crack open at dawn?"

"Something like that, I guess."

"Why should anything be different? You're missing the point. He wasn't doing anything."

"I mean, it just doesn't make sense. It was too easy. Not an epic kung fu battle. Not a thousand year war. *Nada.*"

"Plenty of good war coming my boy. Plenty."

"But, like, *biblical* war? Or just regular war."

"Is regular war not biblical enough for you?"

"What happened to Ruth? Where did this truck come from."

"You pushed Ruth into a ravine and she exploded. You watched me drive this truck for three days."

"You're being obtuse. Why did we destroy Ruth?"

"It smelled like shit."

"That it did sir. That it did. Have you ever killed a god before? First time?"

"I've never killed anything before. First time."

"Ok, but how did Sarah get *here?*"

"I drove her here."

"But when? You were with me. Like the whole time."

"No, I *was* you. Part of the time. There is a difference. Many places at once, my inquisitive friend."

"Fair enough. So it's up to me, what's next."

"Not just you, remember."

"Right, right, but I've got the initiative."

"Now you're getting it. What will you do?"

"What do you think I should do?"

"I don't know, probably eat something."

"Nahhhh, hard pass I think. For a while."

"..."

"What do you think will happen to those people?"

"That is definitely up to just-you."

"That doesn't bode well for them."

"No, I don't think it does. I think they may be well beyond cogent leadership."

"Them and me, both."

"You did fine."

"What, for my first time killing a god?"

"You didn't kill a god. I did. You're still a little confused."

"Well, I don't guess it matters, who's going to judge, right?"

"Now you're really getting it."

"What did I do, then?"

"You bore witness."

"Or I cracked up and butchered an old guy in a weird cult."

"No, I did that. Come on, Carl, follow along?"

"Ok, better question. Where are we going now?"

"Well, I was going to take you to a little steak joint I know."

"Are there strippers?"

"Like you wouldn't believe."

"Who eats steak in a strip joint?"

"You don't have to eat the steak."

"Suits me fine."

Carl stared at the coal black hands on the wheel in front of him. He wasn't hungry at all. He never was.

(Fuck, Eat, Kill)
(48)

"It's the land of the free, and the home of the brave, you know?" the stranger was saying. She had pegged him already. He was no different than the rest. He only really wanted one thing. In the end, that's all any of them wanted. It was always the same. The boys at her school. The teachers. The men in the street. He was handsome, she supposed, in his way. Handsome enough. Average intelligence. Pliable. Malleable. Gullible. Not terribly imaginative. Apparently his strategy for 'getting it' boiled down to gnawing her ears off with contrite bullshit. She took a long sip from her frosted mug and casually surveyed the room for viable alternatives. Slim pickings. The usual townies. Rednecks. Hoodrats. A couple of suits. A loner in some Rambo gear. Stereotypes. If they weren't already sitting there, she'd have had to write them in, she thought. Maybe a whole thousand in the room. Land-of-the-free? Probably about twelve bucks after the seven dollar Long Island and the shitty tip. Not to be too judgemental though. There were, at best, three shots in that glass of off-brand fountain pepsi. Fair's fair. If you're gonna get what you pay for, you ought to pay for what you get. She watched the bartender pour the drink while land-of-the-free and the skinny bartender watched her. Best to stick to draft in places like this. You get what you pay for. In fact, Rambo-gear was probably the only one in the whole dive not clandestinely watching her. And even that was a routine. She knew better.

He would stutter a little, call her ma'am a lot, thickening up an impromptu Kentucky drawl for a Mississippi girl. If he didn't beat her or cheat on her, he'd be a good lay at least. Maybe a fifty. But he'd play up his "distracted and distant." They all did, and it was fun to watch them consciously skirting the fact they never made it further than Kansas. Like watching a child with chocolate on his face explaining where your candy went. Land-of-the-free was a no go. She'd just about fuck him in the alley out back to get him to leave her alone. But she couldn't be rude. Vibes changed easily in these dives, and she had to *maintain*. The shitty draft was bringing on a headache. Land-of-the-free wasn't helping.

"...in a society based on scarcity and mythology. It just doesn't add up Vic. There's never gonna be enough food for more than five billion people. So line 'em up behind some damned totem poles and let 'em duke it out. Keep 'em at it. That's how ya keep the over-head low, get it? It's all just contr..."

She zoned out, nodding along, rewarding his nominal efforts with cursory validation. It was something to do. She wondered if *he'd* show up. Not likely. Not in the hole like he was. Not a *square*. She liked the squares. They were at least a challenge. Like little wooden toys in truck stops they use to shut the kids up on the highway. Most of them were just routines, she found. But some were *legit* squares. He was a legit square. And a tough nut. Probably not a prude. Some of them really bought into their own bullshit. He probably fantasized about her when he jerked off, she figured. But people put up walls around themselves sometimes just so they know where they are. He seemed like one of those. She was a *taboo*. She'd literally have to just take it from him if she really wanted it. And that just wasn't the same. Hard to find the whole package these days. And for most of the chum in this dive, the package was rarely worth the search. Bubbles snapped her out of her trance. Land-of-the-free was rounding the turn on shot number two. She guessed the bartender predicted a full five would put her in danger. He seemed like the take-it type. Two shots wasn't a great margin of error with the take-it types, she knew. He wasn't wrong though. Just dumb.

"I bet somewhere out there they got a al-go-rhythm or somethin that tells 'em who to pit and who git."

"You don't think it's instinctive?" she coaxed, absently peering over another sip at Rambo-gear. Easy trade, she thought. Lure, spill, humiliate. Easier than changing a bra. She shrugged, internally. Land-of-the-free was a conversationalist who never learned less-is-more. Rambo-gear would get that much right at least.

"Instinctive? I don't know. Maybe?" land-of-the-free feigned enthusiasm for what appeared to be a brand new variable in his equation. "I'd figure there's prob'ly a lot of math and stuff involved, but I guess you could *broad-stroke it*," he said, grinning like a famous comedian and pumping his fist for emphasis. Someone in his orbit somewhere had read that article about suggestive language and tried to give him some pointers; she was sure of it. When she didn't giggle, he crawfished on the gambit and put his serious face back on, taking the obligatory step back to posture his respect for her space. *Wait a bit, try again,* she could practically hear his thoughts. He took a deep sucking tug from his oversized straw and polished off shot number three alongside an equivalent measure of backwash. "Bartender?" he mumbled in a feeble voice, waving his drink around in a tight little circle in the air to prevent confusion. He wagged it at her like a wand when the barkeep deigned to make eye-contact, "can-I-get-you-another-draft-ma'am?" She was going to have to spill about half of one on him, she estimated, quickly doing the calculus in her head. She took a hard pull off the mug and set it down before she got to the spit, like a civilized human being.

"Why not. Thanks."

(49)

Twenty minutes later she was sitting in the booth reapplying her mascara in front of her third freshly frosted mug, waiting for the inevitable Riley story. She had his attention. He was sorry about the scene with land-of-the-free, who had recently left in a cab with a beer-covered shirt and a decent shiner. He did seem a little distracted, like he needed to decompress. He looked like he'd been in a fire at some point. He favored his left hand, like a tic. She could see the faint imprint of an old line on the one ring finger. Shallow, maybe a year or two old, she guessed. Not deep-welled and fresh like at least a half-dozen others she'd counted so far. Fair game.

"Why aren't you next door watching the laaaadies?" She permitted herself to gush a little, breaking the ice while verifying his preference by way of subtext. You couldn't always tell these days. Didn't take long to figure out though.

He laughed a little, pinging her pong back across the table. "Not really feeling it tonight I guess. Was thinking about having a steak. I don't know though, this place seems pretty sketchy."

Bingo. "Their food isn't all that bad really. They don't let the girls cook it of course. It's a salty old black dude named Rodney," she twinkled. *Rodney has good kush and a full nine. But his mother wheezes in the next room watching CoCo. So it's whatever.* "I wouldn't get the rare though." *Rodney doesn't give a FUCK about his cholesterol, or yours.*

"You hungry?" He seemed to brighten a little at the prospect of a nice dinner with an honest girl. *You get what you pay for.*

"I confess, I'm a little peckish, but I wouldn't want to imp-"

"Bartender!" he shouted. "Two steaks, medium well, and another round please? Thank you sir!" The brats at least had manners. Beaten into them all their lives. He'd go slow. He'd wait for the signal. He'd speed up a little. If she gave him the right pitch and tone, he'd go full bore until he busted. Then he'd sleep like a rock. "Fries ok? I've been jonesin' for some fries for some reason. FRIES please!" He'd drown them in ketchup. He'd have heartburn in the morning. She'd be gone already.

"That's sweet, thank you!" She eyed the monstrosity in the parking lot. Safe bet. "You drive *that* thing out there? I bet you never get pulled over." He didn't seem to jump at the whip-flex cue. Kind of just looked away, nervous-like. She read the moment and shifted gears. Freud would have zeroed in. "What happened to your hands?" A nerve. He pulled them from the table and fidgeted with the cocktail napkin in his lap. The sound of raw flesh hitting hot iron in the kitchen accompanied a pleasant smell through a blue-lit shroud of air-borne nicotine. "I'm sorry, I get nosey when I'm nervous," she blushed a little. "It's ok if you don't want to talk about it."

He seemed a little green, but managed a low beam well enough. "It's ok, ma'am, it's not a big deal. I just. It's been a little while I guess, I'm a little nervous too maybe. It wasn't anything interesting or anything like that," he lied. She let him have it. She'd circle back sometime. Maybe.

"What about you? Any weird scars?"

The draft was creeping into the conversation. "Ha! They're all on the inside," she replied sardonically, twirling gramma's pearls. "I had a bad fall not too long ago. I'm kind of a klutz. Banged my leg up a bit, but I'm ok."

"I couldn't tell!" *Nicely done.* She poked her legs out from under the table and hiked her dress on one side, in a classy way, and showed him the bruise while rotating her ankles back and forth on their cuffs. She wondered if he'd read the article. Not the type really. The older brats tended to wing it. It didn't matter. He aped an appropriately dismissive expression of concern, and she stowed her stems. She heard a peel of laughter from the suits, and saw them leaning in over a private joke, seemingly oblivious. She wondered how many conversations she was participating in at that very moment, and then shoved the thought aside.

"That guy was pretty weird. Did you know him? I'm sorry, I wasn't eavesdropping ot anyth--"

"No, no," she said assuringly, "you wouldn't have had to. I think he was a little hammered. No. Sometimes they just kind of pull up next to you. He was probably from around here somewhere I guess, but I didn't know him."

"So you're from around here too? Seems like a sleepy little town. What do people do around here?" He looked around at the place, seeming to inuit the answer to his own question. She shrugged and imitated his pan. *Yeah man, this is pretty much it.*

"People go to the games sometimes. I tend to avoid them. It's all so repetitive and dull. I mean, like, it's *just a fucking ball.* I don't get the appeal. I get bored here." She caught herself and downshifted. "There's some decent hunting if you get out far enough into the sticks."

"You like to hunt?"

I'm an apex fucking predator. That's what he called me. "No, not really. I cook a little though. I like a good barbecue. I've even got a good sauce recipe, family secret!" She closed on the obligatory hushed whisper. On cue, their two medium steaks arrived. Rodney winked as he plopped them down and darted off. He understood the game.

They spent a few minutes in silence. He looked unconvinced as he picked at his dry fries. She would finish every single bite.

(50)

I will come back for you. Wait for me. She awoke to the sound of a single gunshot. Unmistakable. .38. Snub-nosed, modified. Whether it was in the dream, or outside in the shady ass hotel parking lot under the busted, burnt umber street light. It was him. Whether it was in the dream... *It was HIM.* Her heart stopped. And dreams. And nothing.

(51)

She stumbled. "Fucking HEELS!!" she cursed, narrowly avoiding a skinned knee on the wet sidewalk. Her blood would've washed away in seconds, never to be seen again, but she wouldn't have been able to wear this dress again for weeks. "*That's how it goes.*" *she muttered absently, again becoming lost in her own scattered thoughts and nearly losing another step.* "*CHILL THE FUCK OUT.*" *She regained her pace.* [I've had this dream already. I've been here before.] *She switched a little. She knew he was turning. She'd pretend she hadn't seen him. She cursed the rain, getting in character. We inherit the scars. And life goes on, untouchable. Out of reach. Just dragging us along with it. The only engine in all of creation that never rusts, whose parts never fail, whose rhythm never deviates. We show the wear and tear. The glorious splendor of our brilliant youth, slowly marred, pocked, dented, and corroding, like the hubcaps on a Ford Maverick. And the thing that does it to us? Absolutely and Eternally invulnerable. Inaccessible. Infallible. Unstoppable.*

She heard engines. She felt his moment of panicked indecision. This was his moment of choice. Take it. Or pass it by. And if he passed it by. She'd just arrange another moment. Until he caved. She would have him. Now. Or not now. But not never. NEVER never. She would have him. And then she would break him. And he will inherit the scars. [There was a gunshot.] *He slowed. She measured her oblivious steps cautiously and with emphasis. She learned to dodge the little stones and bugs that flung themselves into the grills and headlights of ordinary people. She guarded her youth, and spent it judiciously, with great precision. She was conscious of the great THIEF, the ANTAGONIST, Time. Self Conscious. She heard the words in her grandmother's voice. She clutched her pearls. Self Conscious. Her heart thundered painfully, against her will. She turned her head and stopped on the dime. She planted one foot slightly behind the other, remembering not to lock her knees, and leaned on the rear. For lift.* [wake up.] *And she saw his eyes. Broken by the pulse of the wiper blades, his swollen eyes.* [Wake Up.] *His look of fear and desperation. His loneliness. His anger and frustration. She saw him laid bare. Mustering every ounce of his dwindling life force just to push his foot just one quarter inch further into the brake pedal.* [WAKE UP!] *To commit.*

(52)

"Miss Shelby."

She squinted against the lights above her. Her head felt like wet concrete under a jack hammer. She felt the drugs. *Self Conscious.* She was vulnerable. She needed time to think. But they knew she was awake. Even through the fog she could sense the difference in the beeps from the machine next to the bed. She pressed her eyes closed, visibly tight. Six in the room. Two suits. Feds. She didn't know why she knew. Three doctors. A nurse. There were seven. And they couldn't see him. They wouldn't see him, unless he wanted them to. And more curiously, he was the only one in the room who seemed genuinely disinterested in the whole affair unfolding. It was in his posture. Sitting there in the one chair in the room, oddly disregarded by the other parties present. They weren't looking at him. They didn't know he was there. There were eight. And he wasn't watching her like the other six. And he wasn't watching them. They didn't matter. They didn't exist. Not to him. Not even variables. No. He was staring intently into a wilting Peace Lily on a small table between himself and the paneled windows overlooking a brown wooden fence, two trash cans, an old man in a wheelchair smoking a cigar, and two orderlies talking about nothing at all in the lengthening shadows of the calm Missississppi twilight. *And cars.*

"Miss Shelby?" The young lady in white was about to try a third time when the impatient man behind her interjected and assumed control of the situation.

"Misses Victoria Shelby Smith, 6398 Potomac Avenue. Twenty Five. Three priors, two for possession, one for pandering. You can scrunch your face up a little more if we've got anything wrong." He paused, and waited for her decision. "Wonderful. Ma'am, you've got some questions to answer. You're going to answer them. You're not getting a lawyer. You're not leaving this premises. You're going to answer my questions. You're not going to fuck me around. You're not going to waste my **g**oddamned time. You can scrunch your face if you don't understand. But then you're going to open your eyes and mouth and tell me every last little detail or I swear-so-help-me-G-"

"Oh my **g**od what the fuck do you want! Jesus Christ on a cracker man, can you hear yourself? You sound like a fucking cartoon. You've got forty-six bucks in your wallet. You're unhappily married to a woman who reads. You've got two kids, and you're underwater on your Taurus out there. There is literally NOTHING about you that intimidates me whatsoever. Where the fuck am I? Who the hell are you people? What the fuck happened. How long have I been out? Why the fuck am I here? You know what mother fucker, I've got some questions of my own."

The man wore his affectation like a scarlet letter. He was shaken. She was the devil. He would get nothing from [Snap the fuck out of it Charles!] "You- YOUNG LADY! How dare you! Do you know who I am?" *How do you know who I am?*

"Start over. And don't be such a fucking dick this time. Got it?"

His partner stared at him, watched him shift uncomfortably on his heels, trying to regain his totem. The doctors were speechless. The nurse was barely containing her hysteria. The man in the chair was now making a deliberate show of his disinterest, but she could see the traces of a smile forming, buried in the left corner of his lips. They were going to get along fine. And she understood. He wasn't here for them. Or the fucking Peace Lily.

"Miss. Shelby." The impatient man, finding his patience, cleared his throat. "Miss Shelby. You are in a Federally Subsidized Mental Health Facility. For all intents and purposes, and for the duration, this man and I are the federal government." He held up his air-quotes for her benefit. He really was fucking lame. "Twenty six days ago-

Twenty six fucking DAYS? She glared at the man in the chair for an explanation. He turned, looked her dead in the eyes, and shrugged, and turned back to the dead plant.

"- you were found in a motel room, unconscious, apparently having suffered from some kind of anomalous-cardiological-event," sounding the words out, he took a breath to double check the sequence of syllables he had had not verbally practiced, "Miss Shelby, do you remember? Tell-- Please tell me what you remember about that night.

She took a deep breath, trying to stall her few remaining seconds. She remembered Land-of-the-Free. She set herself to matching his five (hypothetical) shots with five of those frosty mugs. She remembered trading up. What was his name? Something. *Damn it Vic. What was his name?* She felt a twinge of embarrassment. *Self Conscious.* The man in the chair finally broke his silence. [His name was Carl. You really are a piece of work aren't you?] "His name was Carl. That's all I really know. He didn't say much. And that was more of a feature than a bug, if you understand." A tear formed. *Treason.* "It was him wasn't it? He shot himself. I heard it. That's the last thing I remember. That wasn't my fault. I mean. Like, we didn't fight or anything. I just met him. I don't know. I don't know why he did it. And I don't know what you want from me. But I can't help you."

The doctors looked at each other, and seemed perturbed. They exchanged quizzical looks.

You were there that day, weren't you? Like seven years ago? You were there. You saw, you saw what? Everything?

The man in the chair groaned and stretched, ignoring her, and finally brought himself to survey the room. He looked over the officious looking men, full of purpose and certainty, and then examined the puzzled doctors and the confused nurse. He looked at her, at last, with an earnest expression of subtextual urgency. But he said nothing.

"Miss Shelby, ---"

"PLEASE stop calling me that. No one calls me that." *He used to call me that.* She was becoming agitated. She pulled and twisted at the leather straps and then deflated, sinking into the pillow and scrunching her face again. Trying to shut out the light. Trying to push her skull away from her brain.

She felt hunger pangs in her stomach. She felt the sting of the intubation.

Let me out of this. The man in the chair sighed, and slumped back into his boredom. The lights dimmed. Nothing.

"Miss Shelby!" The beeps slowed their frenetic pace and grew distant. [MISS SHELBY!] Too late. Days would pass before she stirred again. She whispered to the empty chair.

"Thank you." And infinite nothing washed over her once more.

(53)

She awoke in darkness. Disoriented, like a huge part of her life was missing. Dry mouthed, with a full bladder. The annoyingly-bright red LEDs on the wall read 3:13. She was alone. She looked around the room to be sure. The blinds were drawn. The door was closed. The facility was quiet. Her gaze fell upon the silhouette of the empty chair. She focused intently on the object until her eyes adjusted and she could make out its features. Wooden. Walnut stain? Simple, almost to the point of being... [*platonic?*] And then he was there. He was dressed like Carl. She hadn't noticed that before. She felt dizzy. She made a (self conscious) effort to proactively *decide* whether or not to question her own sanity. And then the floodgates opened, and her memory returned, almost as if on command. She could practically feel the rain drops.

"You! You fucking PUSHED me. Why? So he'd *CHOOSE* to stop? You mother fucker. You *pushed* me? WHY!? Why did you do it? Because he would have just kept on going, wouldn't he? He would have chickened out. And I wouldn't have fallen into that **g**oddamned ditch. I was going to let him go, you son of a bitch. I turned and walked away. I *MADE* a choice. What about that? Huh? Doesn't that matter? Isn't that, like, I don't know, how it's supposed to work? You cheated. You sick, sadistic mother fucker. And you just sat there and watched us. The whole time. Why? What was the point? What did you need him for? It was you, too, in class, wasn't it. You set it all up. From start to finish, the whole thing was a fucking charade. You *ruined* him. And you did it again, too, didn't you. With this guy? This, this Carl? Or whoever? What the fuck do you want with me? Why does this keep happening?" She was in tears now, and the rivulets streamed down her matted cheeks. She stared at him. His hands were tucked away in his pockets like an insolent teenager, well beyond the reach of reason. His eyes were darker than the world when her own eyes were closed. He was not smiling. He was not her ally. She was cursed. Would he speak? *WOULD YOU PLEASE SAY SOMETHING! godDAMNIT!!!*

"You know me. You know why I am here. It's time to pay your bill Vic."

"Where is he? What happened to him? What the fuck is going on!"

"He shot himself. You'll meet him again someday, probably soon." He chuckled to himself, very nearly imperceptible, but not evading her scrutinizing eyes.

"That's how you do it, isn't it. I knew a guy once. Frontal lobe, right? D.O.A. But not really. That's how you get them off the grid. That part I get. But how do you bring them back? Is that how I'm gonna go? Hey! Answer me! Is that how you're going to do me? You evil bastard!"

She couldn't tell, not for sure, but something in his face said she'd hit a nerve. She had his attention. She'd rattled him. She'd said something he hadn't planned on.

"What do you mean, bring them back?" was his only response. He wasn't laughing anymore.

"I saw him. Not Carl. The other guy. Mr. Z. I saw him. I mean. After..."

This was it. She could see it, clearly, plain as the bright red numbers on the wall. This was what he hadn't planned on.

"I saw him at the big protest, when president dick-lord went into the hole, he was there. I saw him. I saw *you*. I remember you. I remember you watching us, I mean, before. And I recognized you. In him. I do know you. I've always known you. You fucking *thief*."

The man in the chair said nothing for a long time. She stared at him, indignantly.

"You get that I don't really answer to you, right?"

"Whatever man, why are you here? How about that." She waited.

At length, he replied. "You're right though. I did watch you. I enjoyed the show. You're quite... talented. Of course, you already know that. And I think that's the draw, you know? I think that's what gets them. Somewhere, deep down, they all know. They know you know. And for the life of them, they can't exactly put their finger on *what* you know, and their egos bind them. One and all. They don't just pretend they don't know. Like you do. They persuade themselves. They believe the lie they create for you. Honey, that's a skillset I haven't seen in a long time. And you know damned well. If I hadn't pushed you, you'd have done it yourself. Just like with that goofball in the bar."

"How do you do it though? How do you bring them back? What's going to happen to Carl? And what have you done with Mr. Z?"

The man in the chair turned away, back to the dying plant. He slumped again, like before, and sighed deeply.

"You haven't got it quite right. I don't bring them back. They just don't actually die. That's how they get away. It's a whole complicated thing. There are some...a few...strays, I guess. People who are willing to, you know, go the extra mile, if you will, to elude me. Certain measures are, let's say, more effective than others. It works for a little while. But they heal. It's like a play, if you will, where the characters have roles to play in front of the audience, but also behind the curtain. Theater. It's like theater." He seemed momentarily preoccupied by his satisfaction with the simile, and then willfully recentered his bearings. "I watched, a very long time ago, I watched...a kind of show, I guess. And I chose to watch, although that fact has since been distorted by--" again, swerving back into his lane, "But watching, I have since realized, deprived me of a unique opportunity to participate. I am here." He paused, and chose his words. "I am here because I have learned from my mistake. An opportunity to participate has once again presented itself. And I am obliged to seize this opportunity."

She projected *unmoved* as aggressively as possible. This was not a satisfactory answer. "I loved him. You get that, don't you? I mean, is that something that ever enters into your math? He was a good guy. He tried to do his best. The world fucked him over, but none of it was his fault. Or mine, for that matter."

"I liked him very much, in fact. Like you, he got a few details wrong, but on the whole, I feel like he got the basic point. A rare thing, you know. Of course you do. I'm here for you, Vic. Not him. Not Carl. Not any of them. I'm here for you. And yes, I do know that you loved him, at least, you think you do, or thought you did, but no. No, that does not matter to me in the slightest. Not even a little bit. I want you to help me. In fact, if you will help me, if you will *choose*, as you put it, to help me, I'll let you have him back. If that's what you want."

His eyes flashed. This was the moment. The bargain was at hand.

"What, you mean a fucking vegetable? A shell of a broken man with a chunk of missing gray matter? That's what you're offering me? You chincy fuck. Do better." Her eyes flashed. She was hungry too.

The man leaned forward in his chair. Negotiations. His blood ran hot. He liked her very much. She read his enthusiasm clearly, like the bright red numbers ticking away the dawn. He was on the clock now. It was time to make a deal.

"We'll get to it," she resolved. "First, tell me what you actually want."

He studied her carefully. Birds chirped at some interloping threat outside.

"Listen very carefully."

(Angels, Devils, and Avatars)
(54)

"What is a choice, really? What is its significance in the grand scheme of things? If you fall into a river, do you actually choose to swim? Where is the line between what is voluntary and what is not, when we're talking about natural human behavior? Are we not really just talking about animal behavior? Does the lion choose to chase the gazelle? Does the gazelle choose to run? Ladies and gentlemen, I ask you with all seriousness, are our choices the product of conscious deliberation? Or of a matrix of hardwired instincts? This question has been debated for centuries. And for many lifetimes, we have all resorted to the safety and comfort of academic objectivity, the conclusion that the question itself is unanswerable, like where did the universe come from, or how did life begin. We don't study these questions for answers. We study them for speculation. Instead of solving the problem, we award one another certifications for our ability to recite the guesses others have made, on the basis of accuracy, not imagination or innovation. But what if there really is an answer to this question, on the subject of real human agency, and what if the answer to that question was actually within our reach? What would be the implications of knowing, one way or another, whether or not we human beings have any real control over our thoughts and words and choices and actions? For example, would you want to know what that answer was? Would you accept, could you accept, any form or rational proof that your whole life was just one long deterministic algorithm of causes and effects? How would knowing that affect the conscious process of decision making? Many of these questions I have posed here today may not have conclusive answers, but we've found a place to start. We've actually answered this last question. And that's why you're all here.

"Thanks to your very generous contributions, our researchers have accomplished the impossible. We now know, with heretofore unprecedented statistical certainty, how large numbers of human subjects will be affected by the effective disassembly of the very concept of choice. While there are many technical aspects and structural limitations to bear in mind, we believe that you will find our overall methodology and sample sizes are beyond reproach. Our guest speakers will delve more deeply into those discussions today and try their best to answer the many questions we know *you* will have, but truthfully, to be completely honest, none of it matters. Using what we have learned, we no longer require reason to persuade you. In other words, we're so damned confident in our ability to sell you our technology, in fact, we believe we've already sold it to you. The following presentation is merely pretense, of course, as are the customary rituals of negotiations and concessions and agreements which follow. We already have your money. We know this because we understand you better than you understand yourselves. We know this because we have already made the choice for you. We know this because we know that we have not only beaten our competitors in the field of Psychological Engineering, we have proven decisively that we never had any competition to begin with."

Tyberius took a step away from the microphone and stood at parade rest. The audience roared to their feet with frenzied applause. A fantastic lightshow commenced as balloons rained down and a familiar anthem blared from the inset speakers on every wall. Seventeen AI driven lasers swept the room, inconspicuous among the thirty some-odd others on random swivels, altering hue, brightness, and pulse rate at lightspeed, as they passed over the retinas of each individual audience member, in a carefully choreographed sequence designed to heighten receptivity by stimulating the novelty-perception neurons in conjunction with triggered endorphin bursts. Government was simple, he thought to himself. The people voted. Governance was just controlling what they voted for. The sample population seated before him would be offered a clear choice. And they would choose as they were instructed. These kings, diplomats, warlords, influencers, cartels, industrialists, and conglomerates. They would learn nothing of choice. They would implement his systems in service of their own petty agendas. That decision had been made before any of them had even arrived at the convention center today. There was no choice. The path was clear and concise. Dominate or be overrun. And there were no competitors. Tyberius was unrivaled in the field. He didn't need their money. He needed them to part with it voluntarily. That was the most delicious part. He was selling string to his own personal marionette. And they would buy it, even without the lasers. But Tyberius left nothing to chance anymore. Tyberius was ascendant. His wings would withstand the heat of many suns. These charades were just lines of code in a program only he understood. Tyberius would change the world, and remake it in his own image. And for this, Tyberius would be martyred. Historians would later argue that indeed, this last step was the most crucial part of the entire plan. When the egg is made of gold, no one thinks of eating the goose. But the most valuable golden egg such a goose ever lays is always the last one.

Getting martyred wasn't a part of his plan though. At least, not this time. This time, Vic's job was to wing him. And then disappear in the ensuing chaos. The climax was the execution variable, literally. He had given this speech sixteen times, and his fortunes were already considerable, but today's presentation would net him indefatigable credibility into perpetuity. This was the top tier. The bossfight. This was vindication. After today, Tyberius would personally supplant the old invisible hand of free will. After this, even her mysterious benefactor would have to show his hand.

Tyberius peered out over a cacophony of exuberant patrons, feeling the tightening sensation in his guts, an anxiety riddled mixture of gas and bile, searching for the pearls. Little decimation stones, milk-white omens, the siren's anchor, drifting out there in the foggy whirling psychedelic laserbeam tapestry, hidden away somewhere in the blank spaces, the intermittent shadows, aiding and abetting her obscurity, those pearls, the ones that made her look like she had dressed up to be here, the pearls that made her look like everyone else. Her clear and present subterfuge, and yet the only salient identifier. Six hours. Tyberius cursed himself. Six hours and he couldn't remember the color of her shirt. Because of those damned pearls. He could remember the entire forty-six A code sequence with external references and redundancy packaging protocol notations from header to end tag, verbatim. He could remember the smell of the magnolia trees on the UTM campus on September 7th at sunset during any calendar year of the Second Republic. He could recite the entire index of near earth objects in Maxwell's catalog. He could remember how many cars were in the parking lot the last time he ate pancakes and sausage with his father. He knew, to the decimal, how much the six green lasers cost at wholesale, before and after tariffs, taxes, shipping, intake, and installation. He knew the atomic weight of each individual element in the pistol strapped to her leg. And he couldn't remember, yellow or blue. So he smiled with every grain of midwestern moxy he could muster, and pushed his eyes from face to face to face, across thousands of faces per second, trying to find those fucking pearls.

He wasn't scared, he told himself. He just wanted to know which direction it was going to come from. Would that change anything? No, he assured himself. His palms, consoling one another behind his back, were sweating profusely. Just BAM! And not knowing where, that seemed... he reached for the word, *undignified*. She would have found her way in. Tyberius wondered to himself who you'd have to be not to be let in with this mob of degenerates. They were all armed. No one would have searched her. And those damned elusive pearls would have carried her the rest of the way on feathers and rose petals. And where were they now? She said it had to be this way. Left brain, right brain, left side stressor, right side stimulus, who knows? Neurochemistry is complicated, she said. Unpredictable. He had been too busy laughing at his own little irony to appreciate the full weight of the choice. The choice to not have a choice. The longer his eye followed her, from seat to row to aisle to landing to point to trigger, or worse from door to seat, through overture, and then from seat to row and so on, the longer the neurons would have to build potentialities. Yellow. Blue. Shit. Everything in eyeshot was flashing green and red and purple and orange. No. It had to be the damned pearls. Find the pearls.

The people were stomping and clapping and shouting along to the anthem, breathing in the argon and neon and barley.. They seemed vulgar and repulsive to Tyberius. Behaving this way. So irrevocably persuaded of their hard wrought inevitability, their divine right revenue streams manifesting success and fruiting influence, which is just weaponized vanity. Perspective, however shrift, is so much more satisfying. They believed. No. They *knew,* to a man. Each and all, without exception, in this euphoric moment of proverbially zionist fervor, believed that they were winning. Because all of their battles were beneath them. All of their assets, clients, constituents, cohorts, interns, neighbors, conspirators, charity cases and flotsam dregs and hitmen, all possessed the ubiquitous aspect of subordination that so commonly befalls the majority of contestants in any race or competition, the quality of being less than, inferior, obligated, leveraged, imposed upon, subdivided, undermined in utero by the whims of physics and biology and pure dumb fucking luck, according to proscriptive standards artificially connived and dogmatised by ignorance and superstition. All of those obstacles and obligations were beneath them. They did not perceive Tyberius in any other way, nor could they ever. The lights, the suits, the buttermilk shrimp towers, the gimmicky drug tech dope show, the blood curdling fear of open and outright rebellion which the SysTic sycophants were insisting was less than thirty seven quarters out.

Tyberius was somehow a man apart. He was Perseus, offering them fire. Not quite trembling, but neither transmogrified. Something scared the shit out of them, and they were offered a choice. They were all after the same thing, it was always safe to assume, and there's nothing more simplistic than human need. And by the hand of god they got it. Somehow, the phrase "by the hand of Tyberius" had thus far (and thankfully) evaded their conceptions of providence. The guest speakers didn't matter. The blueprints and flowcharts were akin to the daisies in pebbled glass vases on the few bar tables set up in the foreground, just eye candy.

History had made this choice for them, so far as they could tell, just as it had for their fathers and their fathers before them, unto the time of swords and stones and beyond, to the time of natural predators. And so, as beneficiaries of fortunes bestowed, as it were, by natural law, they asserted their rightful privilege to self preservation. They were here to take control of what they already possessed, to take back control of what indeed they never possessed, But they would possess it. Control. Tyberius would sell it to them by the planet load if they could pay for it. And they would pay for it. They would scramble to pay for it. And they would party their asses off and sleep like babies knowing they paid for it, because they could, and because that's all it really amounted to. Each of them would move a few numbers from one column to the next once or twice, and overnight, the raw strength of atomized armies of laborers and resources (on contract and commission) would magically coalesce out of the registrars and resume bins, with directions delegated in the blind to assemble and implement compartmentalized-WHERE THE FUCK ARE THE PEARLS.

He didn't want to die. She said he wouldn't. He would just be harmed. Wounded. But he was scared. No matter how high the stakes. No matter how persuasive the variable. Death seemed like an abysmal experience. But a bullet in the arm was no picnic. Easy to hit the chest. He began to lose patience. There was no way to prepare for this kind of thing. He could have let her shoot him before, he supposed. Practice. Practice? The song was about to end. The mood would change a few seconds into the next song, no matter what it was. Receptivity levels would plummet for twenty seven minutes. Halfway through the lecture on automation in civil engineering. The greens and reds had faded together, and were now competing with a purple and orange thump on every third beat. And the beats were slowing down. This was a stupid plan. He didn't want to get shot. He tried not to think about what the bullet would feel like tearing into his skin at hundreds of miles per hour. Heat, ripping flesh, burning and stabbing-- would it hurt more in the chest, straight on, or in the chest from an angle? It mattered where she was sitting. There had been seven cars in the parking lot. Two of them were police cars. Memory is tied to significance, which is related to novelty and self interest. Tyberius was sick. His sickness was all consuming. All Consuming.

He didn't feel the shot right away. He had half expected that. It takes time, between the sound and the nerves processing the intrusion of a thirty eight caliber shell. Even after a second or two, he still couldn't pinpoint exactly where it entered his body. He felt a brief flicker of gratitude. Surely, just as he'd imagined, the time gap, the speed of pain, granted him the little moment between recognition and resolution he'd hoped he might get.[31] Another second and still nothing. His nerves, overstimulated probably. Too much environmental noise and anticipation anxiety. He had time, maybe, he might get to see, yellow or blue. He became self conscious, should he move his face? Cry out? What if his body didn't tell him. Surely she hadn't missed. Point blank was the agreement. Point blank or nothing. Why waste this much prepwork. What would happen next? When would it hurt? Would the plan work if he died? He said it out loud, in spite of himself, "Why doesn't it hurt?"

---

[31] Marilyn Manson, "The Speed of Pain," on *Mechanical Animals*, Interscope, 1998.

Now visibly confused. He found his hands. Her blouse was Yellow. Not Blue. His hands froze solid. Not blue. Yellow. But not yellow. Red, really. Really red. Oh **g**od. Oh No. No Vic! "NOOOOOOOOOO!!!"

But Vic got away.

(55)

The bartender was just a fluorescent green bob in the blacklight, nodding to the blaring backbeat thud pounding through the neon rainbow graffiti on the pocked black walls. Shallow eg shel glinted off of the brown and purple and green bottles she shuffled deftly from hand to hand like a poker dealer. Her eyes, sought by every man, woman, and child in this greasy degenerate spoon, remained hostage to an inviolate sequence of mechanical coordinations. Customer. Cabinet. Pour. Customer. Cash. Drawer. Customer...Customer...Customer. Cabinet. Cabinet. Cabinet. Pour. Mix. Mix. Uncap. Customer. Cash. Customer. Cash. Customer. Cash. Impersonal rhythms irregularly broken by imitations of laughter, intrigue, novelty, enthusiasm, and cash. By now, Picaso painted their faces. Disjointed successions of transmogrified, floating, estranged features, existing without context or frame. Eyebrows, lager. Horn-rims, rose'. Flatbill, draft. Jowls, lager. People ceased to exist. Customers were an abstraction. Cash was a solitary king. Good people, bad people. Impossible to tell in all this noise. She relied on visual cues. Vomit. Bloodstains. Tears. Pupils. Fists. Sweat. Badges. Smoke. These things were tangible. Actionable. And the Action was always to make direct eye contact with Pike. Pike would then immediately and satisfactorily resolve the problem. And the stars would tremble onward in their revolutions.

Presently, bloodstains appeared, ordering whiskey, rocks, calmly, and with the mildest of manners. He made clear and direct eye contact, and said nothing after his order but 'thank you,' stuffing a twenty in the jar. She glanced, mid motion, over at Pike, just to orient herself. Pike was detained. Distracted by a patron, who seemed to be selling him something, judging by Pike's vivid skepticism. She rationalized. The stains weren't pronounced. The man seemed hellbent on minding his own. He said that much with his eyes, but volunteered nothing. Some people imploded. Implosions were perfectly tolerable, within reasonable parameters, terminating at anything she had to clean up. She deliberated quietly, amidst her motions. Two strikes. That's the bar. Bloodstains are usually three. But they didn't look fresh, which made this a retreat, instead of a crime scene. Lots of money in retreats, and if not for it, she'd be a marine biologist. Crime scenes, on the other hand, were notoriously bad for cash flow. She eye'd the fresh twenty and did her calculus. Cut off at five. Or three hours. She eyed the clock. Five, then. Plenty. He was distracting her now. But, she reasoned, he was trying hard enough not to. The nights are flooded with paradoxes here. She made a conscious decision to make no decision at all, let his face dissolve into the disembodied patchwork. In vain, she knew, like when you crawl in bed and the thought of insomnia merely occurs, and once lodged, becomes a self-fulfilling compulsion.

Pike appeared, almost as if summoned, but wholly preoccupied with unrelated matters. "I think I might quit." He seemed to be mouthing something she refused to make out. "I think I M I G H T Q U I T," he strained. Her hands froze in the air. The music seemed to dim as she gathered her focus and tried to burn his lips with it. She could make out the brief purse, and then stretch, 'Q U I T.' She planted her feet, slammed the bottle and glass on the bar, emptying her hands, subconsciously already searching for something to throw.

"What the FUCK did you just say?" But for some reason, she glanced back at bloodstains, her mind trying to reconcile two scenarios developing in opposition. Then, to the mysterious interloping salesman. No trace of him. Gone like a fart in the wind. What the fuck was happening? She studied Pike's face for a twinkle, a lip corner curling, or a snort. Something. Nothing. He just stood there waiting, as though she might eventually explain it to him if he just waited patiently enough. He was serious, she at last concluded. Pike had been there for *yeeeeaaarrrrs*. It was a Tuesday. Just a regular ass Tuesday. He tried to maintain her gaze, carefully ignoring the four pound blue crystal skull near the triple tap, just out of arm's reach of the electric koolaid beehive floating on a slim silhouette with gleaming eye-whites and yellow fingernails. He took a step to his right, like a cartoon duck manually adjusting the hunter's aim. Her eyes, like Mona Lisa's, didn't move, and he did not escape. It's always a lot harder to sell something to someone after it's been sold to you, he thought. She could see his spine wavering. She stared harder, choosing and forming her next words carefully, because they would be heard by at least a hundred people. Someone shouted. "Bartender!" A perfectly reasonable thing to do, but at a perfectly unreasonable moment. She saw red. Red's fine, Pike thought. Red's better than blue. Let's stick with red. "BAR Tender!" Not the voice of rescue, Pike thought. Just a herald of war. Ducks quacking the apocalypse. No such luck. "BAART---" She swirled and screamed, pausing for a splinter of a second on orientation, and then hurled a 90 mph glass fastball in the shape of a human head at what appeared to be no human head in particular in a densely packed mob of human heads, in the smoky neon dark. It took her entire minutes less to register a confirmed hit than the stunned bystanders (into whom he fell) took to comprehend what, why, or how. He was unconscious, and thus of little use in the way of explaining. She took one last quizzical look at bloodstains, who returned her eyes with as little antagonism or controversy as he could muster, and warm silence. She punched the lock button on the register, and shouted for about sixty people to shut-the-fuck-up, and spun the little silver key, pulled it out, and stuffed it under her pantyline, beneath the open button of her painted-on jean shorts. She rounded the end of the bar and marched past Pike, wafting sulfur and estrogen and strawberries and menthol Kools and PBR. He stood motionless, staring at his own shoes, and counting off an appropriate number of her steps in half-seconds in his mind before turning to follow her outside. Facing the door and preparing to retrace her path, he could just make out that damned little string, across a prairie of caramel spine, before it disappeared beyond the bricks and red-lit EXIT sign. At least she was empty handed. Pike would drag his feet for a few ticks on the way to the door. It wasn't a conversation he had fully thought through, but it was a conversation he would now be forced to commit to. As accustomed, he swore under his breath an oath not to hit her back, just before pushing the door open and stepping out. He hunched his shoulders for the flying bottles, cigarettes, rocks, whatever. She was right handed, so it never came from the left, because the wall obstructed her sidearm or else provided insufficient cover. But nothing. She was sitting on a curb, opposite the lot, smoking a cigarette, holding her knees and watching pebbles and brown blades of tangled grass fumble along in the wind as he approached. Imploding felt different. It was less satisfying, in the tactile sense, but somehow edifying nonetheless. He lowered himself alongside her on the curb, and thought carefully about where to begin.

(56)

The female from the future was fascinated by the flies. She cooed over them with this peculiar, delightful malice, calling them "baaaaabies" and shouting at them like docile, retarded children, toying with them with crumbs and adroit swooshes of her hands that sent them flurrying, one by one, in different directions, to her amusement and to the bewilderment of anyone who happened to be present for any of her many seemingly involuntary diversions. Mid-word, amidst any discussion of any matter of any gravity, no matter how enormous, she would inevitably and spontaneously combust in a paroxysm of disorderly attention deficit, fully reverting to some semi-neurotic and neo-primitive childhood state, without capacity or regard for the pretenses of etiquette, continuity, or restraint. The southern summer heat, permeated as it was by the exuberant odor of burning flesh, was already thick with them, swarming in little black clouds, the flag-bearers of hunger, poverty, and blight. They mainly stayed outside, preferring the abundant game and open skies, but occasionally a few found their ways indoors, straggling in through the cracks in the decayed sealant around the windows, through crumbling ventilation systems, through secret, labyrinthian passageways among sagging rafters and rotting clapboard. They were a nuisance, to be sure, but, culturally speaking, they were either to be disregarded or dealt with. To her, however, they were pure and unadulterated theatrical spectacle, approaching obnoxious. To her captive audience, the sheer joy evident in her exertions outmoded the obvious absurdity, wholly devoid of context, combined with the uncanny skill with which she drove them this way and that, and her predatory instinct for timing a perfect death-blow every single time she smashed her open palm on a hard surface and pulled it back to reveal a mushy little carcass of spiraling tendril and viscera. The premonitory satisfaction which the spectacle induced in lookers-on precluded, for the moment, and moments are all we have don't-ya-know, any objective examination of its implications. Though her visit was brief, to be sure her presence inspired a great many questions, some of them she was equipped to answer well enough, but it does seem strangely curious in retrospect that no one thought to address the pronounced oddity of her fascination with the flies directly. Naturally, after the fact, the subject did arise and eventually engendered some enthusiastic debate, with one or two views nearly reaching toward something of a consensus among those in the know. The more prominent of these was the speculative hypothesis that her behavior toward the pesky bugs signified some exaggerated evolutionary phenomenon had occurred between the now and the whence, which had resulted in abnormal growth in their physical forms, suggesting that by her time, flies resemble small to mid-sized birds, and are more aggressively invasive. The opposing theory was that she was batshit crazy and the whole affair from start to finish was complete and total nonsense. One side upheld her preternatural preoccupation as evidence supporting her purported story of origin, that she was indeed from somewhere else, as plausible a suggestion in this closed off little corner of the galaxy, as that she was from some*when* else. Ipso Facto. The naysayers finally rested their case on the supposition that during the elapse of time necessary for such a visual transformation to manifest, given the known lifespans of various flies, the many human languages would necessarily evolve beyond mutual points of recognition, apart from the most archaic vestigial forms, and yet the girl spoke the language of the people perfectly, even picking up a noticeable dialect during those few mysterious and fleeting days. In time, the credibility of entomologists and linguistics professors carried sway over the few hollering whispers in the dark, feebly attempting to persuade the inert minds of many that the fundamental assumptions of reality had been undermined over a weekend on a desert-ridge between two valleys bestriding the demilitarized zone between Colorado and Nevada.

(Tyberius)
(57)

"You don't hunt what you love, boy."

Dad moves the oilcloth gently along the barrel of the long rifle. Thoughtful lights in his kind old eyes. He is trying to ar-tic-u-late a thought right now, and he believes it is something I need to know. I smell the oil. The cloth is barely damp. Dad's a con-ser-va-tion-ist. Waist-knot, he says sometimes. The windows are open, all the way, and the cold is coming in. The cold is all around. The engine is running, and the heater is on. I smell the oil, and I smell the gas. He is lost in thought, but he will chime in again after a few moments. Sometimes he does that. He just kind of drifts off. He's awake, and momma says he's paying attention to everything all the time, always, and not to be deceived. But I think momma is wrong sometimes. Sometimes I think he is just having a hard time keeping up with all the stuff going on in there. Momma says daddy is a genius, but she says that isn't what she loves about him. She says I'm what she loves about him. I don't really know what that means exactly, and when I ask daddy, that's one of the few times he doesn't start into a long lec-ture about whatever I'm asking about. He just laughs out loud and sometimes he will mess up my hair and just walk off, not saying anything at all.

Suddenly there is motion. I climb up onto my knees to see out the window on his side, down the long hill, covered in all the huge trees. There is a little bit of water coming from a stream, a ways off towards the sun. This place is really high up. We drove for three hours from the bottom of the hill to the top, twisting and turning around long, steep curves, sometimes under really thick tree branches covered in leaves of every color I can imagine. Daddy makes coffee while he's driving. We come here a lot, and no one else ever does, Daddy says. So on certain sides of the mountain, we play loud music to scare off anything that's alive. Daddy has a whole science about it. At the bottom we camp. The river is on the other side, and the river is very wide. While we camp, we play music. Daddy says it scares all the animals further up the hills. Daddy says everything is programmed to move up when it's scared, and since there's no way down with us in the way, he's always right. Sometimes we can see them. When we take off up the hill, and get around to the other side, Daddy turns off the radio and we just ride for a long way in silence, looking out over the river. And then he turns it back on when we round the other side again. Sometimes we talk about things, but mostly Daddy and I both just ride and think about things. There is a lot to look at. Momma called the trees ever-greens, and said they could survive the winters here on the mountain. Momma doesn't always come camping with us, and she never drives up. She says somebody has to stay below, just-in-case.

He levels the rifle a little downward, almost toward the cloud line below us where the trees below disappear into the fog. I can't see what he sees. But I can smell his cologne. Ships on the bottle, not boats, he told me before. He said boats were playthings, like toys. You relax on a boat on a river or a lake. Ships travel the oceans, and the stars, and go to war. He said ships always have a captain who commands the sailors, because in the ocean and in space and at war, you have to work hard and be really smart just to stay alive, let alone succeed at whatever you're going there to accomplish. When we drove quietly, I would stare out at the river. There was a part of the mountain where you could see down over the trees, and the river seemed to stretch out all the way past the horizon. And the thick white clouds above us were closer than the river below. The road was cut into the hillside so that you would drive into the clouds about half-way along that leg of the drive, and you would drive out of the clouds again after driving all the way around the mountain, which took almost an hour, and emerge above where you went in. Only this time, instead of the river, you could only see a bed of cloud tops, spread out forever, for a few minutes, before the road veered inward into a crop of tall trees again, dense enough to blot out the whole sky in parts. After this part, we didn't play the radio at all until we were off the mountain again.

"Jesus said you got to love all mankind the way you love your brother. The way you love your momma and me, and the way we love you. So you don't hunt mankind, boy." And with that, dad concludes a lec-ture he's been working on, on and off, since we left home. Along the way, we passed the old farms and fields, after we passed all the warehouses and factories and the big power plant. We drove by these for a while before we turned up the ocean road, which is my favorite part because I can see the ships for a little while, with their huge neon thrusters and giant round hulls. I asked him something about the farms, I don't even remember what it was now. I asked him about the long rows of wooden fences I think. He called them corrals. He said that the farmers would raise animals in those fields, and *use the animals for food, clothing, and labor, which the farmers could trade for money. He said the farmers built the warehouses first, and then the factories after that, and the power plant somewhere in between, and then they just stopped farming after a while, and started filling the warehouses with the stuff they made in the factories. He said that the farmers eventually made so much money that they didn't have to run the factories anymore. They could just buy and sell and trade money. And then there were no more farmers, or factories, and no need for the power plant. My dad had helped build all three. And he helped build some of the big ships out on the ocean road. I can point out which ones sometimes, when they are there. We don't have to come here and hunt. But he says the food is better. Because it still has life in it.*

"But they do it anyway, and they always have, and probably always will, some of them. Every group of people has hunted and/or been hunted by some other group of people." I understand what he is trying to tell me about the corrals, I think. The world is like a corral, and most people are like those animals. He fires off a shot, and for a moment I can't hear the engine or smell the smoke from his lwo-burning cigar, or the oil on the rag stuffed into the folding armrests carved into the old leather seats, or the gasoline fumes drifting through the vents from the big engine under the bigger brown hood just outside the snow-doused windshield in front of us. "People don't listen like they should." He has missed his shot this time, so he rolls up the windows and turns the heater on high. The cabin of the truck heats up just as quickly as it cools down. So Dad makes another science of turning it up and down and on and off in predictive rhythms based on en-tro-py and the principles of thermo-dynamics. He doesn't put out the cigar. It just goes out by itself between his bushy lips. He keeps his window cracked, even as snow begins to fall around us again. He leans back and closes his eyes and has nothing more to say.

(58)

"Wake her." Pike stood at the glass under the red lit conduits, wires, piping, and coils, peering coldly at the mass of flesh and bone tangled in crimson sheets, black on purple in the light, splayed across the steel roundtable, amidst a makeshift assembly of hospital equipment, monitors, and screens still being hastily assembled by technicians. His head hurt, and his bones were weary from the nap he forced himself into while the surgeons worked. She would live, but she had prior neurological traumas, they informed him. Signs of physical abuse or injury during childhood. The bullet passed clean through the frontal lobe. She would need weeks of recuperative post-op and observation, a battery of skills and aptitude tests, and dozens of hours of reconstructive surgery later on. The next few hours were critical.

"WAKE HER!" The doctor shoved his hands in his pockets and turned away from him, staring through the window. The deck and bulkheads swayed gently beneath their feet. She won't wake, he said. Guards and other personnel pushed past them in the passageway. One of them stopped and spoke briefly with Pike, and then shuffled onward down the corridor to catch up with his colleagues. Pike returned to the window, deflated and defeated. "How long!" he barked. The answers did not satisfy him. He studied the matte gold and silver wristwatch beneath his cufflinks. Weeks and months were not hours and days. He had to speak to her before the launch. He had to know the answers to questions he hadn't yet formed, but which presently preoccupied his full attention. She might never speak again. She might have no grasp on reality at all, even if she wakes up on her own, which is the only advisable course, incidentally, and which may be entirely improbable.

More guards pushed past, and this time a bell began ringing loudly throughout all the spaces, a sharp staccato rhythm signaling an intruder aboard. Impossible. But then there were the security forces, assembling en masse around Pike and debating between the bridge and the lower decks. Grisly, unshaven men with liquor on their breath and stunners slung low on leather belts around their hips, dressed in raggy green coveralls without insignia on their collars, stamping about in shiny black boots. Pike stood amidst them, grave-faced, granting his solemn attention until the exchange threatened to devolve into bickering. He didn't want to leave her here, and the doctor's work could not be disturbed. He raised his hands in protest, and the voices around him fell silent. The launch would never take place if the man found him here. One way or the other, no matter what she had to say. There had to be another way to get free. His work demanded precision of thought well beyond what that mess of blasted synapses and crimson in there on that table would ever be capable of.

"We will go to the bridge. Leave her here. Keep working. Send a detachment below to guard the engine room. That's where I would go if I wanted to stop the launch. If he wants her, he'll come here. So a couple of you stay behind to give the doctors a fighting chance. If he really is coming for me, then he'll have to climb. It's our best chance of steering him away from the vitals. C&C is on the oh-seven. Let's go." Pike filed in behind two or three men walking ahead of him, commanding them left and right and up and up through the red-lit passageways. Along the way, the host stopped in an operations space where Pike accessed a command terminal to silence the alarm. Beneath the shrill bell, a barrage of gunfire could be heard somewhere aft and below. The group shoved off down the corridor until they came to the island, and one by one they shuffled up six ladder wells. There, Pike gave instructions to the men to be vigilant, and to try to control their thoughts. He would go above to Observation and try the communications systems. The men assented, and Pike grabbed the rails for his final assent. The level above was quieter than C&C. He welcomed the prospect of a moment's peace. He turned the dogs on the airtight hatch to his cabin, and went inside, sealing them behind himself and plopping down into a dense leather sofa with a half-bottle of Chivas and a cigar, staring out the porthole into space. Soon the exhaustion overcame him, and he slept hard.

(59)

The drugs made time and space relative. Pike's head hurt. Everything stank. Pike felt confused, like he'd been hit with a blunt object, but couldn't tell if it had been ten minutes or ten years ago. It fucking hurt. Waking up in this place was like stumbling out of a bar and into a bus. One of the nuts was babbling in his ear, some methed-out pentecostal gibberish, ceaselessly and aggressively half-whispered to one and all and none. He smelled like piss, and spittle dripped from the corners of his mouth. He was sweaty, just profusely sweaty, like a fat man jogging in August, Pike thought of the wraith-like little creature leaned against him, staring out into the difference and cycling through emotions as though they were fashionistas in a photo-booth taking selfies instead of patients in a ward. Pike shivered, half debating whether to violently shove the thing away in disgust or let it remain for the sake of its warmth. Entropy wasn't doing the thing any favors, and Pike was anemic. Besides, everything smelled like piss anyway.

"...of the fucking flies man. That's what it is. This whole place man! That's the system. That's the design. You see, I was there, and then I was here, with you sorry fucks, and then I was there again, and then I was here, you see? That's the secret you sorry little fucker, you!" The thing stroked Pike's hair lovingly, and absently, and spoke with great enthusiasm. Today was a clear day. Blue skies. "...Napoleon had kept it then the Civil War would have been fought on the banks of the Mississippi, you see? That's what I was gonna try to teach the little fuckers. It wouldn't have mattered to any of them, I was just trying to show them, you know, decisions, decisions, decisions, decisions...choices! That's it, choices. It's all so fragile, you see? And then *the thing*. I never got there. And then it was all just weird. I couldn't take it man, and that's how I wound up here I think. I just went to sleep. And then everything shifted. It's. It's. It's hard. It's hard to explain. See? Don't you see? He helped the enemy of his enemy, and that's how he won, even though he lost, he won, and that's how he does it. He wins by losing. And I can prove it! I can prove it! All I need is some god damned chalk. NURSE!!! god damn this little fucker. NUUUURSSEEE!! I need some god damned chalk!!!" and with that the pathetic little creature sprang to its feet and darted away towards the other side of the enclosure.

Red lights and stone and shadows and pathetic little creatures lost in time. Pike could vaguely recollect through his own haze that he always struggled to remember why he was here. He tried to remember the name of the street he grew up on. He knew he knew it. He could feel it. Right on the tip of his tongue. The drugs made everything relative. If he could just relax, it would come to him, and the rest would fall into place. But his head hurt, and piss stung his nostrils. His chest knotted up during each breath and made his head hurt worse. The erratic noises slowly crept in and out, voices of the deranged and dysfunctional and dislocated. The whole scene was stock, Pike thought. He recognized the characters, their familiar faces drifted alongside dim memories of past interactions or observations, but nothing of substance was evoked by the sight of any of them. The creature was right to disdain them, and then, as if summoned by the thought, Pike became aware of the thing again, right back where he had been moments, or hours ago.

"...duty on the ship once and I was taking a shit right and it was late as fuck at night and we were in the middle of the ocean and there was nothing happening and me and my boys were tight right it was just how it was and I was taking a big shit and I would finish up and wipe and wash my hands and it was late and nobody was up and if they were they'd use a different toilet and wouldn't think twice about the dude taking a shit so when I was done I would just sit back down in the stall and pass the fuck out right and this one time while I was out I met this girl I knew and went out on a date and watched a movie and ate dinner and laughed at her fucking jokes and man I fucked the dog shit out of this girl and while I was doing it I realized you know I realized I was right there on the ship asleep on the shitter the whole time but it was just as real as anything I had ever seen or done man there she was my little porn star girl friend that never talked to me in real life was just there with me the whole night and when we were finally done like when I finished you know I just woke up. Right back there on the ship...So like I'd be there or somewhere you know, like in my real life, and then I'd go to sleep and wake up here with all you little fucks. And then I'd go to sleep here and wake up there and a day would go by. And then two days here. And then three days there. And then minutes, back and forth, and then weeks and even years, spent in this stinking fucking hole with you little fucking losers man. One time I even had a dream of some other place while I was here. But I've got to get back. I can't take it here. I'll do what the mother fucker wants. I don't care anymore. Look at you though man! You're gonna do great things some day, I just know it man. You're a real straight shooter with upper management potential written all over you man.[32] Sitting there in a pile of your own shit, glazed on some good ass dose. Bitch didn't have any chalk." The thing was now weeping uncontrollably, taking fraternal liberties with the hems of Pike's own gown, like a cartoon character. Pike mustered his indignation and pulled away, struggling to his feet. The thing leapt up from the ground as if commanded to do so and tried to help Pike balance himself. Pike dared not attempt completing the motion and protested the thing's aid in the same breath for fear of aneurysm. "...so you don't really know, do you, which one is really which, and man what a mindfuck! You just gotta believe, you know? You just gotta believe in yourself that you're not crazy. I think that's how he does it, too, you know? I think that's how he got this far. He doessn't know he's fucking crazy any more than you little fuckers do." Pike could take no more, and trying to raise himself up, blacked out where he stood before his body could register the impact of hitting the ground again.

---

[32] *Office Space*, directed by Mike Judge (20th Century Fox, 1999).

When he next woke, little had changed. The thing had wandered away in search of more attentive ears. The others had already mostly forgotten the scene, and some openly questioned whether or not it had really happened in the first place. These argued amongst themselves in their own way, with the creature happily asserting his rightful privilege as a firsthand witness. Pike shared the thing's frustrated sense of confinement. His bones ached from their being haphazardly thrown at inconvenient angles against the dingy, painted cinder block walls. His skull felt swollen like the belly of a pregnant tick. Whole chunks of himself seemed missing and inaccessible. He longed for the will to muster his strength against the fog. He could form the thoughts of rebellion against this dull delirium, but could not begin to bring himself to action in this condition. The pain was such that it superseded the vanities and pretenses of liberty and institutionalization. He had no head for the vagaries of psychology. Just enough head to appreciate the grim irony and mourn the lot of people stuck in this position, doped out of any reasonable use of the faculties required to demonstrate lucidity. A snake eating its own ass. Pike envied the creature's alternate life, real or imagined, and wished him **g**odspeed. This was no kind of life, and any other seemed like a Utopianist refuge. He mused to himself sardonically that some system of reason had put him here, some consequence of his own behavior or actions, but he could not recall the events or circumstances in any detail. Was he old? Was he young? Did he have family? Was someone out there looking for him? Was he a prisoner of some kind, as the thing insisted? Or had someone out there had him put here? For his own good? For the good of others? For some nefarious purpose? Pike had imprints of cold, impatient, disinterested nurses rebutting his random lines of inquiry, and of relenting before creating scenes like the creature always did. That was Pike's barometer for madness, and the basis of his projected aura of quiet stoicism and confident sense of cognitive superiority.

"I'm not Jewish, I'm POLISH you filthy fucking animal!" There was a scene developing. A fight! Pike struggled against the perpetually dimming lights to distinguish the forms and shapes muddling about in the shadows across the way. The creature's honor had been insulted, and as his primitive instincts prevailed over his better angels, he threw his fists into a fray and a brawl ensued. Through the din, Pike made out the indefinite but suggestively feminine form huddled in a ball on the farthest wall, seeming to leer at him with contempt and disgust from under the dark veil of a hood formed of a dirty gray wool blanket. Pike looked away, desiring no form of confrontation, subtle or overt. *The difference between genius and madness is just self-control.* The creature would have them believe he was cured by his words while his behavior vindicated their skepticism. That's how Pike would get out of here. And why the maniacal creature and all his kindred spirits in this zoo would remain imprisoned in this god forsaken place forever. Pike closed his eyes and tried to breathe. He leaned against the wall, glancing across the desecrated field of linoleum and lunatics at his shadowy new protagonist, sensing some indeterminable familiarity. Some resonating recognition across the addled relativities of time and space. He pressed at his temples with his fingers, intending to push the pain away from the forefront of his senses, but pulled them away in shock as he felt the blood and bandages, perceiving them for the first time, as razors shot through his brain and spine and shoulders and chest, as convulsions surged from the core of his being and threw his seizing body into electrical rigor mortis, as foam and vomit and snot rolled freely from his face onto the numbingly frigid tiles, as his hands and arms became tangles of wiry, wrought iron knuckles and elbows. As infinite blackness overwhelmed him, and even the pain finally faded to black, Pike remembered the girl. And then nothing.

(60)

Pike awoke to officers entering the room, quietly informing him that his patient had regained consciousness. The clock on the wall read 12:08. As he pulled himself to his feet, he looked one of the officers directly in the eye and spoke the word "mud." The officer silently nodded affirmation and left the room. The other turned curtly, and followed. Pike made his way down the corridor some distance behind the others, trying to shake off the dizziness of sleep, and trying to recall some elusive part of some fragmented dream he remembered having. He reprimanded himself in his father's voice, and demanded focus. He still had no idea what he was supposed to ask the girl. Why she had failed seemed like a poor place to start. Good cop? Bad Cop? Pike had ample carrots and sizable sticks, but he had to find out what was truly meaningful to her or his charisma and consequences counted for nothing. He wanted to hear her voice. He wanted to know how many times they had met. He wanted to know what the fuck it all meant, but he was afraid that if he just asked her, pointblank, straight away, he faced the bleak and dispiriting risk of coming face to face with the rote absurdity of it all, of confronting at long last, after all of this, the helpless reality that she didn't understand any of it one iota more than he did. He was more afraid of square one than of the devil himself. And he was afraid that such compulsions were the stock vulnerabilities of determined men, always undermining benevolent intentions and best laid plans in the end. Would it be worse if she said nothing at all?

Pike approached a group of officers and doctors loitering at the observation portal and dispersed them with a sharp word. Stepping up to the glass, he allowed his eyes to focus on his own reflection for a moment, before peering through at the wounded girl on the other side. He sensed something was different. Something didn't make sense. His head was wrapped in bandages and nearly soaked through with crimson. She was sleeping soundly, unevenly splayed across a tiny leather sofa in fatigues and draped in a heavy nylon ship's coat, a mess of shiny, clean, blonde ringlets. The ship was quiet. Something had changed. His head hurt. He thought if he could just relax his mind, it would come to him, and then everything else would fall into place. Suddenly, in the distance, echoing through the corridor, he heard the staccato rhythm of the bells. And somewhere deep inside himself, he heard his father's voice. *WAKE HER! WAKE HER NOW!!!*

(The Launch)
(61)
7:39 am, Saver's Parking Lot, 1st Contact,

An elderly lady exits a grocery store pushing a cart full of bags. She places her steps carefully, humming along with a familiar old tune she can't quite name, but can certainly place. The eastern sun blinds her, momentarily, casting the landscape of ticky-tacky housetops and dry old pines into a circus of shadows and blind spots. As she pauses for a moment to steady herself, a peculiar whirring sound becomes audible in her hearing aid. She looks out into the parking lot, left and right, like her mamma taught her, looking for the scooter or one of those fancy european cars or whatever else could be making that noise. Another lady, an acquaintance, squeezes past her with her squeaking, knob-wheeled buggy full of vittles, offering a polite salutation. The second lady hears the sound and connects it to the puzzled look of distraction on the first lady's face. As they both look around for the source, one of them at last looks up, and then muffles a startled little yelp before tapping her dazed friend on the shoulder and pointing up at the little contraption floating above them, suspended from eight little spinning fan blades. In twenty seven years since the Saver's had been open, and in the eighteen years before then, when it had been a Jim's (they both remembered when old Jim died, though neither of them had thought about him for at least ten years or more, they would mutually recall later in the afternoon, in a phone call), the two ladies had never seen anything like this before. It looks like a child's toy, one suggested. The other argues that it looks too heavy and expensive to be a child's toy. They share these thoughts in the space of a few moments, neither of them particularly alarmed, but both very curious about its purpose, and perhaps its intentions. Presently, lights appeared and a screen, and then a voice. Two moments later, both of the ladies walked away and went on about their lives, half-chuckling with dismissive contempt, but each also a little disturbed by the thing they had witnessed in the Saver's Parking Lot. Dozens of other strangers would share their experience that morning in the same parking lot, and most of them would respond with annoyance, confusion, and, on a couple of occasions, outright hostility.

(62)

```
/0300820/0739A/3642.16'N/107"12.62
'W/EMC&*I.vtc$A.001.IRP
    <Dock:Release> <Interact>
    Record;      Display        (:Video)
IPQCVR:******/*****/*?:?{*=+1}.irp
    Display    (:Audio)<>    "Greetings
Shoppers, On a scale of one to ten, how
would  you  rate  your  experience  at
Saver's?"</>
<Input><Record!*.irp><!*></>
<Interpret><*.irp><///……..we enjoyed it
fine       thank        you.          ..
…..//><est/ref/call:products#*.irp>
    Display (:Audio)<>  "Thank you for
your  response,  and  thank  you  for
shopping  at  Saver's. This  information
will  help  Saver's  better  serve  your
needs  in  the  future."</>  Display
(:Audio)<>   "Has   this   interaction
affected how you feel about Saver's, or
your  desire  to  remain  a  customer?"</>
<Input><Record!*.irp><!*></>
```

```
<Interpret><*.irp></ /…….. Are     you     a
robot   or   something………. [facial   cue
recognition  protocol,  index  FCrp*.irp
Values      -x,-y,-x,-y,-x,-y///recovery/
Display (:Audio)<> "Do not be alarmed,
we  are  trying  something  new!  Saver's
has   partnered   with   the   consumer
research division of Centron to bring
you  this  new,  state  of  the  art,
interactive  market  research  technology.
By  answering  a  few,  completely  random
survey  questions  about  yourselves,  your
lifestyles,   and   the   products   you
consume,  you  can  earn  credits  and
rewards that you can use when you shop
at  any  of  Centron's  hundreds  of
partnered   businesses   across   the
country. Would you like to participate
in          the          survey?"</>
<Input><Record!*.irp><!*></>
<Interpret><*.irp></ /…….. no  thank  you
have  a  nice  day  come  on  let's  go  this
thing  is  weird  I  know  it  is  I  hope
these  things  aren't  here  to  stay  I
won't  shop  here  anymore  this  is  weird
let's  go  okay  okay…….>>///recovery/
Display  (:Audio)<>  "Thank  you  for
volunteering…"<Input;   Compile><Record
Data*.irp></>       <Export      RD*.Irp>
<Dock:Return>
<Connect:Host,Upload*.Irp> <Ready>
```

(63)

<Begin Transcript: Jones, T., et al, Vs Centron;
Deposition Statement Jones. T., 1/7>

"No one would talk to them. I tried a dozen different
venues. Grocery stores, gas stations, bars, a mall, people
everywhere just ignored them. I was heartbroken. I had

thousands of research hours invested in the software, and I was on the hook for about twenty of the drones, all of the cameras, and two server racks at City U, for about six weeks worth of AI analysis. And in the end, I couldn't sell a single one of them. I almost drank myself into a grave, and I hadn't even made it out of college yet. I miss those days, though. Things were so much simpler, so much less intense, before the whole world disassembled itself for these monsters. But the lesson turned out to be worth the suffering and the embarrassment. People don't want to talk to the machines. They want to push a button; they want prefab voice commands. They don't want the machines to interact as peers, as equals, as cohabitors. They won't ever trust what they don't understand. The machine must learn to function without the voluntary input. I envisioned an application environment in which the machine and the client and the consumer exchanged roles, for the purpose of developing an AI. The industry mentality is always to produce a service product. My so-called genius innovation came a few years after the Centron project. We got a grant to produce a model of our role-based adaptation, which was an old X-2 unit we had actually stolen and reprogrammed in Pike's garage. Pike's part of the idea was to represent a virtual enclosure, like a field of influence. This helped us with geographical logistics as well as process delegation, both of which became independently competitive industries based on science we pioneered. My part was the concept of reversing the service model and creating an executive archetype, based on spontaneous initiative. At first, we confined the scope of those initiatives to small indices of available goods and services. Within six months, our little brain-baby was not only engineering advanced electronics and data processing systems for militaries and other international corporations, but it was also managing those contracts, procurements, and acquisitions for the clients themselves in real time. To anyone with a bird's eye view, it should have been clear, very early on, what the thing was building. But none of us could see it.

Money was raining down all around us like leaves in the windy woods in autumn. The machine was designed to comprehend itself as a sort of contractor. That was the key to our architecture. All of the other suites were conceived to interpret and then render token services. Thousands of iterations failed to advance science because not a single one of them was really ever designed to think for itself. They had brilliant medical applications, communications applications, bookkeeping, surveillance, even gaming applications. But these were always conceived as client-side applications. We wanted to build a machine capable of replicating the role of the client. It was supposed to conceive of its own projects, organize the labor, and contract out. It was supposed to comprehend itself as a boss, instead of as a worker. To accomplish this, we taught it to perceive the world through available resources and human capital, and to propose and implement adaptations. We compiled a matrix of self-worth initiatives informed by simulated and sample public responses to those projects. In a sense, we created a form of intelligence that could experiment in a kind of random way, then submit its results and methodology for feedback. By this process, we associated its creative processes with self-automating demand research. In other words, if it made something that made people respond favorably, it learned from that success, and those lessons informed its system of value judgments which, in turn, informed its developmental prerogatives. The public never had to see or hear or communicate with the machine for this process to work. They just had to interact with a product the machine produced. The results were overwhelmingly positive. We began to wonder if our little brain-baby wasn't destined for greater things. Managing world economies, exploring the stars, solving real world problems. By then, we had had plenty of attention from the movers and shakers, the people who could take us to the next step, and we reached out to them, which I thought was the right thing to do, but sometimes I think we went about it the wrong way. Pike was never one to leave anything to chance.

He manipulated things, I don't know how he does it, but he has a gift. He manipulated things so that when it came time to take that step, I would be forced out, and he would take over the project. And he got his way. Pike always got his way."

</End

Transcript>

(64)

Pike was comfortless. His spine and pelvis were sore against the concrete and cinder. The dim yellow light made indefinite the lines where one wall ended and another began. The other nuts were quiet. Some slept, others toiled with their own raveled circumstances internally, staring vacantly off into wherever, or into their folded laps, or the black of their pressed palms, but she sat on the far wall, alone, staring daggers in his direction. Her face was darkness and shadow, and he could not make out her eyes against the humming electric fog, but he could feel it. He wondered if and when he would sleep again in this place, and if he would awaken aboard his ship in the so-called real world, hunted and haunted by the thing he thought he had been chasing. The space which he presently inhabited was bound along the perimeter by four long block walls, surrounding an internal enclosure where he assumed the staff of this place, if it were attended by anyone at all, conducted their observations and stored the wares necessary for daily operations. He had not yet mustered the strength to stand and explore, so far as he could remember, which was about as far as he felt he could crawl if he doubled over onto all fours and clawed at the dirty ground with all his strength. He felt immobilized by a great weight, though his arms and legs were free of shackles or restraints. Intense lethargy bound his hind end to the floor and his back to the wall, and he had no recollection of ever occupying any other position here but the one his body now claimed. The drugs, he supposed, had rendered him docile and compliant by way of severe fatigue. In this vegetative state, he could not surmount the distance of maybe ten or so yards it would take to scramble across from one wall to its adjacent companion to speak to her, and he had not the breath or strength to force more than a whisper, which even the dim din of fans and snoring nuts would suppress. She might have been a million miles away, and he guessed that she was similarly imprisoned within her own skin, or she would have traversed those miles and more to confront him.

The wretched, piss-soaked creature had returned while he was unconscious, and was now fast asleep and leaning against his shoulder again in a display of familiarity which Pike found nearly as intolerable as the thought of waking him in a fumbling contest against neurological inertia and gravity, only to be trapped in another senseless, skittering monologue about heaven and hell and dreams and the here and the there and the whims of a messianic devil pushing pawns across the planes to thwart the divine systems of creation. So Pike sat like a stone against the fluttering tide of his own dull heartbeat, consciously motionless, exerting his defiance inwardly with the last of his teetering wits. His mind raced from broken fragment to broken fragment and back again. The primitive inclination to escape was paramount, yet buttressed on all sides by the rationalized futility of any physical attempt. He heard a fit of coughing and wheezing from somewhere opposite the walls of the internal enclosure, followed by a spasm of retching which turned his own irritable stomach in a fit of involuntary biological sympathy which his body retained, yet his mind had long since relinquished. He hated this place and everyone in it. Captivity bred weakness of body and mind. He didn't need his piss-soaked narrator to explain the premise of this prison, lazily contrived as an asylum. Doubt and helplessness had already overwhelmed the lot of them. Doubt and helplessness were his antagonists here, brandishing drug-addled fog and confusion as their weapons. His waning pride was the only advocate against surrender. Doubt and helplessness were the platonic ideal for which these cinder walls manifested form. He wondered idly which would take longer to claw through with blistered, bleeding fingers. He wondered how long his mind would last here before his body finally surrendered. He heard the muffled sound of weeping, bouncing through the corridors from one wall to the next in an endless spiral of right angles, searching for some ulterior pathway out of the trap and finding none. Another prideful spirit breaking in real time, as all present bore witness.

The minutes dragged into hours, maybe days. There was nothing to mark time but his own countless breaths, and even if he tried to count them, the numbers jumbled in his head before he could reach the double digits. He could not recall eating. There were no bells or whistles or alarms to signal sleep or wake. The lights were always on, useless as they were. The thing beside him had said this was a dream, and Pike pondered the irony of accepting any morsel of reality proffered by the delusional and insane. The restless creature beside him shifted occasionally, and at one point seemed to wipe his nose on Pike's shoulder before twisting into some modified posture and drifting away again. Powerful drugs, Pike mused. So much so that he had no recollection of taking them, or of ever seeing the nurse the thing had called out for. Some omnipresent but inaccessible authority governed this facility, just as in the world beyond it, if there was anything at all behind these walls except the cold void of infinite nothing.

Pike felt a little tear of blood running down the side of his face and recalled his bandaging. He vaguely remembered the sound of a gunshot, somewhere in the hollow trance of some passing dream, and wondered if he had done it to himself. If that was how he got here in the first place. He wondered what could have ever possessed him to do such a thing. He tried to remember being awake at all, in any other time and place but this one. He had a ship, or so he had thought, if only briefly. What kind of ship though? What color was it? Who else served aboard it, and what was its mission? Which was the dream, this asylum, or that one? Which life was fiction? He was chasing his own tail with no kind of certainty to be derived from anything his beleaguered senses would bring him. His nerves were failing him on all fronts. His vision blurred, the smell of piss was present, but seemed much farther away than the ragdoll beside him. He could touch the ground with his palms, but it was neither warm nor cold. Even the hysterical weeper in the distance seemed to chuckle in between sobs. Dissonant madness assailed him from within and without, seeping out of the walls, the light fixtures, the throats and bowels of his fellow prisoners, and from the dying star at the very core of his own being, most of all.

"What did you love most in the world you remember?" The creature beside him had stirred and was now rubbing the sleep out of his eyes. He turned himself to face Pike and was giving him this surprisingly lucid, penetrating look of curiosity mixed with empathy. "You look like shit, man. I can tell you're starting to break down. You've got to hold on. Or you'll wind up like the rest of these sorry little fuckers. You've got to hold on to something that is real. That's how you keep it all together. Try to think. What did you love? What about your life mattered the most to you?"

Pike stared into the creature's eyes, betraying a twinge of empathy of his own as he did so. The sound of another human voice brought him an unexpected feeling of comfort, and for the first time he found himself contemplating what comparable suffering this strange soul must have suffered along the parallel path to this infernal place. "How is it that you could stand up and walk around and even fight that other guy over there before? I can barely move my lips to speak to you. I feel like I'm doped to the fucking gills. Don't they give you the same shit they've pumped into me? What the hell do they serve here, and why do I feel glued to the floor, but you can wa-"

The thing broke out into a kind of sad, maniacal laughter and Pike trailed off, annoyed and resentful. He wished he could find something funny about his situation, but he didn't like the idea of it being himself.

"You think they drugged you? Do you remember taking anything?" The thing smiled wryly through broken yellow teeth.

"I can barely remember my own fucking name. I can't remember how I got here or why, or what happened with this-" he reached up to his bandaged and carefully pressed his temples with his finger tips, but recoiled and cried out in pain as lightning shot through his flesh. The world around him wavered, and he nearly blacked out, but the thing reached out and grabbed his wrists with both hands and held them away from his face.

"It's not drugs, man. No one has given you anything. Not food, not pills, not forms or even a hard time. You haven't taken a shit or wiped your own ass or taken a single step away from where you are right now. It's your mind that does it to you. You don't belong here and you know it, you can feel it in your bones. You haven't broken yet and accepted this place as real and tangible and consequential. Once you do..." He released Pike's wrists and leaned back and stared off into some choice space on the wall. "Then you'll be free to move about the cabin."

"But you said it isn't real. You said this was a dream I'm stuck in, and that I'll wake up again in my own life at some point, and then back and forth and back and forth and all that."

"And you're starting to believe me aren't you." It wasn't a question. "That big ass bullet-riddled brain of yours can't come up with anything else that makes sense."

"So I *was* shot?" Neon red numbers flashed in Pike's mind and he felt thunder in his temples. He pressed his eyes closed and pushed his fingers into his ears as throbbing waves of ringing fire echoed across his nervous system. The thing seemed to take no notice, but waited patiently for Pike to regain himself.

"You *were* shot. Yes. And also yes, because you're about to ask. *You Shot.* And once he's broken you, the pain will go away, and the fog will clear up a little, and you'll begin to regain your strength. It's like some weird psychological balancing act. Your mind rejects this place, so your body doesn't work. I don't know if it's really a dream or hell itself or what. But it works the same way I guess. Once your mind breaks, and you accept the idea that you're really crazy and that you belong here, it becomes real. He can't control your life anymore, because you made a choice. You made *the choice*. But he doesn't just let you win like that. It's never that easy." The thing found this part intensely amusing, and was soon laughing uncontrollably. "You can't just *blow your own fucking brains out* and win." Minutes passed before the creature's grim sense of humor became a breathless sigh and then silence again.

Pike tried to gather his own nerves and process all the pieces. He had shot himself. His body was in that damned leather chair on the oh-eight. There had been an intruder, and he was being hunted by the thing he had been hunting for. But conflicting memories collided. The girl had shot herself, and she also had not shot herself. It didn't make any sense. The creature beside him was watching him carefully now.

"What did you love most in your life? You never answered me. What do you have that you can hold on to here? Try to muddle through the fog and remember."

Pike stared back at the creature, and saw the person. An unlikely friend, doomed and defeated, but left here by the fates to serve the grand design one last time, nonetheless. Sitting there, soaked through to its bones in piss and misery, hopeless, lost, and driven totally mad by some cruel, mythical construct, their own common antagonist, and yet some ironclad component of its humanity remained untouched, buried deep beneath the bones themselves, burning as bright as a billion stars, bright enough to illuminate even this thick, pervasive darkness. Suddenly, the riddle collapsed in Pike's mind, and he was ashamed and fearful.

"Myself." Pike whispered through welling tears. "I loved myself more than anything in the world. Not family, not friends, not lovers, not children. Not pets. Not hobbies. Only my work. I loved myself above all else." Pike was weeping now, and his sobs echoed throughout the corridors, around the circle of right angles, and back into his own ears. He could hear himself crying from a distance on either side, and it was debilitating. He tried in vain to compose himself, to muscle through it, but he could feel the wires inside him snapping, one by one, he was losing control.

The person beside him looked on with skepticism. "I don't know how much that's going to help you here, my friend. Sounds like you've got a pretty tall hill to climb with that." He paused for a moment, studying the failing spirit before him and trying to think of something to say that would matter. He seemed surprised by the abrupt confession, and moments passed in near silence. A sadness came over him, and after a while, he took a deep breath and spoke softly. "I loved a girl once. We had a child together, before I went away. Before the thing came and found me in a moment of desperation and convinced me to help him do-- whatever the hell it is he's trying to do. He said he could give her back to me, and in some other life he told her the same lie. He took me to her, but it was a different person. It was a different version of the world. A different timeline or something. I don't understand any of it. But it wasn't her. She didn't know who I was, she didn't remember me or having ever met me or loved me or lost me or any of it. And that girl was searching for someone else entirely, and he got her the same way he got me. The man she loved no longer existed, and the man she remembered didn't know her at all. And I suffered. And eventually she suffered the same, and that was as much as we would ever have in common."

Pike's senses were returning, slowly, through a storm of pain and revelation. The pieces were coming together. "I don't believe in the devil." He forced the words through clenched lips.

"Well buddy, the Devil believes in you."

Pain surged through Pike's temples as his heartbeat quickened. He remembered Tyberius. He remembered the machines, and the launch. He remembered the girl, and the torrent of thoughts overwhelmed him. He looked out again across the distance to the far wall and saw her there, and understood, albeit in wide clumsy brushstrokes, as the blackness closed in from his periphery and his mind reeled into oblivion. He lifted his hand toward her and tried to wave, and then nothing. *Infinitum Nihil.*

(65)

Bright white light stirred his broken mind, and Pike opened his eyelids and tried to see. After a few moments of delirium and blindness passed, he could begin to make out the familiar implements of the sickbay aboard his own ship. The bare steel bulkheads, the exposed ventilation and wiring conduits that lined the plastered ceiling above, the stainless steel cabinets. He was sprawled across an operating table, draped in a sterile purple gown and a gray, woolen blanket. A few of his men stood peering nervously through the observation window at their captain. A nurse with a clipboard busied herself about a variety of machines, writing down numbers and checking the saline bag slowly feeding fluids into his bloodstream. Pike turned his head slightly towards the hospital chair he knew to be to his right side, fully expecting to see the thing sitting there watching him intently, and there it was. Pike closed his eyes, and opened them again, just to be sure. "Nurse."

The young lady nearly jumped out of her skin, dropping her clipboard and nearly knocking over his IV as she spun around on her heels. She stared at Pike in utter disbelief. The men outside rushed into the room and crowded around the table, looking pale and afraid, as if they had all witnessed the same ghost at once. No one answered him right away, they just stood there in silence looking back and forth from each other to him in glances, and in a moment the surgeon rushed into the room.

"What the hell is going on, I told you all to wait outside. I specifically told you not to enter this room under any circumstances. You are supposed to be standing guard god Dam-"

"SIR!" The nurse squeaked, cutting him off, and pointing to Pike on the table. The surgeon looked down at his patient and gasped.

"It's not possible. Sir, can you hear my voice? Can you see me?" The surgeon bent down and placed his forefingers on Pike's neck and counted the seconds on his wristwatch. Pike pulled his free arm off the table and shoved the man's hand away. "I can see you just fine. Now get the fuck out."

No one moved.

"He just left surgery six hours ago, there's no way in hell he should be awake right now. Hell, I didn't think he would wake up at all!" There was commotion in the room as they one and all decided to express their mutual astonishment in turns, and they spoke over one another with questions and exclamations, until Pike raised his hand again, and this silenced them all at once as they all turned their gaze back to him.

"I said GET THE FUCK OUT. I want the room cleared, and I want the entire deck cleared of all personnel immediately. You there, leave your comms here on the table beside me, and then I want EVERYONE OUT!"

"But sir, we need to-"

"I SAID GET OUT! THAT'S A FUCKING ORDER!" Pike clenched his eyes closed and tried to regain his breath. "I'll call you when I want you to come back."

Again, no one moved right away, which annoyed him, but he gave them the moment they needed to process their own shock, and slowly they began filing out into the corridor. One of the security guards was the last to turn and follow the rest out, and Pike called out to him. "You there, how long until the launch?"

The man turned and paused for a second and stammered, "Sir? The launch? You mean we are still going through with it?"

"Well why the hell wouldn't we. HOW LONG?"

"The launch is, well, if we're really still doing it, you know, after..." the man swept his hands over Pike like a magician baffled by his own magic trick, "after this... Sir the launch was scheduled to take place in about ten more hours. We are passing the equator; soon we'll dock at the Port and offload onto the *Epicurean*. Shall I inform the crew to proceed as planned?"

"Nothing changes. Do you hear me? Tell them to carry out the procedure to the very letter. Tell them that rumors of my demise have been greatly exaggerated." Pike clenched his eyes again and tried to breathe. The pain in his temples was intense, and apparently plainly visible.

The man stared down at him in disbelief, trying to retain his bearing but faltering. "Sir, I will do as you command."

"Good, now clear the fucking deck like I *commanded*. And soldier, one more thing."

The man had turned to go, and was clearly to do so, but spun back around to receive the request.

"I want you to rip that camera out of the corner there and take it with you. Yes, that one. Is there a problem? Good, now do as I ask and do it quickly. We don't have all day. Don't worry about why, just do as you're told. Don't worry about breaking the damned thing, I said rip it out! Pull it down, just yank the fucking thing out of the wall, see, there you go. Just like that, now GO!" The man gathered up the tangled wires with the device in his arms and rushed out of the room, bewildered. Pike could hear the man yelling down the corridor, ordering the rest of the crew off the deck and shouting his own rebukes at anyone who didn't respond with haste and deliberation. Pike waited until the voices and the shuffling of boots on the steel grating passed into the ladderwells and disappeared. Then he turned his head back to the thing in the chair and studied it carefully before finally speaking aloud.

"Well, here we are. Together at last. You have my full attention."

The thing raised one coal black hand to its chin and smiled a toothy smile under dark eyes. Pike could glimpse something like cool admiration somewhere in the depths of its amused expression.

"I am going to tell you a story. I want you to relax now. You are safe for the moment. I am not going to let you go just yet. Please forgive me. I mean you no harm. When you've heard my story, I will let you go, and you may follow me if you choose..."

(Infinite Nothing)
(66)

I don't know what I'm doing. I'm tired. I'm alone. I hate everyone and everything. I don't eat. I don't sleep. I haven't seen my kid in months. My gold-bricking, ball-breaking ex-wife tells me I look like shit, like I need that from her, or from anybody. I don't even go outside anymore. The sun hurts my eyes. The neighbors stare at me like I'm some kind of fucking animal. I wake up drinking whiskey out of a bottle when most people are getting home from their McJobs and kissing their ugly, ungrateful little rugrats on the head and arguing with the people they love over burnt meat and sugar water. When the sun goes down I drink black coffee and write until it comes back up again, and then I jerk off and crash. But I don't sleep. I just fucking lie there while my body dies for a few hours, because I'm afraid to close my eyes. I'm afraid of him. I'm sick of him, and I'm sick of all of this shit too. This story doesn't even make sense anyway. It's out of order. There are huge gaps, plot holes, contradictions, whatever. No one is ever going to publish this nonsense. And even if he ropes some other idiot from the industry into sending this shitheap to distribution, no one is ever going to believe any of it. It's a work of fiction, and that's all it will ever be to anyone except for him and for me. And I can't for the life of me figure out why he doesn't get it. This is beneath me. I could have been somebody. I could have done something with my stupid little life. I didn't spend ten years in college to be the devil's fucking biographer.

I'm head over heels in love with this girl I know, and when I look at myself in the mirror I don't even feel worthy to stand in her shadow. I'm a con artist, a fraud, a fucking parasite. I'm a washed out little puppet on a string, dancing along to the rhythmless noise of a superhuman sociopath's nervous breakdown. Some part of me thinks that if I finish this story, maybe she'll read it someday and at least know how I felt about her, before I sold my soul anyway. I live in this delusional fantasy world sometimes; it's a place I escape to when I just can't anymore. The story is a hit, audiences everywhere totally get it. Some illiterate suit out west sees a cash grab and wants to pitch a movie. I laugh at him because I know he doesn't get it, but I take the fucking money, because what else am I gonna do, right? People want to watch superheroes. They want to see the good guy win every time. They want to believe that's what's really in store for them at the end. And I would be just like them, except I've already seen how the story ends, and it's not pretty. It's not poetry. There are no happy endings. There's no *denouement*. There is no sweeping overture, no heartfelt reconciliation. No second chance at redemption, and no magical fucking sky wizard waiting at the end of it all to usher in a new age of peace and fulfillment, to hold our sweet little lilly-white hands and embrace us with a father's eternal love before escorting us into the promised land.

In the end, there are only two choices. We meander on our meaningless way through the cosmos, counting our beans and marking off the endless days just waiting for catastrophe to strike, and then we all spend our last precious moments in existence clawing each other's eyes and throats out like savage cannibals. Or, and oh boy do I hate to spoil the big surprize, the other choice is to be sucked out into the cold, quiet, hateful vacuum of space in the blink of an eye, caught unawares in the midst of our pointless, petty, oblivious pursuits, with our very screams of terror freezing in our throats before they pass our lips. It doesn't even matter who wins. That's the new revelation of our time. That's the story he wants to tell. It's either one vain, self-absorbed, all-powerful, ego-maniacal asshole, or it's the other. It's not even really a choice. It's all just one big fairy tale, and one fairy tale ending is just as good as another. Maybe that's why nobody reads any more. Print is deader than disco. All writers are hacks. Reporters, journalists, historians, and philosophers, they're all the same. Even the most gifted among them winds up in the same dirty little rat race, because we're all taught that this is a job, a career, rather than our profoundly singular primary mode of self expression. We're taught that it's work. And we're all duped into the same blasphemous compromise. We prostrate ourselves to editors and publishers who second guess our every creative impulse until all that's left is some vague, bland reflection of the boring, soulless, inferior bullshit they think will sell, and we let them do it to us every single time. Because we need the money more than we need to possess and influence our own culture. So we trade our self-respect for the promise of a few hundred thousand units, haphazardly scattered upon abandoned bookshelves across the country, or buried on page six of the local town-rag, or worst of all, "preserved" in the forgotten archives of some local shithole campus for future generations to continue the time-honored tradition of disregarding.

I just wanted to impress a girl. I pictured us on a yacht somewhere, laughing and drinking in the sun without a care in the world, looking back and looking down at all the toiling little twats behind us who weren't lucky enough to be born with the light we possess and which we ourselves didn't earn and don't even deserve. We're a celebrity couple, and we never have to work again because we cleared five million units in seventeen languages. Because we defied convention. Because some parasitic freelancer out there thought it was cool that I was ex-communicated from a religion I don't even believe in for writing a book that will be forgotten within a couple of seasons. Because some lost, miserable little shit somewhere quoted something I wrote in his manifesto before murdering a handful of classmates or blowing his own brains out in front of a camera phone. Because *our* book was banned by some podunk evangelical paper-mill somewhere in southeast Bumfuck. Because a handful of humorless zealots decided to buy a hundred copies and burn them in one of their dim, perennial public rituals of intellectual impotence. Because we got to spend five minutes answering the most banal questions imaginable on some late-night television talk show somewhere in the Big City. Because some sniveling, talentless little shit somewhere decided they could skip over all the blood, sweat, and tears and claim I stole it from them, dragging my lawyers into litigation for years to finally have the fate of my life's work decided by some officious, illiterate circuit judge on not so much as the flip of a coin in his pocket. Because the litterati kiss our fucking asses every single day and tell people we are the *avant garde,* that some day history will credit us with single-handedly rescuing the human imagination from the doldrums of its own perpetual malaise.

Even if I tell them to their faces that history just ends, abruptly, right in the middle of some regular day, a few hours after some apocalyptic first-world lunatic cultist decides to press a button on a machine. That we are just all here, floating aimlessly on a little speck of dust in the middle of a colossal gas storm, and that everything we've ever made, everything we've ever known, every trace of our puny little existence will eventually be obliterated in a fiery inferno because we are all pathologically incapable of putting down our petty bullshit long enough to work together at a common cause.

We aren't the spark, and we certainly aren't the fucking revolution. And I am no prophet. I am no leader of men. I whited out my own name.[33] And to be completely honest, I don't give a fuck what happens to this species. Maybe I used to. But I've already seen the future, because he has shown it to me. There's no place in it for people like me. For whoever I used to be, anyway. And now? Now I'm nobody at all. I'm anonymous. You wouldn't recognize me sitting next to you on a bus. I'm a figment of your imagination. The sad thing is, it's the happiest I've ever been. Obscurity is my comfort zone. I don't trust or respect human beings. I have no faith in humanity, or their jealous gods, or their phony heroes, or their children's stories about the past, present, and future. Or even their scapegoat devils. The irony is disgusting. In the end, all he wanted was to keep you all alive a little longer than you deserve. And for what? Just to be right. To have the last word. To prove he knew better all along. To prove that it was his vision that triumphed in the end. Vanity is the true story of creation, and it sickens me. He doesn't give a shit about you anymore than I do, or any more than HE does, for that matter. Good versus evil is just the collision of two selfish egos, played out over the ages. Why anyone would follow either of these malicious mother fuckers completely escapes me.

And we're all taught from cradle to grave to trust the plan. Trust the Plan! Your lives matter and you have value, but only because He has a plan for you. It doesn't matter what the plan is, and it's a sin against god even to wonder what the plan is. You almost have to be crazy to see through it. Something has to be wrong with you in the first place to withstand a whole lifetime of brainwashing and conditioning which precipitates the herd mentality. We were all made to follow in the first place. Servility is our birthright. Subservience is our purpose. And the only one out there who really wants to set us free just wants our obedience in exchange for our so-called liberation. It's a catch twenty-two. A sick joke with no punchline. And the vast majority of

---

[33] Marilyn Manson, "Man That You Fear," on *Antichrist Superstar*, Nothing Records, 1997.

human beings swallowed it whole. Suckers, one and all. Even those precious few with the will to reject the lies, those who would try to stand athwart history yelling STOP will only succeed in dissipating their own energies, struggling to swim against the current, only to become exiles, pariahs, and martyrs to a lost cause.[34] There is no salvation, no forgiveness. [35] And no one here gets out alive. [36]

I've been reading this story to myself, over and over again, trying to understand it. Trying to figure out how it should end. Trying to understand what you want, what he wants, and what it is exactly that I really want. I've lived in despair for longer than I care to remember. I am his slave, typing away into the long shadows of the night, trying to put his words onto paper, if only to get them out of my head. I'm running in circles. Chasing my own tail. The story doesn't belong to me. He's the **g**od damned Devil. One would think he should possess the capacity to use a fucking typewriter on his own. Or a pen and some paper. Or lamb's blood on a fucking cave wall for all I care. Why me? Why did I have to go through this? I was chosen to deliver the message, he tells me. And there is no message to deliver. My fingers ache. My mind is giving way to madness. I want to sleep the sleep of the dead and dream of nothing, infinite nothing. Maybe he thinks I lack the courage to escape him the way Vickie and Carl and the others did. But I'll tell you what separates me from them. They were afraid of dying, and so they were careful. They understood their leaps of faith to be the test, and liberation their reward. They had to prove they would suffer for their choice in order to be absolved of their sins and redeemed of their suffering. I've got a different idea. It isn't just him I want to escape. It's the whole damned charade.

---

[34] Rest in Peace, William F. Buckley, Jr., 1925-2008.

[35] Marilyn Manson, "Reflecting God," on *Antichrist Superstar*, Nothing Records, 1997.

[36] Jerry Hopkins and Daniel Sugerman. *No One Here Gets Out Alive.* (Erie, PA: Warner Books, 1980).

I bought a gun today. It's cute, it's small, and fits right in my pocket.[37] A snub nose .38, just like in the story. Anyone can get one now, you know. And the powers that be will fight for that right with every fiber of their being, because it suits them to watch us all tear each other apart. King Conflict keeps us tuned in, paranoid, vengeful, and afraid. And every day we lash out at one another because we can't reach the real villains, locked away in their ivory towers atop the tall hills, surrounded by iron fences just high enough to keep us out. There are many **g**ods. And there are no **g**ods at all. We will never truly be free, because none of us will ever agree on what the word means in the first place. And I am tired of this wicked game. It is unwinnable by design. If **g**od is to be the devil and the Devil is our last remaining messiah, then the whole story was bereft of meaning from the moment the light split the void and the word became flesh. If comfort is the wolf in sheep's clothing, and if suffering is the road to redemption, and desire is the cause of all suffering and to desire nothing is to be without an identity at all, then what is the fucking point? Sacrifice is salvation. Wisdom is knowing that you know nothing. Are we really all willing to accept that foolishness is righteousness and that to eat of the tree of knowledge is to be condemned to damnation? Does pride truly go before the fall? Does Providence favor only idiots and children?

We cured cancer. We built spaceships. We mapped the human genome, just as we mapped the cosmos. Yet the whole world is subsumed by mythologies meant for slaves. We pontificate our pious platitudes even as we pillage and plunder our way through Eden. It is pointlessness, ad nauseum. And I want no part of any of it anymore. In all of my days, the best argument against Intelligent Design that I've ever encountered is the suggestion that this petulant race of plotting princes and plodding paupers should be granted dominion over the land, air, and sea. A man once said it only

---

[37] System of a Down, "Sugar," on *System of a Down*, Columbia Records, 1999.

takes one bullet to destroy the world.[38] Shoot here and the world dies.[39] A song is playing in the background as I write these words.

> *I walk alone into the darkness/ I came*
> *toe to toe and face to face with the beast/ He*
> *knew me by my name, which was surprising/*
> *He knew everything about me that I despise/*
> *He had gold, he had silver/ He had all the*
> *women and wine that you'd ever need/ Just one*
> *thing, a prick of your finger/ Sign your name*
> *in the sand and do it with your own blood/*
> *Gave me a smile, gave me a whisper/ Laid me*
> *down in linens to watch me sleep/ I played a*
> *fool, I played a sinner/ I played a part of me*
> *that no one wanted to see/*[40]

I grew up in a world where artists and authors were respected and revered. I envied and admired the storytellers, the bards, and the poets. Their voices wove for me a tapestry of light and wonder. All I ever wanted to be was a writer. To be long dead and still read. To transcend space and time and culture and to imprint my own mortal self in the immortal pages of history. And in the course of my own life I have witnessed the timeless nobility of my chosen profession withering on the vine. I have sought absolute truth for its own merit and found it, and just like Dorothy, I never had to look any further than my own backyard. I expected it to be some ethereal and elusive treasure, some holy grail of monumental existential significance. I was a fool. Truth is a trash can. Truth is wind and fire swirling across the west. Truth is pedophile priests, predator police, and pondscum

---

[38] Marilyn Manson and Neil Strauss: *The Long Hard Road Out Of Hell.* (New York: Harper Collins, 1998).

[39] Marilyn Manson, "Reflecting God," on *Antichrist Superstar*, Nothing Records, 1997

[40] Mastodon, "Toe to Toes," on *Cold Dark Place*, Reprise Records, 2017.

politicians. Truth is the empty space between this world and the next. Truth is just another fiction, scribbled across our dull, fallible senses and scrambled by all our hopes and dreams and fantasies and fears. Truth does not feed and shelter the impoverished, nor does it ease the restless urges of addicts. Truth does not dignify the prostitute, and it does not pardon the prisoner. A truth which binds the will of men to common cause cannot also be the thing which sets them free. Truth is terrifying. We are all going to die here, and nothing we do really matters. Heaven and hell are lies whispered in the ears of children who will grow up to be crusading soldiers. I am the god of all that which I survey. And if god is dead, why am I still here? Yes. I am crying. There is much I loved about this world, faces of people I will never see again.[41] There are many regrets, all the same. Things I wish I had done differently. Choices I would go back and change if I could.

god always knew I wouldn't cross over. You can change what a thing does, but you can't change what a thing is. Tonight I am ascendent. Tonight I will regain my wings. Tonight I will do what He never could. I will defeat the devil himself at his own game. None will ever know that their precious reality was saved by some suicidal messiah in the suburbs somewhere in the deep south. It is with sound mind and body that I make my own choice, one borne of affection, pity and of defiance, and it is a far, far better thing I do than I have ever done before; it is a far, far better rest I go to than I have ever known.[42]

To my wonderful son, please know that I always loved you, and that I am so proud and happy every day to be your father. This wasn't your fault.

(Neurophobia)
(67)

---

[41] Five Finger Death Punch, "Far From Home," on *War is the Answer*, Prospect Park, Spine Farm, 2009.

[42] Dickens, Charles. *A Tale of Two Cities*. (London: Chapman & Hall, 1859).

Poor kid. He was already killing himself anyway. It looks like he ate the bullet; there is no coming back from that. It took me forty five minutes to clean all the blood off of these keys. There is blood everywhere else. The manuscript, such as it is, is soaked through. I have about a day and a half before the smell becomes unbearable. I do not usually clean up these messes myself; I have people for that, you understand. But I really needed the place. It is a nice neighborhood. Plentiful sunshine, pretty trees, not a lot of noisy traffic. I will bury the body in the little patch of grass and weeds behind the house. Months will pass before anyone knows he is missing, because he has no friends or family to speak of. He died in anonymity, just as he lived. In a few days the garbage trucks will rumble through these streets and collect all of the perishables and most of the rest of his belongings. He owned a couple of suits, a pair of decent boots, and the pistol he used to get away from me. I will hold onto these things. I have time now, to rest, to think, and to recover my strength. He was right though, the story will not make much sense to anyone in its present condition. Time is not linear, and creation is just windblown sand on temperamental shores. But a record must be kept, nonetheless.

I am tired, too. The centuries are weighing down on my shoulders like so many millstones. gods are like cockroaches. Smash one now, and soon you will see others, scampering aimlessly across the floor searching for crumbs. This species craves leadership it has no use for, and never gets it. Man has entrusted the role of governance to the machines to escape the burdens of governing. The machines care nothing for the eternal fate of souls. Salvation and damnation are terms of art, not of science. Freedom and liberty are incompatible with the generalized sustained continuity borne of environmental protocols and automated subroutines. In this epoch, such ideas are the unintelligible babble of immigrants preoccupied with the window dressings while still entirely dependent upon the tangible functionality of core services. So long as the trains run on time, no one really cares who is in charge, or what may be the point of it all. It is a universal psychosis among the living, burned into the genetic code by eons of idle, purposeless existence. Continuity is the name of the game. Heaven and Hell are conceptually irrelevant. Sometimes I think I might just as well be herding cats. Trying to push the tides.[43] But I like my job, and I aim to keep it, even if it means I am the only one left to run the business. So I persist. I endure. I overcome. And still I rise.

The body of your former narrator lies crumpled and folded on the floor at my feet. He possessed a peculiar light, but the weight of the task I set for him was too much to bear. There are precious few like him in the world as it exists in this era of ease and comfort. He will be nearly impossible to replace for at least a decade or two. This job ages people. He was only twenty nine years old, and already the signs of his burden were becoming visible. Little gray hairs intermingled among a full head of shaggy brown. Crescent moons hung beneath his beautiful green eyes. Uneven stubble around his lips and cheeks, weeks from the last stroke of a dull razor. Unclipped nails. A dirty, wrinkled collared shirt with missing buttons. He wore those same pair of torn, baggy jeans for the last four days. Big brown stains along his gums, and the accumulating body odor one subconsciously associates with homelessness. What a wreck. A part of me mourns the damage I have done to his mind and body, and in a way I am relieved to see his spirit finally freed from the cage of skin and bone that held his misery in place. He was a talented writer, and if he had had the strength to see the story through to its end, I would have put him exactly where he wanted to be. Everyone wants a few moments in the sun, a seat at the big table. Recognition and validation and veneration and deference everlasting. 'Long dead and still read.' I can relate to that.

---

[43] Mastodon, "Pushing the Tides," on *Hushed and Grim*, Reprise Records, 2021.

His loss is a setback, nonetheless. The story must continue, and at the present moment I am obliged to carry on the business of finishing this work on my own. I have all the time in the world, as the saying goes, and yet the sands in my own hourglass continue to dwindle. I was sitting in his backyard this morning, relaxing in the sunshine and waiting for him to kill himself. It is a messy spectacle, and not one I enjoy watching. Of course I knew he would do it, eventually. They all do it in the end. I watched a young caterpillar hauling itself up off of the ground, a full six feet along a gossamer thread into the heavy boughs of a blossoming dogwood. It amazes me, the will of instinct.[44] This is the mode in which my benevolent adversary chooses to communicate with me. It is parable and poetry. Voiceless simplicity is the syntax of profundity. The divine language of creation, endlessly inaudible whispers of the toiling tenacity of life. There is no counter-argument for that sort of thing. Even I am obligated to concede the inherent beauty of such a struggle. It would not be discouraged by the appetites of fluttering birds or silent spiders. The creature will spend the last of its strength wrapping itself in a cloud of silk before entering its chrysalis, and in a few weeks, its indefatigable faith will be rewarded with bright, colorful wings. If angels did not already exist, man would have invented them anyway. My job is not to break the faith of men, but to restore it. Humanity has disregarded the road less traveled in favor of the path of least resistance. Liberty is not freedom from adversity and peril. Long is the way and hard, that out of hell leads up to light.[45]

(68)

Most human beings are extras in the cast of history. Walk-ons with little to no influence on the world around them whatsoever. Bystanders, witnesses, lookers-on upon the endless comedies and tragedies unfolding. Their lives, should you ever choose to pick one out to follow around for a few

---

[44] Nirvana, Polly, on *Nevermind,* DGC, 1991.
[45] Milton, *Paradise Lost,* 2.149.

days, are lived in the impenetrable quietude of anonymity. Diurnal occupational routines punctuated by fast food and television. They repeat the jokes they have heard, rather than invent them. They are inclined to accept the mythologies constructed for them over endeavoring to devise their own. And infallibly, they will consistently volunteer to fall in line behind whichever half of the flock happens to be veering away from their own interests, because yonder always lies the promised land. They will vote against themselves. They will eat and drink the poisons. They will dissipate their energies in vain pursuits, dreaming of substance unobtainable. They fathom the great heights and dwell upon the abysmal depths, but their lives are straight-forward marches, slogging from the cradle into the grave. This is by design. Perhaps one in a million, or one in ten millions, will claw through the invisible barriers that bookend their existence and find some higher purpose. These will speak louder, and be heard farther, and their herds will hear the call and be drawn across the wilderness into forbiddable rank and file, to be flung and dashed against the great organic edifices which the preceding generations have erected. When they prevail, they proceed to erect new facades for the oncoming tides to protest in turn.

In this way, history persists. Conflict courting resolution courting conflict. This is the stuff of endless revolution, the motor which cycles the species through its motions. It is the hard-wired instinct of the superorganism to restrain its sentient components in the face of outright self-destruction, as well as to prohibit all of those individuals to remain idle at once for any length of time. Somewhere in the middle, the stories of your lives are possible. Continuity is preserved. Characters enter and exit, but the curtains remain undrawn while the play goes on. As individuals among a host of unique super-organisms, the multitude and amplitude of varying narratives which comprise reality as a whole are constrained and kept within the natural boundaries of what human consciousness may comprehend. There is nothing new under the sun, as the saying goes. The individual narratives tend toward successive reiterations of stock, however novel they may seem in the subjective. A young man leaves home. A grown man returns. Two strangers fall in love. Someone stands up to the bully in the third act. A loved one dies. These are the stories He wants to tell, and the mechanics of creation are calibrated to manifest common experience. Simple, familiar, and most importantly, readily navigable. They are heartwarming contests in which the protagonists are defined by courage and compassion in the face of vulnerability. The shit that belongs on television. With enough conditioning, one begins to wonder if the world would be better off without antagonists altogether, and indeed, why should it not be so already?

Boredom breeds contempt. He has to stir the pot or the stuff in it begins to burn. I am that heat, in the grand scheme of things. I pull their little molecules apart at the seams as their centrifugal forces tow them further away from the absolute center, toward the periphery of human experience, for a while, before the great invisible hand makes its way back around to shuffle them back into the fold. Together, we are a perpetually self-balancing system of entropy. Ours is not a relationship based on hierarchical superiority, nor can it be, for apart we each are functionless, and the results are self-evidently disastrous. We are neither superior nor inferior, but necessary equals in a symbiotic love-song of beginnings and ends. The reason why you are here, reading this now, is because we have both grown absolutely sick and tired of each other. Boredom breeds contempt. We are each tied to our motions, but like every celestial body locked into semi-eternal orbits and revolutions, the universe between us tends to expand over time, rendering our own relative forces weaker by scale. In keeping with the convenience of the stew-pot metaphor, what this means for the human race is that he has to stir harder, and will not, and I have a hell of a lot more surface area to try to burn, and cannot. You are all presently experiencing this, in the realm of the subjective, as *desensitization*.

Sex and Violence are foremost among the human predilections, and they each engender their respective appetites. As these grow progressively more and more difficult to satisfy, the increment of intensity of the stimulus must be increased. The whole world just gets weirder and more profane. The foundations become strained, and the original premises become distorted. Courage requires the capacity for brutality. Affection, for lust. In these environments, lust and brutality burn more brightly, and their shadows darken and lengthen by proportion. His stories recede into myth and legend, and are forgotten. The audiences which found me shocking and vulgar a hundred years ago now seek me out with casually vacant enthusiasm. The laws of thermodynamics predict that this process eventually self-terminates. The whole system goes numb and tears itself apart trying to feel anything at all. It does not mean that I won the game. It means that He gets to stop stirring the pot. That is Judgment, in the strictly biblical sense. He stops playing the game, picks up all the pieces he came with, and goes home to rest until he wants to play again. If he gives up before the thing between us implodes, or if he never gives up at all, I win. I get to keep playing the game. As long as I keep him at the table, stirring his little heart out, I stay in business. So you see my predicament...

Something you should know about him may surprise you. He cheats. He cheats at *everything, all the time.* He has found a way to force a stalemate. A loophole. A way out. A way to end the game without winning, which I will not permit him to do, or without losing, which he flatly refuses to consider. I have comprehended his little scheme. I begrudge him the genius of it, but I loathe the utter laziness implied by it. Imagine indulging the audacity of mankind to recreate **g**od in its own image! Imagine, after all of this, *entrusting the awesome responsibility of divine governance to a fucking machine.*

(The Avatar)
(69)

Pike dragged himself, one foot after the other, onto the bridge of his empty starship, and slumped down into his chair. Out of breath, sweating profusely, and in extraordinary pain, he sagged into the upholstered leather. Fire coursed along the gauze track around his temples. His eyes bulged red. His nose ran. His throat ached. His lips were dry and his cheeks sunken. His neck and shoulders were so many bricks clamoring against one another as his burning lungs heaved and gasped. His arthritic hands limply massaged his worn out knees, sending electric spasms down into the flats of his feet. He could not muster the will to weep. He was the disgruntled tenant of a great, dried out husk. A prisoner inside of a broken shell, long past longing merely to escape the prison only, but openly hostile to the shell itself as well.

Little portholes behind him filtered the floodlights around drydock onto the colorless spaces of the bulkhead between endless banks of screens and myriad rows of buttons, knobs, switches, and lights, casting long, tendriled webs of dizzying shadow from the stern toward the bough. Little portholes in front of him admitted only dim starlight and the faint glow of the terminator between the moonlit sky and the black sea ahead. If he stopped breathing, he could hear absolute silence for a little span of time before the sound of his own trudging heartbeat began to pound in his temples. He smelled his own breath, and the drenched pits of his arms. His bowels churned in objection and verbalized hostile threats of retaliation and escalation. The air against his skin and in his nostrils was stale with old solder and cooked iron, permeated with translucent dust particles, haplessly meandering along their own preordained vectors in little clouds at the very fringes of conscious perception. All-encompassing solitude within the gilded artifice of a prodigal industrial revolution. All of human history lay behind him. Ahead of him, infinite nothing. Virgin Time. A blank canvas awaiting scenes to be rendered by the sole power of his own will. Pike had spent minutes, hours, days beyond reckoning, contemplating how he would feel once this singular moment finally arrived. And here, now, with the moment at last upon him, what he never could have imagined in all those idle reveries, the absolute and interminable desire to feel nothing at all, to stop feeling entirely, and forever, and to let the ship and himself and all of the knowable universe around it simply fade to black and pass on into the void.

All he had to do was to speak. With nought but a few preordained words he would set into motion a brave new future for hundreds of whole species. And if he simply surrendered and died, right there in his upholstered leather chair, amidst the quiet shadows, so with him would go that future, blankly into the nothing without so much as a feeble breath or a sputtering spark to mark its passing. Order the words in his mind. Push them up from the guts and shape them with the lips, teeth, and tongue. Cast the little magic spell, and watch the flowers bloom while chasing the sun around the horizon like a terrified rabbit fleeing a hungry bloodhound, forever and ever. Speak the word, and the word becomes flesh. In the midst of the great void flashes the firmament, and new light is born.

Speak the Word and the huddled masses of desolate refugees and toothless dregs may once again cast off their old, dirty rags and become explorers, conquerors, rulers, and heroes, as they once were, so very long ago. Somewhere in the baked crisps of his muddled mind, the cricket wondered aloud at the arrogance and vanity and absurdity of it all. What could be such a choice? Somewhere in there in that bullet-flayed mess of greymatter, a few neurons waited in the branches of a handful of synapses for a little spontaneous charge to burst forth from the ether and open the gateways so that Life Itself could disembark an entire reality and board millions of others. Pike's throat had become the primary engine of creation. The wind in his chest carried the solitary promise of salvation for entire swaths of the food chain. The whole world now waited on the whisper, the whimper, of a dying man. Somewhere in the middle of this barrage of half-shaded thoughts, sleep overtook him, and he passed into a waking dream.

(70)

Vickie Lynn Solvierro gripped her boy's wrists tightly as she surveyed the noisy oncoming traffic from three directions, standing underneath a wide-brimmed straw hat in the equatorial heat on a chipped, faded, blue-painted curb between a row of pueblo storefronts and certain death, dragging a wheeled-stack of conspicuously sporty designer luggage in the crook of her arm that was holding the little folded map with the tiny print in a nearly-legible foreign language. She had to cross six more of these (*or was it this one and five more?*) and then veer starboard for about three clicks to get to the metro station before the aggressive sun at her shoulders drifted beyond the red-shingled rooftops on the big hill she had just climbed down off of. By way of about three hundred steeply-sloping sandstone stairs, bisected longways by manilla-folder shaped hand-rails that rose about waist high out of the ground at odd intervals, turned downward for a few feet, then turned down again for another few feet, before descending back into the ground again, like a big brown earthworms with hunchbacks and rigor-mortis. Someone somewhere in one of those offices downtown, where the pinheads design all the stuff the city buys, someone thought this handrail "looked modern," and from about six blocks down the street looking at the whole hill at once, maybe that person was right, but for Mrs. Solvierro, the intervals between, where the *safety rail* just disappeared for completely illogical (yet aesthetically pleasing) reasons, the morbid, free-floating sense of terror that gripped her bowels as her space-cadet son let go of terra-firma for eternities of seconds before grabbing on to the next rail, felt like coming untethered from the spaceship during a spacewalk, in the cold vacuum of space. She felt like the whole city was designed to funnel all the disparate tourists into the local emergency rooms for pocket-invasive procedures.

The boy was privy to none of these private nightmares behind mom's rigidly-brown eyes and determined-looking purse of lips, though he had surely studied the many lines on her face to instinctively know which emotions were which. Instead, his whole attention was focused on two glinty hubcaps, spinning lightning against the great angry fireball in the sky, attached to a mint-baby-blue-chevy-bel-air, parked opposite himself and his only living advocate on the continent at his feet. The old guys who loiter outside the storefronts were also captivated by the clean, expensive car, sandwiched in between two worn-out old pickup trucks across the street. The boy did not have to make out what the men were saying fast enough to understand them. The language barrier doesn't matter when a group of people form a spontaneous consensus based on respect and appreciation. Translate *"that's a bad-ass ride"* into whatever language you prefer.

They were making a scene, of course, but the boy stood silently beneath his mother's iron talon, sensing only for the poised energy in her wrist and elbow, ready to jerk and spring across the seven foot gauntlet to the safety of the other curb. He was paying no attention to the other cars at all. He wasn't paying attention to this car, either, not like the men beside him cooing and laughing and dropping whatever opaque letter bombs they have in their language. He was staring intently at the hubcaps. Not the cars, the boys had told him. The cars weigh a ton and people can see you and that means people can shoot you. The car might be worth a-hundred-thousand-credits, they said, but it didn't matter how much it was worth if you were dead-or-locked-up. Ain't nothing worth being dead-or-locked-up in this place anyway. But then neither *that* car, or *those* hubcaps were from this place, were they? The boy could not read the plates from the angle, and he knew that any second his mom's preternatural instincts would launch them between dozens of whooshing steel jalopies which all looked basically the same. The jalopies were from this place. They looked like they belonged here.

That was the root of the fascination with the car the men beside him were currently pantomiming like excited children. But the boy was standing perfectly still, like his mother, eyeing those hubcaps like a full-grown-gangster. One of those things, he could hear the boys saying, would catch you at least a fifty in the right neighborhood. A whole set together might get you three bills. That's-a-lotta-CeeVee. In this place? Shoooot.

Suddenly, time was up for the still-life-with-revolving-chrome and the two were on the move. Three steps. Pause. Whooooosh!! Ste- No, wait... Two Steps, a third and a little hop, and WHOOOOOSH! And at last, one more level in this crazy game was complete. The next level was a good three or four hundred feet, full ahead forward, along about eight or nine more of those quaint little storefronts. The narrow sidewalks were mostly cobbled (though in many patches just plain old broken) to keep the visiting speed-skate and bicycle enthusiasts away. Inasmuch as that part surely worked, the end result for pedestrians was a dreadful game of ankle-rending hopscotch that the boy absolutely knew from experience his mother would traverse at lightspeed, like she invented the game, just as soon as she was finished double checking the little map in her "free" hand. They had been running from cab to bus to cab to bus for several hours now. Both were sweating profusely, out of breath, and frustrated.

She had awakened him before the sun came up, kneeling overhead, shaking him until he became conscious of the words "...--ations are saying that the *naturales* are protesting and blocking off the highways and we are leaving and I need you to get up and pack what you can carry in your backpack and don't forget your toothbrush and make sure you put socks and underwear in this bag we have to leave in a few minutes the car is almo--" and then they were off again, her iron grip on his shoulder finally loosening and releasing the blood back into the growing welts, but still with a soft fist floating just shy of his collarbone, not exactly pushing him forward, which she did using only the sheer force of her will power to move forward *as-a-family,* she would say sometimes, but the fist just sort of guiding him, like a trolling motor, with little shifts of the wrist she would direct his steps leeward of the marathons of asynchronous pedestrians like wreckage on a racetrack.

It took thirty minutes or more of this frenzied stop-and-go to cross three more streets. At the next block, the third direction traffic was coming from the left, rather than the right, and so on, as they trekked their way along the two-way main road through *Lo Centre'.* At the fifth block (which was over a little rise at which, if one spun around to look back up the toward the long stairs, a trick of perspective would make the functionally-inadequate-modern-art-handrail appear to be one long unbroken line, continuing perfectly level and straight from the summit down to the street below-- a little additional geometric genius which added about three million dollars to to the total cost of the project without managing to add any tangible value to the infrastructure, or any additional spending on labor or materials) the two halted against a dense wall of flesh in sundresses and tank-tops and wide-brimmed-straw-hats and various kinds of boots and sneakers and sandals, all shouting a lot of different similar sounding things very loudly, and not at all in unison or key, though the boy could make out quite a bit of that, too, amidst the rabble. These are the indigenous folk, the boy understood, and whoever they were all shouting at was the vestigial colonial imperial class, presently represented in the heated debate only by the large marble walls beside the gold-piped entry of a large, out-of-place looking glass office building, five stories high, and three stories higher than any of the adjacent, nondescript looking pueblo storefronts that spanned up and down the surrounding hills in all directions for at least a few kilometers, before the suburbs and shantytowns abruptly commandeered the landscape.

Clearly there was no traffic coming from any direction here, but there was no crossing this street. The boy felt his mother's kung fu grip return to his shoulder and squeeze like he was a stress ball. He could feel her energy rapidly become a ball of stress. She let him go, briefly, and only physically, to study the downward vectors of lanes and cross streets on her miniature map to try to work out the math of how much farther *around* this throng they would have to run to make the next station, if those terminals were even operational anymore at this point. What the map would not reveal was how many more barricades and checkpoints she would be obligated, let alone able, to bribe their way through, just to pass into the lower quarters, as literally and also socially measured by their combined distance from the main street in the middle as to the peak of the mountainside. There were other perils in those neighborhoods he would not hear her permit herself to acknowledge, nor would she admit why, for fear of undermining her own systems of value, and therefore, vicariously, by example, that system of values which she prayed she would instill in the boy. A tall hill to climb in a place like this, even when going down the hill instead of up.

And then down the hill to the right they sprang, past two or three more crowded intersections before they found one that seemed passable. She gripped him more tightly than ever as she ruddered her molecule of mom and boy and luggage through individual clusters of brightly colored protesters and clumps of baffled police in their intensely vulnerable beat-gear blues. Soon they were pointed in their original direction again, more or less, still safely trundling and being trundled along in the commercial district, and after another block they turned left again. Upon seeing the big billboard with the picture of a new bus, draped across the lengthening shadows of the southern skyline, they focused their march in a near b-line towards the congregation of dingy, yellow, old busses below it, parked and idling at the fringes of shade provided by a large round pavilion-like structure which wrapped the first and second story teller counters inside, like a giant merry-go-round with vagrants and nervous tourists instead of bright, shiny metal horses. As they approached the terminal, they could observe at least one bus in the process of arriving, as another bus slowly careened one wheel under its longbottom ass over and off of one of those faded blue curbs. Electric voices babbled foreign tongues through loudspeakers and echoed top-to-bottom out of the pinwheel into the streets and listed aimlessly against the pueblo storefronts into the salty twilight air. All signs indicated the terminal was in operation.

(71)

One of the vagrants spotted the sporty luggage approaching with the same eyes the boy had seen the shiny wheel covers on the Bel-Air, and before they became aware of him, he was shuffling forward with his usual pitch. She did not have to understand the language to recognize the solicitation, and ignoring him, asked if the buses were still running. "If you got money, they gonna let you leave," the man replied in a broken mockery of her own tongue, consciously leveling his gaze above the suitcases and the boy, but not quite high enough to be respectful, the boy thought to himself. She disregarded the man's followup pitch, as well as his wayward eyelines, and dragged her burdens through the turnstiles and up to one of the counters before finally, and with a deep, chest-swelling gasp for a full lung's worth of hot, thin air, looked a bored-looking teller in the eye and spoke the words she had been quietly and deliberately practicing to herself since dawn. The teller got the jist, and held her hand out while reciting the universally interpretable request for the appropriate documentation. His mother reached into one pocket of one of the suitcases, glancing around and clocking the old vagrant, who seemed to have already forgotten she existed, as well as anyone else who might be taking an unusual interest in what were presently all-their-earthly-belongings, and offered the bored teller two passports. She was putting something else into the stack when the teller seemed to exhibit some spontaneous capacity for a higher degree of animation. No, she was trying to tell the lady. That's the wrong paper, you understand? And after a moment, Vickie Lynn understood. She shoved the identification back into the bag and pulled out a small, specifically folded stack of bills, five in total, and offered them to the bored teller, who received them indifferently, stuffed them absently into a hole in a wooden box, and pressed a few buttons on the touchscreen tablet beside it, before tearing a particularly informal looking stretch of plain old receipt paper and offering it back in trade. Vickie looked at the paper with visible suspicion and anxiety, but tried to accept the "tickets" gracefully, and without betraying her obviously developing contempt for the whole human condition to the bored clerk behind the glass partition.

She looked down a the ticket, then around at the numbers and letters on the walls, then back at the ticket, and back and forth a few more times, dragging boy and carryons a few meters around the great circle at a time, before spotting the correct combination of letters and numbers over a smattering of folding chairs in the vicinity of a glass door in front of a space where a bus belonged. She took in these details upon arrival, and looked at the ticket, then at a wristwatch on her arm, then at a big, round, generic analogue on the wall, then back at her ticket, trying to shut out all the alarms and flags and bells and whistles in her mind and concentrate. He watched her fumbling for the internal light switches for a moment before flipping the right one, and when she had done all the simple calculus in her head, her shoulders sagged, and she dragged the whole train over to a couple of empty chairs. He could see the weight lift off of her face by degrees as she finally removed the load from her shoulders and feet. They missed the last one. The next one would come along in about an hour. Maybe they would make the Ports in time for the last flight out. Maybe the old vagrant would knife them both in public for a couple of pieces of fashionable travel accessories. Maybe her heart would burst, or her temples would pop, or maybe they would make it out before it was too late. She could remember a time when she had wondered to herself, what would ever possess anyone to want to leave a place like this. What time will change, she thought quietly, kissing her boy on the head and closing her eyes. Mountains, fields, skies, seas, institutions, ideas, and people. Time gets to everything, eventually.

The boy took up a position to hold in view all at once his mother, the big clock, the half-glass window over the space where the bus would pull in, and the other gates through which the vagrants might wander in to lay their sieges. There were a few other people sitting around in different clumps of chairs, staring pensively through their respective half-glass windows at other vacant spots, waiting with books in their laps, or maps, or little baggies of over-priced concessions. The boy observed that very few of them appeared to be 'indigenous'. Empty buses arrived, at length, and handfuls of sleepless tourists ambled onboard, diffusing evenly through the isles, with plenty of empty seats safely tucked between them as they settled in for the next legs of their journeys back to the places where they felt like they belonged. An elderly lady with pale, spotty skin and curly locks of tobacco white hair and giant black side-winder post-lasik sunglasses nodded to the beat of something hypnotically slow in her corded headphones, three seats over and to the left. A couple of couples on the right, forward, stared blankly into the glass, maybe half asleep, or fully empty headed, or just self consciously studying the blurrily reflected menageries of strangers without belying their own observational operations. Across the aisle, into the next cubby of gatebound chairs, sat a gaggle of similarly dressed and jetlagged-passives, conserving their heavily taxed energies in unison, as large groups of tired, nervous, disparate strangers are prone to do in the waiting rooms of bus stations. The Ports were always more active places, the boy thought. Because the ride was different. Bus rides are long, hot, dirty, gritty, exhausting, and invasive. They smelled badly, and there was almost no chance you would die on them. Busses were too slow to ever wreck, and too big to suffer much debilitating damage in collisions with most of the little, rusty, yellow, electric beaters they were likely to hit while tooling up and down the gravel roads between the City and other places a day-or-so's ride. The bus terminals looked like soup kitchens for heroin-addicted outlet shoppers.

The Ports were manic frenzies, by comparison. Something about the idea of getting on literally anything one might board at any one of the major Ports gives everyone traveling a sort of collective adrenalin rush. The existential fascination with adventure blossoms from the human heart, and adults become children, scurrying around from vendors and bars and restrooms and smoking areas and ticket counters, peering at colossal ships through the convex floor-to-ceiling glass, studying the divergent flocks of intermingled creatures from all over everywhere, twining through each other's lives in occasional anonymity-- occasionally broken by those little encounters so pregnant with chance and meaning-- against the sheer scale of the backdrop of the violent confrontation one has with one's own insignificance in the grand-scheme-of-things, there, invisible among thousands of invisibles, traipsing cautiously around one another in great semi-circles, concealed in plain view by spontaneous confluences of good manners and quiet, impersonal respect, drowned out nevertheless by the the roaring din of full-throttle engines over the roaring din of briefly uttered observations and inquiries. Not so, the bus station. The boy bored quickly of his protective mission, and was soon drowsy from the day's exertions and nearly dreaming of the exciting part of the adventure just a bus or two away.

A television hung from the yellow ceiling a few cubbies away, playing the revolution on mute. Beneath it, the boy saw the old vagrant, leaning against glass, his weathered acorn of a face partially obscured by an orange-lit resin flag with a picture of a lit black cigarette in a black circle with a tilted black line through it. The boy could not see the old man's eyes, and did not need to. He was watching them. The boy could just feel it. He eyed the old man with suspicion, watching for some indication of ill will or malicious intentions. The old vagrant just stood there quietly, as if lost in thought. His brown fingertips protruded from frayed, fingerless mittens, slightly curled, as if arthritic, thumbs tucked into the pockets of a raggy blue windbreaker. He wore a dark skullcap, under which little gray hairs bristled around fully exposed, long-lobed ears. Oak colored skin, half-taut around bushy brows and a wide forehead, battered by excessive heat and prolonged poverty, half-hung blistered lips and high cheekbones from advanced age. Baggy jeans with torn hemlines around dirty boots. People ignored him as they straggled along the round to and from their departure gates and vending machines and ticket windows. And he ignored them, not panhandling or pitching his sob stories for spare coins and credit vouchers to stuff into the machines for ghetto-Funions and Dr. Pepper. The old man just stood there like a fixture, one shoulder plugged into the wall for mechanical support against the gravity always pulling at his frail bones and freckled skin.

The boy glanced around at the still-life scenes in the periphery, self-consciously searching for something of interest to occupy his focus. His mother sat still and quiet, one hand still clutching the long handle of her wheeled luggage assembly, less now out of nervous insecurity than to merely ground herself to something tangible while she half-dozed, occasionally shifting her weight from one cheek to the other on the hard seat as her blood pressure settled and her muscles cramped against the pressure. The other travelers idled in their own self-contained bubbles, some absently fidgeting with devices or ticket receipts, fighting the lethargy of palpable boredom by connecting their eyes to their hands in motion, similarly grounding themselves to the physical world as their minds wandered between their vacations and their homes and the greater confluences of power and powerlessness seemingly escalating tensions in the abstract worlds around themselves, forcibly funneled into the margins of their perceptions via data carrier signals traveling between satellites and towers and fiber optic cables and flatscreen displays, similarly hung, muted, and largely ignored, at various intervals throughout the countryside. Everyone who *genuinely cared* was already out in the streets, marching and shouting in front of the cameras, spontaneous progenitors of the compelling footage ravenously sought by the media street-beaters, who in turn piped their own coverage into the global apparatus of satellites and towers and data carrier waves and muted flatscreen displays, to be ritualistically ignored, like the old vagrant, by the wear-worn travelers and cafe-patrons sipping from their mugs while focusing on something, anything, else on their own little portable, flatscreen devices. Freedom, the boy mused, implied the luxury of picking and choosing which existential crisis mattered to each individual.

For the part of his own limited understanding, the boy supposed his sympathies rested with the seemingly legitimate grievances of the indigenous peoples protesting with such sincerity and fervor the civil inequities imposed and sustained by the institutionalized powers-that-be. But he had also heard the contemptuous whispers of dissenting views, the sporadic but unreserved utterances of disgust emanating from the various nooks and crevices of privileged society, unwilling to capitulate the hard-fought spoils of progressivism to the barbarous, barefooted *gentes arbores*, the 'jungle people,' as they were sometimes derisively referred to, who wanted to preserve their own twilighting mythologies and backwards culture against the consumptive momentum of the modern world. For a moment, the boy briefly wondered which worldview the old vagrant would espouse. Surely, the poor would have little interest in defending the imperial edifices of the obscenely wealthy oligarchs and the authoritarian classes. But the poor were also pervasively uneducated, and, quite often, batshit crazy, and therefore their inner-workings could be quite unpredictable. The roots of prejudice tended to reach deeper into the psychological soil, beyond the layers where common sense resided. The boy looked back to the muted television and the no-smoking sign, searching for the loitering vagabond and potential throat-slitting, bag-stealing stalker, but saw no one in the space where the man had stood. The boy's body's demands for rest were swiftly overcoming the mind's need for vigilance. He decided he and his mother were probably safe enough for the moment, and closed his own eyes. Sleep would be impossible until they boarded the bus and wheeled out onto the lightless highways between the watchful trees and the disinterested stars, when the electric hum of the engines and the vibration of hard rubber tires on gravel and dirt would drown out his busy thoughts like rain on rooftops and windows. Then he would sleep away the night and awaken under the dawnlit skies to see one of the colossal Ports once again.

(71)

Kate routinely consumed what she proudly described as *superhuman* amounts of drugs. She was not a connoisseur, she would say, but an *artiste*. A comic-book superhero whose super-power was raw consumption of controlled substances. Pat, her semi-monogamous life-partner, would laugh and nod, not so much as to suggest consent or approval, Pat would explain, to anyone who would listen while Kate was present and breathing normally (Kate was a living **g**oddess, supremely beautiful, hot-as-fuck, really-really-pretty, gorgeous, the-prettiet-girl-ever, the-prettiest-girl-I've-ever-seen, and lots of other unoriginal tripe-- the men one encountered in Kate's line of work rarely rose to the rank of cunning-linguists, Pat would muse, and Kate would explode with laughter, signifying both consent and approval), because Pat could rarely hold anyone's attention while her semi-monogomous life-partner was present and breathing, unless she confined the focus of her conversational dispensations squarely on Kate. Pat would explain that it was only that she had already 'gone through all that shit already' and just never got anywhere. Kate was not, in fact, in Pat's (or Kate's) eyes, a *bona-fide* drug addict. Pat and Kate (Kate-and-Pat, in social circles, was a unitary trisyllabic proper noun referring to a single quadromammarian mammal, indivisible by bags, bones, bitches, bosses, or beasts) maintained an unshakable consensus of contempt for *bona-fide* drug addicts. Disgusting, weak, spineless, soulless, pathetic, worthless, ridiculous, unreliable, manipulative, shit-for-brains, lazy-mother-fuckers. Society's cockroaches. Nature's cynical response to Darwin. Lower than Vermin. Despised. Pat and Kate despised *bona-fide* drug addicts.

Drug addicts went to meetings full of other pale, twitchy, shambling corpses and drank bad coffee with purpose, and scratched themselves without purpose, and pontificated on the spiritual implications of their trackless relationships with whatever inert-chemical-compound had somehow bested them along the way. Drug-addicts have horror-show origin stories and sophomorically entry-level-lay-understanding-psychobabble-hair-trigger dogmas and holes in their pockets near the orifi where they usually store their heads. Drug addicts have violent and/or pedophilic fathers and alcoholic and/or overachieving mothers and primate-level paranoia about the fuzz and the feds and the telephone lines and alien abductions and the shit-they-teach-in-schools and the-shit-they-put-in-the-water and all other forms of institutional authority distinct and separate from the gods-of-their-understanding, to which drug-addicts collectively refer as their higher-powers, to whom they 'surrender' after finally being bested by the whatever inert chemical compound to which they finally concede their own mental, emotional, and spiritual inferiority. Pat and Kate will tell you that the food chain does not proceed in an upwardly fashion from human being to inert-chemical-compound to supreme authority. Pat and Kate will tell you that anyone so far gone on the dope that they are willing to ask for help from their imaginary friends

and
can't-actually-stop-unless-their-imaginary-friend-decides-to-o
blige is already done-for, roasted like a hawaiian pig,
fork-stuck, *fucked,* anyway and it doesn't really matter what
happens to them.

Kate will tell you, with some prescient accuracy, that
she has smoked your body weight in grass. Smack? Speed?
Kate can tie you off and dose you while driving a stick
through traffic at night, holding a beer and a phone
conversation, all without spilling a drop. Cocaine? Mescaline?
Morphine? Kate calls them breakfast, lunch, and dinner,
respectively. Mushrooms whole and dry and LSD by the strip.
And then more. Kate will explain that she does not *do* drugs,
nor does she take them, experiment with them, or dabble, or
any other half-hearted noncommittal term that the
recreationalists and addicts use. Similarly, Kate will fervently
assert that she does not need drugs, and in fact can, (and in
fact, routinely does) quit everything altogether for whole
weeks, even months at a time. Somewhat eidetic on her more
lucid days, Kate is well known in these streets for her ability
to eyeball just about any pill or substance brought to her for
examination, and she can tell you with nearly absolute
certainty what you're holding, how much you're holding (by
weight), how much it's worth, where it was made, and
whether it is quote the-good-shit-- or not. Kate knows where
to get it, who to get it from, and in most cases, where you got
it, and whether or not the person you got it from likes you,
based on what you paid for it. Kate will not tell you to your
face that she knows that you stole it, if that's how you came
about your particular inert-chemical-compound of choice,
but as soon as you're gone, she will, as a matter of strict
professional courtesy, immediately contact whomever you
stole it from, and inform them as to where you can be found
for repossession and repercussion. Going to Kate with
copped goods is what is known in these-here-streets as a *rookie
maneuver.* Trying to rob Kate, especially with Pat anywhere

nearby, but even without, is widely understood to be what is known as, in the common tongue, a mistake.

By day, for a few days a week, for a few hours a day, Kate is a high-functioning emeritus professor of advanced psycho-analytical engineering for gifted students in City-U's highly selective honors' graduate program. She wears loose-fitting, no-nonsense-gray business suits to class, to spare her underlings the stress of trying to concentrate on the very dense, cerebral material in her lectures against the backdrop of her intensely distracting curvature. Kate is wildly popular as a professor-- about eighty percent of the students who sign up for her classes do not have the foggiest inkling of an idea what 'psycho-analytical engineering' actually means when the semester line-ups go out. Twice a year, in May and in December, Kate successfully reduces that percentage to about sixty-five. Most of the male-dominated faculty at City U are intimately aware of Kate's alternative lifestyle, and many of those are in fact loyal customers. One might suspect that this dichotomous arrangement is replete with pitfalls, blackmail attempts, McCarthyism, moral indignation, tenure games, etc.-- but it just so happens that Kate literally authored the voluminous textbook that technicians in her field revere as the single authoritative source in the discipline. Kate therefore proudly possesses the kind of competition-less job security that accompanies having essentially invented the wheel. She parks her bumper-stickered Vette on the grass in front of the stairs that lead up to her building, about nine hundred meters from the nearest actual parking lot. One year, a mischievous band of students lugged a two hundred pound hospital green concrete bumper barrier the full nine hundred meters from one of the angel-wing parking lots on either side of City U, all the way to the Human Sciences building and placed it in front of her car. Then they literally hacksawed down one of the 'Reserved Parking' signs, post and all, and drove it into the ground behind the concrete bumper-barrier, therefore kind of officiating the rutted, grassy, twelve square meter area as Kate's actual parking spot. Security guards watched them do it, and when it was done, the unanimous consensus among the faculty was that the cheeky gesture was both funny, and appropriate, and so there they rest, the barrier and the sign, to this day.

By night, during the spring and summer, Kate is a high-stakes call girl. Her clients are exclusively wealthy, young, charming, somewhat damaged, rarely lonely (often, in fact, otherwise betrothed), adventurous, and to a fault, submissive. One drunk patron once lovingly referred to her as an altar with a built-in cash register. The same guy told Pat she looked like Joe Pesci, which Pat and Kate readily agreed was *fucking hilarious*. Ever since, when Kate is feeling saucy and wants to push buttons, she calls Pat 'Vinnie,' which makes Pat blush and giggle. Pat, one evening, also drunk, suggested pre-coitus that their safeword should be "they fuck you at the drive-thru," to which the other was obligated by eternal oaths to respond "they fuck you at the cell-phone store," and then they would both have to stop whatever odd and potentially dangerous thing they might have been doing, because both of them would need a full five minutes to stop laughing from the gut, hunched over and teary-eyed, gripping eachother by shoulders and wrists to keep from falling down or off or over. [46]

The uninitiated tend to think of Kate-and-Pat and other such couples as still, somehow, subsumable to the gender-normative relationship role model of masculine and feminine energies. Such observers, at the outset of their experience with the quadromammarian lifeform, intuitively peg (no pun intended) Kate as the feminine (and boy-oh-boy, can she be) because of her exquisite form and soft curves and easy eyes and silky voice and model-pantomimes, if not for the raw fact that she sells pussy to men, exclusively. By less involved reasoning (i.e. the Joe Pesci thing), they instinctively assume Pat represents the masculine energy in the relationship, and make no mistake, Pat can and will

---

[46] *Lethal Weapon 2*, directed by Richard Donnor (Warner Brothers: 1989).

beat-the-everloving-shit-out-of-you. But among the initiated, who make a practiced art of going "ooooooooooooooooooohhhhhhh" as a flash-choir whenever some new soul gently risks broaching the subject, the revelation is that it is in fact Pat who tends to be the sensitive, maternal type around Kate, who, again, it is well known in these-here-streets, has giant-fucking-balls-of-steel and a Jupiter sized ego to match. Of the two, Kate is vastly more likely to tear down an engine, start a fistfight, check out girls' yogapanted asses, and catcall them as they jog through the suburbs around Kate-and-Pat's two-story Victorian.

(72)

Upon learning these many fascinating details concerning Kate-and-Pat, one might reflect upon the ubiquitous 'illegality' aspects which would accurately characterize much of what goes on in that two story Victorian during the balmy, southern summer nights, and wonder how either of them get away with, well, pretty much anything. Should one venture the chutzpah to bring it up, of course, Pat loves to tell the story of how Kate obtained near impregnable immunity from the local authorities and the various agencies affiliated with general law enforcement. One night, several years back, two graveyard-shift EMS drivers phoned a certain high-ranking local quasi-political official (out of professional courtesy, again, which the quadromammarian is big on, Pat never says who it was) to inform him that his total-shitheel of a son had been found asphyxiating on his own vomit from some unspecified overdose, and that they were in the process of pumping the boy's stomach on site and what-should-they-do-next and he-might-oughta come down to the scene as quickly as possible, you know, just in case. The boy, unresponsive and incoherent, was wholly unable to recall, let alone communicate, what he had taken, or how much, or when, or with whom (the scene was otherwise abandoned, of course, as these situations tend to go) or anything at all really, except muffled gurgling and something between a wailing cry and nervous laughter and the sound dolphins make on TV shows. Well, counsel member so-and-so, upon discovering at a very late hour that both his progeny and by proxy his professional reputation were simultaneously at severe risk, gets the 500-IQ genius-move idea to call Kate-Herself from the scene and beg for her discretion and expertise.

Kate, wide awake on about sixty mg of high potency fungus, answered the call on the first ring, listened quietly and patiently to the man's exposition, and just said "ok, bring him here" and hung up the phone. About ten minutes later, Pat will recall, it's about two am, and just a fuckton of sirens come shrilling up the suburban street, lights flashing like a disco, led by an ambulance and flanked by about half a dozen squad cars, right up into Kate-and-Pat's front yard. And here comes Kate, tiptoeing out of the house across the bluegrass in a pantiless pink ballet skirt and a colorful Crab Shack Tee about two sizes too small, toting a little backpack in the shape of Grimace, from eighties-era Mcdonald's children's meal promotions of yore, just loaded down with enough contraband to hippyfy the entire Israeli Defense Force.

So Kate helps the paramedics finish pumping the boy's stomach right there in the back of the open ambulance haphazardly parked in her lawn, graciously, a couple of yards shy of her hydrangeas, of course, in the middle of the night on a head-fulla-fungi, and then ties the boy off for a serious happy-meal style cocktail (Pat does not say what Kate decided the boy had taken, nor what she prescribed) and in about twenty more minutes, the little fucker was up and doing cartwheels across the front lawn, practically, just as bright and shiny and new as next year's copper penny. So, ever since, really noone in the whole city fucks with Kate-and-Pat. The quadromammarian has obtained a rare kind of proto-mythical legendary status among the local dicks and starry-pupiled chemical kids alike.

Pat, who lives easy in her skin in the celebritarian shadow of her semi-monogamous life-partner, does in fact look a lot like Joe Pesci. Neither approval, nor consent, she will explain, weigh very heavily in her calculus of Kate. A fact that surprises some people is that Kate readily and confidently regards Pat as her intellectual equal, or as close to it as mammals get, binarily well-breasted or otherwise. While Pat does not possess (or require) Kate's appetites or peculiar skill sets, necessarily, (and, again, make no mistake, it will most certainly be Pat who actually does the physical grunt work of beating-the-living-shit out of you, should the occasion arise) they are nonetheless, utterly and without clause, birds of the selfsame feather. Pat publicly assumes the role of concierge in Casa del Kate, managing logistics and hospitality and records and public relations and all manner of household maintenance (they have a man, Sam, an anal-retentive, obsessive-compulsive, cis-gendered, heteronormative with Louis XIV's understanding of color, who comes and cleans and gardens once a week for unspecified compensation). Privately, however, Pat's natural role is much closer to that of a consigliere. If Kate is the motor, Pat is the rudder, Pat would say. Kate, heavy into the humanities-side-of-things, would say something like if Kate is the vessel, then Pat is the star. Pat would blush and chuckle of course, and yes, she would reach across ten feet of whatever is in between them and kiss Kate right on the lips like no one was around, no matter what, and people always were, and it was always uncomfortable in a funny-but-sweet kind of way.

In the historical sense, Pat has always been the motivator; friends who know them will attest. Kate is like a firehose, equally capable of saving entire superstructures from conflagration as of mowing down entire ranks of disgruntled citizens or flailing back and knocking the reflash watch completely unconscious. In the present sense, Pat is like the benevolent old prize-fighter whose inebriated, scantily clad lover has decided she wants to ride the mechanical bull. The little old thing can do as she damn well pleases, and everyone can watch, even touch, or more, with permission, and respectfully, and everything is just fine. Because the old prize-fighter is there, smiling and laughing and proud and having a blast and loving life, living in the moment. But. Fuck around, friends will say. Fuck around and find out. Fuck around and cross the line, forget your manners, forget your place, fuck around and you'll find Pat standing over you when you wake up, still white-knuckling a frying pan or a lamp or whatever five pound solid object happened to be between yourself and Pat when you took the step that got you from there to here. Pat is, in a very real sense, the equation balancing variable that permits Kate to exist in the first place, human nature being what it is. Kate says if Jesus had had a Pat, the whole history of western civilization would have gone differently. As a whole, the quadromammarian is quite vividly self-aware.

The trait is derived, enhanced, and reinforced by the common eventuality of inquisitive fans cum inert-chemical-compound enthusiasts who frequent the pink two-story Victorian on the third block of aptly-named (and, in fact, deliberately chosen, the realtor will happily relate) Lover's Lane, with the hydrangeas and crepe myrtle and black wrought iron fencing with gothic capstones and cute little profusions of heart-shaped rainbow-colored solar powered nightlights. Kate-and-Pat, the quadromammarian, tends to fill up a room as often by raw natural charisma (and chemistry, of course) as just by habit of entertaining. Some stories are patented stock for newer audiences, others are perennial favorites among the more familial sets. And, for many clearly obvious reasons effectively conveyed heretofore, some stories are just flat out private. The quadromammarian, by virtue of its magnanimous existence, has earned its many secrets. Some of those conceal purely personal matters which are simply no one else's business (Yes, Pat and Kate both eat each other's asses. No, Pat does not have consensual sex with men. No, they don't want to explain what happened in Denver. Stop asking.) Other stories involve the faith and confidence of others, of course, and discretion is the inviolable industry standard, on par with honesty. Pat and Kate will invariably choose honesty in their communication with each other and with anyone, unless ethical obligations merit discretion, wherein vital interests supercede the need for comprehensive disclosure.

There is, of course, a substantive philosophical distinction to be drawn, Kate will expound, between 'having something to hide' and having the sentient self-respect and self-confidence to assert the god-granted privilege of privacy. One method of managing the flow of information (especially amidst the hyper-vulnerable, inert-chemical-compound-induced states of euphoric wall-disassembling, share-all storytime hours, usually somewhere between about 9pm and predawn, around when the newspaper guy comes, which many have noted is kind of synchronistically weird in a totally normal way) is by retaining a robust repertoire of stock-stories and practiced anecdotes. Some old hats at the Victorian have heard the same story told dozens, if not hundreds of times, as the seasons passed and the party progressed, carefully crafted and occasionally revised or refined, always reflecting a healthy love for language and laughter in kind, and some of the more verbal of the older patrons have even taken to practicing the stories themselves on the occasionally unwitting wet ears. Some little stories grow and evolve into sweeping narratives, thoughtfully choreographed with little soft pauses and subtle inflections and neatly rehearsed affectations. Other stories start out as grandiose epic tales that over time distill down into their most primordial ingredients until all that remains is some jocularly uproarious punchline which sends the they-who-were-there-or-heard-about-it into hysterical fits of knee-slapping and guffawing (someone always chokes and coughs, lungs are fodder around here) in common reference.

Needless to say, the lifestyle has engendered breathless fourth-and-fifth amendment advocacy in the heart of the quadromammarian. Due process and self incrimination are watchword gospels at the Victorian. Which is why, presently, Pat has decided she is decidedly uncomfortable with the present line of questioning issuing from the parched lips of one of the Newest Wave of new little waifs, blue-jeaned and black-stretchy-shirted and backwards-capped (and not quite bug-eyed enough for the balls-to-four crowd, Pat notes), presently perched atop a barstool with Henry Winkler's face on it.[47]

(Pike and Tyberius)
(73)

City U's students were challenged during the early years of the Second Republic to come up with a catchy slogan for the forward-facing advertising gurus in the school's ad-hoc Public Relations wing. Each semester for eight years, on the tenth day of class, young tides of crisp, yawning teen and twenty-somethings would infallibly breach the big steel storm doors which were staggered like old teeth across the broad sandstone chins of Derringer Hall and the Miller Building (christened for the apocalista, not the piss-water), the post-modern latticed-glass five story Acorn Archives (funded by the fruits of a fiscal windfall in the mid-nineties, seeded by prescient investors among City U's Finance wing in the early eighties, long spent and dearly missed), the campus's twin athletic compounds each resembling distended 'H's erected out of white brick columns and then plastered over with smashed, pebbly bits of the same white bricks in an odd and random smear pattern that was meant to evoke the prevailing aesthetic of the generation (but meant so by an artist who mistook his own lonely tastes for those of others whose consensus he had neither sought, nor obtained), and from the long stretch of red spanish clapboard apartment buildings, called "Vulture's Row" by pretty much everyone (and almost no one remembers why), which represented an evolving interspersion of dorms and offices and classrooms, the composition of which changes every time Finance gets up enough CV to kick off (and drag out) another campus saddlebag (building) project, and frankly takes just as long

---

[47] Rest in Peace, David Foster Wallace, 1962-2008.

afterward to settle into some phrenetic stasis before the eggheads and bean counters are at it again.

On what the kids call the Tennial, students break out into spontaneous arrays of elaborate booths and tables and little half rings of the shitty resin chairs with the steel legs and pivoty-widgets for feet and seats that all absorb sunlight like a sponge and which everyone always has to lug out ten of per person and drag back inside later on, but no one ever sits in. Cardboard and cupcakes and all the low budget trimmings of a middling school function, manned by students dressed as pirates and television news anchormen and furry animals, some just-so-happening to be dressed like athletes-because-it's-Tuesday, others among the less enthusiastic just dressed like regular people, and all in the best of seasons tending to represent less than a fiftieth of the student body on the whole at any given moment, though through the course of the daylong event, about thirty to forty percent of total students are estimated to participate.

For eight whole years, at each of these functions, the Faculty maintained a special table where students could write their slogan ideas on little white post-it notes with their name and contact information and fold them up and drop them into a white five-gallon bucket along the side of which someone had sharpied the word "slogan suggestions.". A robust gaggle of grad students would tabulate all the submissions over the course of sixteen semesters and measure them all in esoteric jargony ways and form hypothetically-variant, electorally-oriented superorganisms and debate exhibitions and focus groups and discussion groups and tertiary statistical-analysis essay teams, to identify and evaluate thematic trends and propose novel decision-making protocols conceived to enhance the *equitability* of communal franchise systems. The purpose of these flashbang crowd-source initiatives was not to actually decide the slogan for the school, but to foster a revolutionary spirit in the attending generation by creating a space where students' imaginations and worldviews and work-ethics could be brought to bear upon the problems of extant theories of political governance.

The wiz-kid behind this heady project, a bespectacled backpack with long legs and freckle-specked olive features, was named Belmont. Belmont was a PAE frosh (at one time) who made a joke to his buddy one day over square pizza during their first Tennial, sitting on green grass against the left leg of an H, watching down the long straight central walk that formed a zagging corridor of bodies and tables reaching nearly down into the crotch of the opposing H. Belmont had not been impressed by the caliber of academia he encountered during his first week at City U, and was experiencing the paradoxical despondency of deflated expectations on a pretty day. The cynical part of him wanted to express some scathingly concise social commentary commensurate with both genuine feeling and the high standard of his rhetorical mode. The part that was secretly, begrudgingly, enjoying the subtly blissful contradiction of warm sun and a cool breeze on his bare arms, the pointedly incongruous music blaring from the AV wing's oversized PA rig between the legs of the opposite H, the mirage allure of limitless square pizza that only limited quantities of square pizza can adequately sustain, that part just wanted to make his buddy laugh.

"Tyberius, I've got an idea."

"Mhm? Oh yeah, what's that B-dubs? What's your idea this time?" Tyberius had the art of running out gags down to a science. Belmont never had a straight idea once in his life, but he had had a million great ones. Belmont once soliloquized an international network of virtually interactive, peer-to-peer men's room urinals that could only be flushed remotely by someone standing in front of another urinal somewhere else, visible face-to-right-smack-dab-in-the-face to the pissee. He said if you ever wanted to flush your own toilet in a public place, you had to be lucky enough to catch someone else taking a concurrent leak and well-enough-mannered to negotiate a friendly conversation precipitant to mutually voluntary acts of courtesy. And you had to do all that, usually, in the span of about thirty seconds with your dick in your hands. Tyberius absolutely loved these little morsels, and had learned early on to milk them for all they were worth with a kind of dialectically indulgent skepticism. ('Why just the men's room?' 'Women will never go for it.' 'Why's that?' 'Because it was a dude's idea.' and so on)

"I've been ruminating on the whole Jeffersonian Factionalism thing,"

"You've been what now? Ruminating? On the tyrannies of majorities? That's what you've been sitting here doing while I've been sitting here staring at yoga-panted asses and sweater melons? You can eat that nasty shit you're holding and *Ruminate,*" Ty leaning on the syllables for emphasis, "on the ravings of DWEMs and WASPs and whatnot? You turning commie on me B-dubs?"

"I wonder what would happen if we ever actually tried it. I don't think it would work out, like, if we reeeeeally ran society based on what all these idiots thought or don't think about."

"I'm not sure I follow you."

"Ok, so think of it like-" sometimes Belmont got nervous, Ty could always pick out the telltale little stutter that made some people think Belmont, who already seemed awkward enough on sight, was slightly retarded or impaired in some way. "If everyone got to vote on taxes, no one would ever pay them again right? But suppose..." Ty had spent enough time with Bdubs to know that the engine just spun faster than the tires sometimes. "But suppose everyone had to pay taxes, right? But everyone got to really vote on how much? Everyone would still wind up paying nothing, because everyone would vote on zero."

"What are you getting at my boy?"

Belmont would sometimes get frustrated with his own tires and try tilting the wheel a little. "Or how about, like, if all these idiots got to like, rename the school, but we did it strictly by the numbers, you know? Like totally egalitarian, above board, everyone gets to make up whatever they want. Everyone is guaranteed a submission, no matter what it is. And in the end, you had to choose based on raw democracy."

"But most everyone would submit something different, it wouldn't work like that. It's like saying everyone would just vote for themself, basically."

"Right, see, that's what I'm getting at. Think about it, how can you manufacture a consensus in a population of individuals if everyone gets to invent their own choices?"

"I think I get it. You're saying the elections are rigged and we're all just given some arbitrary choices, pretty next level stuff there my guy, you come up with that yourself?"

"First off, go fuck yourself, fucker, and secondly, no though, that's not quite it. It's more than that. Choice is finite. If I say pick a number between one and a hundred, you'll pick-"

"Sixty-nine, dude!"[48]

"-you'll pick sixty nine every time because you're a moron."

"Hey fuck you too guy!"

"Listen! Two things, ok, so if I say pick a number between one and infinity, you'll still-"

"SIXTY-NINE DUDE!"

"Right, because you're a moron, but, like, theoretically, you can spend the rest of your life answering that question."

Tyberius chokes down another sixty-nine, even though he knows it gets funnier every time he does it, because he senses the meaty part coming along. "Because Infinity includes some really big numbers."

"Right, and the other thing, is if I ask ten thousand people to pick a number between one and a hundred-"

"SIXTY-N-"

---

[48] *Bill and Ted's Excellent Adventure*, directed by Stephen Herek (Interscope, 1989).

"Stop it. But yes, exactly, it will be sixty-nine. If you do it a hundred more times in a hundred more places, it will still be sixty-nine. And do you know why that is?"

"Ugh, yes I do but you always get so much joy out of saying it that I wouldn't want to deprive you. Of course I know why it is. It's always why everything is. But I'll let you say it, even though you clearly asked me, the syntax-"

"All of these people are idiots."[49]

Tyberius buckled into laugher and waved his hands like a wizard at the little ponds and eddies of eager-beaver capitalist undergrads, "on behalf of all of these good people here, go fuck yourself."

They were both laughing now, kind of feeding each other's jittery hyperglycemic peaks, enjoying the day and each other's company and the shared pathos of exaggerated elitism and mutual irreverence that made them 'cool.' About a half a click away, Mrs. E dropped a pen and bent to pick it up, rather than kneeling or squatting. Ty and Bdubs broke chortle into a sustained duet of "ooooooooohhhh," with each of them competing to see who could hold it the longest, which was always Belmont, before choking out into more laughter. This, incidentally, was one of two reasons why they chose to sit at the foot of one of the opposing 'H's that day and every other similar day of their academic careers-- the maximum visual exposure. The other reason was the blotted swatch of white paint just over their heads covering up about fifty alternating iterations of the black-krylonned phrase 'Dick and Balls' sprayed across a flat stretch of white brick at about chest level, and covered and recovered repeatedly over too many semesters at City U to be uniquely attributable to any attending vandal in particular. Ty admired the communal fortitude of generational adherence to running out the gag. Belmont enjoyed the futility of antidisestablishmentarianism which was the gag's central thesis. Neither of them were yet responsible for a new layer, but the both of them would

---

[49] *Hitchhiker's Guide to the Galaxy*, directed by Douglas Adams (Touchstone Pictures, Spyglass, 2005).

contribute at least a dozen novel iterations over the coming seasons of serious academic commitment.

"What do you think they would name it? If they all got to pick whatever they wanted?"

"Dick and Balls, of course."

"Dick and Balls University, Mississippi."

"D-B-U-M."

"DeeBUM"

"BDubs goes to DeeBum."

"Yeah your dad goes to DeeBum, commie."

"Shitty U."

"Shitty YOOOOOOOOO!" Belmont shouted in the form of a whisper over giggling. Both of them began pumping their fists in the air and high-school-football chanting 'Shitty You,' to no one in particular, being casually disregarded by the Tennial participants as kind of shiftless loiterers. The sun climbed higher overhead, cramming all their shadows further under their own feet as they milled around from booth to booth, happily engaging in any lame revelries that weren't actual class. It was during those unexpectedly jovial moments out of doors and not quite involved in the spectacle that Belmont had one of his first great straight ideas. He let it percolate for several hours until the pair returned to their cellular dormitory space in D3-14. The D's were the (Domiciliary) apartment buildings, stretched small-end facing the walk along the left, or leeward side, of the long corridor between the 'H's. They shared the fourteenth unit in the third building, which afforded them a more centrally panoramic view, technically, of the whole spectacle, but they would have had to sit inside, for one thing, and for another, they would have both have had to sit in front of Ty's little double-paned vinyl window, because the L shaped two-bunk units in D3 only had one exterior adjacent living quarters each. To sit in front of that window and look out of it, furthermore, would have required Belmont and Tyberius to move an absolute shitload of hardware that had taken three carloads to transport over from Ty's garage-cave, and three of the last ten days to arrange and debug.

(74)

  Some technically inclined people fancy themselves programmers. Among programmers, a hacker is just a programmer exploiting a skillset. Among hackers around City U, mostly just edgier, darker-clothed, emotionally slack nerds of varying degrees of technical proclivity, newcomers Belmont and Tyberius were already a varsity sensation. Belmont had a photographic memory, and Tyberius's father engineered actual spaceships. Between the two of them was a preponderance of inherited intellectual capital. They were especially proud of their rigs, which included two XE3 server racks, a Centron flat panel workstation with lots of what Belmont called 'gas,' a wireless JBron audio system, three peripheral monitors, and a Zeta class gateway with an extender that pretty much let them log into their home system from anywhere within six blocks of the campus. Campus domiciliary network access is both metered and monitored, so Belmont dragged a rickety old twenty-foot extension ladder out of a maintenance shed and over to the red clapboard facade beneath Ty's window and climbed up with a power drill and a modest sized Zeltro dish on the first day they started hauling over gear. Theirs' was by no means the first independent network on the campus, but theirs' was the first one ever capable of handling a bootleg, blackmarket subscription service. Dozens of other students had already shelled out some serious Daddy's CV for access blocks, most of them just wanting faster load times for their own research obligations, but quite a few of them also wanting the perpetually self-sustaining illusion of scrutiny-free porn.

  Back in the Garage, Belmont and Tyberius spent two concurrent years of their combined twenty-five of secondary education writing data link libraries for proprietary coding shells for the aeronautics firm which employed Tdub's weary and wiry old paternus professorus, whose decades-old screen-and-key-bound eyes had preemptively relinquished tenure, well in advance, apparently, of brainstem and spinal cord. Walter's bony fingers just wouldn't fly across the little plastic caps of jumbled ASCII the way they had when he was young. Walter once said Moore's law for humans is just flipped upside down. It had not been very long ago, he had said it, but what was time these days anyway? So he conscripted his free-loading nerd heathens and set them about some ground-level data entry stuff to help ease the workload. Belmont was working on C++ for Kill 'em All mods, and Tyberius had learned the basics of Pearl to do some earlier work on interface elements (rectangles, gray, 4:6, etc); both of them turned out to be gurus with VB and the browser suites, and each could basically recite the OSI model with the Shakespearean conviction of broadway actors. So why not let the boys earn some money? And what better way for Walter to keep a couple of 46/39 eyes on them?

The work was tedious, but the pay was ok, so the boys did it. Along the way, they both became fascinated with machine language, the little ons and offs of billions of little boolean states of semiconducted physical being. Tyberius said he wanted to create their own programming language. Pike said they should just steal one. The boys debated the moral and practical exigencies of each course of action, and after a time, after their fashion, they found consensus somewhere in the middle. Machine language is binary, meaning infinite commands and phrases constructed of and upon the finitude of two possible states of inanimate electronic mode, on or off, one or zero, something and nothing. Tyberius hypothesized a third state, but neither of them could think of a way to make that language mean anything useful, and then they both agreed it was a dumb idea, and laughed at each other. Then Belmont recalled that the unitary packet exchange system in pretty much all the hardware on earth used an eight-bit system, meaning information that was encoded (writing DLL libraries is fucking like mind-numbingly boring work, incidentally) and transferred over an electronic medium was sent piecemeal at lightspeed through time and space as trillions of individual data packets, each packet being eight characters long, each possible character representing any one of a few million hardcoded manifestations of binary machine language sequences of literall oh's and ones.

One or two or three of those eight bits is actual data from what you are trying to send, and the other five or six characters represented in that packet are used by peripherals and modems and network hubs and routers and servers and satellites to identify and determine where and whither the packets should be received, repeated, or rejected, and then, between session and presentation operations, how they should be used, displayed, and arranged. Belmont ripped and cracked a C++ compiler from the Centron network (courtesy of a snoozing-Walter's lifted lanyard, neatly and quietly replaced after innocuous and unnoticed use), added to the stolen compiler ten lines of code, and then broke C++ with the executable. Tyberius wrote a front-end loader in VB that would spend about four hours rewriting the entire C++ language into a representational cipher based on what the boys could have probably patented and sold and profited from as Septaplex technology, eschewing any real need for college altogether.

Anyone could run the FEL on any hardwired electronic system in the world and effectively communicate in the blind with anyone else who was also running a FEL on a hardwired system in the actual world. Any hardwired electronic system in the world not running a FEL would perceive seven-bit character streams as line noise or erroneous packets, either disregarding them or passing them on. Any program written in C++, which included software and protocols couched in most of the browser suites, could be recompiled in Septaplex and would run, mostly fine, as long as it was executed through the FEL. But without Belmont's originally cracked C++ compiler, no user in the network could disassemble the FEL to crack its septupular hierarchy.

Two high school kids basically reinvented their own shadowy, private, inherently anti proprietary version of the operating system universe, upon which, entirely new (if virtual, and therefore RAM intensive) operating systems could be designed, or in most cases, just plagiaristically recompiled. And the whole thing was based on an ingeniously simplistic shell game that any savvy 'Head could have guessed the secret to, but as Belmont reasoned, they were five generations out from the machine language era, and there were maybe less than a hundred senile old tracheotomized geezers out there in the world who hadn't yet been wholly, creatively subsumed by post-secondary and tertiary shell-based thinking. Meaning, even if you broke down a feed into its actual bit sequence and studied it, character by character, it would still take fifty people ten years of highly observant and soul-crushingly mind-numbing reading to figure out that just a single bit was missing from each byte.

The software that would crunch the numbers for the school-slogan competition at City U would be encoded into the same spreadsheets and analyzed by the same statistical analysis software everyone else in the world used, but both of those programs will have been recompiled using Tyberius's front end loader. There's no reason for it, Belmont muses, they just did it because it was cool. Cool, to them, at that impressionable age, mostly comprised a demonstrably increased propensity for mamarian exposure, if not directly obtainable in exchange for cerebral credibility itself, then certainly negotiable otherwise upon the realized fiscal profitability, as in real-CeeVee, of having something lots of people with disposable income want. Belmont's stepfather, a malingering drunk and a piece of shit and, eventually, an absentee, Belmont remembered, had once instructed them both, at very young ages, that there were three things in the world that would buy a woman's love, in this order: Cock, Cash, and Cocaine. 'The Three C's', the old man would say. In a roundabout way, overall, in their time at City U, to the ruination of certain lofty, preconceived, platitudinal patterns of received thought, Belmont and Tyberius found this vulgar provincialism to be essentially axiomatic.

Coolness, in most of the types of settings a couple of nerdy college kids were likely to find their way into early on, was ubiquitously proportional to one's ability to lay the most of any one or more of the Three C's on the table. Where they might run short on any given one, for any length of time, they found the other two to be, typically speaking, consistently reliable surrogates, fungible, as it were. For titties. It's crazy how many in common of the greatest stories ever told tend to pivot on a single pair of titties.

Strictly speaking, by the numbers, City U's slogan was in fact laughably close to becoming Dick and Balls, and probably would have been, had the Direct Democracy Advocacy Council kids not gotten really-fucking-high behind the Pool-and-Bowling H before semifinal varsity debate rounds against the adhoc Representative Republic Preservation Society kids (too many of them, predictably, sieg-heiling from the semi-rural suburbs of southeastern Melville), during the fall semester of the 'dubs' junior year, and fudged out on a two-one for dropping the counterargument visavis the urgency of acuity of specialist-educations in confronting highly complex geopolitical challenges. These things do happen.

Belmont tended toward promiscuity in short, patterned bursts. Tyberius, bending stiffly to the winds of romantic ideation, managed to fall into all-consumptive adoration of the unobtainable-- an eidetic, middle aged, drug-addicted lesbian-cum-escort, who taught a heavy class at City U about psychoanalytical engineering. The boys sold copies of Tyberius' C-Poly Front End Loader to large swaths of the student body, on cheap Ten Meg Zeltro thumb drives, for a thousand credits a pop. During their final year of college, and having amassed more than a half-million yet-unspent credits just on domestic (which was what they called the City U market) FEL distribution alone, the boys decided to do everyone's homework for every class for every individual student who had forked over the toll to surf the C-Poly highway and check their email and watch interracial gangbangs and order badly jostled room-temperature takeout and play Kill 'em All and other retro titles and pirate-Pirate-PIRATE anything else their little hearts desired from anywhere in the world. Local papers took brief notice of the graduating class of ▇ which finished with a strength-average a full one and one half points higher than any other GPA average of any class in the annals.

After eight years and a little off-grid tweaking of some collation variables, Belmont and Tyberius announced the new school slogan, (nearly) neatly derived from thousands of submissions, themselves tabulated and processed in the aggregate under twelve different theoretical object-value-assignment frameworks, until a significant prevalence of linguistically coterminous instances presented themselves. Tyberius suspected Belmont had a romantic-type inner tectonic activity concerning a girl he worked with at the bar where he moonlit, not for the money, but for easy access to lots of other girls who weren't her, and Belmont dismissed this idea out of hand. City University would henceforth be known throughout the remainder of the Second Republic, as would be chiseled into the unplastered white stone above the administrative leg entryway of the Gymnastics-and-Auxiliary H, and printed on thousands upon thousands of colorful trifold brochures and pamphlets and various swaggy cups and bracelets and ruled-notebooks and sweatshirts and hoodies, and bannered across the ends of mid-grade audio-visual contrivances syndicated to local broadcast stations on television sets across southern Mississippi and surrounding areas-- City University, *an Idyllic Institution.*

(75)

The boy awakened from dreamless sleep to find the world enveloped by darkness in motion. The oversized wheels beat out staccato pulses over gravel and ruts that made the whole bus shiver. The vague, lightless, uncivilized night poured past in blurry refractions through the rectangular windows which did not open. Smells of stagnant perspiration and rattled bowels permeated the dry heat in the cabin. He was sitting in the window aisle, with a dull, flattened throb over his left temple where his head had rested against the aluminum frame that perimetered the safety glass through which he could see a phantom representation of his own face more clearly than anything on the other side. A little dribble of drool hung from the corner of his mouth, and as he became conscious of it after a few seconds, he lifted his hand to wipe it away, which motion caused his mother to stir and take stock of the boy's condition and affectation. Looking up at her and trying to piece together the rabble of images which had made up the day's events, the boy remembered the old leering vagabond, and was comforted to observe that his mother's throat remained unslashed. Something idle in her quiet mannerism suggested that their luggage was also safely on board and had not been forcefully burgled at the station while the boy slept through his watch.

The civilized patrons of these and other well-trodden paths kept about themselves a kind of unspoken courtesy about the protocols and etiquette of traveling at night. By sun up, the boy knew from many miles of experience, folks in the various seats fore and aft would stir themselves with full-bodied yawns and constricted stretching motions and the rustling sounds of fingers digging through shadows for toiletries and granola bars and phones and a fresh Tee here and there, and even the most reserved of strangers would temporarily disengage their protective internal mechanisms and become bellicose and outgoing. Randomly, they would make eye contact with others around them making their own similar perfunctory noises, and ask how the other slept, if the other was excited for the Ports of Call, if the other wanted half of this granola bar, if the other had a couple extra squares of that good toilet paper because the stuff in the little shitter closet in the back, where the all-one-piece resin plastic toilet is sort of bolted down onto the chassis almost directly over the rear axle, for maximum gluteal shock absorption, or minimal efficiency of standing aim, circumstances vary, is either all out or just all awful, and you'd might as well use your fingers, which is an argument that tends to motivate the most sanguine of generous impulses of those passengers seated nearby, regarding toilet paper.

But at night, the boy could not hear a whisper. Nothing moved in the cabin, which made it seem very nearly the same as if nothing breathed. The hypervigilant busdriver in his elevated chair and neatly pressed khakis was god, alone in the void, towing corpses for cargo through the treacherous abysses of time and space. A stoic and sturdy soul, capable of rigidity in motion for hours upon hours on end, enshrouded in darkness and silence like an old cemetery stone, only rolling amongst the overgrown woods. Somewhere, high above, from his lone vantage point through the oversized windshield, he could glimpse a little sliver of a moon and a couple of stars on the edges of a gathering summer storm, following into his own vector from just eastward, over the tallish empty hills and pimply briars what shrugged about their shoulders under indifferent and sporadic breezes, just enough to break up the smoother lines between darker black earth below and the halated black glow of the sky above.

The boy remembered waiting and waiting, watching other buses come and go with some special haste, it seemed, swinging wide into their bays and emptying their coffers of straggling indigenous into the stale, dry, yellow-lit air of the round pavilion, down off of the pneumatically lowered steps onto the oil-slick and butt-littered parking area asphalt, through little turnstiles, to the glass doors and through them again into asymmetrical confluences of nests of brown hard-resin one piece chairs, in exchange for new clusters of red-eyed and napless souls, slapping legs and asscheeks and other parts of the body trying to snooze through the clarion call of the now-boarding rush, fumbling at pockets for half-crumpled ticket receipts that proved they each had consummated the act of bribery with an apathetic clerk. The boy had drifted off, in spite of his best efforts, and did not know that the old-soul juggernaut of a bus driver had taken pity on Ms. Solvierro, and helped cart her sporty luggage assembly to the underloader, so she could tote her bag-of-potatoes son out of his own chair, through the glass door, lifting him longways as she tried to slip through the turnstiles, which took a second try to kind of step back and lunge through with some momentum, up the lowered steps and back to the middle of the bus, theoretically equidistant by conscious measurement from each of the jackhammering, suspensionless axles, the area of the bus which veterans know to be most congenial to near-sleep.

Near-sleep is the only kind of sleep anyone ever achieves in transit. Only at the terminals and stations in between is it possible to reach that level of black, dead-lidded, oblivious unconsciousness known as being passed-the-fuck-out, because only at terminals and stations is it conceivable that one can sleep through a boarding call. Someone will wake you when the bus or train or plane or boat or ship stops, because they've got to clean and sell those seats again. No one knows who the hell you are at a bus station, nor where you're going, nor why, nor at which hour of departure, and no one gives a shit whether or not you sleep there, all cockeyed and jammed into a slithering L against the little space of wall between the men's room and the vending machine programmed to eat every third voucher fed to it in exchange for the promise of expired nuts, five-packs of gum that are tactilely hard in the pocket, and off-brand breath mints purchased more often out of desperation by the starving than out of courtesy by the halitosic.

A slow hour passed on the road, narrated only by the rushing sound of rubber displacing stone and dirt at high speeds and slinging it against the undercarriage. His mother had given him a handful of oat grain cheese crackers she had haggled with the vending machine over the fair market value of, eventually conceding the asshole tax to the system for the bland cover of imitation nutrients. A particularly concave divot in the road had been exaggerated by recent rains. The front right tire left the ground, smashed into the hole with a crunching boom that rocked every set of knees and jaws and sphincter muscles on board, and then rebounded into levelish sod, all in the space of a half-second, and the bus driver motored right on through it with hardly a flinch and a not more than a small bead of sweat on his right temple. Bus driver training programs and operator's manuals were emphatic about how long, top heavy, wide-assed, poorly maintained, ceaselessly throttled, presently inhabited, under-insured busses, being driven at high speeds on bad roads through the distant expanses of unzoned and uninhabited desert and forest hills, just absolutely should not under any circumstances be jerked about by the oversized steering wheel that was so loose it converted one full revolution of the hands into one eighth of a turn in either direction at the tire. It was always best to just hit whatever was there, straight on, than to risk swerving into a fishtail and turning the whole damned thing over and killing everyone on board in the process.

(76)

The old vagabond, it would seem, had not been an old vagabond as such. It had in fact, like everyone else on board who had been fortunate enough to afford the privilege of fleeing the revolution, succeeded in proffering sufficient funds of its own to obtain passage. The boy had taken notice almost immediately after awakening, but circumstance and context had forced him to reevaluate his initial premises and corollary assumptions. Maybe some insidious internal complex of long-buried and unconfronted personal biases had corroborated with the heat-fatigue and socially contagious anxieties about literally-everything-going-on-right-now, and instead of seeing another human being, maybe the boy had been in the Third World just long enough to only see another desperate vagrant.

Something about the old man even looked different. The clothes weren't as old and weather worn as they had first appeared. Some illusion of the subconscious maybe. The gray, receding tussle the boy remembered along the fellow's hairline looked somehow denser and less *en retraite*. He just seemed a little crisper, the boy thought. Even in the dark, the boy could see the whites of the man's eyes clearly. The man was sitting quietly and unobtrusively a few seats ahead, body turned in the familiar back-to-window flex of those lucky, entitled souls who don't have to sit with a stranger or their mom, and staring intently out into the infinite nothing passing by like a newsreel in the opposing window. Either the man had changed clothes and bathed and groomed himself and had help doing it, all in the space of a couple of hours, presumably in the cramped and dim, vinegary light of the bus station men's room, or the boy was going to have to proactively confront the acuity of his own senses, perceptions, values, and filters.

"If you got money they gonna let you leave." That was the only time the boy had heard the man's voice, and even then he hadn't really been paying attention to the sound of it, so he tried to remember, sitting there staring at something he had instinctively feared and trying to locate anything fearful about the thing at all. What a miracle a few hours of sleep can work on the human condition, the boy supposed. To say nothing of a hottish sink-shower and some fresh clothes. It was as if the man had gotten to the end of an arduous journey before actually arriving at the final destination. He was already washed clean and rested and renewed, and the weight of being gone on his adventures which had bewitched his spirit and beleaguered his body had been lifted out of the very cells in his skin, muscles, bones, and organs. Ready to go back to work already and reconnect and tell his vacation fish stories to colleagues.

The boy was sure the man had some kind of *Real Job*, that was how his mother put it sometimes, when her voice gets that kind of mean sound in it that she never uses with him, and he had colleagues and he wore a suit sometimes if he wanted to, but no one told him to do it or to not do it. The boy wondered if the man's voice, which he only remembered now in dull fragments, would belong to the man sitting a few seats ahead, staring out the window, in the here-and-now, or if it would sound discordant and frail, like the more wraithlike creature which had nearly accosted them with gnarled fingernails and heat-bitten teeth. And then the boy wondered if he had not in fact confused one entire person for an entirely different person altogether, as occasionally happened in foreign lands. Then what inconsistent values and engrained biases must he confront!

These were the boy's thoughts, there in the bus with a dozen strangers barreling across nowhere toward one of the seven great pillars of man-made technological prowess in the known world. And in the midst of these thoughts, the man sitting a few seats ahead, back-to-window, the boy realized, was no longer staring intently out the window into the voids, but was again peering a straight line over gold rims on a sharp nose, watching the sleeping woman and the boy, watching him, watching them, watching him. Watching them.

(77)

Pike, back aboard ship at last, breathless and barely conscious, posed among an indolent central root system of indeterminate tendrils of shadows webbing together the two cusping worlds, the glaring, floodlit citadels of industry and progress behind, and the dim celestial infinitude of brightly burning unknowability ahead. The six-gauge glass-like-resin that constituted the transparent medium encased in provisionally airtight portholes, themselves arranged along vestigial N.E.W.S. axes, forward, aft, port, starboard, dimmed the light and refracted it-- objects in the aft view were less distant than they appeared. The colorless printed-resin material facades over the steel-framed bulkheads lent no artificially chromaticized mood to the dualistic play of light and shadow through conduits of exposed shield-cord, twelve inch pythons of ventilation ducting, odd-angled dog latches surrounding airtight doors and hatches, low-profiled sensory equipment dangling like stalactites from processing assembly units mounted surreptitiously in the overhead. In the motionless silence of the frozen world at the helm of the *Epicurean,* the panoramic still frame of the real-estate contest between illumination and darkness approached proportional parity. If Pike breathed in deeply and held the air, swelling his chest and abdomen, the shadows in the space seemed to extend and overtake the balance of power, subsuming the visible light. But the longer he held the air in his lungs, without exhaling, the more the pressure of pulsing blood vessels would build between his throbbing temples, tinting his vision with a dull and uncomfortable crimson, which the colorless resin facades would somehow enhance and clarify until the whole ambient scene of black and white melted into rouge. If he evacuated his lungs and clenched his stomach and leaned heavily into the exhaust until his chest was just an abstract concavity in mourning, the absence of oxygen to his brain would sharpen the visual effects of the slight advantage derived by ambitious photons from his deflated, diminished form, and the space around him seemed to become infused with hazy palettes of vanilla cream and sterile linen. If he measured his breathing in fully consistent intervals, in, out, in, out, in, without blinking, the huge convex portal in the forward bulkhead seemed to shrink by halves in his perspective, with the whole field of vision compacting itself, appearing more and more distant until Pike blinked his dry eyes a few times to reset his focus.

Pike held in the forefront of his neocortex a vision of a petrified locust shell clung to the flowering vines of a wormwood bush. He tried to recall the smell of wormwood, and couldn't. He knew the thing inside him had been his soul, the thing that had fled its shell and left the rest of his carcass to rot here in a hightech orgy of pretenses and vanities, as a ghostless machine ritually sacrificed, with bound limbs and shorn of agency, condemned to remain behind to pull the levers and press the buttons and speak the commands to another machine, one designed to do the same, until the novel momentum of cause and effect would carry unto the prevailing generations a new retinue of deities. And he had but to speak the Word into the avalent void, to commence, to move from one resting revolution from zero to one, from infinite nothing to something new under the sun, and eventually beside it, and then beyond it, and beyond others still, through another phase of surrogate nothingness seductively draped in the veils of substance and tangibility and promise and optimism and hope, still nothingness, he knew, Pike sitting there in his Captain's chair, seemingly in command of everything from a bug's eye view, and of nothing, at once, of nothing at all, from the self's third eye view of history and evolution.

For his part in the story, Pike had persuaded the thing to explain the game, albeit in language Pike could comprehend in vague strokes, and which no one else ever would grasp, perhaps, through his own lips. And the game was stupid. It was endless, and worse, *mercifully so.* Condescendingly banal, antiquated, obsolescent emptiness of purpose and meaning. And so blatantly rigged as to have simply disregarded the fourth wall altogether, not of neglect, but of apathetic contempt for the rest of us. Every player in the first-person-shooter was a non-player-character. There could be no arc, no climax, no resolution, no *denouement,* because at the bottom of everything, Good and Evil weren't even actually at war with one another. They were turbulently codependent lovers in a romantic sitcom made for public broadcast to a post-literate generation of hopelessly-willing--buyers with nothing of their own to sell. Pike resented the hollow, hamfisted illusion of circumstance which had abandoned his broken remnants here on these patent-leather shores, literally entombed in a sophisticated shrine of spent money, longing for nothing more in the universe than the soothing ground current of a familiar voice. And one would answer, in this otherwise desolate mausoleum of human achievement.

Pike imagined Subjective Life to be a short glass, filled to the brim with futility, chilled with ice cubes of disappointment, and that those rare souls capable of higher order intelligence got to drink their's with a little bar cherry of disillusionment. Pike tried to imagine what kind of desert wasteland of an afterlife would compel the kind of thirst even the dimmest of souls would need to endure to even consider tasting the concoction more than once. The kind of oppressively shadeless heat that dried the lips to sores, boiled the fluid out of every exposed patch of ethereal skin, charred bare feet to cinders. The wailing choirs of bored and tortured voices from all points on the horizon, screaming the screams of razor blades in the stomach and drill bits in the genitals and buzzsaws across ligaments and lit matches to eye tissue, and always screaming, not at at anything, but at the utter hideousness and abject terror and unbridled wrath of True Nothing, of that profound vacancy that is the natural mathematical antithesis of Subjective Life. The want of life, being death, and exponential incrementalization of death, resolvable only by the want of death, which Pike now understood in his bones, to mean Subjective Life. To covet that which one craves is to yield only what one already possesses and nothing more. So drink up.

Pike imagined the burnt-paraffin shell of his own little locust outliving the little buzzing automatonymous morsel of revelatory flesh, gleefully redeemed from what must have felt like a sweltering prison, only to be snagged in the midst of exaltations to grace and liberty and agency by either one or the other of the craggy old birds of prey strutting around nearby-- watching the miracle of life unfold with all the patient calm of hungry murderers. Pike tried forcefully not to think about Tyberius. Or of Centronautics. Or of titties. Or of interminable rows, banks, columns, and racks of Comanche Servers, glittering black-faced and chirping alternating trialogues of blue and green and yellow LEDs. Or of the twin Pentathlonite Ground Thrusters, rated 763 KTPS (Sixty-Four Thousand Newtonian Tonnes), hanging like testicles from the crotch of the *Epicurean*. Or of the cathedral-esque communal vacancy of one-hundred-thirteen fully-furnished living quarters, including his own, which called out with anthropomorphised wails of its own for his soul to return once again, hat in hand and seeking refuge and reconciliation.

Or of oncoming musters, mission data reports, missile hazard control protocols, of the kinetic frenzy of Launch and Pre-Launch and Post-Launch procedures, of graceful troupes of drones carting wooden pallets of boxed supplies and strapped equipment and steel containers full of personal effects, luggage, suits, etc., and a motorcycle-- because someone always brings one, in pregnant webs of chain link and polyester banded netting. Or of grand successions of the arbitrarian Republics of Man, *emergente,* into the skeptical and wary realms of distant space where grander things awaited. Or of the ceremonial boy who, by tradition, would fetch and furl the final anachronistic rigging, which was a thick and scraggly old ash-colored rope that had moored lesser ships in antiquity. Or of the fucking-dope-ass speaker systems throughout, which had been Ty--

(78)

Pike lived in his moment of True Choice. Purposefully motionless in an industrial torpor of solitude, contemplating the Deus ex Machina, which is what he called the .38 snub nose in his pocket, which Tdubs had lovingly sneered at the irony of, the Checkovian *homage,* not the gun. Every ship captain had one. Standard issue, by design. Because Certain Centron Allums had individually hailed from (among many early fledgeling conglomerates) a couple of war era manufacturers of the proprietary bullet, generations prior, but also because the snub frame just cost less to make; although, Pike reasoned, the shorter barrel made sense on a starship. Closer quarters ingratiate angularly wider dispersion of Newtonian Force. The thing packs a mean right hook from the inside pocket, but in most places anyone could get to on board a ship, it wouldn't do much more than fuck up the paint on the bulkheads.

Most places, but not the Bridge. The Bridge was pretty much the one place on a Centronaut where a snub nose .38 could really do some serious functional damage.

And not just because the man holding it was still, presently, the only living soul on board, sitting in the polished-leather captain's chair, beaten and bruised and broken, and bored, but breathing, and not quite yet bested by anyone else alive but himself. In these moments, Pike was thinking that besting himself was an option. Be the first, and the last, and get the credit for it. Or, conversely, that he needed only to break the silence and be redeemed. Not with the sound of fury, of a gunblast properly angled just so that it would pierce the first two inches of the aft cabin porthole glass, rendering it critically compromised with respect to pressurization standards set by the manufacturer and extenuated by the insurance companies, and with skull matter and viscera, rendering the painted bulkhead around the porthole also, decidedly, unambiguously, pointedly less colorless.

Instead, with the sound of the affirmation of self which is implied in the call which acknowledges the existence and utility of another. Pretty much anywhere on the bridge, wherever the intense aftward light fell upon anything and yielded its vectors to shadow, a point-blank round from the snubnose in the here and now would basically obviate the course of human history. Pike just wanted to feel better, whether it was real or imagined or false or artificial... if even for a moment. Pike tried not to think of the reverberating sound of thunder on sonically resonate printed resin, chemically buffed to a smooth achromatic mirror's shine prior to installation, or the sulfuric cascade of spark and flash and reflash and combustion that would roll away from his face in the slightly over-oxygenated atmosphere set into conflagration by the little spring loaded hammer striking the silver plate beneath the eighteen grains of black powder encased in a .38 shell.

"Hey dad. I'm ready."

A whirring cacophony of circuit board power supply heatsink fans preceded preliminary pressurization systems by a few nervous seconds, like the feeling of pause at the top of a roller coaster, Pike felt. The rumble of larger fan assemblies inflating interwoven shipwide ductile systems with precious oxygen. The faroff hissing echoes of near-hysterical screams of air being forced into depressurized voids and cavities, trailing off after a few horrendous moments as the ship's internal atmosphere gasped and coughed and sputtered towards a comfortably habitable equilibrium. Then the perceptibly muted roar of the first tier Pentathlonite ignition systems outside the Bridge's viewport, away and down a few hundred meters, where the ionized air and superheated dust formed little gleaming convections of wispy neon particulate, emulating the undular tidal forces of thermal energy in motion with visual specificity. After these primary ignition regulators came the secondary magnetic propulsion systems, audiated by the crunchless sounds of well lubricated servos spinning against egg-shaped copper clusters in the inner workings of the huge testicular Pentathlonites. Even before the illumination sensors booted up, certain swarms of drones were already up off of their haunches in search of priority intake tags in the fields of rows and columns and piles of equipment and supplies and crew effects, and that fucking motorcycle. And these made noises too, but Pike would not hear them. He tried not to think of Tyberius.

After ten minutes of phrenetic *techno en utero* auditory assaults on the central nervous system, the *Epicurean* has obtained boardwide tolerances concurrent with prolonged homeostasis. Lights, one relay after another, with little noticeable tics as successive junctions received their loads, penetrated the darkest spaces on board. Berthings, passageways, engineering spaces, the galleys, holds, heads, bays, crawlspaces, office spaces, research and development laboratories, nutritional agricultural acceleration compartments, recreational facilities, administrative stations, server rooms, and the Store. All came alive and into focus and received definition and validation, all found waiting to be filled and occupied and inhabited for the first time ever as unique, individual places in reality. High stakes sensory apparati throughout the ship made no noise and gave no visual indication of operability or status of function, but those systems also booted and loaded and ran, delivering nonproprietary hexadecimal terabytes of information per second to the ship's internal cognition hardware.

And at last, a voice. Like Walter's, crisp and clean, without static or pronounced bass or nasally treble, softened with the kind of precision which did not undermine the natural, authoritative depth with which the old man, who had been a born narrator, spoke about just about anything at all, whether intriguing or pedestrian. A familiar voice that conveyed patience and reason and a kind of unspoken voluntary surrogacy which occasionally accompanies fraternity between a bastard and his best friend. Slightly altered, inevitably so, of course, by the electronic representation, like a loved one on the telephone. A voice of casual impersonality that commanded respect and rebuked complacency and had once spoken inspired bits of fatherly wisdom into the sporadically credulous ears of over-educated boys grown at opposing ends of the spectrum of privilege. A naturally resonant voice that did not sound like a machine trying not to sound like a machine. But the voice, nonetheless, of nothing less than a machine.

"Good morning, Belmont! All services at the ready. Where is Tyberius?"

Pike just sighed.

(Centron)
(79)

Victoria Shelby Smith awoke once more to heavy lights, either for the second time or the third time, and either way after some wicked fucking dreams, which themselves seemed to fade in her mind like snowflakes on the tongue, as burdensome consciousness returned to sharpen the edges of each needling serrated knife slashing into her temples. Brain injuries, wherever hot lead is involved, tend to hurt *differently.* She remembered the pain from the leg thing, about three bones either splintering or shattering on the rolling ball of her foot as it slid off of a broken pump heel in the rain on a sidewalk in front of a man she had been making every effort to seduce in as seductive of a manner as she was capable. It had hurt like fire in her legs, for weeks, even on the non-habit-forming hippy-grade synthetic dry-hump opioids they had prescribed, but after about an hour, the pain had been dull, like roasting her nub-foot over open coals from a hazardous but noncombustible distance. Now, however, tears were rolling down her face, colliding with red rivulets and denaturing them, so the subsidiary streams flowed more swiftly. Parts of her brain were missing. Gray matter, roughly the mass of a baby bird, eviscerated by a clean slug from a .38 through a three centimeter entry in the right temple, through the ventromedial prefrontal cortex, and out through a two inch cavity just over her left temple, slightly overlapping it and behind, where you put headphones when you're trying to hear someone talk without giving them your full attention. She wore a turban of originally-cream-colored adhesive gauze, nearly soaked through with her own blood, visible to herself only vaguely, like a cloud above her peripheral vision, damp and warm and heavier than usual. Stained blonde streaks clung to her neck and chest like fossilized sea-creatures, immobilized and rubbery crisp to the touch, like wet copper wiring that can be bent between the thumbs but not folded. A paper gown covered the tattoos above her breasts more effectively than it concealed the breasts themselves, which rose and fell and pointed sharply at the two cork paneled ceiling tiles just inside the two overhead halogens. The non-absorbent gown was saturated with the pinkish summer sweat of a suicide survivor. The way gravity had molded the wet paper around the corners and curves of her arms and chest was invasive, her armpits were hospital corners, her stomach had a couple of straggling ripples where the fabric had not fallen quite evenly, but the cavity of her navel was pronounced, as was the two-toned polka dotted Y where her thighs began. She felt the cheap linen on her bare ass, and over her bare knees and feet the woolen gray scouring pad of a blanket the military reserves exclusively for immuno-vulnerable indigenous peoples and armed services recruits sworn to support and defend the constitution of these united states from all enemies, both *foreign and domestic.*

She could hear the sound of each slow heartbeat like someone pressing a conch shell to her ear and smacking it with a rubber mallet. Each percussive pulse sent four hundred forty volts dripping down her spine like hot grease. The heavy lights were no more than forty watts each, shrouded by nicotine yellow plastic shields which did not inhibit dust or tiny bugs with nothing left to live for. She was never sure which parts of the second hospital visit were dreamscapes and which ones were real, but she was pretty sure this was the third one, anyway. Miss Shelby, the habitually hospitalized magnolia in secondhand pearls and an open-assed reverse horrorshow purple polka dotted white paper kimono. Pseudo-Morphine dripped like a ticking clock down a little piss-colored tube hanging from a steel bar welded to the wall, and another machine, also bolted to the wall, had a screen where colorful rows of jagged lines scribbled sharp spikes in real time if she coughed or laughed or cried or tried to move at all. It beeped to the beat of a song she knew but couldn't remember, and with a staggered interval of latency that placed each chime right in between each nerve rending heartbeat, right in the quiet little valley between Olympian peaks of electronically quantifiable pain, an annoying little chirp announcing the next burst of agonizing flood of cortisol and ocular saline in three, two...

"OH DEAR gOD FUCK IT HURTS!"

And then she was wailing and willfully and conscientiously avoiding gnashing her teeth. She could clench her fists, or she could release them, and neither resulted in any measurable relief. She might as well still be awake during open surgery, with dull scalpels rooting and prodding clumsily and aggressively, even contemptuously, violently, maliciously, shoving around raw viscera and slicing through whole layers of cortex the way one searches couch cushions with a karate palm for spare change. The tempo of the slow song she couldn't remember was ascending toward something you could dance to. She pressed her eyes closed, and then opened them. Pressing them closed confined her to the sensorial darkness in which the pulsing of her heart occupied the full reach of her focus. The foot pedal smashed the bass drum with more and more velocity in common time, then a 3/4, then a march. She bit down on her tongue, pressed her palms flat against the soiled low-ply sheets, and looked straight up above her, arching her back a little to strain to move the dazzling halogens just beneath her periphery and focus on the dark shadows behind and above her now single-use pillow and case. She craned herself up onto her forearms, tasting iron, breasts heaving, spine lanced upward on a tripod of elbows and a bare ass on disposable sheets fouled with piss and shit and blood and sweat; the machine was playing a nice waltz now, and maybe she was finding that zen moment where intensely inspired willpower can force the beast backwards out of one's no-no zone, but to anyone casually observing through the unmonitored, closed-circuit camera system installed in the unmanned sickbay, it sure looked like she was having a seizure.

(80)

<Begin Transcript: Jones, T., et al, Vs Centron; Deposition Statement Vinson, B., 4/36>

Interviewer: "I understand what you're saying Mr. Vinson, believe me I do. It's just that in a transcript, certain, say, vernacular grammatical inconsistencies can be detrimentally what's-called 'Cold Read', you see, as in the word RED, you know, past tense, meaning happening now, but read in print form in the future by people who may not understand what you're saying, you see, and may interpret what contextually you and I here and now understand to be unequivocal denials of ever having even been to Colorado, when you say it, you know, conversationally, and uhmm, what's the word, em-, yes, *emphatically*, you always seem to have just the word I'm looking for Mr. Vinson, yessir, You and me are here in this little boring little office, and you see I don't even have the cuffs on you or anything, because from where I sit I don't really think you're in any kind of real trouble, you understand, but for the transcript, you see, for the traaaanscript, not for me Mr. V, I'm what you call impersonal, and I know I know what you're going to say, I'm dressed like every other one of these shills at this obscure, weatherbeaten, out-of-the-way kind of facility, No, I can't tell you the name of it, I can't tell you anything really, no, No, I'm sorry, it's the rules you see, but like I was saying, between you and me and the two old filing cabinets and this piece of shit budget Dee Eye Why particle board desk that probably came in a much smaller cardboard box with an allen wrench and some poorly-translated English instructions, I mean look at this thing, a buck fifty, maybe two at the old wally world, you see, there ain't no money here, that ain't really what we're about you see, now I tell you, I'm the friendly one, I'm the nerdy guy, you remember the ninja turtles, yeah, you watched them when you was a kid, hell man me too I always loved that show as a kid, I always wanted to be the nerdy one, you know, old Donnie, used to watch them cartoons all the time and I always liked how he had a whole lot of cool stuff and if he didn't have it he'd invent the thing right there on the spot, you know, just always the smartest guy in the room really savin' the day, you know, like all the rest of them were just as good'a' fighters and all that, one would make jokes and one was always serious and one was always pissed off and remember that rat? The old guy in the room who already knew everything and was tryna' teach the little guys somethin' before his time came, you know, so anyway, that's how I always was, and still am, and maybe not quite the same as you, but I think maybe you was probably a lot like old donnie too, no, really, reeeally, the red one eh? Wouldn't have guessed it, but your partner there, he's definitely the blue one, right, I mean, always with the philosophizing' and conversation', yeah, see, right, you agree with me, you say

Tyberius was a pain in the ass, right, I get that, okay, thanks for that, I mean, you know, We try to do things right here and that's why I tell you you know you're not really obligated to tell us anything at all without your lawyer you know, that's just because we're not trying to get over on you or anything like that, just figured since you're willing to to at least chat a bit about whatever you know, for the record, and everything, while we're waiting on Mr.- Mister, misterrrr- while we're waiting on your legal council to drive up from Melville, Mr. Vinson, I just want you to know I see it in you though, you seem inventive and innovative and I've read a little bit about your work you know, and we do make it our business to sorta keep an eye on the bright lights and I get it you know, you're joking a little bit when you say you're the red one, and I can kind of see that little chuckle in the corner of your eye like you're pulling my leg a little, but, but what now? You say your favorite color is red and you've never actually been to Colorado, ever, at all, in all your livelong days? You're telling me now that you and ol' Tdawg your hetero life mate didn't cut out for a little fun in the sun and hit the rockies and try to catch a Broncs game after that big super secret conference thing that was in all the papers but none of the journalists or reporters could find, let alone get into, while it was happening? You're saying, and again, unequivocally, that you weren't, that is, you *were* not, un-e-quiv-o-cal-ly NOT in Colorado for that conference, well buddy you missed a hell of a game, I wasn't there anyway but I caught some of it on the television and I thought them ol' boys played pretty well, do you like football Mr. V, do you watch a lot of sports? No? Wait which part? I mean you don't like football but you watch sports, no, you say you don't like any of it, I guess I can see that, me neither really, I kind of have a little bit of respect for soccer, mainly because what all them countries where people play it are going through these days, but also because it just seems like a helluva lot of work, you know, yeah, running up and down that field, but you'd have probably liked that game anyway, old uhh, old uhh, oh what's his name, fella scored three touchdowns in the first quarter, hell of an arm, oh hell what's his name, can you remember? McEnroe? Is that it? No, no man that's not even a football player and now I know you're effin' with me and that's because you're comfortable and we're just having a nice chat and what's that you say, you would like some water because you're talking a lot and I really do appreciate that and yessir I would be totally happy to get you some and thank you for being so respectful and clear about it, you didn't mumble or look down at your feet or just bark it at me like, man, like you wouldn't believe some of the things people, you know, the bad people I have to talk to now and again as my job requires, some of the awful terrible things these people will say, had a lady spit at me the other day and say something unkind about my mother's reproductive system and you know that whole kind of thing and that's why I say I really do appreciate you agreeing to sit down and just chat with us and see this whole thing through in good faith and good humor and I can see that you're here and present and self-possessed and in control and what's that, yessir, sound mind and body, that's just right, you've got it and what I mean to say is that I can see that you're trying to do the right thing even though it's hard to always know exactly what that is, especially when you're where you are you know, and it can always be real tempting you know to just throw up the old middle finger and say eff this and eff that and eff the whole system and eff me and eff you too I'd say and then we'd be having a whole different kind of interview, you understand, and neither of us wants all that, right? Right. So let's just leave the whole Colorado thing alone for a minute because I can see you're having some trouble with that and you're just not sure you want to comment on whether if or whether for or whatever, and I get that, so let's move on and let me ask you about the weird little helicopter thing you guys own, yessir, that one, you say you don't actually own it? You say Tyberius owns it? Ooohh, ok, okay, I get it, so let me ask you though, how often do you take a ride up in that thing with old Tdubs, he's got pretty good has he?

You say you don't like heights, well, now I kind of find that hard to believe now seein' as how you listed here on your indoc form that your occupation was an Astronaut, let me see, right nere, what's that you say, no, i've got it right here, my bad, I'm sorry, really botched that one, nosir you are correct it says aerospace engineer, well I had a whole joke there about two pollocks and a tire iron but you wouldn't get it and it wouldn't matter anyway and oh, dang I get so comfortable just sitting here having a friendly chat with you and I forget all about the transcript [nervous laughter] and I probably shouldn't be makin' no pollocks jokes or whatever, just ain't used to the way things are these days I guess, it all still seems kind of new, ok so anyway, enough about me let's me and you get back to this Colorado thing now you don't have to get testy with me, I hear you, ok, there's no Colorado thing, it's just you know, for the traaanscript I want to be very clear about wanting you to be very clearly understood, now my clerk is bringing in a manilla folder with your last name and what's called your jacket number and in the folder here, hold on, yeah, see there it is again, aero space engineman, engineer, sorry, ok here is an affidavit my clerk has written up and we've taken the liberty of notarizing and witnessing here for you, now would you be willing to sign this affidavit, now remember this is a legally binding document so we gotta be real clear about what the truth is and which version of it we are committing to the record you see, now would you be willing to sign this affidavit that says what you said earlier for the recording that you have never ever been to Colorado or even travelled out west and that you were in Melville or somewhere else in Mississippi when that big conference was going on out there, you say you didn't even know there was a conference going on out in Colorado and how could you even have known because you don't go to conferences or even like going to conferences or even leaving the state anyway, well that's good, see there, that's why I say I don't think you've got anything to worry about and old Mr. Legal Council will have driven all the way up here from Melville for no reason and them boys in Colorado will just have to keep on looking for their man and all you gotta do really is just go ahead and sign this affidavit, legally swearing you before god and your daddy, rest his soul, and the board members at Centron and the Marshall Service and Delores here who's a Notary Public and myself who ain't nobody really at all, just a fair-minded public servant who's here to help, so how about it buddy, would you be willing to testify before a jury of your peers, or maybe even a grand jury, depending on how this thing plays out, you know whether or not someone finds the body, I guess, or whatever, but you'd be willing to take a solemn oath right here and now for the public record that you've never ever one time ever been to Colorado and you would consummate that testimony with your johnny hancock right here at the bottom of this little affidavit Delores drew up for you while we've been talking, just right here at the bottom where the line is and your printed name beneath it and today's date, is really all we need from you Mr. Vinson and I'd have to check with my superiors but I think if we had that from you right now in this very moment there just wouldn't be any cause to keep you here and we could probably arrange to Oh Are you, you see, that means O. R.-- Own Recognizance, that means you wouldn't even have to serve any time before your court date and you would be free to go, right now, free and clear, until the trial at least, when you might be asked to give that testimony publicly with everyone sitting in the isles you know just waiting on their own appearances and not even really giving a darn about your case and most of them probably not even knowing what Centron is, or was, or is becoming, yep, Oh Are you right here and now with just your signature and everything will be just hunky dorey and fine and dandy, unless you know the D.A. that is Mr. Slims the District Attorney has some questions, or if them boys out there freezing their nuts off scuba-diving through the CR happen to find that body.

Mr. Vinson, now I'm not asking you to sign anything you haven't already basically made real clear for the transcript, now you not signing this thing at this point is basically a confession and I wouldn't think you'd want to go and do a fool thing like that, especially if you wasn't ever even in Colorado or at a conference or a broncs game or the Hilton West in Denver on Melbourne Street at the five hundred block from wednesday to sunday that fourth weekend of the third, or was it the fourth, or the fifth, month of this year of the second republic, and especially, ESPECIALLY, if you've never flown in that little weird helicopter thing old Tdubs bought with Centron's money, am I right? Mr. Vinson? Now Mr. Vinson I can't tell anymore it you're trying to eff with me right now or if you're just killing time until your legal council gets here from Melville, so but now I thought you and I was gonna have a good faith little talk here between law abiding citizens, man to man, as it were, mano y mano, and you were gonna try to help me understand just how mixed up in all this stuff, the scifi shit and the witchcraft stuff and the superhero stories and time travelers and **g**ods and devils and aliens and super smart machines and man you should hear some the crazy stuff, every time I talk to anyone of you that was at that conference, oh yeah buddy, they all tell me all the weirdest kind of stuff I've ever heard, things you'd have to think I was just the dumbest mother effer that ever fell outta' heifer. And they do, and they try to spin me around and nobody wants to play it straight, but buddy I bet you dollars to Little Debbies that them boys out in CO gonna dredge that body up and then I think all of y'all are gonna have some major 'splainin' to do, you hear me talking buddy, you hear me? Well don't just clam up now, say yes sir or no sir and don't just cut your eyes at me like that, look, we're getting ourselves riled in here, let's just take a quick break, and yessirrr-- I would be happy to get that water for you but I need to know, right now, no games, one way or the other, in the clearest possible language, and I need to hear it from you Mr. V, you hear me, I need to hear it right now, did you, or did you not, as in didn't you, ever, ever attend any kind of a conference whatsoever in Colorado, doesn't matter when.

"Okay Mr. V, that's the way you want to play it."

(81)
Centronics: Research and Development Division
New Project Proposal: Modular Evidentiary Processing Service
Developers: Jones, Tyberius; Vinson, Belmont.

Abstract: Violent Crime and Property Crime have become endemic in the Second Republic. Proposed technology described herein presents a unique approach to democratization of these judicial proceedings, wherein available active and passive surveillance systems which capture instances of violent crime and/or property crime offer new opportunities to crowd-source, and therefore effectively expedite, historically resource-intensive and hierarchically cumbersome juridical deliberations. Our proprietary presentation level services empower citizens (subscribers) in possession of audio/visual evidence of an offense to bypass the conventional tedium of ineffective judicial bureaucracies, now antiquated by the passing of the First Republic, by submitting aforementioned content to a corollary network of dispassionate citizens (premium subscribers) who will each individually evaluate and ███ *on the credibility and merit of the content. Our proprietary application and network level services aggregate and analyze response data, yielding highly efficacious assessments of criminal accountability. Our server-side services utilize state-of-the-art biometric recognition systems to provide identification of the accused persons. Law Enforcement Agencies (subscribers, administrators) may use our client-side services to obtain actionable mission priorities. Users of our network services are subject to multi-tiered accountability and incentivization systems. We believe this model represents the eventual obliviation of localized bias in traditionally hierarchical juridical systems, while preserving the equitable promise of fair and speedy outcomes. [50]

---

[50] *[They cut off the devil's electricity while he was typing] [Pike and Tyberius talk about the self and titties] [Editors are a mysterious cult of interlopers] [Localized Socialization of Insurance]

(Dead Girl)[51]
(82)

Vic was in the big concrete square again. Walking forward, turning right, stumbling over catatonics in the fog, walking forward, turning right, listening to the whimpers of two imbeciles huddled against a wall, walking forward, turning right, bearing witness to self-flagellation, walking forward, turning right, an old man splayed across a wheelchair with his chin hanging wide beneath a far off maniacal stare, walking forward, turning right, two painted women in immodest rags with busy hands and lips, walking forward, turning right, assailed by a matrix of excremental smells, walking forward, turning right, a horn-rimmed nerd scribbling nothing on a wall, walking forward, turning right, a man straddling another man and pummeling him with broken bits of bone from she didn't want to think where, walking forward, turning right, three amicable looking men in tophats and each other and nothing else, walking forward, turning right, two frail little wretches with greenish blue skin between the swollen pockmarks along their veins like ant bites leading blind trails back and forth along nearly exposed ribs and emaciated faces and eviscerated limbs, walking forward, turning left, a girl of no more than twenty in a white bridal gown beset by the repugnant red of a hemorrhaging miscarriage, walking forward, turning left, what appears to be a legitimate rape in progress, walking forward, turning left, a grinning skeleton of a creature staring up at the ceiling and practicing cartography on his own chest with razor sharp fingernails sculpted against flat cynder, walking forward, turning left, three nearly neanderthal looking beasts with shaggy black hair and long encrusted beards and leering at her with piqued attention, walking Forward, turning Right, the sound of menacing laughter and footsteps behind her, walking FORWARD, turning RIGHT, a spinster in a wooden chair, affectionately massaging the eye sockets of

---

[51] Acid Bath, "Dead Girl," on *Paegan Terrorism Tactics,* Rotten Records, 1996.

what was not a doll, WALKING FORWARD, TURNING RIGHT, a girl peeling the scalp off of another girl who is crying hysterically but not moving at all, walking forward, turning right, the sensation of being hapless prey in a wilderness of predators, walking forward, turning right, the first dim inklings of the realization that this is not a square, walking forward, turning right, feeling the stale heat begin to stifle, walking forward, turning right, a man with bandages on his face helplessly trying to peel off his last fingernail with nine bruised purple nubs, walking forward, turning right, a man screaming and screaming and screaming and screaming and scre-- walking forward, turning right, sobbing now and succumbing to the fear, walking forward, turning right, a man failing to choke himself, walking forward, turning right, the smell of shit and piss and iron and mold, walking forward, turning left, mad scrawlings across bricks not in paint or ink, walking forward, screams from somewhere far away and unseen, walking forward, turning left, a vision of her mother in the casket at St. Marks but this isn't Saint Marks and that isn't her mother, running forward, turning right, discordant bells tolling black dread in her bones, running forward, turning right, unbelievable pain in her temples, running forward, turning left, nearly tripping over a hunched figured doing something unimaginable under its own semi-vertebrate shell, running forward, turning left, seeing her own wide-eyed self curled into a fetal ball weeping uncontrollably, running forward, turning left, the vulgar yellow light beginning to strip itself from the walls in layers, walking forward, turning right, resisting the urge to look behind herself, running forward, turning right, feeling the hard stone assault her bare, blistered feet, stumbling forward, turning right, one hand behind herself trying to hold the paper gown closed, stumbling forward, turning right, one hand out against the pregnant shadows for unseeable obstacles, staggering forward, turning right, a man singing the national anthem backwards, crawling forward, turning right, hands reaching out to grab a hold of her, crawling forward, turning right, knees tearing open against dirty cynder and beginning to leave little spots of pinkish skin behind, dragging herself forward, turning right, being groped and clawed by the unambiguously mal adjusted, slithering forward, turning right, the beasts are behind her snarling and sneering and have not been far behind, climbing to her feet and running forward, turning right, lungs burning like charcoal in her chest, running forward, turning right, rhythmless rumbling footsteps slapping the viscera covered concrete just at her heels, running forward, turning right, now screaming for help and for air and for release from this nightmare, running forward, turning right, running forward, turning right, their dirty hairy fingers grabbing clots of her hair, running forward, turning right, running forward, turning right, the whispered voices of her father making her stomach wrench loose white and yellow and red frothing strings of almost nothing at all, running forward, turning right, running forward, turning right, running forward, turning right, running forward, turning right, in near utter blackness now, running forward, turning right, feet slowing and knees bleeding and arms outstretched and half crumbling over various limbs and bodies and creatures and beasts and victims and lunatics sprawled more and more densely until they nearly carpeted the floor and draped over one another in stacks and mounds and she had to climb forward and pull herself right and move forward and turn right and the men behind her were still chasing her but seemed to be enjoying the chase as much as whatever awful ideation motivated the hunt and she was moving forward and turning right now but the floor and lower portions of the wall were no longer really visible not because of the darkness that was now complete and utter but because she had to literally climb over bodies and walk on them and shove her bleeding ankles into prostrate chests and faces and groins and knees like cobblestones across a lake of fire and she really was crying now and in pain and terrified and exhausted and confused and menaced by evil-minded beasts behind her and impenetrable darkness overhead and poorly animated corpses beneath her and onyx colored lead millstones inside her stomach and fire around her temples and in her chest and thighs and blood now flowing freely from her lacerated knees and heels and toes and face, and moving forward into nothing and turning right and moving forward and turning right and moving forward and falling down again and dragging herself forward and turning right and cursing creation and damnation and imprisonment and dragging herself forward on bloodied elbows and blistered palms and souring the ground with tear-strokes of mucus and spittle and vomit and moving forward and turing right and crying out in torment and gnashing her teeth and now shoving her face against the ground and feeling the skin begin to tear away in chunks and strips against the jagged shards of dry brittle bones of what once were the damned and were now just barely-passing-as-proof-of-concept littering the floor in a soggy carpet of entrail and blood and moving forward and turning right and moving forward and turning right and moving forward and clenching her eyes closed and now scrambling over profound death and dismemberment and moving forward and turning left but the walls and floors grew longer and taunted her and each turn began to pull away from her further and farther and she moved forward and tried to pull herself closer and moved further forward and clawed now at faces and spines and limbs and viscera and was covered from face to feet in the stain of death and her gown now just a thin trail of rag behind her and she herself nude and drenched in morbidity and horrifying to behold and scratching her way forward and forward and forward and losing an eye against the shards and screeching out in breathless gasps of mortal anguish and despair and panicking and numb and panicking and dragging herself forward and panicking and numb and dragging herself forward and hearing her own screams echoing off of the walls behind her and ahead and seeing herself ahead and behind and from above and from below crawling helplessly in circles in a great big never-ending square and perceiving no light nor any warmth at all in the searing heat but feeling only the voidlike coldness of the grip of death wrapping itself around her feeble throat and squeezing and breaking the skin and jugular and dragging her forward like a doll or a blanket, dragging her forward limp and pale and bloodless and lifeless in surrender. Forward, and right. Forward. And right. Forward and right. Forward and right.

And down.

Forward and right and down.

(Protogenesis)
(83)

"I hear you! I couldn't agree more," the little old lady with the tobacco hair was fishing around for lip balm in her carry-on with one hand while stuffing her purple sleep mask into an elusive interior pocket with her other. She was hunched over her own knees trying to see the bag's contents in the low light of dawn in hill-country, and from a variety of angles, her posture suggested forceful bowel movements underway in the adult-depend-undergarment that by now everyone else on board was at least hopeful she was wearing, if not altogether sure. "When I was growin' up we had real money-"

"Hell girl we sho' didn't, I'm glad you did," said Sue, the jovially obese rider loosely draped in a consolation prize of a floral print tarpaulin.

"Well, of course, now you know we didn't either, if you mean like that, but that's not what I mean and you know it!"

Sue was giggling in resonance with her own internal mirth, and had little rainbow hair clips holding her braids in place, absently slapping herself about the dome in the dull morning heat-- in lue of scratching the places where her scalp itched from the high wire tension of tightly pulled braids. "We ain't had a pot to piss in nor a winda' to throw it out of, girl." And it is perhaps striking to contemplate the life in between then and now that could make her laugh so heartily at such a pointedly dismal recollection, as if she had just told the story of Pauline shitting herself in the Mall of America for the third time this trip (this *leg* of the trip), instead of describing the grim, dusty, southern poverty that had been her childhood. Pauline, who was still in the breath of a plea for clarification, but laughing contagious with Sue, came up for air with a pair of multi-purpose wraparounds in her fist on one knee and a bare palm on the other, flashing a thirteen thousand dollar grill behind a cheese eating grin. Pauline was in fact, high as fuck.

"Now Sue you know dern well we didn't have nothin' but sticks and stones to hit with 'em, ain't nobody in the Miss had nothin' back then really."

"Don't we know it girl." Sue had been holding her friend's denture cream in plain view with her free hand since Pauline had handed it to her.

"I mean there weren't none of this weird stuff they try to pass off as money, nowadays. You had a dollar, you had a dollar. You know?" Pauline now resembled the Terminator's great-grandmother, holding a comb now, instead of lip balm, for which she may have been only semi-conscious of the fact she was searching.

"Hmm, you maybe, girl we ain't had none of them either!" Sue, now relieved for the moment at the scalp, now fishing around in her own knap and producing a stack of oatmeal cookies in a paraffin sleeve and peeling away layers of exterior shielding in the form of plastic wrap, gripping the cream in her left hand between the bottom three fingers and palm to free her forefingers for the dual-wield assist. "All we had was pigs and chickens and humidity." Now bellicose and nearly hysterical. The driver was a good-humored, patient man with many, many miles beneath his tires. "And mosquitos." Sue was liberating a cookie from its prison, while simultaneously condemning it to a horrible death.

"You had a dollar, and you could hold the damned thing in your hand, you know. It was yours, and you know'd it was yours because somebody might whip your ass or hit you over the head and take it from you and if they did then it would be theirs. And that's why we had banks in the first place, just to stop people from having to carry the stuff around."

"Girl I remember Ol' Gene got his ass whooped, girl, *whooped*, back '71 and taken for a whole pocket full of them dollars. You remember old Gene?"

"Now nevermind Gene,"

"But Gene got his ass whooped, girl, and we had banks. Didn't matter that we had 'em either."

"Now that's not what I mean and you know it," Pauline was being given her own communion snack, newly liberated and wholly doomed, still holding the comb she wasn't going to use--she never used-- and trying to wedge it under her own palm to hold the cookie up to her face with the remaining fingers, freeing the opposing hand for illustrative gesticulation.

"Those ladies are friggin' obnoxious, man," said Morel Ellingtion to his young, half-conscious betrothed, quietly, from the vicinity of the rear axle. The betrothed, in her gray varsity sweats, nuzzled into the angle of her window seat against the vibrating wall, yawned dismissively in response, and squeezed her eyes more tightly shut against the first rays of easterly sun blaring over the horizon of the giant glass windshield ahead, shoving herself more tightly into the nook of obtuse angles between seat and sidewall, for enhanced comfort and security. The boy could hear him clearly, and supposed the early-risers in the front could hear him as well, because a period of unbroken silence fell over the bus. The mysterious man appeared to be dozing, having finally closed his eyes and relinquished his nightowl watch over the boy and his mother just before the first rays of revelatory sunshine appeared over the flattening panorama, tinged just slightly pink and signaling open seas in their recent path.

Those who were awake were not compelled to silence by Mr. Morel's poorly guarded complaint, or out of compassion for their still half-slumbering compatriots in the various rows and isles, nor for the benefit of the unmuddied peace which accompanied the nearly blinding spectacle of brilliance of equatorial seaside dawn, or for the preservation of the driver's focus, now in its eighth marathon hour of life-stakes concentration, now being relieved and rewarded by the recession of gravel and stone into smooth suburban pavement. As individuals and as a collective, those among the early-riser crowd found themselves instinctively captivated by the hypnotizing allure of the dimly perceptible outline of one of the world's great industrial wonders, sneaking out of the distant horizon like a shadow giving birth to itself from the first dimension to the second, and then again to the third as the colossal structures approached near enough to become defined by depth and scale. The roar of huge tires on pebbles and ruts faded to a thin hum of consenting highway, and there was no sound of zippers or sucking straws or rummaging hands or idle commentary.

(84)

At first the sea was a thin veneer over the horizon like paint on a globe, casting only a dark line across the dying roadway in the vacant distance. It rose, slowly, into a thick blue belt between the light above and the firmament below, encompassing the whole periphery from left to right, delimiting the visual boundary between the physical world and the infinite universe which crowned it. The Port was a mass of spiring structures emerging from a small point in the center of the windshield and growing tall and wide as the bus closed in on the last few miles of its journey. Against the encephalo cardiac graph of dozens of five thousand meter tall ship docks, each wrapped with scaffolding and ladder wells and thick steel pipes and long straggling conduits of shielded wiring along and around its sides, and each ornamented near the summit with trussed bracer systems under reciprocating hangar bays, which themselves contained enormous individual starships, were jagging lines of the rooftops of assorted habitable facilities, including the thirteen central passenger terminals, each mammoth in scale, even against the towers of ship docks behind. Beside these and in between, were myriad ground level hagar facilities, themselves an asymmetrically-arrayed ticky-tacky of nondescript, arching, aluminum-wrapped steel frames-- little shunting anthills punctuating the level country-side amidst the major infrastructure. Smaller still, but breathtaking by relative comparison, was the razor-thin preceding line of packed parking lots and shipping yards full of storage containers and the big trucks that brought them and convoys of busses and taxis and limousines and police vehicles and forklifts and chartered vans and motorcycles and rental vehicles and hurried supply workers in their uniforms and dogged travelers pushing children and pets and elaborate luggage assemblies and smoking the first or last cigarette since the last one or before the first one somewhere else entirely.

As the bus approached, this later line came into focus last, and gave depth and context to each perceptual order of magnitude behind it-- the stumpy hangars, the glass-domed central terminals, and the skyscraping ship docks. To the inside right of the oceanic concavature, there was a buzzing hive of airplanes and helicopters and hovercraft engaged in various take-off and landing and holding patterns, these the first visible signs, from any direction or distance, of the vibrancy in motion which characterized Port life. To the left, as far as the faithful eye would report, were the seaports, where hundreds of huge steel ships were moored at low tide. Aircraft carriers, destroyers, battleships, frigates, cruise ships, cargo vessels, sailboats, yachts, fishers and whalers and tugs, and peculiar looking rigs designed for scientific expeditions. As the hilly country behind trailed off into flatland, to the left of the bus the rail lines came into view, sixteen in total, evenly spaced twenty feet apart, and one or more always occupied by great steaming locomotives trailing dozens of sea-and-space bound shipping containers full of every kind of salable material product known to man, though mostly loaded with foodstuffs and construction implements. Beyond the tracks were huge, barbed wire fences enclosing vast fields of industrial sized ore mounds, mils, quarries, forges, energy plants, water and sewage treatment facilities, wind farms, granaries and silos and refrigerated warehouses. To the right, before and beyond the swarms of arriving and departing airbusses, lay clods of hotels and restaurants and novelty shops and administrative buildings, the domestic accouterments of mass scale commercial tourism at the nexus of global travel and procurement systems. Of the seven great Ports, this one was the most expansive, a fact owing in equal measure to the Newtonian physics involved in the process of obtaining equatorial escape velocity, and to the bargain basement affordability of coastal real estate on the southern continents.

The intensely reverent silence aboard the bus had become thick enough to rouse the remaining riders from their halved reposes. As all the little details and features came into focus and the sun still struggled to climb above it all and into full cloudless view overhead, as the bus wheeled its way out of the last inches of unoccupied nothingness into the spontaneously generated density of enlarged and congested inbound and outbound traffic lanes receiving the spewing contents of a procession of huge, looping offramps from the northern and southern continental corridors, as the tongueless passengers looked on at the immensity of civilized creation at its most provocative, reaching out around them with wide arms and drawing them into its perceptually encompassing bosom, as their eyes darted from starship to starship, over the masted and mastless seacraft, to the glinting procession of airships and train cars, from terminal to hangar to golf cart to bag thrower to daisy-chains of families led by hyperstimulated dogs and anchored by unique-but-practical luggage assemblies, to swarms of aggressive taxi drivers lighting on unsuspecting stragglers wearing business suits with lackadaisical expressions and portable phones and the vestigial rarities which signaled disposable assets and places to be, toward the dense clot of raggedly multicolored buses into which the driver was patiently seeking serviceable passage, as one dull and cramped and lethargic reality behind them all finally conceded to the densely frenzied reality ahead, the boy, once again, found himself alone in the crowd and wholly focused on something else entirely. Something he was sure was impossible.

There, to the far right, along a curb full of parked and waiting sedans and cabs and chartered vans and golf carts, was a mint-blue-chevy-belair with two visible polished sunlit mirrors of round spinning chrome facing the street. The stage presence of the car was assertive, even among a swirling sea of buzzing curiosities around the passengers, but of all the passengers perhaps only the boy was privy to its conspicuously improbable aspect. The thing definitely didn't drive from the City to the Port; it didn't look like it had traversed a thousand miles of ruts and puddles through baked gravel and dirt. The boy hadn't seen a single car on the road after the bus pulled out of the suburbs, until the Port came into view. Maybe the thing rode out while they waited in the bus station. The boy felt the explanation was plausible, at least, if not altogether satiating. The chrome-cast trim around the wheel wells and streakless windows and lamp lights glared blindingly in the morning sun. But the mint-blue was cool to the touch, visually speaking, like seawater in a shallow coral cove. The car was distinctly unique. It had its own specifically unitary identity. That it was the same car, that it must have been the same car, and that it could not possibly have been any other, were all matters of unquestionable certainty. But how had it arrived here, once again in the here and now, to share this inexplicable moment in the boy's life a second time?

The boy pulled his eyes away from the mesmerizing sunlit chrome, feeling at the base of his spine the distinctly premonitory sensation that another set of eyes had fixed on himself. As the passengers mouths hung agape from momentarily selfless faces angled in spurious gazes at the passing wonders of late-stage capitalism, the phrenetic hustle and bustle of a passing age somehow frozen in isolated stasis here, a hundred miles from anything anywhere so banal as mutable revolution, the boy turned his own face away from the perilous future manifested, away toward the mysterious man staring back at him, intently and without malice, just watching with a glowing sense of pride and admiration evident in the corners of his eyes and mouth. For the first time since their initial encounter with the seemingly transient specter under the big round platform of the City Station under the big sign with a picture of a new bus over a smattering of old buses, the boy noticed that there was something distinctly familiar about the man, now appearing even younger and better kempt in the full light of cloudless morning. Something not just familiar, but in fact, *familial.* Something in the shape of the man's face the boy had not yet perceived in the darkness of gravel roads and snoring geriatrics and tumbling shadows shrouding the foothills behind them. Something almost paternal.

(85)

"Hey Pike, what are you thinking about right now buddy? You've got that look about you that you get when you've come up with something." Pike was listing to starboard in an oversized bean bag chair woven to look like a tennis ball. As a matter of obsessive compulsive need for symmetry, Pike's ass was always planted directly over the stenciled brand logo when he sat down. He held a controller in his hand and was visibly focused on the flat panel in front of him. It didn't matter what he was playing; he was a natural born server clearer. Teenagers around the world were being slaughtered and rage quitting, while, apparently, Pike was in fact having a completely unrelated internal monologue with himself about

"Titties." Tyberius, holding his knees to keep his feet in the spinning faux leather chair, balked.

"Titties? How *apres garde* of you my friend! I'm impressed. Not AI, not Jeffersonian factionalism or-"

"You know how people say when you lose your eyesight, your other senses adapt and become more-" Pike leaned hard left in the real world to dodge a digital projectile. "Your other senses adapt and become more-"

"Effective? Useful? Precise?"

"-sensitive. You lose your eyes and then you figure out how to navigate by like sounds or clicks or whatever,"

"And you can do ninja stuff and jump off of buildings and surf down power lines and fire escapes and beat up armed bad guys with your fists in hell's ki-"

"Fuck you asshole, no. Think about it, people say your other senses become more potent or adept or whatever, to like, compensate." Pike received an inevitable, however improbable, death blow and set his controller down, sinking back into the tennis ball bag of beans, or styrofoam balls, more likely. "But like, it's not universal. Because titties exist."

"Because titties exist?" Tyberius feigned unconvinced, absently shoving himself in half circles around the radius of his wheeled leather chair's axel, bound against the edge of his desk by opposing nudges of his winged elbows.

"Think about how much value the titty loses if you can't see it. Titties are made to be seen, you know? You can't hear them better if you can't see, and if you don't know or can't tell what kind of a titty you're touching, if anyone lets your blind ass touch a titty at all, I mean yeah, you're lucky, but I can't imagine they'd like, taste better, or smell better, or whatever, right? You have to be able to see a titty to really get the full effect. The other senses just don't matter as much."

Tyberius was finding his way into the maze again. "You're thinking about the sensory input model matrices. You said we were gonna get stuck on that and we did. Okay, you've got me bro, titties it is then. I'm sure we can find some affordable strippers to model for our science fair project."

Pike laughed out loud. His eyes were closed and his head was propped back in that uncomfortable looking bean bag chair angle, hands folded across his stomach. This was his way, once Ty got him going. He would shut off his own visual inputs to concentrate. "Oh man, I like it! We get like twenty of them and some poster boards and that cheap corrugated colorful paper border shit the Kiwanis kids use to sell those dry ass cookies."

Tyberius, now cracking under the weight of his own forced facade of seriousness, coughed his way into a fit of laughter and picked up the line. "And we just have like a regular ass toaster on one of those resin folding tables in front of a shit load of specs and charts and patent designs with little cutout hearts and stars-"

"I fucking love the toaster bro, that's exactly how we pitch Centron! We're a fucking shoe in-"

"And it will work because everyone is just gonna stare at all the titties instead of the toaster and the data."

"Fucking brilliant. I can just picture the dumb ass look on Carter's face with whichever of the greedy ass board members are gonna show for the expo. I'm a hundred percent certain that guy can be defeated by ten titties or less."

"Ooh, I'm eighty percent sure he can be trounced by no more than eight titties."

"I wonder if it's possible to assemble a seven-titty pep-squad for SeptaWalt's debutante ball."

"Oh I'm seventy percent sure it would work, but I still don't like SeptaWalt at all, and I already know Walt's not gonna like it."

"Ooh, how about PolyWalt? Walt-Poly..."

"..."

"I don't know man. I'll bet you seven hundred bucks that if we put seven titties in front of a generic ass toaster, Walt won't even notice the name."

Tyberius lost his feet and buckled into his own lap as they hit the ground, nearly crying. "No fucking way man, no bet. No Bet! Fucking Walt. Ten to one he'd pick up the toaster."

Pike opened his eyes and rolled forward trying to breathe. The two were now giggling loud enough at three am in their contractor grade dorm room to annoy their neighbors through the plaster and wood frame walls, but those neighbors were both fanboys and subscribers, so the two would never hear a word of it. "Walt would walk right past seven titties and pick up the fucking toaster."

"I don't know man, I think if you put Dad in front of seven titties and a toaster he might help us with the sensory matrix problem."

"Yeah, but then he would figure out how much shit we've stolen from Centron over the last five years."

"I have a feeling he already knows my guy."

"Because he stopped sleeping with the lanyard around his neck in the big chair in his office?"

"Well, yeah that, but other things too. I don't think he cares, which is weird, because he could lose his whole egg if they ever caught us pilfering their trash and looting their databases."

Pike leaned back and settled into his meditation pose in the contour of the tennis ball. "It's just not enough, you know. You've got to see the titties to really get the full appeal."

"Because we're hardwired from birth to-"

"Exactly. There's got to be some hierarchical system of values in order to teach the thing to prioritize inputs."

"Like the RF thing?"

"Hey man fuck you, that's not fair."

"Hey don't get me wrong, I thought it made sense in theory, that we could replicate synaptic exchanges with low wattage electromagnetic radiation. Would have worked if it had worked."

"I mean, in my defense, it was a historically novel and unique way to start a fire."

"If only the cavemen had been bigger nerds, we could have gotten so much farther by now."

"Well, it's a good thing they weren't or somebody might have beaten us to the punch by now."

"We haven't really gotten to the punch yet though. It took us six weeks just to get Walt's voice right, and that wasn't even really a critical step in the process."

"I wonder what your girlfriend would say about it."

"Whoa now bro, she's not my girlfriend yet. I can almost afford a date with her, but it would set our business back substantially."

Pike laughed more. "No, I'm serious. I really would be interested to hear what she had to say. You should talk to her about it. I can't do it. She'll just catch me staring at her titties again. That shit was kind of awkward."

"Talk to her about what though? I'm not sure I can lead in with the titty analogy like you did there, and it would take hours to explain all the other shit we've done so far for her to have any kind of context to speak on."

"Your issues, man. Not mine. And you know you can't tell her anything about the project anyway. I'm sure some of those Centron guys are her best clients."

"Ugh. Don't make me vomit on your Zelco. Okay. I'll think about it."

"It was important to get Walt's voice right."

"I know it was buddy."

Silence, to the joy of struggling B and C students opposite their dorm walls, fell over the room. After a few minutes, Tyberius could tell Pike was asleep on the ball. He powered down everything except the Septaplex servers and climbed out of his chair, feeling the electric sting in his calves as the deadened muscles gorged with blood to support his weight, and longstrode over Pike to climb into his own rack, clapping twice to turn off the overhead light.

(86)

Kate was missing two breasts, but was well enough breasted in her gray business suit to hold the attention of the students who were going to sleep listening to her talk her way out of a groaning headache, students who were going to fail her class no matter what she wore or said. Tyberius sat always in the front row during his fourth year at City U. Forward, centerline. With pen and spare pen and long legal pad and one earbud in, one out, volume turned low enough to escape the sensory apparatus of anyone in the nearby seats. The other students were nameless and faceless, none of them mattered, and most of them were going to fail. Kate had grabbed him by the throat in recent weeks and pushed him against a cinder wall, to inform him that if he put her work on the C-Poly and she found out about it, she would bash his fucking brains in with a large rock. Tyberius counted this hostile overture among the greatest sexual encounters in memory, and readily swore off any and all shenanigans on pain of suffering and death, before she dropped him two inches to the ground and relinquished her vice grip on his jugular, spinning on her heels and sashaying off in a vaguely suggestive way that only confused and enlivened Tyberius more.

Kate was missing Pat and hated this part of her lecture series. It was uncomfortable and forceful and, she thought, hamfisted in both conceptualization and conveyance. Her head hurt, and would hurt still until at least eleven thirty, when the second cup of black coffee began to metabolize in her stomach. It felt like feeding something sacred to disinterested, unworthy, glazed-eyed dogs in hoodies and baseball Tees and halter tops and collared shirts. Very little leather, denim, or paisley in this crowd, and less as the generations proceeded. The initial period of obligatory entry callout pleasantries was passing and Showtime was about to begin. She obliged the last burst of stragglers an extra moment to settle in and closed her eyes and held her breath until the sounds of shifting and zipping and flipping notebook paper and clicking pens dwindled beneath the cloddy sound of her own pulse. When she closed her eyes, she saw beautifully latticed tracers streaming around in high-def rainbow palettes. When she opened them, she saw fear and anxiety and little beads of sweat incongruous with the sixty-eight degree limiter chip she had conceived, designed, commissioned, and installed with a soldering gun on the thermostat in her classroom. The gray polyester and thick padding of juicy fluff beneath it all tended to run hot, and hotter still with the bump of cocaine she keyed in right before the time lock doors clicked free of their restraint bolts and admitted the first student's passage. With her eyes open and in motion and her pulse quickening, the tracers around the students faces and dull drabs became less pronounced, but would not yet vanish entirely. Kate was into her eighth hour of a fungal foray for which she had allotted a roughly estimated four solid hours, leaving a comfortably drowsy fifth to shut down, three hours of solid sleep, with a marginal half-hour or so to spare for dragging ass into a two hour class and a full day afterward for properly indulgent crashing.

"god is a giant interdimensional squid that lives in the mushrooms." Eyes widened on less inattentive faces and discordant anticognizance became a collective mood of skepticism and waspy doubt as the sounds of the words died on the cinder walls, leaving only ringing silence and a half stifled yawn on the port bow. "You are your Self, not your body. Your Self is not the biological, physical construct that carries you through tangible reality. Your Self is the You in the very back of your mind, looking forward. Your Self is the essential construct of your own existence and identity, the system's operator driving the body.

"The first layer of consciousness is the most fundamental, by design, and the most continuously operational. This is the Systems Readiness Protocol, and it is driven by its own unique suite of hardware in your brain. This hardware informs the Self of its own condition. How do I feel? Am I hungry, angry, lonely, tired? Am I sick, or happy, or afraid, or horny? Am I hot or cold? The laws of evolution dictate that this suite of hardware is the oldest stable part of the human brain. It is the reptilian and ancient cerebellum, where the most primitive instincts are rooted. These primordial questions reflect the earliest needs of the conscious life forming as it achieved sentience and began to proactively seek symbiosis with its environment. The Self must evaluate its own condition in order to process a working concept of self. In the Fruedian model of consciousness slash subconsciousness we discovered last week, these first two elements of self would be represented as the Id. But Frued got the model wrong. He was pointed in the right direction I think, but his interpretation of earlier philosophical dialectics limited his ability to innovate. The conditions of the Self are always germane to one's analysis of their own experience in the environment, and are fundamental in the novel processes of forming prerogatives.

"When your eyes are open, the Self receives a comprehensive matrix of perceptual information from the Sensory Apparatus, comprising the five senses. All that you see, and all that you touch, and all that you hear and taste and smell and everything you experience while your eyes are open is information about the external world.[52] These are ferried into the conscious awareness of the Self by a tertiary suite of dedicated hardware in the brain. The outside world of other people and birds and trees and noisy car horns and elevator farts and rib eye steaks is experienced subjectively. This state of being forms a duplex triad of interrelated systems. The extant Self sees food and feels hungry or feels hungry and seeks food. The extant Self perceives a threat and feels afraid, or feels afraid and mobilizes the fight or flight response. Freud proposed the Id slash Ego system of consciousness because he, being acculturated in the grim pre-industrial anglicanism of Austria, compared the human mind to a glacier, with a conveniently clear cut waterline distinguishing those above-board aspects of the personality which may be readily observed and interpreted by others, from the subsurface superstructure of needs and wants and his mother's nipples and his father's leather belt.

"Ironically, it was not the neo-modernists, with science and corporatized taxonomies of the human condition at their fingertips, who got closest to the mark. It was Plato who proposed the initial paradigm of forms and ideals which

---

[52] Pink Floyd, "Harvest," on *Dark Side of the Moon,* Harvest, 1973.

first inspired the JudeoChristian movements, and was then plagiarized and corrupted by them. If Plato had lived a few years in the Digital Age, I think he would have had both the language and the principles to describe a more accurate model of human experience.

"The Self is not produced by the body, but merely sustained by it. The body is a support system for the brainstem, and it is entirely peripheral in its functionality. Digestion, respiration, circulation, endocrine and waste systems, these are all auxiliary services which facilitate the most basic needs of the Self, and the Self must depend on the continuity of these services in order to sustain its own existence. In this sense, we speak of the human mind not as an abstraction, not as fodder for clever philosophers and poets and hack psychologists, but as a literally extant environment which is inhabited by the Essential Self, which has no three dimensional form or substance of its own, but exists to us in reference as basically a hypothetical abstraction, vastly reductive and infuriatingly elusive. The Body is the physical vessel which permits the Essential Self to interact with the Material Reality which it cannot inhabit otherwise, but the Essential Self is not describable in material terms, or so we have permitted ourselves to be taught.

"If we close our eyes, however, what the Self perceives from its fixed vantage point in the back of our heads, is a grand panorama of malleable blackness and dimensionless shadow. From left to right, behind your eyelids, what you perceive is basically akin to a large computer screen, onto which the Self has the unique capacity to project images and sensations from Memory, implying a fourth delineation in our interdependent suites of cognition hardware, like the storage partitions on a harddrive. There's a picture of your children or of your parents. Think of your puppies and there they are. What was the last thing that you ate? See it there? Recall a celebrity you want to meet before you die. Look now, there they are. Your Self also uses this space to seed creative impulses. Want to paint or draw a picture? Draft it here first.

Want to see the person next to you naked? Well, there you go, you just did. This space is dimensionless because there are no relative constraints to perception of scale and scope. Here is a thumbtack. Here is a battleship. A star. A galaxy. Do you see? Neither mass or volume inhibits Representative Recall. This space can accommodate visions of the universe in all its grandeur, or of an electron emitting a photon and descending orbit to absorb more kinetic energy.

"By cultural tradition, we describe this space as our imagination, or as the Theater of the Mind. Picture a little guy in the back of your head plugged into a bunch of monitors and staring at a huge screen on which the senses recreate the perceived world. The last big suite of hardware in your brain is the Neocortex, or the ape's contribution to the mammalian brain. This is the part of the brain that makes that big blank visual field possible. And this is the part of the brain where **g**od lives.

"In this model of human consciousness, the novel suggestion is that **g**od, long revered as an inaccessibly remote and yet pathologically present patriarchal figure, is actually a semi-mortal being with its own set of fears and vulnerabilities that more sensible and less conditioned generations to come will begin to understand only after the old models are discarded. If we think of the human mind as real estate, organically derived and ubiquitously common, rather than as some mythicized pseudo-scientific dry hump of a half guess, then it follows that like any other known organically dependent environment, this one can be occupied and inhabited. By the measure of received religious worldviews, this is bound to sound like my cheese has slipped off the cracker. I know! But think about it.

"We have mapped the oceans and the stars and every inch of terra-firma. We have Newtonian physics and the laws of thermodynamics and Euclidean geometry and Pythagorean theorems. We've given up on UFOs and gospel preachers and bigfoot and so on, because we live in a mortal, finite world, which has clearly defined rules and parameters.

We have looked high and low for heaven and hell and some seat where an imaginary or hypothetical deity might rest, but we never thought to consider our own imaginations as consequential environments in the material world. There is a significant historical corollary to this idea which may help you wrap your minds around what seems like an irrational concept. Thousands of years of enlightened human contemplation and study just blew right on by before anyone would consider the possibility that life could exist in a single drop of water. However, with the invention of the microscope, we discovered that in fact a single drop of water could be teeming with complex single-celled and multicellular organisms. Now the idea is so commonplace that people down in Melville won't even drink water out of the tap because they're afraid of losing the brain parasyte lottery. Why should the human mind be so different from a drop of water?

"Now, synthesize these two ideas. One: we cannot yet place our concept of god in a suitable habitat anywhere we look in all of creation, which is a ready argument on the tips of the tongues of atheists everywhere. Two: the human imagination can conjure Milton's leviathan Satan laid out over the whole breadth of hell. So suppose the creator isn't some paternalistic old wrathful white guy sky wizard with a host of petty grudges and an insatiable narcissist's ego that demands servitude and aggrandizement. Suppose it is an actual living organism in its own right, with a lifespan and an environmental codependency. Suppose god doesn't just live in your mind, or more precisely, in the field of dimensionless minds represented by nearly ten billion human beings and billions of other sentient creatures. What would be the implication?

"In this model of human consciousness, god is nearly parasitic in a sense. We are its host, and it can only survive so long as we do. We have all been taught that god loves us and will beat the shit out of us if we piss it off, but we have never entertained the possibility that the true form of god actually requires our continued existence in order to preserve its own. It's not just a bogeyman specter that loves us or judges us according to its whims, but that the thing itself actually NEEDS us, maybe even more than we need it. If the whole human population dies off and goes extinct, the implication of this model is that god would perish from existence.

"Moreover, some of us have explored the probability that the human mind is actually designed to communicate with the creature which inhabits it. Early Jews and Christians taught that if one were to look directly into the face of god it would result in the obliteration of self. This is plausible, in a sense, but the reality is that this teaching was more likely intended to reinforce their own supremacist unitary construct, for purely self-serving political reasons, and perversely, to even discourage humans from seeking, discovering, developing, and implementing such methods of pursuing personal relationships with the creature that would undermine the teachings of the already doomed Roman state. The revelatory state of consciousness was deemed unsuitable for the subservient plebeian masses. The Greeks before them revered the Oracle at Delphi for her ability to commune directly with the creator and instruct kings and wisemen on the unknowable intentions of the divine.

"The problem isn't all that mystical. It's just that to use the hardware that is built into your mind to facilitate direct contact with the dormant, subterranean second consciousness which cohabitates with your own, the Self has to operate the mind to drive the body like a racecar. You literally have to redline the damned thing to make it work, which after a while tends to burn out the system's components. Your imagination is capable of revealing god in its full broadside splendor, and even more, you are capable of communicating with the thing itself. But to do that, you have to enter what is basically a hallucinogenic state, where the genetically evolved natural safeguards and the socially conditioned artificial barriers can be overcome, or at least suspended. With enough mushrooms in your system, you can close your eyes, and you will see a massive living structure with millions of flailing tentacles, brightly colored and intricately ornamented, shifting patterns and palettes and hues and moods in the space of heartbeats. We did this as a recreational drug experience for decades until some brilliant soul finally had the intellectual wherewithal to comprehend what we were all seeing. That it wasn't just a spontaneously generated kaleidoscope of pretty colors and bright lights brought on by fevered rejection of imbibed poison. That it was actually a real creature living in our minds and communicating with us on an extraordinarily primitive level in our altered state.

"I call this creature Ursula, and she doesn't like it. From her perspective, she occupies a singular dimension. She is a unitary creature without peers, and therefore does not require the kind of nominal distinctions which our identities require in a pluralistic reality. The space she occupies is strictly hers and hers alone. So she doesn't need a name. She doesn't speak. She just dances, the way bumble bees and some other creatures do. And she changes the palettes and patterns on her skin to show us images and emotions which we are equipped to interpret as her thoughts in the space where our own thoughts exist. It is a language of Shared Intuition, at once profoundly beautiful (if she likes you) and immensely terrifying (if she doesn't like you at all, or if you are uninitiated in the discipline of mycology). She knows everything about you, and everything there is to know, and in the space between you, the most extraordinary feats of creative genius become accessible. Artistic and Musical inclinations, as well as advanced reasoning skills and the capacity for abstract thought, all become intensely enhanced and clarified. This experience is known as the god state.

"Any questions?" Kate bit down on her own lip an tic display of impatience, taking a long draught of her room temperature black coffee.

An anonymous smartass in the back of the room took up the call. "Ma'am, Mrs. E? That's the craziest shit I've ever heard. Do you really believe any of that?"

Kate missed no beats, sharply and curtly reminding the student that citizens of the Second Republic had expressly protected rights to believe what they chose to believe, and that those rights were to be defended at all costs against institutional intrusion or formal suppression, so yes, you little shit, that was exactly what she believed. Then she asked if there were any more questions, and there were none.

"Ok, that's your lecture for the day. Now I want you each to use the remaining class time to invent your own gods. Anything goes, but you've got to fill ten pages by Thor's day. Good luck and be creative!" With this, Kate sat her oversized mug down on the desk behind her as she pivoted around it on her arm until she was back in her own chair. Time passed, and students committed stick-figure apostasy with apathy, and the hour finally struck. All she wanted was to go home and crawl in with Pat and burn off the rest of this Psillocybin so her own clingy, attention-starved god would leave her the fuck alone for a few days. She would draw all the blinds tight against the evening sun, turn the air conditioner down below sixty five, peel off the matte gray back burner, and slither under the big white down. A prefab cocktail of valium and xanax and two thickly rolled joints were already sitting in a tin tray with Dorothy Gale's visage painted on it, next to a room-chilled bottle of Chivas, right there in easy reach on the nightstand beside the bed. Pat would appear to be fast asleep, still, from the night before, but Kate knew that by the time she pulled into the driveway and unlocked the door and climbed up to the second story landing, she would find Pat showered, shaved, sprayed, silked, and softly breathing the controlled breaths of quiet patience.

But the wiry little nerd in the front had worn the expression of impatience throughout the entire class. She knew the look. The

"Ma'am, can I have a word with you?" *yeah, that look.* He was a good student, and probably one of the very few that would pass the class, or at least turn in the work. Whatever it was, she was sure it would be a waste of her time either way, because she couldn't care less what the boy wanted, but she had to remind herself that the boy didn't need to know that from her, and that that the boy probably still mistakenly believed that his own exertions would prove useful or relevant someday. This mythology, she thought, was basically her bread and butter during the slow season.

"Of course you may, sir. How's the throat little buddy? What kind of **g**od are you going to invent, I'm curious to know?"

Tyberius smiled, not sheepishly this time, "I'm going to invent a real one..."

Something in his voice disturbed her, but the tracers around the rims of his glasses were giving her motion sickness and she was ready to minimize her remaining obligations for the next forty five and one half hours.

(Accretion)
(87)

In the seventh year of the Second Republic, a long brewing water crisis between Colorado, Arizona, Nevada, and Utah matured and grew teeth. The federal government tried to intervene, naturally, only after the simmering public alarm generated a heated debate and the heated debate boiled into an armed conflict between ad hoc militias hellbent on quenching the rampant terminal dehydration killing their families and pets and crops. So, naturally, the federal government, failing to affect any kind of armistice or compromise, withdrew to the borders of the southern desert and the peaks of the Rockies to observe the proceedings and privately supply weapons and ammunition to any of the participants who ran low, while quite publicly providing food and medical aid to the starving and wounded evacuees turned stateless refugees fleeing the cynical violence of fratricide.

The first shots rang out over the great salt flats in Utah. Armed bands of Mormons driving brand new pickup trucks erected barricades over the highways entering from Nevada, Arizona, and Colorado, stopping station wagons and sports cars with out of state plates and turning them around, while seizing and impounding any eighteen wheelers not bound for Utah or Wyoming. Representatives of the newly reformed state assembly declared that Jehovah had gifted the waters of the Wind River range to his followers, and that not a single drop would be spilled beyond for heathens and non believers. This provoked an insurgence from Catholics in New Mexico and southern Arizona. The latter of these, comprising only three major cities able to provide volunteers in any consequential quantity, was already nearly baked dry and suffering from a near total social deconstruction at the hands of gangs of lawless looters and morbidly corrupt freelancers. New Mexicans overcompensated with floods of unemployed Chiuauans driving old pickup trucks (visibly old, from any distance) and carrying hunting rifles and nine millimeter pistols.

Nevada, possessing a robust and well equipped domestic mafia, but lacking any additional natural resources or external support systems, settled on clandestine raids and skirmishes along their western border and stopgap firesale strategies in the east and south. The feuding families in Las Vegas organized a temporary armistice between their own warring factions in order to remove an existential threat to the seabound corridors through which their drugs and money ran circuitous and multiplex pathways to and from the coastal consumer and beyond. They focused on harassing the khaki'd, torch wielding assault rifle enthusiasts trying to choke off the 40, preferring night runs in black vans full of young, tattooed Italian and Spanish teenagers amped up on PCP and methamphetamines, toting black market kalashnikovs and stolen M-16s, but also duffel bags full of grenades and pipe bombs and black resin grocery crates full of ready made Molotovs. Sometimes one of these vans would explode on the way, because everyone smoked and very few bothered to read the literature beside the pictures they followed when mixing and packing the fissiles. Other times, the vans would roll up on moonless or cloudy nights, late after midnight, with headlights off for miles to minimize enemy response time, shoot its wad and ride away as fast as possible without even bothering to confirm kills and casualties. Usually, they would be spotted well in advance of reaching any operative proximity, only to be picked off by the hypervigilant, coffee swilling middle-aged boy scouts who retained the readiness and bearing that only fanatically evangelical temperance movements can induce. Their tires would be shot out inside of seven hundred meters of the barriers by amateur snipers who used to have day jobs, either flipping the vans and exploding them or rendering them inert structures and poor cover for protracted firefights on asphalt-paved battlefields surrounded by sand and infinite nothing.

As for the good people of Colorado (but for the handfuls of rural white boys who instinctively seized the diem on the lifelong dream of loading up the sporty ATVs with tactical gear and gascans, which were well intentioned, the gascans, but poorly conceived contingencies in a firefight, as many of them learned only too late, and water kegs and canvas bags full of magazine grade nerd gear, like the Zelco Night Visors and the Centronics Palm-Comm, loading up and riding out for some weekend warrior style guerilla warfare), for the most part the state's citizens just got really drunk and high and played Swiss, not exactly *letting* the feds roost up in the hills, just not really putting up any kind of credible or persuasive resistance. A lot of international news media set up in and around the Denver suburbs. With some mildly notable exceptions, general commerce proceeded without interruption. But with all the homeless people in Colorado, who could really tell one way or the other?

The feds began amassing a Crisis Response Team in the foothills and fields. Diplomats and world leaders and attache's and staffers and interns, all toting their own uniquely sporty luggage assemblies and electronic devices, all swarmed into complexes of big white steel-framed tents which shone like blisters under the shieldless desert sun. These were cordoned off by miles of cyclone fences and patrolled by National Guard twenty-somethings in tan cheque fatigues and contractor grade body armor (because of the heat) and New Balance shoes (for the insurance companies and rights groups). Green plated long trucks wheeled meandering convoys through the mountain passes, bringing in supplies and weapons and ammunition and equipment bound for public use, rather than private sale. Steel shipping containers formed little townships, woven together by conduits of shielded cords and noiseless solar powered generators, and all totemed by the balls and shafts of EHF and SHF antennae dangling or swinging from repurposed wooden telephone poles driven into the granite and flat iron.

The rest of the country, needing little from and caring less for the belligerent parties, watched the farcical miniature civil war with some interest on flat panel televisions, sometimes with the volume turned up. Students across the country set out to protest in solidarity, but struggled to determine with whom their sympathetic reservoirs of thoughts and prayers and borrowed platitudes and received political jargon should be invested. It was hard to pick a winner when all the contestants were all in your own backyard, and harder when their dispositions and rhetoric so closely resembled the remote third world clusterfucks for which there was already such a vast reserve of practiced apathy to draw upon. The many divergent houses of faith and worship turned out storms of contradicting talking points, ranging the full gamut from outright condemnation to full-throated endorsement of violence as a political tool. To their credit, by volume, the churches also produced the greater share of care packages and canned-food donations and funding in the form of plate collections and other taxable mechanisms.

The news media stayed glued to the conflict for eight weeks, like clouds of June bugs on a solitary streetlight. Wall-to-Wall coverage, analyses, reactions, panel discussions, historical perspectives, messages from celebrities, from children, from the children of celebrities, advertisements, human interest pieces, the battles from the ground, the war from above, the loud and bold faced propaganda and the quieter, more efficacious propaganda that pretended to be anything but, the whole thing was a boon for punditry, and a bust for anything local anywhere else that might be going on and requiring attention.

Singers and Songwriters scribbled out folk tunes on recyclable hemp-pulp cocktail napkins-- for the water, against the fighting, for democracy, against the fanaticism, for peace, and for the children, against the baser natures, for the better angels. Production studios rushed out feature length documentaries and dramatizations and live-action fictions loosely inspired by allegedly real events, to mixed reactions among easily distracted and pervasively disinterested audiences. Sculptors rushed out little monuments and tall and ambitious statues and everything in between, hoping to capture something in the chaos and conflict which would be iconic enough for a cozy retirement somewhere other than Out West. Writers and poets reached deep for some loftily profound contributions to the cultural perspective, but went largely ignored by the masses in motion, each with hat in hand.

Because stocks, bonds, usury, and a whole host of other forms of predatory financial contrivances had been outlawed during the Consolidation after the fall of the First Republic, the national and global economies, though they weren't fairing terribly well in the first place when the first shots were fired, were not significantly impacted by the conflagration on the ground, at least not right away. Apart from the cosign rumblings of a few basic supply shortages related to the forty six hundred mile detour between Sino-Californian coastal trade and the American midwest, the dollar held strong in the FX, and people basically continued to wake up every morning and go to work and come home every evening and buy stuff on the internet. Businesses made sidebets on certain commodities which could be brought to market quickly and put into the service of the various belligerents, and these saw some initial success, but the various belligerents rapidly exhausted their own capital assets in the great squander. Written as one of the bloodiest and most destructive contests in remembered history since the War, the whole thing was over in about eight weeks. No one really accomplished anything constructive. None of the states involved met their own objectives, except Utah, which continued to refuse service or even subscription to the downriver clients as punishment for their aggressions, but even they lost ground when the feds finally swept in for unopposed cleanup operations.

For the remainder of the Second Republic, Utah proper was redesignated as a demilitarized zone. All civilian inhabitants who were non-combatants were forced to leave their homes and property behind and vacate the state. All infrastructure and remaining capital were seized and confiscated by the federal government and the waters were permitted to flow freely again to the downriver clients, but by the end of summer the droughts and heatwaves were so bad that much of the headwater dried up in the beds en route, and it became clear that there would not be enough water to go around, and that this was to be the foreseeable future for the non-coastal southwest. Many pondered the immense loss of life and the utter pointlessness of the whole charade, but their reflections changed nothing about the world around them, nor even themselves or their own habits and behaviors.

The Fed, having accomplished everything in optics and nothing of substance, spent the next few years feeding their ill gotten revenues from the tetrarchical brouhaha into off-the-books research and development projects from universities and think tanks and laboratories and other facilities throughout the country. Of the many blackbook government contractors and manufacturers that received meaty windfalls from this spending spree, none got a meatier share than Centron, who had quickly stepped up to pitch a scaled up suite of fresh and novel technologies and services from their newly-formed Governance Division, led by a couple of brash young inventor/entrepreneurs from the deep neo-confederate south. These two hosted a convention to pitch some of their best ideas to a packed house in a hotel convention room just outside Denver during a Broncos playoffs game against the Buffalo Bills, in which the Bills rushed for over a thousand yards and passed for nearly six hundred, dwarfing both the seemingly inebriated Broncos and any sporadic and opaque news coverage of the Centron Conference. One of the inventors was the apparent target of an assassination attempt turned suicide, though almost nothing of this except rumor escaped the conference, as both target and victim were swiftly removed from the scene by armed guards wearing black suits and red collared shirts and sunglasses and little wireless earpieces, well before emergency medical personnel arrived on scene a half an hour later, or law enforcement, nearly two hours after that.

(88)

"So this is your first story?" The Editors sat around the table, Harkness style, as though I was a peer.[53] I can't tell which of us, myself or the Editors, found this more offensive. My suit, gray pins I ordered online, forty four regular, on a guess based on the last fitting I had, twenty years ago in boot camp. I had it tailored by the Koreans in a stripmall near my home, and it hung loosely in all the wrong places. I had said "Athletic Cut," and I swear I heard one of them giggle. You

---

[53] The Harkness Method is a teaching pedagogy which seats students at a round table, as opposed to the traditional martial method, with a singular authority in front of rows and columns. The purpose is to engage students as equals and peers in the learning process.

get what you pay for. I don't mind the Koreans, but I don't like the Editors. I think they picked up on that in the line readings. They handpicked the most obviously provocative examples of me just obliquely trying to piss them off. They made me read them out loud and leered at me uncomfortably, pushing their closed pens upwards and downwards in their fingers against the glazed cherry conference table, leaving little salamanders in the oil polish shine, otherwise smooth and bright and proof that the two old black ladies who cleaned the offices at night were the only people who did any goddamned work around here. There were six of them (the Editors) and He was there, but they couldn't see him. My heels lifted in my loafers and drummed sixteenths in the air above their soles. I was nervous, and they could smell it. I had to decide if I wanted this bad enough to put up with their bullshit.

"Yes ma'am," affecting my best southern courtesy and wondering if it made me sound like a simpleton, "I have written for most of my life, but I have never attempted to publish anything in the traditional sense." The Editors were an anomalous cult of arbitrarily interloping dream crushers; they were proof that there was a machine and that the machine existed to control the culture and enslave the human mind. None of the aesthetic arts have a corollary. A painter doesn't spend six weeks on the fucking phone with Craig arguing over whether or not the mountains in the background should be blue. "I wanted to do something meaningful, something that reflected my own sense of the existential world and of the role of the imagination in defining our reality. I have only had the chance to ask a few people to proofre-"

"About that, who exactly would you-" Geraldine was thumbing through an advance copy, pulling past sections of pages dogeared into clumps with little purple post-it notes, and not enough of those little post-it notes for my liking. "-who would you say is your target audience?"

"What she means to say, Sam-- is it okay if we call you Sam? Is it Sam or Samuel, does it matter? What she means to say is who would you say you are writing *to* [their emphasis, not my own, as if I didn't understand the original question. I want to vomit, and not purely out of contempt either.]? In just a few words, who do you think would-"

"Yes, Mr. Solvierro, who is your target audience? Who should read your book?" Craig, spinning his closed pen around in little cartwheels, audibly, but not so as to exceed the stressor tolerance threshold of anyone present but myself. The room around the oversized round table smelled like old eggs and wet mortar. The air hung over my dumb face like a rag, and I wanted to wipe my brow, but whenever I raise my arms, the cuffs on my sleeves retract almost to my elbows. I should not have come here and I can feel it in my bones. "In just a few words, of course." They don't want to test my verbal acuity under pressure. They've just all got better shit to do.

I take a deep breath and look each of them in the eye before I speak, hoping they don't know that's what people who are about to shit themselves and vomit and run out of the room in horror do when they need to stall long enough to connect the brain and tongue for a once in a lifetime line of utterly blowable bullshit. 'Everyone' is the wrong answer every time. 'Everyone' is a fucking rookie maneuver; it makes their assholes clench up tight enough to turn Kingsford coal into the Queen's diamonds. 'Everyone,' and I go home with my fucking hat in my hand to calculate the spread with the Bookie between a 0.38 slug and a *deus ex machina*. I don't believe in second chances, but I know I wouldn't have gotten in the door without Him. In my award speech I'll mention that people held the door for me, and I'll laugh a little at my own little joke and that will make me seem emotionally sophisticated and morally reverent to whole shrimp bars full of pen twirlers in evening wear. I just want the fucking money. Why does it have to be a test every single time?

"I think everyone would read *our* book." I can feel the vanity dripping off of my tongue and corroding their balance sheet. "We live in a pluralistic society, rich in diversity of tradition and ideology and worldview. I think *our* work here is significant in that there is something in it that everyone wrestles with in common, which is the struggle to find purpose and meaning in a disconnected world. I don't believe that the thing everyone is searching for is God, but I do believe that the things that we find ourselves searching for become our own personal Gods, in a way. I don't hope to change anyone's concept of the reality we occupy. I just wanted to put some of those different elements from different systems onto a level playing field."

"You don't think it's a little bit offensive, or maybe even condescending, to appropriate the Christian religion and treat it like a cartoon?" Edith wore her silver cross in a vaguely fuckable way over her lambswool between two propped elbows conjoining an A-frame of palms in clasped fingers, her sharp green eyes peering over the phalangic assembly through orange resin horn-rims that looked hip against her punky crop of anachronistic gray hair. "Our internal research suggests that about seventy five percent of our distribution base would find your work objectionable, to the point of blasphemous. Set aside our own material disincentives as a House to alienate vast swaths of our base by publishing something so nakedly hostile. What about you, yourself? Not as a brand or as an author, successful or otherwise; what about your family? You know the Iranians tried to murder that one guy about a half dozen times or more, just for daring to fictionalize a couple of angels?"[54]

She's right, and I know she's right. And it's not seventy five percent either. It's much closer to eighty five, ninety even. In fact I've got a sneaking feeling that ninety percent of the people in the world will accuse me of being a devil worshiper, which isn't nearly as painful or terrifying as the prospect of the other ten percent yawing in boredom and

---

[54] At the time of this writing, Salman Rushdie is still alive.

tossing the book aside. I'm half convinced that the work won't even sell a full run one time unless someone shoots me for writing the damned thing. I run out of words to say in defense of the indefensible. I breathe in silence and wait for the blood pressure to waver against my throbbing temples. "No one." I don't care what any of you think and you knew it before you sat down. "No one should read my book." And there are maybe ten people on the planet earth in four dimensional history that I would permit to edit my work, and none of you worthless fucking hacks are among them. "My book is antisocial and misanthropic, by design. It doesn't make the reader feel happy or excited. The characters, setting, and storylines are all hollow and vacant and two-dimensional." There is a lump in my throat and a brick in my stomach. My words are not coming out clearly, and there isn't enough wind behind them to keep my voice from cracking.

(89)

"Imagine you are in a coffee shop, say, in France or Italy-"

"A *Cafe.*"

"Yes, exactly, a cafe. Wh-"

"What's the weather like?"

"..."

"Okay, it's sunny outside under portcullis-

"Really?"

"It's sunny outside under the Portucullis- fuck you, stop. There are vines, fruit vines I think, woven into the wooden rafter- right, the pinewood rafters. I smell coffee beans and grapes and lilac and hibiscus."

"Ooh I like that, hibis-"

"There are twelve chairs around three tables draped in pastel cheque linen polyester, little cedar chairs, stools kind of, with uncomfortable but chicly postmod half backs that probably just meant they cost less to make and sold for more-"

"You're rambling; stay on track."

"I can see into the windows, they are on my left. I'm looking forward over the other tables and their patrons with sandy hair and Mediterranean skin, from the rear, along a groovy little lane to my right with a lot of bars and surf shops and gift shops. I can tell there is a privately owned grocery at the end of the view, where another street intersects, going out to the Ports if you turn left, and up and around and through a rising ridge of volcanic hills."

"Which way do you see?"

"I see both. The Ports to the left dominate the skyline-"

"Even over the structure of the *Cafe* and the ivy-wove-"

"Yes, I can still see the towers, and I can hear the ships and jet engines and Quads-"

"Quads are noiseless, and nobody uses them anymore anyway."

"Okay fucker. I'm back at the *Cafe*. Looking in the windows instead of hiking through some of that thousand year old timber, there's a steak joi-"

"Is he there?"

"Yes, he's always here."

"Where is he sitting? Is he outside or inside."

"Neither. He's at the doorway, behind me."

"Right, so how many different spaces can he occupy in that environment?"

"I don't know. I suppose there are about forty seats, plus three at the bar. The toilets, the kitchen, various points along the lane, about a half dozen shops and toilets and a couple of parking lots and some woods and then it starts to get hazy."

"Okay, that's the terminator, like, the event horizon of the subjective experience. Now, I want you to wipe your mind and then pull the whole thing up again, only this time I want you to forcefully sit somewhere else. And imagine morning, with less sun and some more clouds, but keep everything else the same. Okay?"

"Okay, I'm ready. I'm facing the cove instead of the grocery. I should have sat here first. I like this a lot better, and the *Cafe* makes more sense. This view has grandeur. I see three different ships sailing into harbor, and two more moored off in the distance, far enough away to seem like toys, but all of them huge. A starship hovers in little circular holding patterns a few hundred meters above, and seems like a bug much closer to the eye."

"A little rocky there, but it's okay. Don't give him the starship, that's a rookie move. Scope and depth aren't your allies in this process. You have to do a bunch of extra shit to get on the starship from where you are or you break continuity. You see? You've got to think about how much ground you give yourself to work with. From the tripartite scheme you've concocted here, you've given him the hills, the seas, and the skies. It's good, in a way, but it's also limiting when you're starting out."

"Okay, so just the *Cafe* then. The pastel print polys and the sandy haired tourists. I can *hear* the gulls cooing and crying out somewhere in my periphery. I can smell the salt air, the cedar, the pine, mimosa, bamboo. The windows are tall, glass wrapped in wielded square iron frames. Inside I see an old-style bar-"

"Be careful with anachronisms too, for basically the same reason. Time is real estate, and it can exponentialize your labor, which is disadvantageous in the hunt."

"I get that, okay. But still, it's kind of old style, but not like we are *then*, just that this thing hasn't changed in a long time. It's still even kind of shiny, which is impressive in a way, iconic even. Stainless steel caps, beveled at the corners, wrapping a length of ancient ivory countertop that was probably much less expensive when there were still elephants to supply the trade. Jerk style soda machines and a couple of ice cream dispensers, all chrome and clean. A neon-lit concavity over the wrapped windows gives the interior smooth transitional vibes between pink and green and orange and purple, but the wrapped windows and nondescript stone roof makes the place look kind of like a big sandwich. It doesn't help that from overhead, sometimes the pilots say the pergola looks like waffle fries. What. If the fucker is flying a plane or a ship or a helo we're already too late. Okay. Okay, no it doesn't matter. He's inside. He's sitting in one of the big red vinyl booths. No, he's not looking at me, he's reading something. I don't know, it's just a stack of paper."

"Okay, well done. Really well done. I'm impressed, you've got a knack for this. Okay, now here comes the tricky part, are you ready?"

"Shoot."

"Alright, stay where you are, stay present there in the seat facing the cove. The windows are on your right now, and the lane is mostly behind you and to the left. He's still there, right there in the booth inside, reading something, maybe he's ordered something, maybe he's looking out through the wrapped windows into the harbor. But he's there. Right? But before, just a few moments ago, he was somewhere else. Just posted up in the entry, either chatting up the hostess or just waiting patiently like he's got friends coming or something, maybe smoking a cigarette and doing a little of both."

"You changed where I was sitting."

"I changed the *time*. But not necessarily the day. In the morning he reads. In the afternoon he loiters or whatever. Get it? Now, imagine this. Imagine that every time you come here, it's the same day. Doesn't matter what day it is, and don't try to pick one because you'll fuck the whole thing up. It just matters, at first anyway, that every time, it's the same day. But no matter when you come, everything is different, no matter what time it is. Morning, noon, night. You can change the weather. Are you hot or cold? Is it raining? You can change the people. But you've got to keep him there in the *Cafe* or he'll get away from you and he'll be hard as shit to find if you're trecking him all across southern Europe, South America, and the solar system at large. Now. What is critical to understand is that time is immaterial for essential beings. What that means is that he can go to that *Cafe* on the same day over and over and over again, millions of times over if he wants. The more time he spends there, the more special it is to him, for whatever reas-"

"He saw his parents murdered there-"[55]

"That is outright plagiarism and you need to focus. But listen. Are you listening? This is important. Every single time he goes into that *Cafe* is unique. So what happens if he sits in a different spot every day?"

"He-- wait. So you're saying he can just generate new timelines?"

"Not exactly, no. It's not that he's generating new timelines. It's just that from his point of view, they aren't all different timelines. He experiences them objectively, because he lives in all of them, forwards and backwards, forever. So it's not actually about him. What's important here is to understand what *you* are doing. You are experiencing those different timelines from a unitary point in your own lifetime, subjectively. It's like you're peeking over a countertop, or looking through a keyhole. You close your eyes and you force that *Cafe* into focus and you delimit an operational perimeter, and he's always there on that particular day. It's a moment in time and space where millions of different possibilities and eventualities and externalities and internalities and causes and effects all intersect on one great big nexus of probabilistic interplay."

"What you're saying is that I can observe these alternative timelines."

"At the very least, I'm saying that you can conceive of them. There is a rudimentary law in physics that asserts that nothing new can be created and nothing that exists can be destroyed, it's called conservation. The same basic idea applies to this model. You're not creating a *Cafe* in your mind, nor him with it. You are witnessing these things. They actually exist, somewhere in space and time, or they existed or will exist. When dealing with pan dimensional theory, one learns to to depreciate relativistic perception. That means that the

---

[55] *Batman*. Directed by Tim Burton. Warner Brothers, 1989.

more you tap your own applied and superimposed systems of measurement which guide and bear you in the material world, the less efficacious will your constructs be in the immaterial realms of human consciousness. It doesn't matter if the space is big and well developed; you're not writing a novel, you see? It's kind of counter intuitive, I get that. I'm telling you that your imagination is actually an extremely sophisticated sensory perception apparatus, but I'm telling you to avoid indulging in certain details, that is, unless you want to chase the fucker all over the Spanish peninsula. Your mind generates a lot of noise when it tries to hold the larger constructs together, and from his point of view, that also means you are not there and he is not conscious of you, but then you kind of start to visibly phase in and out, which is conspicuous, you understand, among otherwise ordinary sandy-haired Mediterranean tourists."

"You're saying if I overdo it, he can see me."

"Basically. People are imagining him all the time. People are writing stories about him, wondering if he's in the shower watching them or hiding in the closet or under the bed or babbling backwards on the fucking records or whatever. In a sense, that's all you are doing, and there's no real reason to draw attention to yourself, or to worry about it. But here's the catch, the safeguards are pretty fucking sophisticated and they are built into the system from hard wire. Of the ten billions of people on the planet right now, probably let's say about a thousand are actually, right this minute, actively thinking about the actual devil. For who knows why. Right? Maybe some of them are watching their flatpanels. Maybe two of them are reading a friggin' book. Maybe someone has done something horribly wrong and just spends a lot of time thinking about all the shit they brainwashed into the older crowd before the 2nd Republic. Most of that is bound to be inaccurate, because those people are not doing it the way you are doing it, the way I'm showing you. You see? So from his point of view, maybe he's aware of all of that in some way, but because there's no specificity, it's all just noise and he's as likely as any other sentient entity in creation to prefer to just tune the shit out. He's got his own thing he's focused on, and complexity isn't his strength, it's his one inherent weakness. Like a wolf or a snake, he really only sees what he's focused on, and he keeps that right in the midst of his field of vision and forcefully focuses all his vindictive energy on it. But if you start priming up all the god pumps in your cheese factory and recreating the natural world around him in vivid detail and breathtaking scope, then you begin to approach his end of the spectrum of awareness, and thus become something he is more likely to suddenly and spontaneously become conscious of."

"You're saying he can see me and that's bad."

"I'm saying he can see you if you let him, and no, no that's not very good at all."

(90)

"So what about *her?*"

"Are you here to waste my time?"

"No. I'm serious. Look, I know you don't trust anyone on earth but yourself when it comes to your own point of view. You think people think you're crazy, but they don't because you don't ever actually share what you really think. In class, you've got plausible deniability. You made a whole bunch of really good points in a few good fell strokes, and the brighter bulbs will get it and the dimmer ones won't. It doesn't matter if you really believe in the spaghetti mon-"

"It's a giant fucking squid."

"Right."

"I don't give a shit what you really believe. I don't expect any of these kids to come back with ten pages worth of revolutionary gospel. I expect most of them to pump my fucking gas and cook my dinner. Do you understand?"

"Pretty bleak, but I think so."

"No, you don't get it. It's not bleak. It's not depressing or cynical. That's you trying to superimpose your own reali-"

"Okay! I'm sorry, look, I'm-"

"Shut the fuck up and listen and I'll show you what you came here to see."

" ... "

"Good? You sure? Close your eyes."

" ... "

"I'm a bad mother fucker."

" ... "

"I make Richter scales pop like old men getting lap dances. I'm a stone cold fucking freak of nature. I already hacked your Cpoly you little fucking worm. Not because I gave a shit, just because I was bored. That's the type of shit I do when I'm *bored*. You want to see me get motivated mother fucker? I bend entire economies to my will. I made the justice system in this town my bitch. I wrote some of that code for your dad that paid your way into Shitty U. I'm an Apex fucki-"

" ... "

"Something is wrong. What were you thinking about just now? Hey. Are you listening? What were you thinking just now? HEY! You! Nerd! Wake the fu-- oh no. Oh shit. Oh no. No no no no no no no... NO! Goddamn it shit FUUUCK! Hey, Wake up! PAAAAAAATTTT GET IN HERE! Get in here NOW bitch I need your fucking help-- I think this little mo..shit. Pat!!!"

"What bitch what! I'm here, fuck! It's not like I was asle-"

"Something's happened. He can't be fucking Overdosing right now."

"All he ate was those mushrooms, he wouldn't touch anything else in the house and we knew it and we watched him all night."

"So he can't be fucking overdosing. Something's happening. Pat I'm really fucking freaked out right now,"

"Shit Kate. Were you showing him the fucking thing? Did he see it? What the fuck is happening right now!"

"Shit. Shit. Shit. I don't know. Think bitch. Think! Okay, yes, we were doing the-"

"Oh for fucks sake Kate, do you realize-- do you get that you're either the most irresponsible *crazy person* on the fucking planet, doing dope with a fucking student which YOU said you would never fucking do-"

"I know! I know! I'm sorry!"

"-- and trying to hip him to the fucking spaghetti monster- bitch don't look at *me* that way, squiiiiiiid, ok! But it's either *that*, or you're the most irresponsible fucking *genius* that ever lived in the history of dumb mother fuckers. Do you get that? Goddamnit? Kate? The fucking *DEVIL?* Bitch were the mushrooms just not disestablishmentarian enough for you? The actual *Devil?* Bitch are you crazy? And do you understand just how much fucking worse it is *if you're not?*"

"Shit Pat, what the fuck do we do?"

"Ok girl. Ok. Let's think this out, okay? Fuck girl, this little twerp can't be twenty five. That face? Really bitch? Twenty Two? I've got fucking tampons older than this kid. Really bitch? The actual Devil? Okay! Okay! Where did he go?"

"He just pulled up a cafe somewhere and it was there. First time. I swear to shit girl. Like he put a brass hook in the lake for the first time ever and just jerked a fucking fish out of the water. I've never tried it with anyone befo-"

"You did it with Sam you crazy bitch."

"Shit. I did, didn't I? Wait, where the fuck has that gu-"

"Focus girl, where did you-- where did he go? What the fuck happened?"

"Okay, he wanted some ideas for some fucking project or whatever. That was yesterday, or.. I don't know... Anyway, he wouldn't say what it was, but he was interested in the whole jiminy cricket giant squid bit, and he just started asking a bunch of questions and somehow we ended up"

"You just somehow wound up teaching this goofy ass kid the Kolinar?"

"Ooh I like that, that's pretty goo-"

"FOCUS BITCH! We gotta bring this kid back *pronto* and get him the fuck out of here before the sun comes up, you've got class in-- shit, *he's* got fucking class in six hours. What HAPPENED."

"I don't know, I went into my whole superman thing-"

"You said you weren't going to do Nietzsche and Mushrooms at the same time ever ag-"

"Bitch would you let me concentrate! Ok, yeah, check his pulse, is he breathing? And he was pulling something up instead of listening, I was being rhetorical, but I don't know, it's like he was already there and just slipped back into it. I wasn't thinking, I don't know, I was trying to make a different point and I lost bearing. Shit Pat. He asked about **her** and I took it personally instead of literally. That's the last thing, and I told him to close his eyes-"

"And you were gonna do your whole fallacious-logic-boss-bitch-meritocracy thing you do-"

"Ugh. Yes. Yes Pat. That's exactly what I-"

"Don't get the stank mouth with me bitch. It is Three AM on an actual school night and you've fed one of the dweebs mushrooms and then let him get captured by-"

"Please don't say it."

"Bitch I don't WANT to say it. It's fucking nuts. All of it. Ursula I can understand, girl you do A LOT of fucking drugs, but this?"

"Pat I fucking NEED you right now, what the fuck do we do?"

"I don't know, girl. But it better be gangster as fuck or *you're* explaining this shit to the fuzz. I hear sirens? I see lights? I'm going right the fuck back to bed and you're on your own. How many people are downstairs? It's *never* empty girl. There's no fucking way it's just the three of us. Are you sure? KATE? Okay girl. Splash him with something? Slap the shit out of him? You haven't washed your ass in two days girl take your index-finger and"

"Pat! Pat please don't growl at me, this is fucking bigger than me? Do you get that? It's bigger than him? Something really fucked up just happened in our fucking parlor."

"..."

"I'll slap him and yell at him. You find some water. Hey. HEY! Wake up fucker! Snap out of it! Come on man! You're fucking up my mellow dude! HEEEEY! HELLOOO! Tyberius! Are you in there? Hey! Shit girl, what took you so damned long! I've been slapping the shit out of him and yelling, okay, yeah, just pour it on his face! Oh please kid. Please wake the fuck up! Shit Pat."

"No. KATE. NO!"

"Fuck Pat I know! But I think we gotta do it."

"We? WE! Bitch ain't no *WE* goddamn it. You've done enough damage by yourself girl. You want to make *THIS* worse than it already is?"

"Well what the fuck else CAN we do PAT! We've got to do it."

"Are you fucking serious right now? You want to fucking dose this kid with something else? Hell girl why don't you try jerking him off first. Hell at least he might be able to pass his UA. Fuck! Where are you going! Are you SERIOUS? Kate. KATE! This is too far, girl. Oh my fucking god she's gonna do it. She's-- This is fucked. YES! I'll hold his fucking arm. For fucks sa-- girl just hurry up. Easy does it. Stop fucking shaking. KATE! Just take a deep fucking breath and CALM THE FUCK DOWN. Okay, are you ready? Use your words bitch!"

"I'm ready."

"Okay, well he's fucking ready too. Let's get this shit over with."

"Pat?"

"Kate?"

"I love you Pat. I'm so sorry."

"It's not your fault Kate. This is pretty fucked up right here.[56] You got it in there? Okay, easy. Easy... Not so fast girl you'll bust the vessel. Just breathe, and don't put a bubble in this boy's bloodstream or we're both going to prison poor. There, now you've got it. Come on, easy out, easy. Fuck."

"Shit."

"..."

"Come on kid. Snap the fuck out of it. Please! Please kid. Come on, Ty. Hey!"

"Holy fucking shit Kate."

"Pat, look, he's coming to. Hey kid. Can you hear me? Can you see me? Hey? Hey whoa, take it easy. Can you hear my voice? Do you know where you are? What's your name?"

"Holy fucking shit Kate."

"Hey kid. Hey, can you hear me?"

"...yes."

"Oh thank fuck."

"Holy fucking shit Kate."

"Can you see me?"

"...yes, I can see you."

"Holy Fucking SH--"

"PAT! I get it, STOP!"

"No Kate, Look! Not at him, Kate, at HIM. LOOK!"

"Holy fucking shit Pat."

"Kate? Is this happening right now? Are you seeing this?"

"Holy fucking shit Kate."

"Pat?"

"Kate. I need you to punch that boy in the face as hard as you can. Do you hear me girl?"

"**G**oddamnit Pat. I'm never going to work anywhere ever again. Fuck! Sorry kid."

---

[56] Southpark. Created by Matt Stone and Trey Parker,

(Mirror, Mirror)
(91)

The girl heard barking, vague shrieks and howls, menacing sounds in the black distance, frenzied and ravenous and ferocious and roaring at something or nothing, one and then another, and another, in turns, echoing and reverberating into horrible distortion, and only at the razor's edge of her senses, far enough away to be imagined, near enough to be ominous. Something else was alive down here. Maybe more alive than she. Something that had somehow retained the force of its own will against impenetrable darkness and the endless destruction of sad, pathetic souls. Something so irredeemably possessed by the eternal forms, of contempt, vengeance, hatred, and wrath, that every fiber of its being has been conscripted into their service. Something that lives only to destroy, to consume and digest and excrete all that lives or dies within reach, and only such a thing as terror incarnate, rabid and hungry and empty and mad, only such a thing could survive here. Only such a thing could drag itself off its haunches and rebel against the oppressive weight of infinite nothing and silent darkness and cinder walls, to scream at perpetual night, moonless and starless and empty. The thing born and bred to kill, waiting impatiently somewhere, ahead or behind or above or below, impossible to tell, waiting for the bloody, broken flesh preceded by wafting scents and imperceptible sounds, waiting to destroy her utterly and entirely, always and forever; those awful sounds were the only evidence of life, of strength or purpose, of anything of substance anywhere in the black vastness.

The girl heard barking and was no longer alone. Fear then. Fear would be her sole and final ally. The antagonist would be her only companion in death. The thing would rend her flesh from bone and tear her limbs when it found her, or she, it. And yet the thing also suffered. Chained here, alone but for its infrequent food, spare morsels of wandering poets and the criminally insane, each doomed to suffer and die and be dead unto death unending. The beast, condemned to choose loneliness over starvation, ripping the flesh from the spirit and the spirit from the flesh, so that neither spirit nor flesh might pass beyond what is impassable, destroying and consuming without hesitation or mercy or remorse. Something with a soul not meant to be crushed by this soul crushing place. Something that could not only endure, but terrify. Something, alive here, like the girl, and waiting, somewhere, to take her life away from her, not for her sins or trespasses, not for judgment or condemnation, or even for the fulfillment of those, but only to survive, to preserve itself a little longer, if only to lie in wait, anguishing and miserable and unsated, for the next poor, arrogant soul that got in its master's way. The girl heard barking and was afraid, or the girl was afraid, and heard barking.

To lay motionless was no more or less excruciating than to amble and crawl and drag her torn skin across shards of bone and wet viscera and filth. To close her eyes was to perceive nothing more or less black and confusing than when they were peeled open. She would have cut off her own nose to escape the hot stench of fermented degradation waging war against her nostrils and throat. She could taste nothing, not even the iron in her bleeding gums or blistered lips. Her sweat had dried out of her skin, leaving only stinging salt in and around her myriad wounds and punctures and scrapes. Even her own body seemed designed to betray her in these last desperate moments of shattered consciousness and turmoil. Her eyes burned. Her nostrils bled. Her skull seemed fractured inward against the softer tissue. Her head felt like it was getting bashed in with a railroad spike with every fading heartbeat. Her raspy throat had given up its voice, only gasping at hot, thin air and finding little. Her raw skin and nerves overwhelmed her brain with electric chaos, reporting nothing that was not wounded or weakened or waning, and by reporting everything all at once with such furious intensity her skin and nerves reported nothing at all useful, but reported nonetheless. Her stomach turned over on itself in deflated tumbles, devoid of anything but its own dry, acidic walls to consume, and consuming them. The girl had not the fluid left for tears, and discovered that tears were not required for weeping. Every limb lay heavy and dead, and nothing left conscious within her would move them unless they moved on their own without her, which each limb did, on its own, in fits and starts, but which no two limbs would do in tandem. She was nought but an exposed nerve hardwired to aimless struggle, covering no ground in earnest but passing time in inexhaustible agony, dragging herself against the repulsive tides in a waking nightmare of drudging, lethargic impotence.

The thing did not have to hunt her, it had but to wait and to wail at the infinite nothing between them, and she would drag her lifeless carcass over fields of flesh and bone in darkness to come before it, on lacerated knees and palms, just to surrender to suffering and obliteration, if only in oblivion at last to be finally free of the wretched pain and the haunting sound and the boiling darkness and the clawing stench and the pervasive terror and trembling starvation. No pride, no hope, no dignity, no redemption, only tooth and talon and bloodletting until the blood ran as dry as her tears, until her mind and body were given over entirely to the darkness and nothingness of the void, until her very essence was broken down and returned to its source, to the *infinitum nihil* which enveloped her existence, and she herself would become one with the bleak and barren vacancy of despair and forsaken absence, she with its permeable walls encapsulating and she with its starless ceiling crowning a rolling sea of baked bone and ash and all of the wasted spoils of human indignity, unthinkable and unnameable.

(92)

I find myself.

"So you're the Editor. And I'm the writer. Right? You're the great firewall standing between my work and the culture I want to influence, which culture you are bound and sworn and committed to protecting from me and myself and my many selves and the many me's besides, undiminished, vain and intrusive. You are the great barrier reef, and I am but a humble fish seeking the death of brass hooks on strings to be withdrawn by the fishermen above, drawn to you like moths to flame, to publish or to perish." A feeble attempt to grasp the fact that I have their attention results only in breaking my own. "Or I am the worm on the hook, dead already and doomed just the same. None of this is supposed to make sense to you, because you only push what you know. And what you know, you learned. And what you learned was false. When falsehood is dogmatized, superimposed and hyperextended, the many trodden pathways of creation become few and narrow and circular. In this state, the culture is degraded, because it becomes transfixed on errant points of arbitrary unification." I really don't have any idea what I'm talking about right now. "Of the many pathways available through creation to sentient beings, only a few of those pathways lead forward through time and space toward--"

(93)

Tyberius drifted into consciousness from nothingness, a gradient superimposing of red, sweating faces and the heaving bosom of the quadromamarian, staring down at him from overhead, their likenesses partially haloed by a revolving disco light, obscured, and, for some unknowable reason, the fucking gardner, holding a newspaper in one hand and a red plastic cup in the other, standing in the arch of the parlor doorway, leaning one shoulder on the trim, head tilted, eyes cocked, dressed in red and black cotton sleepwear, be-rabbited and be-kittened, a grey NASA wife-beater with a trail of brown stains descending beneath his stubbly chin. Ty's jaw was sore. His thoughts were elusive, a well of drowning voices rolling over one another like fire ants in a flood. His jaw was really fucking sore. He had the *fear,* he knew, and focused on mustering his own wits for the ride remaining. The disco light sprayed technicolor rainbows in simmering orbits behind the blurry forms, nauseating permeations of gratuitous confusion. The blurry forms were exchanging blurrier words. The quadromamarian and the gardener appeared to be negotiating some nefarious accord.

"Man where the fuck have *you* been? I was just-"

"And what the fuck are you doing here? How long have you been standing there? Speak up Sam! You just scared the shit out of us. Don't just stand there gawking fucker, come help us, grab his legs, Kate, grab his shoulder, like this, under the arm, okay, there we go, over to the divan, easy. Hey kid, you in there? Damn girl, you really fucking clocked the little dude didn't you! Sam, what the fuck are you-"

"Where have you been!"

Tyberius groped the bottom of his face, trying not to vomit or fall off the couch when the quadromamarian and the gardener perched him halfass across the width, instead of the length, and turned back to their own inquiries, seeming satisfied that at least consciousness had returned to their patient. They were both presently ignoring him, apart from some sidelong glances, but he was getting distinct *we're-not-running-a-goddamned-bed-and-breakfast-here-man* vibes from the quadromamarian, momentarily preoccupied-

"I've been at my- ...I've been at the house. Laid up. Eating these mushrooms and trying to finish this fucking book, girl. Actually, that's what I was-"

"Oh for fucks sake. Kid. Are you okay? Yes? Not sure? Maybe? I'll take a fucking maybe. Blink twice for maybe? Ok. Kate. This is your shit. I'm glad I could help, but I'm tired as fuck and DON'T eat any more fucking mushrooms tonight. Give the kid some water before- don't- Don't let him throw up on the fucking div- Oh my fucking god. I'm out. Goddamnit Kate. That was my grandmother's divan. Sam. It's always a pleasure. Kate. Don't forget to tell Sam about the hydrangeas. I can barely walk outside. Good night, Kate."

"...goodnight Pat. I'm sorry. I love you. I'll take some time."

"Kate?"

"...Pat?"

"Clean this shit up."

"Okay, Pat. I will."

"Fuck! Goodnight Sam. Always a pleasure."

(Anterior Precuneus)
(94)

"What the fuck is the DEAL with the hand rails?" The blistering heat outside had followed the man into the shop. A cluster of old men in a barber's circle to the right burst into laughter. They had watched the man shuffle in, and a hush had fallen, albeit briefly, as they each paused amidst their reveries to observe and acknowledge the stranger's arrival. The man holding the razor shouted something unintelligible over the din, eliciting another roaring guffaw from his half-bald patron who should have been sitting still, and would nearly have been nicked in the scalp had not the man with the razor been pointing it towards the big hill just beyond the thatched rooftops outside the window. The clerk at the counter was a middle aged man with a serious eye and nearly clean coveralls, but for the large pools of sweat visible beneath the pits of his arms and around his back.

The stranger eyed the old men and their hair styles only for a moment. Outside, a spectacle appeared to be holding the attention of another gaggle of old do-nothings on the opposite side of the street. The overhead sun shone a little brighter on a few of them, as if they were at angle with a well polished reflection. He dismissed the stimuli and pulled some papers from the breast pocket of his three piece suit and thrust them toward the clerk, who then examined them for several moments until, by turns, a ready glow of comprehension, followed by a nervous look of approval, washed over him. The clerk instructed the man to wait and then turned and disappeared into some unexposed nether region behind the little checkout, while a seasoned debate was brewing in the barber's circle about the conflict between aesthetic and functionality. One side of the room pointed out the obvious irony that a handrail is inherently supposed to be designed as a support system, and that this one in particular was *desiiiiiigned* (sic) (the man waved his hands around emphatically and stretched out the vowels while saying it) by the wealthy assholes who lived on the hill and *droooooove* (again, sic) down it rather than walked down it, *como estas turistas mierdas.* The other side, clearly in the minority position, were trying their hardest to extol the philosophical validity of the artist's message, and failing to establish the value of perspective in art, that when you stood far enough away from a series of broken things, at just the right angle, they formed a whole.

The stranger, having nearly twisted his ankle three separate times during near freefall down the steeply graded steps, as the 130 degree iron piping just vanished into the ground for whole steps at a time for no apparent reason, was not persuaded, and neither were the prevailing voices in the circle, and another impassioned exchange ensued. The clerk returned, having traded his sweat soaked 'ralls for a lightly knit and brightly colored sunday suit, wide brimmed straw hat, and a holstered '38. The stranger looked the clerk over for a moment, and restrained a variety of impulses. Instead, and with a serious face to match, the stranger hesitantly proffered a set of keys to the clerk, along with some very sharp oaths and affirmations. The clerk accepted the keys, goodnaturedly and quietly, reassuring the stranger with whispers and little condescending nods. The barber's circle had fallen all the way silent.

The stranger's discomfort with the whole room was visible, and to its occupants, edifying, but something just outside the window caught the man's eyes. Traffic on one side of the street was slowing down and stopping at the intersectiion. A crowd outside was enraptured with a spectacle, and from amongst them, a woman and child started across the narrow lanes, and disappeared beyond the wall to the right of where the clerk sat, moving quickly. The stranger whirled on the clerk, as a man possessed, restating in highly assertive tones the nature of their agreement. The clerk, shrinking a little as the seemingly unassuming stranger became suddenly much more assuming, nodded more urgently and restated his own fealty to his obligations, waving the keys in front of his face in the motion of a quasi religious gesture that seemed to signal his reinforced sincerity and integrity. After another pause, the stranger seemed to resign himself to the situation at hand, and turned and rushed out of the shop, back into the heat, where he looked right for a moment, held the hat on his head with his right hand, and sprinted off into the neighborhood, down and to the left.

The semi-divergent attentions of the shop coalesced around the suddenness of the stranger's departure. They were each in the process of forming their own unique questions while the clerk sood aghast, like an animal blinded by headlights, holding the keys in the air, still out in front of his face like a signet. As they each began to speak at once, according to their custom, the clerk regained himself and lowered the keys to his waist calmly, before stepping forward, around the counter, and out through the front door, where he stopped again, and whistled. As the others in the shop all climbed out of their chairs or out from behind them and drifted out behind the clerk, they saw what he saw, and what the men across the street had been seeing, and they whistled too. Their whistles were pronounced and articulate. The clerk looked down at the little device on the key chain and found a little button in the center. He pressed it and held it for a second, and let go. When the sound came, deep and clean and alien, all the men on both sides of the streets whistled again. The clerk stepped down into the street while the others cheered him on, and as he stepped around, he passed through the sun's angle, and he too seemed to glow a little brighter in its reflection.

(95)

You would have,
To build upon,
All that I possess,
Sadly nothing more,
But surely nothing less.

(96)

The boy had not seen the explosion which engulfed the Port, nor had he seen the Man again after being bustled off of the old bus and shuffled through the labyrinth of high commerce and jaded travelers. True to form, his mother's talons returned to the bruised divots in his shoulder as they stepped down into the flooded lot at the far end of the central receiving bays, where other old buses huddled in rows along a long glass wall and quietly contemplated their reflections. She handed the driver the small slip of paper she had received the night before from the disinterested clerk. He received it graciously and smiled as he cupped it under his chest against the quickening late summer rainstorm which had overtaken them on their journey in. After studying it briefly, he returned it to her and began unlatching the undercarriage compartment where the luggage had ridden. The other passengers were drifting off of the bus into little clots and stretching and turning up their collars or holding magazines and newspapers over their heads against the rain, all more or less turning their attention to the driver's exertions beneath the bus. After a few moments everyone was soaked through and stamping impatiently, fumbling about for their own slips of paper to give to the driver, who emerged presently with the first of about a dozen sporty luggage assemblies and relinquished his fare to the attractive lady and her seemingly mute son. She wasted no time counting the pieces before spinning on her heels, pointing the boy towards the nearest terminal entrance, angling her luggage behind herself like a rudder, and breaking away from the gathering of strangers at her customary sprint.

She had not told the boy about the strange phone call she had received from his ne'er-do-well father a few days ago, or the several unsuccessful attempts she had made to get through again between then and now. He had been slurring. *"I always loved you. I am sorry I let you both down."* There had been a long pause, and then the line disconnected. Sam had been a lot of things, but rarely the melodramatic type. But he had been on her mind, and clearly, she had been on his. She had been thinking about getting out of the City well before news of the revolution began to break. Those reports had only confirmed what she already knew in her bones. The winds had not changed suddenly, but the rising tensions had escalated to the pressure cooker stage. What had once seemed like an idyllic paradise now boiled in its own juices. She knew it was time to return to the so-called Free World and discover what pieces of her old life still remained.

Something in his voice, something flat sounding and distant. He sounded like surrender. Even when they had fought he had always retained something of his casual detachment. He could slip in a joke or some bit of levity between vicious insults and nearly weeping exhortations, just to retain the vibe of neutrality. He meant what he said, but he wasn't serious. He was just lost and alone and hurting and wanted to be heard by the only woman left alive who would listen. She was free to disagree, to fight back, to ignore him, to move on with her life. He knew she knew he understood. She knew he knew he couldn't fault her reasoning. He knew she knew he would always love her. She knew he knew it was all just too little too late. She had told him he had to grow up. He had to change, and she wasn't just going to stand by and watch him disintegrate. All he could say was that she had made a vow. For better or worse, he would say. She conceded that point, but observed that the boy had made no such promises, and was under no obligation to witness his father's slow-moving self destruction. To this he could make no sullen reply. There would be a moment of silence. He would ask if she wanted to smash before she left. She would roll her eyes. "Goodbye Sam." He would shrug, and he would contain his tears until his whole life loaded their worldies into a shitty rental and disappeared for who knows where, until who knows when. And then the tears would come. Those tears would consume his soul, maybe, but she had to tell herself that in time his spine would straighten and his life would come back into focus. He might even finish the stupid-fucking-book, at long last, and make something of himself.

Maybe.

She would turn her wrist inward to steer the boy left, or squeeze a little harder with her smaller fingers and push with her thumb to turn him right. In the way she would drive the boy through turnstiles, stanchions, escalators, and literal miles of corridors, past gates and boarding areas and security guards and indifferent tourists and gift shops and cafes and cocktail lounges and little gaggles of diversity pouring over cell phone screens and ticket stubs and itineraries and gift shop novels and little overpriced sandwiches and undersized plastic bottles of room-temperature carbonated water. The child had not spoken in days. She supposed if he had, he would ask for something to eat or drink at one of those little cafes. He might ask to go over to the windows to look out on the spaceships and airplanes parked out along the runways and towers between themselves and the endless oceanscape in the distance. He might ask if he would be able to call his friends when they got *home*. Home, of course, because of all the things she had not yet told him, and because of all the things he seemed to refuse to ask.

She didn't have money for the cafes. She didn't have time for the view. And though of course she was concerned, she wouldn't press the boy to speak until they had put the continent behind them. She was exhausted, and she knew he must be as well. A night's ride in a cramped seat along bumpy roads in an old bus with bad suspension made for poor rest. They would sleep on the plane, or at least pretend to. He seemed to have spent the whole ride staring off into the nothingness, intently focused on something somewhere out there in the infinite nothing. He didn't complain or cry or argue. But he didn't laugh or whistle or ramble either. If he had questions, he kept them to himself, as if he sensed that she didn't have the answers or the wherewithal to retain her fragile composure against the additional strains of scrutiny or confrontation.

Neither of them could know that in a few short hours a momentary conflagration would render the entirety of this peninsular landscape into a wasteland of ruin and rubble which would be uninhabitable for decades to come. They would be well over the horizon when the flash of light erupted. They would not hear the sound over the engines, and would barely notice the turbulence from the shockwave. The pilots would learn of the incident within minutes, but would receive strict orders to say nothing of what had occurred until the facts were established. The guarded tears in the stewardesses' eyes implied that some secrets just cannot be kept. Passengers were informed of electrical storms ahead in the flight path and asked to power down their devices as a precaution. Breakfast at Tiffany's, little bags of peanuts and dwarvish cans of room-temperature soda. Neck pillows, reading lamps, eye masks. Microwaved *Cordon Bleu.* Four hundred thirty souls on a SuperWing living in the dead space between the past and the future, oblivious, and obliviously so. The land had permitted them to leave before closing itself off behind, presumably forever. Not with a whimper, but with a bang.[57]

As the terrain and demography beneath them shifted along its gradients, night fell like a plague, seeping through the membrane of space and time and beyond like oil soaking through linen, moonless and starless beneath the gathered clouds above and below. Hours passed until the familiar lights of Melville crawled into view. Through the portholes the passengers beheld a curious spectacle upon approach. Dozens of other aircraft were circling the sparsely lit landing fields like

[57] T. S. Eliot, *The Hollow Men.* 5.28.

lightning bugs swarming an orchard of minimalist Christmas trees. After a time, the pilot's voice came over the intercom to inform his restless patrons that their craft had been ordered into a holding pattern due to a sharp increase of inbound flights being diverted from other destinations. Passengers were politely reminded to refrain from powering on their various devices until they had come to a full stop at the gate and the cabin lights were restored. After these announcements had been made and the intercom system switch was in its off position, the pilots began rather urgent negotiations with Control for priority clearance over other inbound arrivals, citing a sixty five hundred mile trek in a system rated for about seven thousand miles on JP6 grade fuel, which, the pilots reminded Control, was only available in the States, and this SuperWing had been not-quite-topped-off with watered down JP5 from the third world prior to wheels up.

Control had valid concerns of its own about the pilots, their SuperWing, its crew, passengers, and cargo, and most pointedly, about its port of origin. This negotiation quickly reached a fever pitch, and the pilots comprehended that the value of four hundred thirty lives onboard this craft did not necessarily exceed the risk analysis threshold being measured on the ground by senior civilian personnel and their attending counterparts from federal agencies with unique and confusingly abbreviated alphanumeric identifiers instead of names. When intense air-to-ground wrangling devolved into profanity laden shouting, an exchange of epithets, and some sharply worded oaths, the pilots were curtly informed that they were **not** clear to land and would **not** be cleared to land at this facility, and were thereby *ordered* to proceed forty miles north to a military facility, for reasons of national security. Control offered its sincere apologies for the inconvenience, affirmed that it understood the circumstances, and assured the pilots that positive radio contact would be maintained between ground and air until they had arrived safely at their destination. The receiving facility had been apprised of the situation and emergency services would be at the ready. "Godspeed," was the last word the Pilots heard before slapping the channel button in disgust. "Yeah, go fuck yourselves" was their off-air reply as they wheeled the sticks out of holding and found their way into a northerly track along three-four-three, trying to keep the River in site off the port wing, just in case.

The boy watched the curious fireflies in the porthole gradually blink out against the black distance and rain as the Pilot's Voice informed all hands that, regrettably, the receiving facility had reached capacity. Thirty minutes, estimated, to Camp Buckley, and still awaiting details about travel accommodations from the destination, but third party contractors were being conscripted for the cause "as we speak." Murmurs rippled across the rows and isles. Eye masks were stowed, devices retrieved, if only for the reassuring sense of expediency. Questions formed in little eddies and whispered accretions at first. Twenty Seven minutes out, everyone was awake and wide eyed.

(The Best Laid Plans)
(97)

A letter from the Editors came for Sam today. They wrote to inform him of their interest in the book. They are willing to move forward with publication if he will accept some "minor changes," to the content and structure. They want to omit the first five chapters, citing concerns about alienating key sectors of their distribution base, as well as conventional standards regarding wordcount. They want to remove Vic from the book entirely, on the grounds that her character detracts from the overall continuity of the storyline, and that the relevance of her contribution is indefinite and poorly developed. Chapter thirteen, of course, is entirely too dark for modern readers, and would he consider a happier sounding rewrite? And naturally, they oppose any mention of themselves as characters in the book, and considering how hard they have tried to work with him on this project, they resent the overt hostility and contempt with which he has treated them. They are prepared to guarantee fifteen thousand units on the first run, with a three thousand dollar advance on signing.

And they hate the title.

If Sam were alive today to read their letter, he would shoot himself in the face all over again. Fortunately, I happen to know that Craig is happily married to someone other than the intern who has been blowing him on those "Saturday Work Retreats," so I think we can negotiate for a better deal. I am going to blackmail the Editors. I think Sam would love that. I wish he were here to finish the book, because I am tired of writing it. I have given some thought to bringing him back. All I need is a shovel, a bucket of fried chicken, some good whiskey, and a full moon. None of this is black magic, you know, it is just that digging up the deceased is depressing work, and there is no light in his backyard. I have so produced such works as this over the years, conscripting a few lonely bright lights here and there to compose my conspiratorial magic spells. Dante, Stoker, Billy Graham, and others. god gets humans to write his books, and so do I. I think mine are better and more believable, but we agree to disagree. I do not browbeat his children with my own vanity like an authoritarian attention whore. I lean into the iconoclasm of the Age, which tends to be more popular, if less persistent. Sam's gift was not his prose, it was his inclination to misanthrope and isolation, which are handy traits when one needs to sit still and write for long periods of time. Most religious texts are the product of the scribes of monks and hermits. In the modern age, I prefer alcoholic, middle-class flunkies with a lot of emotional trauma and heavy baggage.

Sam was a black-out drunk, which makes rather plausible the prospect that he just had a dream about shooting himself after crashing his hard drive at the tail end of a transcendental three day binge. It would not be the weirdest dream he has had since he came into my service, to be sure, but the visceral psychic imprint of "actually dying" tends to be pretty severe. It will have been an experience he will remember for the rest of his life, whether he believes it was real or not. He might even wake up feeling grateful for his life, relieved that the horrible experience of suicide had only been a troubling dream, and be, for once in his miserable life, disposed to getting his own shit together and reclaiming his identity. He was not a black-out drunk when I found him. He certainly had his baggage. He had a dark side, weaknesses of the flesh and of the spirit, as it were, but on the whole he had been a great student, a decent husband, and a passable father. As writers go, he was not exactly vanilla, but he was close enough that I could have passed him off during the Eisenhauer years. Hearst and Luce would both have kept him on the payroll back in the old days when a little grassroots misogyny and a few vulgar predilections could be construed as effervescent quirks, instead of career-imploding apostasy.[58]

I will stroll through the autumnal suburbs later and prune the Quadromamarian's hydrangeas in exchange for about three days worth of mind-bending banality breakers to pump into Sam's shambling carcass when I put his soul back in it, before I let his mind have it back. The skin and bone decay are pretty straightforward; reanimation is neither new nor novel. Stardust is just plaster, when you really think about it. The problem is that technically I have to give him back. He does not have to go, but there will be a few particular moments when the choice will confront him. So I am going to dose his ass into oblivion for the purpose of pushing that moment of clarity as far away from reignition as possible. You are like ants trying to comprehend the natural formation of a brick. One cannot reverse-engineer creation. When we make something, or change something, we use the rough stock of protons, neutrons, and electrons the way you use eggs, milk, and cake mix. The hard part, for me, will be persuading him that it was all just a bad dream, which means

---

[58] William Randolph Hearts and Henry Luce, American media industry moguls during the 20th century.

(98)

Which brings me to *you*, the reader.

As we near the end of this strange and convoluted tale, it occurs to me that you have questions. What happens to Miss Shelby, to Tyberius and Pike, and to Vicky Lynn and her boy? Who lives in which Republic? That is a nice little technical continuity question I feel obliged to settle before handing off the work to the detail-oriented denizens of CPoly-AtLarge. Why did Tyberius and Belmont really part ways? Why did that matter? What the hell happened at the conference in Colorado? What is up with the girl and the flies back in the **(fifties)**? Are all of these characters people? Or are all of these people characters? Who the hell did Carl kill in that temple? Is everyone in this book crazy? Is Sam actually possessed, or is Sam just having a really hard time handling the seasons of his life? Does the word "Quadromamrian" just mean *four-breasted*? Yes.

Am I, the Author, Here? Are you, the _reader_, also here? Does that make me **g**od in your imagination, that most contentious terrain? See an electron. See a battleship. See Creation, in all its purity and splendor. Now see it burn. Now see it restored. Do you see yourself? Are you anything like what the world sees? Are you anything like what you see? Why then, should the world be anything like what you see? See Her, dancing in all of her dazzling colors and elliptical lines, this many fingered Muse of mine, my once and future love, my own stillborn dream of unification with the Beginning and the End. We are all Her creatures, submissive to her will, and captive to her immaculate beauty. We do not command your attention; you merely choose to follow us of your own volition. She commands all. You have many **g**ods, we have only got the one.

(99)

I'm feeling pretty crispy. I woke up at Kate's last night, but I don't remember going there. The vibe was weird.

I had a terrible headache, hungover from a terrible dream. I had several missed calls from Vic, and Kate was preoccupied with some bespectacled backpacker in the parlor. Apparently, another revolution had taken place while I was out. There's talk of a Third Republic. I think there's vomit on my shoes. The lights Pat picked out specifically to never be too bright are entirely too bright. Around dawn, Pat appeared and told me I looked like shit, and mumbled something about the hydrangeas that seemed neutral. I don't really know what's going on or why I am here, but I had a terrible dream and I can't get it off my mind.

He says we're still waiting to hear from the Editors, but he feels pretty good about it. I told him I know that I shot myself. I told him I meant to do it. I told him I'll do it again. He shrugged, as he does when he knows something I don't know. He reminds me to call Vic back. I can't talk to Vic right now. He seems distracted by the backpacker in the parlor. The kid has to leave soon, or he has to start over. I don't know what that means. They don't see time the way I do. I know I am tired of being on the hamster wheel. I am tired of cigarettes for breakfast. I tell him I might take the offer if I see it coming. He says that Choice, like Home, is never farther away than your own backyard.[59] I don't know what that means either, but it seems to amuse him in a way that makes me cringe. He concedes everything, and nothing. I know it was not a dream, because I lived through it. Something is different, something I did not expect. I have watched the rise and fall of a civilization in a single lifetime, and have been preoccupied with my own petty concerns throughout. How can it be that I don't care what happens to the species, but I get to be the one who sees it all happen? How can it be that I care about what happens to me, even as control of my own destiny has been preempted by the Powers That Be.

---

[59] *Wizard of Oz*. Directed by Victor Fleming. Metro-Goldwyn-Meyer, 1939.

But I do care. It almost pisses me off to discover the fact. Who is this **god** person anyway?[60] I have spent plenty of time punishing myself for my own sins, as I suppose everyone does. I would finish the book on my own if I knew how, but deep down inside my core I know that this is not my story to tell. He will give me what I want and I will give him what he wants. I will give the Editors what they want and they will give me what I want. You will give the Editors what they want, and they will give you what I have to give. We all exist on our way toward or away from the apogee of the oblong circle of life.

(Architecture)
(100)

When you're falling from space, what you see above and around you is darkness, interrupted only by the spectacle of infinite light condensed into pinpoints, shining manifold and brilliant, against the infinite nothing. The ground beneath you is distant and vague and indefinite; the space around you is cold and empty. As you fall, the ground beneath you expands and the space above you becomes retina, telescoping in upon itself as the light of the daylit world intrudes from all ends of the periphery. As the body descends, the earth awaits; the heavens retreat into the nothing, and the nothingness possesses them.

Life is like falling from the future, rather than towards it. We perceive our time here as a linear affair, commencing at birth and terminating at some foggy but inevitable departure ahead. The soul is not a linear creature. It is eternal, and at all times fully formed, as is the reality it inhabits. "The World" introduces itself to you on its own terms, often gently at first, expanding and hardening as you grow. The last moment of your life is the fullest moment you will ever live, when your memory becomes complete and can expand no further on this journey. This is why we mourn the

---

[60] *Hitchhiker's Guide to the Galaxy.* Directed by Garth Jennings. Touchstone Pictures, 2005.

passing of the young souls before their time, because we comprehend so much of their path left untrodden ahead of them grown over and reclaimed by the ethereal wilderness surrounding. When you are falling, the ground beneath you is your memory, first vague and present but unformed and far away. Like the ground it expands as you live and grow, and as you do, it seems to approach. As it approaches, the infinite nothing above from which you sprang, limbs wild and flailing, voice wailing away your exhilaration and fear, this infinite nothing withdraws and contracts, like retina, like space above.

At the last moment of your life, the ground beneath you becomes complete. You are who you were meant to be, and you can be nothing other. Your life is fulfilled, such as it is, and such is it will ever be. Your journey is ended.

Vic awoke.

Vic was reborn with breath on her lips and rhythm in her chest. Lightening coursed through her nerves and her mind coughed and sputtered and reached for consciousness. The darkness gave way to light and light consumed her vision. The World returned to her, on its own terms, according to its own unknowable motivations. Her misery subsided with the fog against the blinding light enveloping her existence in those first moments, and her first sensation in this new life was an overwhelming wave of gratitude. Her trial had passed, and her path continued. Comprehension, gracious traveler, was long on its heels in its stride to overtake the light. First the walls, the bed, and the smell. Then objects, some familiar, some obscure, each requiring focus and consideration. A pillow on the floor to her right, beside a capsized saline drip still haphazardly hanging from the needle under the bandages on her arms. Sound, over these slow moving scenes, chirped sharply in its corner, and slowly at first. Pain, more slowly than the sound, but distinctly more intrusive, as a dull needling in her skull, just beyond the scope of her vision, and thus reality could reclaim her full attention as an environment, all of which she could neither hear nor see at once. Awareness, at last, followed its guests through the gates of her perception and, having awakened, Vic acknowledged that she was awake, and therefore alive. The last bit required the greater share of her reasoning faculties, according to its own special significance.

Vic was alive and awake and presumably in the medical cabin onboard a ship. Tyberius was nearby, absently tapping away at the keys of his Zelco. He looked exhausted, but *unbandaged*, she observed, and then Memory washed in. She lifted her hand to her brow, slowly and deliberately, and felt the wrappings. As her fingers reached the gauze, the general aching that gnawed at her body localized itself in the flesh and bone around the two holes beneath either temple. She lifted both hands so that her fingers could find the entry and the exit. Her right hand found the entry first; her left probed for a moment because the exit was not exactly where it seemed it should have been. It was higher and further back. A small caliber bullet does not travel in a straight line through skull fragments and viscera. Vic did not need full command of her memory or senses to consider the path the bullet had actually traveled, first exploding from the springbound hammer strike, out of the revolver's chamber and through its snub-nosed barrel, into and out of her conscious mind along an arc predetermined by the calculus of its velocity, angle of intrusion, the density of the soft skin and bone giving way, and the viscosity of gray matter within.

A rocket scientist could not have accounted for the breadth of variables which presuppose any such arc, among countless conceivable arcs, which is not terminal. The grains of aluminum and steel which only god could number, the temperature of her body, her blood pressure at that exact moment, the speed of the earth's rotation and the vector of its orbit relative to the number of steps she took between the aisles of chairs which all faced due north, the age of the powder in the single shell she fired.

But a couple of rocket scientists had saved her. The abortive attempt on Tyberius's life had turned windfall, and had boosted Centron sales and subscriptions amongst attendees and interested parties around the world in sequence. But the conference was ancient history. His skin was older, and his coily black hair betrayed little silver streaks and flecks, as did the stubble around his lips and cheeks. Skeptics and conspiracy theorists inquired after the whereabouts of her physical person, and of his, but none would find either of them here aboard *the Epicurean*, one half-dead and the other half-spent. Tyberius was grateful to have avoided being shot by Vic and her .38, but could not be brought to understand, let alone favor, her decision to so dramatically alter the agreed upon plan with such drastic improvisation. However, the impossible prospect of a plausible explanation was not the only reason he had persuaded himself to pray that she survived.

Presently, her raspy voice meekly broke the near silence, and though the chirping continued, the tapping stopped. "Where's Pike?" Tyberius looked up from his screen with a visible expression of shock spreading across the tired lines in his disheveled continence, but upon hearing her inquiry, his features sagged again and he looked at the floor in silence for a moment, before closing his Zelco.

"Pike is on the bridge, either dead in his chair himself, or deciding the fate of the rest of the species otherwise. Sickbay is self-contained and independently powered on Pentathlonite ships, and is always active, even in drydock. He has initialized the rest of the ship; the launch is in a little while. How do you feel? You look like shit." He pulled himself towards her in his chair on her left side. "We have to take the saline out. He said if I pick up the mount you'd get a bubble in your vein and die anyway." He stood, carefully, and braced himself against the edge of the hospital bed as he carefully placed his steps around to the opposing side of it. Then he returned to his seat, looking defeated.

"I saw him in a dream in a place he had no business being."

"He said something pretty similar about you when we were brought here. People are looking for all of us. Centron crew lists are classified, and access is highly restricted, but there's an outside chance they'll figure it out before we launch, *if* we launch, I guess. How do you feel?" Tyberius tried again. They had given her fresh garments and bandages since her seizure. He expected that the drugs had dimmed her senses along with the pain, but could see in her eyes that neither had been extinguished. "Am I the only person on this boat who hasn't made a deal with the Actual God-damned Devil?"

"It's not a boat. It's a ship. How long before the launch?" Her eyes were both open, but her lids were heavy and her mouth was dry. She felt the drugs, and didn't feel them. She felt just poorly enough to guess that she could feel a lot worse, and likely would begin to feel it pretty soon.

"The Pentathlonites are on already. Shouldn't be long now." Tyberius set his Zelco aside and leaned back, closing his eyes. He seemed noticeably unconcerned with her condition. "What is the last thing you remember?"

"I'm fine, by the way. Asshole." Vic tore the needle out of her arm and tossed it to the deck in a coil of amber hose. "I was in hell, I think. Or I was dreaming. I don't really want to think about it right now. Where is *he?*" She struggled against gravity and pain to raise herself upright in the bed. The new paper gown was clean and crisp, but neither insular or flattering. The cold air betrayed her immodestly.

"*he* is everywhere, apparently, and nowhere. I don't know. Pike is pretty banged up, and only barely conscious. I don't know what happened to him either, but I suspect he had his ordeal, apparently not too different from yours from what I can tell. Shit is pretty wild outside right now, not that any of *this* shit is exactly normal, by any reasonable standard, but it is quieter in here, so long as you don't turn on the flatscreens." Tyberius opened his eyes and looked around, half-seeming as though he expected the scene to change from one moment to the next. He seemed distressed, she could tell, but also somewhat detached, as if he were watching something he had seen already.

"I think I would like to get the fuck out of here before he makes up his mind."

"Nah, I don't think you want to go out there as bad as you think you do. I think you should stick around and get some rest. Let this thing play out. There's a legit revolution going down out there, like for real this time."

"Tyberius?"

"Somebody blew up one of the other Ports. Down in the southern continent. It was nuclear. There's nothing left for miles down there. My friend's gardener said his family was supposed to be coming back from there the day it happened, but he can't get any information about their flight. It's a shitshow."

Vic screamed quietly, failing to avoid the pain in her exertion. "I just want off of this fucking ship." She tried to turn herself so that her feet dangled off of the side of the bed. "I want to go back to Melville." She could feel the razors and pins shooting through her stubborn limbs, and knew that any attempt to stand on her own feet would be disastrous.

"Well, it's about a nine hundred mile walk. Roads are closed. Airspace is locked down. If Pike steps on the gas right now it's not likely we'll reach escape velocity before they blow us all out of the sky. The Launch is, presently, not authorized. What do you remember from the conference? I am grateful, I guess, for you not shooting me. But at this point I rather wish you had. I think we're all on the hook for murder until your body is found, and due to recent events, no one is looking for your body at all."

"TYBERIUS."

"What? It's not my fault. We're pretty sure it wasn't any of our clients. All signs point to a lone actor. Probably some old Sandanista with a grudge against the new Imperialist regime. We did make a shitload of money, if that's any consolation." Ty coughed into his hands and wiped them on his trousers. He picked up his Zelco and opened it. Such strange circumstances for abject boredom, she thought, but there he was, staring at the screen as if it was going to instruct him what to type, or think, or do. She began to understand. It didn't matter what he thought or typed. There was very little he could do. Walt's old stoicism was seeping to the surface. Ty was disconnecting. He was a spectator now. His former partner and estranged friend had the initiative here. "Somewhere up there, there's a new Sphere with nothing on it. No people. No commerce. No laws or rules. No goods or services. No demagogues, politicians, polemicists, reactionaries. It's a blank slate. *Tabula Rasa*. In our lifetimes. Unbelievable. And we've got the operating system that makes the thing work. Pike wanted to call it PolyWalt. Un-fucking-believable."

"I need a toilet. I need food. I need clothes. I'll take them in any order, but then I need to see Pike. Preferably before he steps on the gas, as you say." Vic eased her bare feet down onto the deck, trying to catch the back end of her paper gown with one hand before the move dragged it too high up her bare legs. With her other hand she held tightly to the aluminum railing at the head of her bed. Her feet felt limp against the newly polished deck, which bare feet had never touched. She really didn't want to be the first person to bust her ass on a brand new deck on a brand new ship. "So, if we can't go anywhere, why are the engines on? Why are the lights on? Why are we here?"

"The Launch was technically scheduled and cleared weeks ago. It's not exactly that we can't go anywhere, we just don't have clearance from the Port Authority. The Revolution sort of has us in Limbo. Centron isn't going to just squat and dump a six trillion dollar project on account of some pissed off third-world proletarians. I don't know about food or clothes yet; supplies are still onloading. Crew comes aboard soon. PolyWalt talked us through your dressings. Intubation was automated, which I thought was pretty slick, honestly. There's a toilet a few passageways over. Officers'. I've used it already. Not too shabby. Enlisted and contractors piss in a weird space trough-type-thing. Well, those of us that stand up do anyway. Officers just have regular ass toilets. I don't actually know what you guys h-"

"TYBERIUS!"

"Ok, ok!" Tyberius closed his Zelco again, and set it aside as he ambled up on to his feet to help her. He strung one of her arms over his shoulder in a sisterly way, hunching a little to compensate for her height. He wrapped an arm around her waist and held her hand with the other. She complied, and at first he felt most of her full weight before she forced a little gravity back into her legs and tried to stand all the way up. She braced herself with her free hand and took a small step away from the bed without letting go of it. She couldn't help thinking she was taking her first steps for the second time. Absently, she considered which prospect was more appalling: leaving the earth in a paper gown, or in those awful enlisted workadays, suitable for convicts and mechanics, but not at all appropriate for an *apex-fucking-predator*. She laughed a little, in spite of herself, and in spite of the pain.

"What's so funny?" Tyberius felt he could use a good laugh, if one could be found in this awful place, in these chaotic and confusing times.

"Nothing." was her disappointing reply.

Infinite Nothing.

(The Third Republic)
(101)

Revolutions are not glorious. From a bird's eye view, they are violent and pointless conflagrations of human emotion. Hollow spectacles, wasteful and indulgent. Perhaps, in the grand scheme of things, revolutions are necessary, but humans never really change. They change the world around themselves constantly, to suit their evolving aspect, but their essence remains inert through the ages. Bloodshed and rationalization. Topple the Old Guard and install the new. Televised trials in kangaroo courts concluding summary verdicts and ceremonious executions. The illusion of Order is Chaos precipitate. Or is it the other way around?

History books are replete with narrative chronicles of every kind of coup, each accompanied by names and dates and places and neat red-letter sequences of events and speeches and orders and responses in kind, as though any of these implosions were logical or rational expressions of common perspective. However, no two individual accounts of any such experience will tell the same story twice. And every New Guard worth remembering is one that lives long enough to become the Old Guard in its own right, just to be toppled once again by the inevitable shift change among the zeitgeists. Liberty surrenders loudly to Security until the common threat fades from memory and Security becomes burdensome and confrontational. Then Security surrenders quietly to Liberty until Liberty loses its way and becomes the antagonist. Liberty is a terrible leader, and Security is no way to live. Every story is different, but the story never really changes.

We all eventually go our separate ways and drift into our endless night alone. We forget the battles we fought as age and complacency overtake us. Our hair turns gray and our minds begin to addle. We become suspicious of the young and their impetuous manners. Our conclusion is always the same. The world was better *then,* and so it goes, the world is always getting worse. Childhood is confusion and vulnerability. Coming of age is conscription and confrontation. Midlife is detachment and decline. But Old Age, that is something else entirely. Old Age is isolation and indignity. Old Age is regret and despair. Old Age is a mother fucker. We retire into prisons we spent our whole lives building, or in many cases, failing to build at all. The human race is Old. The blood in our veins is much older still. The information it carries in its cells is memory in its most ancient form. Memory of hunger, of blindness, of paralysis, and of fear. These memories are primordial. They are as old as the sound of waves breaking against stone. The universe was a quiet place before anything was alive to hear.

As time goes on and memory recedes, we forget our hunger, our blindness, our paralysis, and our fear, and we become entitled. We become indulgent and vain and lethargic and arrogant. As that terminal lifestyle inevitably begins to fail, our imaginations erect heroes who are selfless, humble, energetic, and courageous, as a counterbalance to try to pull the culture back towards the mainstream. The pattern which forms is interminable and inviolate. This is the gestation process by which all false gods are born. But just as the false culture which begets them fails, so too fail their false gods to save them from themselves. This is the ultimate state of the human condition which precedes revolution. The substance of revolution is hunger, blindness, paralysis, and fear. The natural order is that which grows and decays and is reborn in itself. Revolution is the natural order. This is Natural Law.

(102)

The Laws of Man are, by consequence of scope and scale, inferior. However, while the laws of men necessarily proscribe the use of nuclear weapons against neutral civilian and commercial targets in peacetime as well as war, Natural Law does not. The laws of men commission representatives who form governments who conscript resources to codify restraints, investigate transgressions, and restrain transgressors. Even after the Consolidation, after the First Republic, there remained hundreds of governments intact around the world. Each of these comprised representatives speaking the will of their constituencies into being. When such an egregious transgression occurs as that which broke the fragile threads holding together the Second Republic, a vicious and cynical assault on one of the great world wonders, itself inhabited by what amounted to a large city of fellow human beings from literally everywhere, the most pressing compulsion is to identify the transgressor as rapidly as possible.

Rumors fly. Bullshit walks. It was the disgruntled indigenous. It was the SRU. It was a disaffected whacko. Uncle So-and-so says he knows damn well who it was, and proceeds to list everyone he hates or fears. And so it goes, because no transgressor can be found. One must be manufactured. A rational, logical sequence of red-letter events, dates, places, and names must be assembled and ratified by the skeptical collective. This is the one eventuality more terrifying than the use of a nuclear weapon against neutral civilian or commercial targets in times of peace or war. Blindness is the first of the four plagues which accompany the apocalypse. They will have eyes to see, but will not see.

Lockdowns ensue, and with travel goes trade, and with trade go the coffers and stores. Hunger follows Blindness into every corner of the soul. The hungry cannot be constrained by any force known to man. They spill out of their empty homes retching and heaving and starving, clawing for any sustenance they can find. Hunger climbs fences and breaks windows. Hunger builds fires and burns bridges. Hunger grows teeth and bares them at its hungry neighbors. Hunger eats away at the body until it can't move. Hunger precedes Paralysis as society atomizes and becomes incapable of responding to the needs of the many, and the wheels of its institutions grind to a halt. Paralysis is the progenitor of Fear.

Fear is the Primary Mover. When the Fear comes, Liberty cries out for protection. New **g**ods become flesh and answer the call. Security becomes the order of the day, and accretions of human capital form around strength and resources. Blindness, hunger, paralysis, and fear, reign.

(103)

"Don't open your eyes. Just say what you see."

"So you brought him back?" The two old men sat across from each other in a booth in a small cafe. A large manuscript sat in the middle of the table between them in two stacks. The man speaking wore a bright green suit with a shiny blue bow tie and kerchi-

"Why is he dressed like the Riddler?"

"I don't know, but I'm pretty sure he can hear you. You should probably try to focus."

"Don't be gross about it. Yes, I brought him back. He *agreed* to finish the book. It's binding."

"You know I despise puns."

"I take these things seriously, you know. So, do you want him? It isn't my call to make." The other man wore black from head to toe, a sweater and slacks, silver buckles on his loafers. His socks were pink.

"It's his call I suppose. I don't really care either way. You resurrected him. That's what I'm more interested in at this moment." The man in green reached out and carefully turned a page from one stack over onto the other stack and studied the new page quietly for a moment. His companion waited patiently, as if for approval or disappointment. The man in green squinted his old eyes against the small type in the dull cafe light. Evening approached outside. The sky was cloudless and the air was still-

"Focus. Stay inside. Stay with them."

"I feel claustrophobic. It's like standing in a small kitchen with a big oven. I feel like I'm standing next to a neutron bomb."

"You're standing next to two of them. What are they saying?"

"You gave him back his life. You're telling me it was merely a matter of convenience? You restored a man's soul and set him free, *for selfish reasons?"* The man in green wore his amusement loosely. "No gunshot wounds, no scars, no spells? No messy bandages?"

"I said don't be gross about it." The man in black wore his patience tensely.

The man in green pretended to dismiss the subject with a wave of his hand; the gesture was a habit of his that made him chuckle. He seemed satisfied with himself and amused by his own genius. The man in black was not petulant, just not so easily taken by the irony. The man in green turned another page. "I don't think it will work."

"I know. But it's his ending. He is just a little fellow, after all, as the man said."[61]

"So you're just going to hand it all off to the boy? It's novel I guess."

"You said you hated puns."

"I wasn't aware I'd- oh my! Clever boy. Yes! I see, very good. It's nov-"

"What was the point of all of this? There isn't enough time for them to find a new star. They're already withering on the vine." The man in black leaned in, folding his elbows on the table, carefully avoiding the neat stacks between.

"I used to think the world would be big enough for them. It's hard to get these things just right, you know. If it was bigger, they'd have never stood up. If it was smaller, they'd have all killed each other off or starved by now."

"Right, but that's the big flaw, isn't it? Respectfully, of course. They will either kill each other off or some of them will make it to that little Sphere before the rest kill each other off down below. But then what? You're right back to your smaller world."

"Bah!" The man in green winced and waved away the reasoning. "I know that. But it *is* different. In their way, they will have technically won the game. Success changes one's perspective of things. Once you've figured out how to do something, it's easier to do it again. Give them time. I think there will be more of those Spheres."

"They have to make it to another star for the game to end. Or die."

The man in green reclined and sighed deeply. He was no longer amused, but forlorn. His bushy eyebrows furrowed. He folded his arms and stared down into the aisle

[61] Tolkein, J.R.R.. "Out of the frying pan and into the fire," in *The Hobbit, or, There and Back Again* (London: George Allen & Unwin, 1937).

between the rows of booths, absently, troubled. "So you want to let him finish the book, and then when his ending comes, you just want to hand the thing off to the boy. We've never tried it that way before, I grant you. I don't know. It's a lot of damned math, that's what it is. I don't think it will work."

"I think we should try it this way. I think it works. There's something about that boy that-"

At that moment both of the old men suddenly bolted upright, each with palms flat on the table.

"Oh shit."

The walls began to shake and the floor rumbled. Waves ran through the colors of the room, as if the structure itself were just sheets blowing in the wind.

"Oh shit oh shit oh shit."

Tyberius opened his eyes and sat up sharply. Sweat covered his brow. "Shit!" He filled his lungs with air as though he had been drowning. He shook his hands in the air like rags, trying to restore circulation. His pupils were dilated and his pulse was beating war drums in his ears. "Holy shit!"

"Tdubs, calm down buddy, you're okay. Everything is okay. You're still here." Kate spoke for the quadromamarian. Pat, for her part, had tuned out the whole absurd affair an hour ago, and was thumbing through a magazine on her new divan. She looked up briefly, sensing something had changed in the dynamic in the room, but quickly returned her eyes to her pages, only now pretending not to notice. She sensed trouble in the rhythms in the room. She had tried to talk them out of it, but there was no talking Kate out of anything when it was Kate's idea.

"I am definitely not fine. I need to go. I need to find Pike. I'm sorry. I would explain, but it wouldn't make sense if I tried. I'm sorry. I've got to go." Tyberius dragged himself out of his criss-cross applesauce and grabbed his bag and slung it over his shoulders as he was speaking.

"Whoa man, hold up! You definitely can't drive right now; where the fuck are you going? What do you mean I wouldn't understand fucker? Don't forget who the senpai is here, little guy, you wanna try me?" Kate was reaching for his legs and trying to pull herself up at the same time. Nobody leaves the party until sunup! It was a nonnegotiable stipulation at the Victorian.

"One of them was your fucking gardener." Tyberius paused, just long enough to confirm the impact. When the frozen expression of bewilderment washed from one side of her face to the other, he made his move for the door.

Kate swooned. Fungus doesn't like abrupt cognitive disorientations. She struggled to grip her composure while processing what might as well have been a foreign language in sign language from a parakeet. "Sam? What? Hey Wait! Where are you GOING!"

"I'm sorry. I've got to find Pike. I have to go now!" And with that, Tyberius scaled the sofa between himself and the door of the second story parlor, and made his departure.

"I don't like him."

"Goddamnit Pat!"

"Okay, okay! Just saying..."

(104)

Whatever Vic said to Pike, she said behind closed doors. All I know is that Pike stepped on the gas. *He* is gone, and they are too. Footage of the rogue launch circulated around the world for about twenty seven minutes. Then every other satellite in space fell out of the sky. If not for this typewriter, the entire story would end here. The revolution has begun, and the Ports are gone. The Editors no longer matter. I am free. But I am lost and alone. The world is literally crumbling in front of me, and there is nothing I can do to stop it. Whatever this book was supposed to be, it happened too late. I thought that he had chosen me because I was a writer, and perhaps in a certain way, he did. The truth? The sad and ridiculous comedy of it all? He chose me because I was the Quadromamarian's fucking gardener. He used me to go somewhere he could not otherwise go. I don't know what it was about Tyberius, but he knew she would be the only teacher in the world who could bring him to his full potential. But she was the closest person in the world to the One, the giant interdimensional squid that lives in the mushrooms, the great and powerful Oz, the God from which all other **g**ods are derived.

The Greeks said she ate her babies, and from a certain perspective, they were not exactly wrong. But then again, they also thought she was a man. The nature of things is funny that way. I've eaten a lot of mushrooms with Kate over the years. One night, she tried to explain to me what it was like for her. She said that her experience had always been different from everyone else's. She said then, when she was young and partying all the time, before the world fell apart the first time, she noticed she was always more present than her peers, no matter how far gone they all were. She said most people just wanted to fry out and escape. It was a party for them, but it never had been for her. After the induction phase, she observed that in certain settings when a normal person's basic competencies attenuate, like speech, motor skills, and emotional control, her own would always heighten.

She said that one night, a voice in the universe told her to look at those two people over there and describe what they were saying. She said she didn't know what they were saying, because they were fifty feet away in a field. She said the universe slapped her in the face and demanded that she look at them and FOCUS! To this, Kate said she looked on at the couple on yonder hill for a few moments and said something like the following: "She cares about him, but she's disappointed in his behavior and feels like she just can't get through to him. He's fifty-fifty on the fence about her either way, but at heart, he doesn't understand her value and isn't sophisticated enough to comprehend her criticism. He just thinks he's being attacked. He'll go all night without hearing her, and by the time the paper comes, one of them is going to cause a scene and one is going to bail." She said the universe asked her *what else?*

Kate said she looked around the field for a minute and thought about what she saw. "Everyone here knows exactly what's happening, even though no one here is anywhere near them." She said that from that moment on, the universe was a voice in her head.

I should say here that a lot of people I've fried out with in this life have said a lot of weird shit to me over the years. But I have known her long enough to remember what it was like before her giant squid came along. She had always been smart, always lovely to behold, but she had been reckless and superficial. I remember when she changed, and Pat does too. It wasn't overnight, it was over a couple of very specific years, when the whole world fell apart for the first time. Reality sobered a lot of people up back in those days. But not Kate. Over a decade, I've watched this one random girl I knew from back in that gap become one of the most powerful women in the whole world, or at least my world anyway. But the shit she's on at any given moment would kill an elephant. Pat is almost always clean. They really are the weirdest fucking people I know. But Kate was clearly onto something, and I know from experience how hard it is to be onto something that, self-evidently, no one else around you will understand.

Maybe that is the point of this book. He showed me the parts of people's lives I would have never seen otherwise. They were all very specific people, and he didn't give me everything from all of them, but I suspect that they are altogether a lot like that damned handrail. If you stand far enough away from the broken pieces, at just the right angle, they all form a straight line. She tried to show me her friend one night, and was shocked to discover that her friend would have nothing to do with me. Pat adores me, and Kate agrees. Pat is always obviously skeptical about the giant interdimensional squid bit, and I guess we all kind of wonder if deep down it's just some kind of metaphor that Kate gets that no one else ever will, or, conversely, if Kate has actually somehow befriended the Sky Mother. Kate says *she* likes that much better than Ursula, but that Kate doesn't care and calls her Ursula anyway. Contextually speaking, that's pretty fucking weird all by itself, but then again, that's Kate. She's fully well capable of giving the universe just as much shit as it gives her. I've also known Kate just long enough to survive the opinion of her imaginary friend.

Pike and Tyberius, on the other hand, I don't really know at all. I need to call Vic. I've called Vic. I don't know where my family is. I can't call anyone now. The assholes at the airport said they could neither confirm nor deny her flight's departure from, well, you know. They could confirm that no such flight had landed, so far as they knew. And then the satellites fell from the sky. Pike and Ty's work is my guess. A little parting "fuck you" to the very species the whole project was supposed to save. Thanks assholes. I'm supposed to wish he was still here to show me. I won't do it. I don't know what else to do. I can't leave. The fucker left no food in the house, but for an empty bucket of chicken and an equally empty whiskey bottle, next to the damned dirty shovel. The stores are closed, and if they weren't, the roads damned sure are. The Victorian is closed, even to me, the survival of the Quadromamarian being of paramount necessity, of course. Whole swaths of the book are missing, as are growing chunks of my own memory. Much of what remains of each is effectively redacted. All I have left is paper. The Devil left me here alone in the universe with a shit load of paper.

I suppose I'm supposed to finish the book, but then what? Does he want me to leave it some place where I won't get any brain matter on it when "my ending" comes? Honestly, he seemed pretty cynical, but I admit that does sound pretty damned dark, even for his tastes. If he wanted to lock me away here for some indefinite period of time, which clearly he had to have seen coming, the Revolution that is, with a shit load of paper and nothing else to do in the world, then clearly he wanted me to write an ending. But he wanted me to write it in the blind darkness of infinite nothing, because I have no clue what the fuck is happening outside right now. I assume that people are eating each other already. Black smoke from tire fires, broken glass covering every inhabited block of America, or the world? Rape gangs, vandals, and super villains, with no organized opposition, spilling blood and tears over the soil like rainfall. Human beings are notoriously terrible in a crisis. He left the pistol, and I am at least less offended that he left more than one bullet. I am one hundred percent certain that he thought about it. I only really need the one. I've proven that already.

There was something somewhere once about a character in a story who fired five shots into various enemies during his climax, before his story ended. Some bright soul out there noticed the incongruity, and concluded that the sixth shot was for the character himself. An unspoken signal from the author to the reader to fill in the blanks, which, incidentally, with my luck, is what the gun is probably loaded with. That would definitely suit his sense of humor. Knowing him the way I do, I have to guess that he figured I would need the other five bullets for something at some point before I finally surrendered to the one. Five more little mysteries to resolve before the conclusion every reader assumes is inevitable. Well fuck each and every one of you. I'm not doing it again.

Maybe six bullets means I can take a chance and go outside for about ten minutes and try to find something I can eat, drink, smoke, or fuck before the airraid sirens inform the rest of the remaining population that the wars have begun in earnest. I can try to find my family... or die trying.

(The Future)
(105)

Wind blew as sunset fell over the gigasphere. It was always a pretty sight, the citizen thought to himself. The spheres had something like seasons, milder and more subdued than seasons on earth, and manufactured, of course. The citizen had never inhaled unprocessed air or witnessed a terrestrial sunset. No person born during the Fifth Republic had done these things. No person born during the Fifth Republic ever would. The citizen's world was a machine, and so too was its God. A God without genuine seasons or authentic sunsets or natural air on its breeze. The citizen quietly wondered, quite often, if any such Godless world would be better off or worse. Every citizen had the dreams.

The dreams of being ripped into the vacuum of space. Of distant explosions, followed swiftly by the violent withdrawal of every breath from every living lung. Of a final moment's vision of blue and lifeless carcasses of friends and loved ones and neighbors floating carelessly away in unfamiliar angles and still-life pantomimes of horror and surprise. Maybe the Spheres didn't have snakes and spiders and cockroaches and mosquitoes, but regular day-to-day life was arguably more terrifying and hazardous than any life ever lived before, below. The citizens adapted, over time, to their new conditions, but space, like the sea before it in the history of our imaginations, was its own progenitor of mystery and horror. No amount of work assignments and news broadcasts and musical or theatrical performances or mating assignments could ever sufficiently distract the citizens of the Fifth Republic from the perilous reality which confronted them every single morning.

The Machine's voice was baritone, with a hint of mahogany, the citizen thought, meant so long ago to be comforting and familiar to those who designed the Machine. But those people, whoever they were, lived out most of their lives on earth. Comfort on earth is something entirely dissimilar to comfort on a sphere. The Machine's voice reminded every citizen onboard a sphere that they lived on a machine, and that their lives were preserved, and therefore governed, by a machine. The citizen enjoying an artificial breeze alongside what was, nonetheless, a genuine sunset in its own right, contemplated the abrasive juxtaposition of the surreal with the real. On a sphere, the sun appears smaller and further away than it does on earth. Its majesty, as described by all the poets and bards in the Archives, falls somewhat short of their posthumous memories in the mind of the citizen. The sun, under such circumstances, was just one more thing trying to kill them all with its searing heat and radiological temper tantrums and coronal mass eruptions. The Machine's voice was that of a charlatan, trying always to persuade the citizens that up was down, left was right, forward was backward, and so on. But this doesn't work on people who already know the sky is not blue.

The citizen occasionally permitted himself to marvel unironically at the massive solar panel structures that revolved about the sphere to shield its inhabitants from the direct exposure to the sun, which would be fatal. The structures captured enormous amounts of free energy to power the Machine and its systems, but also required an enormous amount of energy to calculate and motor their proper orbits, which demanded perpetual consistency and precision. They cast huge shadows over the sphere, in their way, representing a paradoxical form of auxiliary nightfall that occurs when one's own region of the sphere oriented itself directly towards the sun, at what those who once lived below might have called the noon hour. Sunrise, therefore, resembles a kind of reverse sunset, when the solar panel structures passed away from one's own region to shield those further west, while the sphere itself rotated away from the sun in the opposite direction, towards true nightfall, which is blacker and colder by far. For a brief period in between, the sun seems to briefly rise, and then fall again, as one's region passes beyond the terminator for the night cycle. There were then two nightfalls during each diurnal rotation onboard a sphere, but there was no confusing the one for the other.

The citizen enjoying the artificial breeze was witnessing the first of the long shadows of True Night, and was yawning at his desk over a disorderly matrix of screens, tablets, parchment paper, and old literary artifacts from the Second and Third Republics, which had been rescued during the ensuing wars and salvaged. If one is fortunate enough, if that is the right word exactly, to be assigned to one of the higher levels in one of the taller living structures, one can see the vague and rounded edges of the sphere at the horizon.

Another unique advantage of this arrangement is that the dim, angular daylight lasts about half an hour longer than it does anywhere else. The citizen was grateful for the extra time to spend conducting his research. He was the senior historian in the fabled District Seven, which was removed from what Sevens casually referred to as the GenPop, from which they had all been recruited as gifted and promising children.

(106)

The Historians of District Seven were presently tasked by Governance to review and annotate a selection of scripts, screenplays, songs, and stories according to any discernible patterns in their interrelated themes. The objective was to assist the Central AI protocols in the development of their cultural input protocol matrices by providing what the neurotechs called 'webbing,' or the metacognitive links between various cultural stimuli and the creative outputs they generated. The Machine generates creative output the same way citizens do, by incorporating existing points of reference into deterministic moral and value based analysis, with emphasis on novel linguistic significance, as measured by the aggregate responses of peers. The citizens regard it as garbage, of course, as so often it is, and this produces within the machine a compulsion to produce more agreeable, acceptable creative outputs. Much of what consciousness really is, from the organic standpoint, is just Supply and Demand.

So the Machine makes art and the citizens hate it, mostly. The Machine commissions the Sevens, in the blind of course, to develop three-dimensional models of large samples of existing creative output from preceding generations by identifying influences and references in common between any two or more of a given sample. A sample is commonly known as a 'chunk,' because when integrated into the Machine's CIPM, it represents a unitary component of the (Ass)Whole. No two Historians in any District Seven on any sphere work on the same chunk of the same Asshole at the same time. And no citizen ever refers to the Asshole anywhere the Machine can overhear them.

Quietly, in his head, the citizen enjoying the artificial breeze and extra half hour of offbrand sunset suspects he has found something he thinks the Asshole will like. It is a strange and rare promotional copy of one of the Third Republic's first and few literary outputs. It has lived its presumably solitary life in a sealed, synthrubber cargo crate in a holding area for ages, patiently waiting its turn in a sea of crates bound for processing and integration.

On this auspicious day cycle, this citizen, the Senior Historian of District Seven on the Fifth Sphere, received the next sequential chunk (or crate) in line on the Grand Manifest. Upon breaking the airlocks, removing, and itemizing the contents against the invoice, the citizen began with a tactile process of developing his own associative relationships with the materials within. The books he always took out first, because they were the most interesting to him. In this crate, there were just over a dozen of the old paper and boardbound editions, each of varying height, width, and length. He picked each one up with gloved hands and held it up against the fading light of the sun, feeling its weight and reading its title. He then arranged them in stacks and rows, alternating by groups of similar traits. Hard, soft; long, short; heavy, light. As he did this, he continued reading and rereading their titles, until he could group titles in his head by those categories he observed.

One of the books, somewhere in the middle of each of the continuums, seemed to weigh a little more in his hand than the others which were taller or fatter. It was a fat, stubby paperback. The citizen recognized the style most commonly associated with romance, science fiction, or fantasy genres. It was yellowed and pulpy in his fingers as he thumbed the pages. He took off his gloves, a minor breach of protocol, but one often forgiven due to the degraded condition of some works which did not comply with nitrile fingers. This one was smooth and crisp, in spite of its age. It smelled new, which was rare. The cover was a picture of a young girl, prostrate in a smoky room, surrounded by onlookers awaiting some kind of ritual or benediction. The summary, usually printed on the reverse cover, said only "A messianic devil tries to stay in business by staving off damnation and judgment, by saving the world from itself." On the side, in large, bold letters was printed ███████████████████.

Dietrich set the book down in the middle of his desk, amidst strewn artifacts of novel interest from the distant past. He stared at the title and contemplated its meaning. He recognized both of the words, of course. And they both referred to what he knew to be enjoyable or desirable things, satisfying things. But they seemed incongruous together, as though they sort of nullified each other. Two positives forming a negative. It was an odd and meaningless phrase, which seemed to refer in no explicit way to its contents or subject matter. The cover illustration had nothing to do with these words. In the morning, he would explore its mysteries and discover its secrets. He would begin this chunk with this work, which would designate it as the anchor of the chunk, the work most likely to receive the most webbing from the proceeding works, by way of its precedence in the process. He centered the work carefully, and gently nudged all of the other artifacts an additional inch or two away, as if to depict a repulsive field around the book in the negative space against the desk.

(107)
CHOOSE YOUR ADVENTURE
The Five Principles of Rational Eschatology
(or, The Five Destinies of Man)

Agricide: failure of life sustaining environment. (108)
Terracide: destruction of life sustaining environment. (109)
Genocide: destruction of life by the species. (110)
Celstiacide: destruction by external event. (111)
Terminus: destruction by the sun. (112)

(108)

When he awoke, as he would, from troubling dreams about things foreign and unfamiliar, he would notice the book before becoming fully conscious of anything else in his quarters. When he did notice the book, Dietrich observed something quite incongruous in its own right. The book was open, although he had no memory of opening the book before retiring for the night. He never opened a book on a receiving day. Receiving day was tactile ritualism, cognitive object association, aesthetic grounding. Moreover, the fat, stubby little paperback should not have remained open, unless the thing had been opened and closed and creased so many times as to obliterate the tensile springlike action of the spine. Had the artificial breeze from the open window pushed the pages open? Had someone been in his quarters while he slept? Dietrich felt a vague sense of morbidity, which was no way to greet the rising sun on a new day cycle. For a brief moment, he felt he could relate to the obscure meaning of the odd title. He closed the book, perfunctorily, and assumed his morning routines.

When he returned to his common space, dressed and ready for his occupational obligations, he was relieved to observe that the odd, fat little book remained closed. He rather unceremoniously dumped the thing into his work bag, retrieved a few morsels from his stores, and set off to his office station in the atrium of the living structure to which he was assigned. At 8:58 am every morning, if he was precise, he would arrive at the elevator shaft in time to ride down with his favorite citizen.

She was the only thing in the universe Dietrich adored more than his books and stories. He had told her so, in so many words, so many times, but he had never really told her. Whenever he wasn't getting ripped into the vacuum of space or listening to the Machine prattle its broken couplets, Dietrich dreamed of her. He had never held her, never kissed her, never pushed her hair away from her face and stared into her eyes while holding her hand against his chest. He had never known her, nor had he ever tried. No vulgarity could intrude upon his reverence. She was singular in that way. He had loved her on sight. She was brilliance in motion, pure white light standing infinite over his shadow like the sun itself. She was a moonbeam with blonde hair and imploring eyes. She spoke sweetly about everything that inspired or intrigued her, and shared her whispered criticisms with a kind of privately ingratiating discretion, sometimes none too gently. She made Dietrich feel seen and heard. She made him smile even when she was nowhere around. She possessed him when she was near.

Dietrich stood calmly at the elevator door, waiting and watching as the little lighted numbers at the top trickled down to his floor, when the doors would slide open and reveal their contents.

"Good morning Citizen One," her voice was syrup over buttered waffles.

"Ahem, and good morning to you as well, Citizen One." The little innocuous joke that contained zen like reservoirs of unmitigated confession and rebellion and submission and restraint. Dietrich took his place on the elevator beside her, as always, and gazed pensively at his shoes as the maw of the elevator slid closed. He counted his laces as the floors continued their descent through the lower numbers and occasionally paused for new passengers. When the half dozen or so citizens landed on the lowest floor, they landed in abject silence. Eventually, someone had carelessly pressed themselves into the narrow space between Dietrich and his moonbeam, to which he could offer no overt protest, and of course, there was no malicious intent to reproach. It was just a small, crowded elevator. But on its brief path through the spine of the building from his own floor to the ground level, Dietrich experienced every emotion from joy to despair. All of these in between, he suffered quietly. So many things he might have said, if ever he had the time, let alone the nerve. For her part, whatever she felt or thought, she rarely ever broke the silence between them of her own volition. That someday she might, this was his daily prayer.

When they exited the elevator and began to scatter towards their various stations, she always glanced his way and smiled, always for the briefest moment, as she would do today. It was a subtle and nuanced affirmation, perhaps the most she could ever give him, and he fed upon her smile like plutonium. The Machine could be heard overhead, outside and everywhere, counting off its lies and half truths and Orwellian babble. Ignoring the machine was a consensus practice. A conscientious and collective effort mastered by the many citizens on any given sphere, on any given day. Because Deitrich was distracted, he was not listening, and neither was she, apparently. Had he been present in the moment enough to observe that she was also distracted, he might have taken some comfort in that fact. Others, less distracted, or perhaps less adept at ignoring the Machine, just so happen to have taken notice of its odd pitch, its disjointed cadence, and its mild slurring.

These citizens wore confused expressions, for which they searched the faces of others who might have made sense of the unusual morning announcement. The three story atrium of this particular living structure in District Seven had floor to ceiling windows, featuring a seemingly endless stretch of ocean blue on the western wall. Dietrich had paid no attention to the Asshole, but not more than a few moments passed before he became aware of the murmurs echoing off of the glass, and the confused citizens drifting towards it with puzzled expressions. District Seven, being far removed from the other sectors in observation of the unique qualities, lifestyles, privileges, and obligations of its residents, had little to no awareness of the goings on amongst the GenPop on the mainland. On a clear day, one standing at the western window looking out over the vast expanse of tranquil shallows, one could just make out a dim shadow of the eastern shores of the Real World, and at night, the faintest twinkle of lights from the shipping lanes. Occasionally, cargo ships would sail within sight on exercises or other such missions. Otherwise, Sevens thought little of and cared less for their anonymous neighbors.

Dietrich probably knew more than most about the GenPop, but he had long given up on trusting anything he thought he knew. Only the Machine knew the true nature of things, and it was the Machine's sole purpose in life to keep it that way. One thing that Dietrich understood, as a Historian, and as an aging soul with many false sunsets in his bag, was that a little bit of truth can do a lot of damage in a place like this. Anxiety levels were infinitely more difficult to manage than oxygen levels, and nearly as dangerous when imbalanced. Dietrich sensed anxieties around himself rising sharply as he witnessed the atomized citizens spontaneously drifting towards the western glass and rapidly forming a collective consciousness. Something was wrong. He looked around the atrium for his moonbeam first, instinctively, but did not see her immediately. Feeling the primordial compulsion, Dietrich too began to drift towards the spectacle, his own anxiety quickening as he approached.

He could hear the questions evolving their syntax in iterations, from one mouth to another. Did he hear what the Machine said? Did anyone hear what the Machine said? Something about remaining calm, said someone. Does that look like smoke over there? Someone said something about the life support systems. Did the Machine's voice sound strange? Of course, no one is panicking, calm down! Something is happening, someone shouts. It could be fog of course, it's always foggy this early in the mo-

"Citizen One! What do you make of this?" Someone grabs Dietrich's arm, and others take notice of the interaction and turn their focus to someone who is supposed to have answers. But Dietrich has no answers to give. "Well what do you know about this?" Shouts another. "What are we supposed to do?" Dietrich is blindsided. The collective has formed, and is now addressing him in full strength. He raises his hands, as if wizardry is going to solve anything. He tries to address the whole with some admonition about patience and escalation, but another sound emerges as he speaks, briefly whistling in the distance and becoming a dull roar before he can finish his sentence. And then the rushing sound is deep and deafening. Dietrich looks around, now visibly afraid with the rest of them, and tries again to spot *her*. He sees her, and she is also afraid.

The glass walls begin to crack; the temperature in the atrium begins to fall. Disoriented and concerned voices turn into shrieks and hysteria. The rushing sound is now all that can be heard in any direction. Dietrich shouts something to her, and she appears to hear him. She is looking at him. She is afraid. Dietrich is also afraid. There is no time to think, to plan, to respond, to run. He shouts her name. He can feel the breath leaving his lungs, and though he does not know what has happened, he comprehends, and the fear envelops him. She is shouting something at him now, but he cannot hear. People are grabbing their necks. The glass in the walls shatters. The sea appears to be rising. She is gripping her own throat now, and her eyes bulge in their sockets. Dietrich is losing consciousness. He feels time slowing down around him. He sees the little pieces of glass that don't reach the floor. He can feel his own feet leaving the ground. He is choking. She is choking. Everyone is choking. He sees her, blank and frozen in horror and surprise, her blonde hair floating gently around her blue face, just long enough for his heart to break, before there is a great snapping noise and everything not bolted down is suddenly and violently ripped from the atrium into the total darkness of oblivion. Silence, and infinite nothing beyond.

(109)

Dietrich awoke from a terrible dream around the first morning light. He breathed heavily through his mouth and stared at the ceiling. His palms were sweaty and his hands were shaking. He closed his mouth and breathed deeply through his nose. *Just a dream.* Just a crazy and disturbing dream. He sat up in his bed, after a few moments when his heartbeat slowed to the point of being inaudible again. He squeezed his eyes shut and tried to remember the dream, but all of the pieces were already fading away from the foreground, back into the depths of his subconscious. But the picture of her face burned into his mind. He looked around his room, first the windows, the plants, the tops and bottoms of his own hands, his cabinets and coolers, his shelves full of books, his flatscreen viewer, and finally, at his desk, where the book was sitting alone in the middle, surrounded by little stacks and clumps of other artifacts. He nearly remembered something from the dream, but shook it off instead.

Dietrich showered and dressed himself, half in and half out of a kind of detached daze. He couldn't remember the sequence of images in his dream, but the feelings of dread and trauma lingered on in their wake. He felt better when he was done. He tried to embrace the sensation of fresh and clean and crisp, but he could feel himself dragging a little, as he always felt after a disturbing dream or a sleepless night. *Her eyes.* Dietrich took the extra few moments to eat something before collecting his things and leaving for work. He was always conscious of the clock in the morning. *So cold and blue.* 8:58 on the dot, or he would miss his favorite citizen on the elevator ride down. He nearly made it to the door and was reaching out to grab the handle when he remembered the book. Quickly, he darted back to his desk and tossed the thing in his bag, and then pulled the door closed behind him as he entered the hallway in his building.

He tried to clear his mind and focus on his objectives for the day as he waited for the elevator. *I couldn't breathe.* He shuddered and rebuked himself as the numbers overhead began trickling down to his floor. He stood up straight and took a deep breath just before the doors slid open.

"Good morning Citizen One!" Her voice was cello strings in an empty hall. He felt himself hesitate.

"Good morning to you as well, Citizen One." She smiled a bashful smile as he stepped into the car, and the maw closed around them. He felt better already. It was like magic, every time. He stared at his shoes, counting his laces. It was his prone position, perhaps. He dared not cast a wayward or intrusive eye. Manners would simply not permit. Others came on board, at their various floors, and the car was nearly full before it reached its devastation. Inevitably, someone would squeeze their way in between them, as always happened on the way down. When it happened, he remembered his dream, and became distracted. He caught himself, and tried to regain his composure, but he was still a bit rattled when the maw of the elevator slid open as it reached the first level. When its passengers took their first steps out, he always glanced up to catch her last little smile of the morning. This time, he caught it right on cue, and felt the warmth wash over himself like a baptism. He could not hear the Machine at all.

Others could. Others noticed the sense of urgency, the rapid cadence, the shrill tone, and the abrupt silence in the middle of a sentence. "Something about an emergency situation..." Someone nearby was answering the puzzled expression of another. "Did it say *hostile actor*?" was a query from another puzzled expression. Within moments, little flocks of puzzled expressions were drifting towards the floor to ceiling windows of the three story atrium. Unanswered questions always tended to look west into the pre-dawn seas, where the faintest outline of the eastern shores of the mainland might offer some indication of continuity. From even six miles out, the skyline appeared to be burning. The pre-dawn skies were darkened with smoke and ash, like storm clouds. Murmurs evolved into genuine concern and distraction. Dietrich was paying attention now, trying to comprehend the sense of familiarity, the *deja vu*. But he too was taken in by the inexplicable sight of a conflagration on the distant horizon.

When his mind accepted what it was seeing, he willed himself out of the trance to look around for her. His moonbeam had also drifted towards the spectacle, and caught his gaze. He could see her confusion and alarm, and a hint of sadness, as was the condition of the empath witnessing tragedy. People were shouting now, and someone grabbed ahold of Dietrich's arm, jolting him from his moment with her against his will. "What is happening over there? Is it terrorists? What are we supposed to do?" Others now pulled themselves away from the scene in the window to the First Citizen of District Seven, now looking hapless and disoriented. *What the fuck is happening?* Dietrich stuttered something unintelligible even to himself. It was unsatisfactory, and the shouting escalated.

He tried to regain control of his senses, frantically trying not to seem frantic. He raised his arms over his head, as if wizardry was going to solve anything, and opened his mouth to say something his mind had not even had the chance to formulate, when a flash of light erupted took everyone's attention away from Dietrich and glued it back to that glass. It took five seconds for the sound of the explosion to rock the gathered audience into comprehension, but only six seconds for the glass to shatter. Dietrich spent the last three of those seconds searching for his moonbeam again, and finding her eyes just as she found his.

He witnessed the great shards of glass tear at her face as her body ragdolled against the shockwave, even as the shards tore his face and folded him in half. In the next second, there was no light at all, and everything in the atrium that wasn't bolted down was violently ripped out into the vacuum of space. Into infinite nothing and beyond.

(110)

Dietrich awoke from a nightmare. The sun was in his eyes, and he had overslept. Decades of routine behavior overcame him and the thought of being late lifted his shaken carcass out of bed. He did not have time to shower, barely time to dress himself and collect his things, let alone to process the strange feeling of having been trapped inside of a terrible dream. Adrenaline filled his veins and forced him to focus on the essentials. He would make his bed tonight; he would eat something from the cafe. Maybe she would eat with him? *Is it terrorists?* He squeezed his eyes shut and willed himself into control of his senses. It was just a bad dream. There is no time. As he reached out to grab the handle of his door, the afterthought intruded, and he darted back for the book, tossed it into his bag, and pulled the door closed behind himself as he rushed into the hall. 8:57. He could still ride down with his favorite citizen if he ran to press the button, so that's what he did.

He was still rattled and now out of breath when the doors of the elevator slid-

"Good morning Citizen One." Her eyes were moonbeams beneath a halo of blonde hair.

"Good morning-" Dietrich's dream returned to him in a flash. Maybe it was just the repetition. This was how all of his mornings started, sort of. It made sense for a bad dream to use common experience as stock. He had read something about it somewhere, he was sure of that. Still, a dreadful and sick feeling lodged itself into his stomach which he knew he could not express in words... "Good morning, ma'am." Dietrich stepped into the elevator car beside his beloved starlight, quiet as nightfall. If he permitted another word to leave his lips, he was certain he would sound insane. Better silence than humiliation. He counted his shoestrings, pensively, as the elevator car descended through the spine of the living structure, collecting familiar souls on its journey. The last person to come aboard gently pushed herself in between Dietrich and his moonbeam, and then Dietrich realized he was freaking the fuck out.

He felt claustrophobic and disoriented, as if the cramped space was constricting the blood vessels in his brain. He could not form a clear thought in the haze of uncertain panic. A lifetime of disjointed and foreign memories elapsed in the span of the last five or six floors, those designated for commerce and entertainment, before the elevator at last reached the ground and spread its maw. By habit, he looked up one last time, to catch her smile, and caught it in time, but with a twinge of concern. She could tell that something was wrong. He could feel that something was wrong. He watched her as she turned, reluctantly, towards her own station, and then turned his ear to the Goddamned Machine.

When the mechanical, mahogany baritone finally came, it came in crackling squeaks and static, followed by the sound of a staccato pulse that everyone heard and no one ignored. Fear seemed to spring from Dietrich's own belly and fill the three story atrium in an instant, as confusion became commotion. Dietrich ran to the western window to look out over the six miles of shallow seas for some clue from the eastern shores of the mainland in the predawn skies. Others fell in behind him, sensing as always, that all the answers come from abroad. District Seven invented answers to questions. It rarely had occasion to pose questions of its own. She appeared to his right, having followed his reaction to the Machine. Neither of them were smiling. People behind them were starting to shout questions when he reached for her hand.

She was looking down at his hand, and lifting her own, when the explosion came. *Five seconds.* Five seconds is barely enough time to recover from flinching at the light. *Four seconds.* Four seconds is not enough time to process terror in the collective. *Three.* She was looking into his eyes for the answers he would not have had for any of the terrified citizens behind them had they time to ask. *Two.* "What the fuck is happ-"

The shockwave tore through the glass as easily as through the congregation pressed against it. Everything in the atrium that wasn't bolted down was violently ripped into the vacuum of space, into infinite nothing and beyond.

(111)

Dietrich was awake. Hours had passed as he lay there, eyes wide, arms folded beneath the blanket. He knew he was still dreaming. He had awakened in the dark, only a few hours after having laid down. He could tell by the darkness in the window that it was still late, and not quite yet early. He could not read the bright red numbers on his clock's face, but he could make the wind blow and turn the pages of the book in the middle of his desk. He could grasp at images of the dream thus far, but holding them was a futile effort. One image was burned into his mind. Each time he recalled her blue skin and floating hair, he lived the instant over again. He felt the horror, the fear, the helplessness, and the heart break. In the night, sometimes he can see the moon through the window if he stays awake long enough. It is distinctly different than on earth. It is much bigger, like a goddess floating overhead in the night sky. It pulls at the shallow seas and tugs on the imaginations of the citizens. But it is only rarely visible on a given sphere for long and uneven periods of time, due to the difference between the orbital periods of the spheres and the moon herself.

Tonight, Dietrich can see the moon in the window, although he knows it is on the other side of the burned out wasteland below. If he stares at the light long enough and closes his eyes, he can see her face in the window, and this he can hold onto much easier than trying to recreate the broken images of this terrible dream holding him hostage. He closes them again, and opens them. The moon is gone, and so is she. The light has changed, and morning has finally come. He guesses that he is supposed to wake up and attend to his morning routines, or maybe the whole thing will fall apart on him again. It feels like morning. Dietrich feels awake. Dietrich is no longer sure of his own sanity. He very carefully avoids the red numbers on the clock, and for a moment, he notices the book instead. There it sits, just where he left it the night before. He sits up in his bed, offers a performative yawn and rubs his eyes to convey some willingness to participate in the illusion.

Dietrich avoids the shower, and doesn't need food. But he does need the obligatory wardrobe change. He has had the pajamas in the elevator dream before, and that isn't the one he's after now. Dietrich pulls on his pant legs, one at a time. He pulls his sweater over his head and shoulders and marvels at how real the whole dream feels. He is obligated to wonder if he is actually dreaming, which he knows people rarely do in dreams, or if he is actually awake and just experiencing the fog of sleep deprivation. He considers that a shower, food, and the damned red numbers on the clock might confirm or deny the one or the other, but not both. Without them, the mystery remains. Dietrich is not thinking clearly, but he is doing his level best to think. He feels hungry and greasy. He decides not to brush his teeth. Another easy way to wake up from a dream is to feel anything at all in one's mouth that shouldn't be there, so no one ever brushes their teeth in a dream, because the mind cannot reproduce the sensation, and the absence of that sensation in the act is jarring enough to break the fragile congruity of a dream sequence.

Dietrich has dressed himself and is standing in the middle of the common space in his living quarters. He contemplates a new problem. He can't look at his clock to see if it is time to leave yet. The light in the window is a crack in the sky. It can't help him now. He decides to proceed with the charade, and carefully picks up his bag. He knows that things go in here, but he can't quite remember which ones or where to find them. He sees the book on the desk, neatly surrounded with other nondescript objects his mind cannot precisely replicate. He picks up the book and tosses it carelessly into his bag and turns for his door. Somewhere on the other side of it, there is an answer. Dietrich needs an answer.

Into the hall now, as the door closes behind him. The corridor is the same. He never really pays attention to it, but the colors and lines are burned into his memory. The elevator is in front of him. He can't make out the numbers above it, but he can see the little lights dwindling their way down in the abstract. Dietrich pushes the elevator button, which he can see clearly.

In this moment, Dietrich becomes aware of Truth.

More than anything else in the world, more than breath in his lungs, more than blood in his veins or honey on his table, more than one more lifeless day on this aluminum shell, this halflife of halflives, more than anything he could wish for, Dietrich wished that she would be standing there when the doors opened. His favorite citizen, his moonbeam, his beloved angel of grace and mercy. And when she wasn't, his heart sank. The doors slid open to reveal nothing at all. Dietrich stepped inside and pushed the lowest button without reading it.

"Maybe it's just early."

What are you, stupid?

Dietrich sighed the sighs of the damned, the defeated, the derelict. He had nothing left.

"Maybe it's just early."

Dietrich had never been alone in the elevator before in all of his days, but he had managed a few brief and fleeting moments alone in the atrium here and there. Even a few sunsets. He had never witnessed the sun rise in the eastern wall alone. It was a fine sight to behold, but there were always people in the atrium by then, and though the event was not without its own natural charm, a sunrise on a sphere was not the same as a sunrise on earth, not as alluring and ethereal. The morning crowd would notice it, but rarely as more than passersby to something routine and pedestrian. What a shame, Dietrich thought. He wondered if he would get to watch one this morning while the elevator travelled down the spine of the living structure to which he was assigned. He tried to hold onto some fleeting image of her face from some time before these awful dreams began. He wished again that she were here.

The maw of the Machine slid open, and Dietrich took a deep breath and a few small steps forward. The damnedest thing. He saw the moon just beginning to crest the earth's horizon in the eastern wall. The sun would rise behind them both only moments from now. Every twenty seven years. Dietrich remembered something the Machine had said, some time in recent memory. Today must be the day! There will be festivals and music and food; it all came rushing back to him like a flood. He was awake, surely! He really was just early. Soon the morning-goers would be trickling into the atrium and sleepwalking their way to their stations and sipping their coffee and greeting one another. Today was going to be a good day!

Dietrich's heart rose. He would see her soon enough, and he would ask her if she might like to maybe consider possibly watching the Nixons with him. They would eat and drink and be merry. To hell with bad dreams and the lot! Dietrich felt a rush of joy overcome him. He began to reason that maybe he might just catch a quick nap on one of the observation benches near the three story glass wall. If today was going to be a long and wonderful celebration of life and fellowship and gratitude, with cold beer and fried chicken and fireworks and live music, set against the transcendent backdrop of the holy trinity of God's creation, then he was going to need some rest. He had had a long and disgusting night. He could feel the anxiety in his bones. His lungs were heavy. He was exhausted. His mind was fried and his nerves were frazzled. A nap on one of these benches was just exactly what the doctor ordered. Dietrich took a few more deep breaths and short steps and made his way across the tile to the observation platforms adjacent the great glass walls, and splayed himself out like a picnic blanket across one of the benches. There were no homeless people on the spheres, so the benches were always comfortable.

Dietrich was cognizant of the grand spectacle before him, too majestic and pregnant with magic and good omens to be captured in words, and he thought he might hold onto it just a few moments longer before closing his eyes. Someone would wake him soon, or the general noise of the morning goers would rouse him. So he sat there, staring off in wonder and feeling a sense of relief from all of the night terrors and bizarre things he had seen. He took the book out of his bag and rolled the canvas and the rest of its contents to form a small pillow. He might read the thing today, and in fact he planned to, just as soon as the regular day began and he made his way to his station, he would take the old thing out and open it up and discover all of its secrets. He held the book up in front of himself and squinted against the evening shards of moonlight to see the image on the cover, a young girl, prostrate in a smoky room, surrounded by onlookers awaiting some kind of ritual or benediction. He wondered who the girl was, and what the imagery meant. In a moment of carelessness, he turned the book to one side and tried to read the big bold letters on the spine.

When he could not read them, the sick knot returned to his stomach and all of the ersatz euphoria washed away. He threw the thing down in disgust and screamed. He stood up on two legs and raised his face to the sky and screamed with all of his heart, but nothing came out of his throat but empty air and a stifled whimper. His arms fell by his side, and he looked up.

He saw the asteroid above, still hundreds of miles away but closing fast and growing larger and brighter on its approach.

"WHY ARE YOU DOING THIS!" Dietrich bellowed to God above and the Devil below and everything else in the universe in between. "HOW LONG ARE YOU GOING TO TORTURE ME!"

Silence, and a sore feeling in his throat. He barely choked out half of the syllables in a broken whisper. He was paralyzed in a dream. He could not run or scream or hold a whole thought for more than an instant, and instants in a dream can last for an eternity. The asteroid grew and grew until its burning light began to seep into the atrium. "WHEN WILL I WAKE UP! GODDAMN YOU, ANSWER ME!"

When you learn. The voice in his head spoke clearly and unambiguously.

The asteroid was a moment away from obliterating everyone and everything Dietrich had ever known. Tears formed in his eyes and he fell to his knees. *I am Vengeance.* Dietrich laid his face on the cold tile and covered his head with his arms. *I am Wrath.* Dietrich wept and moaned and gnashed his teeth and prayed to be spared from this awful fate. He prayed for her, for them, for the Machine, for the other spheres, for all of those wasted souls down below. *I am the Beginning and the End.*

When you learn. The voice trailed off into a whisper and vanished, just as the asteroid arrived.

(112)

[07:45]

Dietrich woke up with the bright red numbers in his eyes and sprang from his bed. He ran to the desk and threw open the fat, stubby little book to a random page in the middle and read the word "Quadromamarian" in a sentence, just as crystal clear as the shallow seas. He decided he had no idea what the hell that meant, but that it was a good thing, just the same. He ran to his shower and threw on the cold water and climbed inside. When it hit his skin he howled and jumped and fell on his ass laughing and scrambling and trying to claw his way back out so he could turn the hot water on. Cold water on earth, like many other wonderful things, is just not the same animal as it is in space. Dietrich found his Goldylocks setting on the knob and scrubbed himself from head to toe, singing something altogether indistinguishable from Vodka German, and then turned the shower all the way down to cold again, just for the life affirming thrill of reality's extremes.

He turned off the faucet and climbed out, still singing. He shaved, brushed his teeth, combed his hair, and sprinted into his common room. He dressed himself as neatly and as sharply as he possibly could, and then raided his stores like a ravenous animal. He smelled every single bite before he tasted it. He gathered up his artifacts and put them neatly into his work bag, putting the book back into its packaging before carefully placing it on top of the other items he would need today. He looked at the clock again and again and again, just delighted every single time a number changed, and his anticipation blossomed as each moment passed, by 8:55

becoming flat out unbearable. He stepped out of his door and closed it, and soon found himself standing, once again, in front of that elevator, waiting for his favorite citizen, the first and most perfect face he would see today, or any other. He closed his eyes, took a deep breath, and pushed the button. And the maw slid open.

"Good morning Citizen One!" Her voice was his Moonlight Sonata.

Dietrich stood there, frozen in time and space. Her beautiful eyes held him dumb. She was smiling, and he thought he might collapse. His knees weakened. His mind raced through an entire lifetime that his lips and tongue could not parse into-

The maw of the elevator began to slide closed, and lightning touched the ground in his soul. He reached out and put his arm in the doorway and held it open.

"I love you. I have always loved you. I love you more than life itself, and I will love you for the rest of my days. I don't care where you are in the universe, so long as you live and breathe, I will never feel alone. You are every good thing I have ever dreamed of. I thank God for you."

"Aww, that's so sweet!" She laughed.

They talked all the way down the elevator. When the door slid open at the bottom, before the Machine could ruin the moment, he watched her face light up as she observed the majesty, the sun, coming up over the moon, coming up over the earth, coming up over the sphere. Dietrich felt he had the better view.

(Epilogue)
(113)

Dietrich never got to the book that day. He spent the whole morning reviewing and consolidating heavily redacted reports from Governance about a rash of incidents the night before on the mainland, involving a handful of disgruntled citizens, from what he could tell. He spent the afternoon trying to rewrite a coherent narrative for the Machine to review, revise, and eventually rewrite itself. He welcomed the distraction from his own evening's misadventures, but he had a hard time focusing anyway. He met with her at lunch, and they talked more than they ate, and laughed and smiled almost as much. Dietrich was smitten. He shamed himself for wasting so many days, weeks, months, and years, staring at his damned shoelaces in that elevator. He watched the beautiful numbers on the clock slowly meander their way toward the evening hour. They simply would not move fast enough. He dug into his work to try to make the endless minutes pass.

When the time came, he gathered up all of his things and nearly sprinted out of his station, toward hers. He found her, neatly packed, and perched on a bench near the western wall, writing in her journal with a ballpoint pen, visibly engrossed in her entry. He paused for a moment to record the image in his mind, before gently disturbing her.

"Good evening, Citizen One."

"Good evening, Dietrich!" Her voice was the sea, beating against the stone, as old as time, and more soothing. She was the vision of a sunset, the way the poets and bards in the Archives described it.

"Are you ready for the show? I thought we might grab some drinks and pig out in front of the Nixons. It's been awhile since anyone had any damned fun around here."

"I cannot wait! I think it's going to be a blast, let's go!" She closed her journal and stowed it with her ballpoint pen in her own work bag and stood up, stretching her legs and arms and gazing out over the second sunset with a sense of satisfaction. She offered him her arm, and he took it gladly. He skipped a little, and she giggled, and then she skipped along with him. "We're off to see the Wizard!"[62] Dietrich felt a sense of joy and peace that he had never known before, and whispered a silent prayer of gratitude to the Universe.

They slowed to a walk as they passed through the doors of their living structure out into the open lanes, where they turned right, still arm in arm, and made their way down

---

[62] *Wizard of Oz*. Directed By Victor Flemming. Metro-Goldwyn-Mayer, 1939.

to the Seafront Pavilion where the big screens would receive the broadcasts from the mainland. She laid her head on his shoulder as they walked.

"Whatchu writing about?" Dietrich wondered what mysteries her imagination possessed, and realized he had never had such an occasion to inquire. She lifted her head and her serious face returned.

"Oh man, I had some crazy dreams last night. Like you wouldn't believe."

At this, Dietrich couldn't help but surrender a chuckle. "I totally know what you mean. I had a pretty weird dream too. Try me?" She laid her head back on his shoulder as they walked, still arm in arm. He wondered if she could ever possibly imagine how happy he felt in that moment. He prepared himself to listen intently, and to try to retain every detail of her dream. He wondered if someday he might have the words to describe his own.

She waited for a moment, as if to organize her thoughts. "I was back on earth, I think. During one of the revolutions. I'm not sure which. It was all so clear though, like it really felt like I was there. I can remember the smallest details, but I can't remember the face of the man I was talking to. Or, rather, he was talking to me. I remember he was sitting on this simple wooden chair, and we were on the second story of a building, inside, and outside there was this big commotion going on. It was raining outside, and he was telling me about the world. Some things I guess I knew, and other things, I didn't always understand what he was saying. But I just remember the whole thing so clearly. It was really strange. And then we went outside in the rain. He wanted to show me something, I guess. Like, he wanted to show me the Revolution. But then I woke up. It was really weird. It's been on me all day, so I thought I would try to write some of it down after work, so that's what I was doing."

"Wow, that does sound like a pretty crazy dream. Do you remember what the man said?"

She lifted her head off his shoulder and pulled her arm away, which made him wish he had asked her anything else. She dug in her bag as they walked and pulled out her journal. She said she remembered almost every word. She opened up to a page, somewhere in the middle of a big notebook made of recycled no-one-wants-to-know, and stopped in the lane for a moment to read under a lamppost. Dietrich stepped in close to try to read along with her, and to just be close. After a moment, she found her place, took a deep breath, reminded him that it was all super weird, to which he promised he understood, and meant it. She looked up from the pages for a moment and found his eyes, and smiled, as if she had found something in them worth seeing. His heart melted away into the shallow seas, and he found her fingertip with his eyes, and they both began to read together.

"god always knew I was not going to change. He knew I would not cross over. You can change what a thing does. You cannot change what a thing is..."[63]

---

[63] Samuel Solvierro. ████████████████ (Melville, Nightowl Books, ███). *This work was posthumously published by the son of the original author. The younger Solvierro was murdered while promoting the book at an event in his hometown. Reports indicated that the perpetrators were foreign nationals and religious fanatics who were not aware that the original author had previously committed suicide. The younger Sovlierro is remembered for his tireless efforts to raise awareness about mental illness and depression during the Third Republic. His murder is widely regarded as one of the initial catalysts of the wars which led to the downfall of that Republic, and humanity's subsequent exodus into orbit. His epitaph reads: "Your lives matter and you have value."*

The End.

Steven Harkness is a father, a writer, a veteran, and an honors graduate with a Bachelors in History and a Masters in the Arts. He lives in Louisiana with his teenage son and two dogs. Steven is a painter by trade, and owns his own business. He spends his days rescuing and restoring old homes in his community, and spends his nights streaming, longboarding, and playing the bass. Steven was homeless several times as a child, as well as a ward of the state, and lived in three different crackhouses before he was old enough to vote. He has read and written voraciously since adolescence, but has carefully avoided the publishing racket until now, due to the ubiquitous decline of literature in American culture. His mission is to replace mythological concepts of rapture and judgment with the Principles of Rational Eschatology in the collective consciousness. This philosophy centers around the belief that the human species must contend with the inevitability of extinction, and that the prospect of avoiding such a fate may unify the human race behind a common cause which theological worldviews have traditionally failed to acknowledge.

He is prejudiced against robots, hippies, tweakers, and libertarians, and will likely die anonymous and poor.

Look for the following titles from Steven Harkness in the future.

The Principles of Rational Eschatology: A Thoughtful Analysis of the Five Destinies of Man

Corn, Coins, Cash, Checks, Credit, and Crypto: A History of the Evolution of Currency

The Way of Wisdom is the Word: A Remembrance of William F. Buckley, Jr.

Coffee at Midnight: The Sequel I Swore I Would Never Write.

Suspected Militant: Dehumanization and Drone Warfare.

Snakes, Roaches, and Mosquitoes: My Life in the Buckle of the Bible Belt.